The White Wolf

The White Wolf

by
Paul Féval

Retranslated by
Jean-Marc & Randy Lofficier

Annotated and introduced by
Jean-Marc Lofficier

A Black Coat Press Book

ISBN 978-1-61227-832-2. First Printing. June 2019. Published by Black Coat Press, an imprint of Hollywood Comics.com, LLC, P.O. Box 17270, Encino, CA 91416.

Introduction

Le Loup Blanc [The White Wolf] is Paul Féval's fourth novel, and the one in which he defined the (melo)dramatic archetypes that he reused throughout his prolific and extraordinary career.

It was first serialized in the newspaper *Le Courrier Français* from 23 September to 27 October 1843 under Paul Féval's name, before being reissued as three slim volumes by publisher L. Chelndowski under the title *La Forêt de Rennes* [The Rennes Forest] under the signature of "Sir Francis Trolopp."[1] It was reissued again in 1856 by A. de Vresse and in 1878 by V. Palmé as *Le Loup Blanc* under Féval's own name. It wasn't reprinted until 1965 when Belgian publisher Marabout released it in a handsome paperback edition.

Le Loup Blanc was adapted for French television, relatively faithfully, in 1977 as three one-hour episodes by Jean-Jacques Decourt, with Jacques Rosny in the eponymous role and Claude Giraud as the villainous Hervé de Vaunoy.

In 1843, the 27-year-old Féval had been living in Paris for only about four or five years. After having obtained a Law degree in his native Brittany, but deciding that he wasn't suited for a legal career, he had briefly tried to succeed in the banking business.

---

[1] A *nom-de-plume* Féval reused when signing *Les Mystères de Londres*.

Jacques Rosny as The White Wolf

But in the end, Féval's love of literature proved too powerful and he quickly found employment as a proof-reader at the magazine *Le Nouvelliste*. From that perch, he began to publish literary reviews and few short stories which were very well received.

In 1841, Féval published his first novella *Le Club des Phoques* [The Seals' Club] in which a Breton Marquis is forced to reclaim his title and fortune stolen after a shipwreck. *Le Club des Phoques* was published in the prestigious *Revue de Paris*, and was both a public and critical success. However, *La Revue de Paris* paid very little, and it was Féval's ambition to become a full-time writer. So, in 1843, he sold two full-blown novels, *Les Chevaliers du Firmament* [The Knights of the Firmament], a Walter Scott-inspired historical novel taking place at the Court of Portugal in the 17th century, to *La Législature*, and *Le Loup Blanc* to the more popular— one might say downmarket—*Le Courrier Français*.[2] *Le Loup Blanc* became a huge success and Féval's literary career took off spectacularly.

Féval's timing was excellent since, the previous year, Eugène Sue's *Les Mystères de Paris* had launched what might well be dubbed the "golden age of the roman-feuilleton." Sue was quickly followed by Alexandre Dumas, and Paul Féval was only too eager to make himself a name to rival those of his two contemporaries.

The success of *Le Loup Blanc* is what made Anténor Joly, the editor-in-chief of *Le Courrier Français*, who wished to imitate the colossal success of Sue's epic, published by the rival *Journal des Débats*,

---

[2] That same year, Féval also sold a collection of previously published short stories and novellas entitled *Le Capitaine Spartacus* to L. De Potter.

ask Féval to pen *Les Mystères de Londres*, which he did from December 1843 to September 1844, while signing "Sir Francis Trolopp" in order to preserve his literary reputation for what he thought would be his future, more worthy works.

Le Loup Blanc is a remarkable novel, in which Féval transitions from the influence of Walter Scott—faithfully continued and expanded by Dumas—to the darker type of criminal intrigue that would become his trademark. The trope of the hero betrayed, wronged and despoiled, who returns under the guise of a new identity to obtain vengeance and reclaim what is rightfully his, was already well entrenched by 1843, having been large-ly exploited in the *romans noirs* or gothic novels of the early part of the 19th century.

After *Le Loup Blanc*, characters such as Fergus O'Breane/Rio Santo from *Les Mystères de Londres*, Edmond Dantès/Monte-Cristo from *Le Comte de Monte-Cristo*, André Maynotte/Trois-Pattes from the first vol-ume of *Les Habits Noirs*, Lagardère/The Hunchback from Féval's eponymous swashbuckling classic are all perfect exemplars of this type. But what makes *Le Loup Blanc* so groundbreaking was that Féval didn't limit himself to milking that well-used trope, but added the notion of a criminal conspiracy, the so-called Wolves, led by a mysterious, masked avenger, the eponymous White Wolf, a daring hero who cultivates a secret identi-ty hiding behind a seemingly ineffectual personality.

Seen in that context, the White Wolf cleverly antic-ipates future characters such as Zorro, created in 1919 by Johnston McCulley, and its predecessor and inspiration, The Scarlet Pimpernel, created in 1903 by Baroness

Emma Orczy. It may very well be the first novel in the genre.

One of the essential elements of the plot of *Le Loup Blanc* is the history of Brittany, reimagined by Féval as a near-utopian medieval society.

At the beginning of the medieval era, Brittany was divided between three kingdoms: Domnonea, Cornouaille and Broërec. These realms eventually merged into a single state during the 9th century. This unification was carried out by Nominoe, considered as the Breton *pater patriae*. His son, Erispoe, secured the independence of the new kingdom and won the Battle of Jengland on 22 August 851 against the French King Charles the Bald. The Bretons won another war in 867, and the kingdom then reached its maximum size, including parts of Normandy, Maine, Anjou, and the Channel Islands.

Brittany was heavily attacked by the Vikings at the beginning of the 10th century. The kingdom lost its eastern territories, including Normandy and Anjou. Nantes was seized by the Vikings in 914, but was eventually liberated by Alan II of Brittany in 937 with the support of his god-brother, King Æthelstan of England. Alan II expelled the Vikings from Brittany and recreated a strong Breton state. He paid homage to King Louis IV of France, who was Æthelstan's nephew and had returned from England in the same year as Alan II. Thus Brittany ceased to be a kingdom and became a duchy—but a sovereign duchy.

Several Breton lords helped William the Conqueror to invade England and received large estates there. The French kings maintained envoys in Brittany. The dukes were usually independent, but they often contracted alliances with England or France. Their support became very important during the 14th century, when the English kings began to claim the French throne, resulting in the Hundred Years' War.

The Breton War of Succession, a local part of the Hundred Years' War, saw the House of Blois, backed by the French, fighting with the House of Montfort, backed by the English. The Montforts won in 1364 and enjoyed a period of total independence until the end of the War, because France was weakened and stopped sending royal envoys to the Court of Brittany.

English diplomatic failures led to the Breton cavalry commanders Arthur, Comte de Richemont (later Arthur III, Duke of Brittany) and his nephew Peter II, Duke of Brittany playing key roles on the French side during the deciding stages of the War—the Battle of Patay, the Treaty of Arras (1435), the Battle of Formigny and the Battle of Castillon). However, Brittany lost the so-called "Mad War" against France in 1488, mostly because of its internal divisions, which were exacerbated by the corruption at the court of Francis II, then Duke of Brittany. Indeed, some Breton lords were fighting on the French side.

At that time, the French justified their sovereignty over Brittany based on historical precedent: In 497, Clovis I had united the Franks into a single kingdom; then, in the late 8th century, Charlemagne had incorporated Brittany into the Carolingian Empire; and finally, in the 11th century, William the Conqueror had expanded into Brittany. But the Bretons defended the opposite view, arguing mainly from settlement of the territory at an earlier date than by the Franks; forgetting the lack of a treaty with the Roman Empire permitting such settlements, as well as any agreements with the Frankish kings following Clovis.

They also argued for the sovereignty of Brittany based on its status as an ancient kingdom, although Nominoe never had the formal title of king, and the fact that the homage paid by the dukes to the kings was one of alliance rather than as lieges.

The King of France, Louis XI, felt a great hatred for Duke Francis II following the latter's involvement in a series of anti-royalist conflicts, such as the League of the Public Weal (1465), the conquest of Normandy (1467-68), the war of 1471-1473, the Mad War (1484–85), and the Franco-Breton War (1487-1488). Also, Francis II had taken advantage of the historic enfeeblement of the French monarchy to endow himself with symbols of sovereignty, such as a royal seal, a royal crown, the adoption of the principle of lèse-majesté, the establishment of a sovereign parliament, independent and direct diplomatic relations with other major powers, and, especially, the eviction of the King's tax collectors!

After the Mad War, Francis II could no longer marry off his daughter, Anne, without the consent of the King of France. Nonetheless, he married her to the Holy Roman Emperor in 1490, which led to another war with France. Charles VIII of France besieged Rennes and had the marriage cancelled and eventually married Anne himself. After he died childless, the duchess was forced to marry his heir and cousin, Louis XII. Anne unsuccessfully tried to preserve Breton independence, but she died in 1514.

The union between the two crowns was formally carried out by King Francis I of France in 1532. In so doing, he granted several privileges to Brittany, such as exemption from the *gabelle*, a tax on salt which was very unpopular. Brittany and France remained governed as separate countries, but under the same crown, and Breton aristocrats at the French royal court were considered foreign princes.

Francis I sought to enfold Brittany into the Kingdom of France through parliamentary maneuvers. He formally invited the Duchy of Brittany to join the French crown.

The union of Brittany and France was almost achieved by Francis III, Duke of Brittany, the eldest son of Francis I of France and Claude of France, and therefore the Dauphin of France. Francis III inherited the Duchy when he was 6 years-old after the death of his mother in 1524. That Francis I allowed his eldest son to carry the title of the Duke of Brittany supports the perception that the Duchy of Brittany remained separate from the Kingdom of France. On 13 August 1532, an edict of union was signed by the Estates of Brittany in Nantes. Some members of the parliament (the Estates of Brittany) were either intimidated into co-operation with the union or bought off, with the demand for union in fact being inspired by Francis I.

However, before the kingship and dukedom could be joined under a single ruler, Francis III died in 1536, never to inherit the French crown. The duchy then passed to Henry, the second son of Francis I and Claude. The Duchy of Brittany was thus considered incorporated into the Kingdom of France upon the death of his mother. When Francis I died in 1547, Henry succeeded him as Henry II of France, and the kingdom and dukedom were finally united.

From the 16th to the 18th century, Brittany was in an economic golden age. The region was located on the seaways between Spain, England and the Netherlands and it greatly benefited from the creation of a French colonial empire. Local seaports like Brest and Saint-Brieuc quickly expanded, and Lorient was founded in the 17th century. Saint-Malo was also known for its corsairs; Brest was a major base for the French Navy and Nantes flourished with the Atlantic trade. The inland provided hemp ropes and canvas and linen sheets. However, Colbertism, which encouraged the creation of many factories, did not favor the Breton industry because most of the royal factories were opened in other provinces. Moreover, several conflicts between France and England led the latter to restrain its trade, and the Breton economy slid into recession during the 18th century.

Two significant revolts occurred in the 17th and 18th centuries: the Revolt of the *papier timbré* (1675) and the Pontcallec Conspiracy (1719). Both arose from attempts to resist centralization and assert Breton constitutional exceptions to tax.

When *Le Loup Blanc* begins, in 1720, Brittany may have been French for two centuries, keeping its privileges, franchises, and Parliament, but the real power lay in the hands of the Governor of the province and the Intendant, representatives of the French royal power. The Intendant had just declared the Forest of Rennes royal property, thus preventing the local people from exercising their trades as cloggers, coopers, coalmen, etc., condemning them to a life of misery and hunger…

Now, read on…

Jean-Marc Lofficier

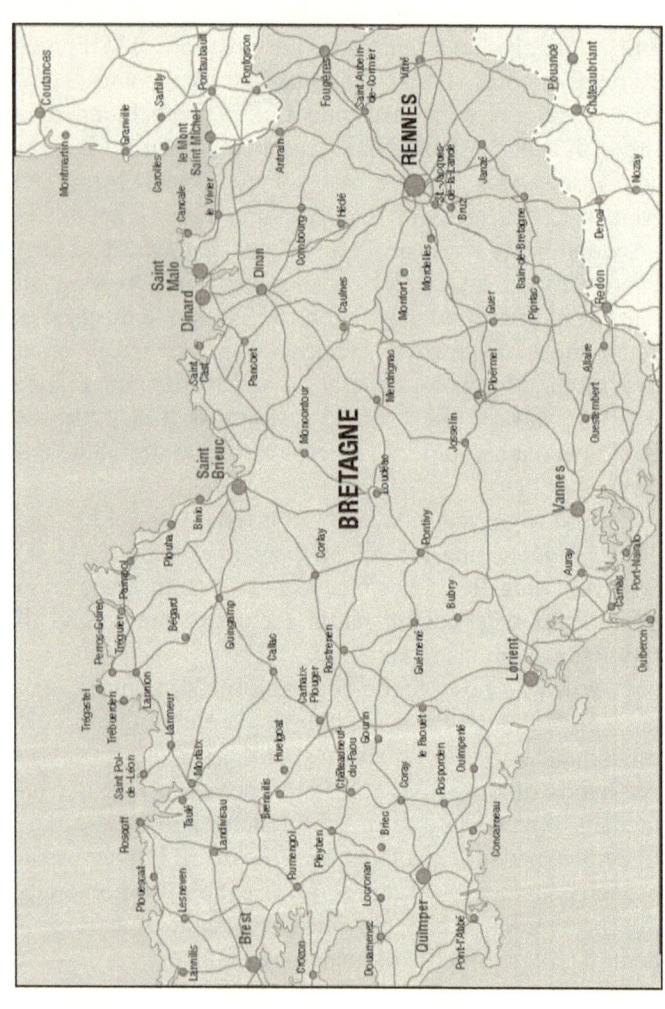

THE WHITE WOLF

CHAPTER I
The Lament

Not so long ago, a traveler journeying from Paris to Brest—from the capital of France to one of its chief seaports—would fall twice into the arms of balmy sleep, rocked by the cumbersome stagecoach, and awaken twice, before he would behold the scanty harvests, the thickly-planted orchards, and sturdy gnarled oaks of impoverished Brittany. He would first awake in the fertile plains of the Perche, near the Beauce, that paradise of traders in corn and other cereals; and then, he would fall asleep, lulled by the bittersweet smells of cider from the Orne and the nasal strains of the maids of Lower Normandy. The morrow's sun would bring him to ancient Vitré, a gothic town with its dark houses and the ivy-covered ruins of a lordly castle, tottering upon the summit of a steep hill; in the distance our traveler would perceive the meandering Vilaine, with its silvery thread softly flowing with a thousand undulations through a chessboard of verdant meadows, studded with graceful willows, and dotted with innumerable waving beds of rushes. At close of day, the sky would start to lose its azure hue and turn to slate grey; the horizon would diminish and the air would become impregnated with saline humidity; far off to the right, our traveler would at last see a dark outline standing out in bold relief against ranges of small, sandy hillocks crowned with flowers of purple heath and golden broom. It was what had once been the great Forest of Rennes.

Nowadays, that forest has fallen from its former high estate, for the majority of its massive trees have since felt the dreadful edge of the woodman's axe, due to the voracious demands of the new industries.

Messieurs de Rohan, de Montbourcher and de Castlebriand once hunted the red deer in its shade, accompanied by the Seigneurs de Laval, expressly invited, and the Royal Intendant, whose presence was usually not welcomed. Now, it was with the greatest difficulty that the ruddy employees of the new Forge Masters might kill a miserable hare, or a lean fallow-deer, scarcely worth powder and shot.

The once verdant glades no longer ring with the baying of noble hounds, the shrill echoes of the cheerful horn, the tramp of fiery coursers, champing on their bits, impatient till the game should be afoot; the cries of the joyous cavalcades are no longer heard, having been replaced by the monotonous sound of steel hammers and steam pumps, breaking dully on the ear.

The utilitarian might say, rubbing his hands, that this result is far better for society, that old castles never did anyone any good, while factories produce bowls, nails and other useful domestic utensils; for my part, gentle readers, I have my own opinions on the matter, but I shall wait for a more suitable opportunity to express them.

However, it is enough to state that, about one hundred and fifty years ago, instead of a few measly patches of trees, which gradually grow fewer and farther between, the Forest of Rennes boasted a surface of eleven leagues of land, and its trees were so tall and leafy, and its underwood so thick, that even the gamekeepers occasionally lost themselves in it.

Instead of the modern factories, which now clutter the site, one would have found artisanal shops making the wooden shoes called *sabots*; and also, amongst the chestnut groves, a few huts where men cut hoops for hogsheads and other barrels. In the center, there was a clearing where ten or twelve huts lay embosomed, the residences of the charcoal-burners; taken altogether, the population of the forest was said to amount to four or five thousand inhabitants.

They were almost a race apart from their fellow men, half savage and warlike, the born enemies of all innovation, and detesting, from instinct and usage immemorial, every law but that of ancient custom which gave them a prescriptive right over all that the vast forest produced, except the game, which belonged exclusively to the superior lords of the soil.

Since long gone times, the shoemakers, the coopers, and the charcoal-burners, had not only rejected every attempt to limit their rights, but they appropriated for themselves the materials necessary for their respective trades, in the full belief that the forest was their hereditary patrimony, to which they had been born, and in which, without let or hindrance, they proposed to live and die. Whoever was bold enough to contest that right became, in their eyes, an oppressor.

And they were not of the type disposed to be trodden upon, without the most determined and desperate resistance.

When our curtain rises, Louis XIV was no more, and Philippe d'Orléans, despite the testamentary dispositions of the Sun King, had become Regent of France. This Prince, whom history has censured so severely and yet so justly, had instantly abrogated all the regulations for the internal government of the kingdom made by his predecessor. Yet, those regulations generally withstood the test and continued, at least everywhere clumsy or perfidious hands did not try to undermine them.

In Brittany, the long and valiant resistance of the "States" had long ended.

An Intendant appointed to collect royal taxes had been installed in Rennes; the "Edict of Union," broken in its most important stipulations, was virtually a dead letter; Brittany was entirely subdued; and the province had now become, to all intents and purposes, an integral part of France.

But passing a publicly distasteful measure in a Parliamentary assembly was a very different thing from thrusting it upon a proverbially stubborn and courageous population; and although Monsieur de Pontchartrain, the new Royal Intendant, had taken up his permanent abode in Rennes, he found the execution of his odious functions attended with the greatest of difficulty and danger.

Resistance to the collection of the newly-imposed taxes sprung up in every nook and corner of the ancient Duchy; the "States" were accused of intimate connivance with the rebels.

During the Cellamare conspiracy,[3] it was amongst Bretons that the Duchesse du Maine found her most ar-

---

[3] The Cellamare conspiracy of 1718 was a conspiracy against the then Regent, Philippe d'Orléans (1674–1723). Concocted in Spain, the plot was the brainchild of Antonio del Giudice,

dent defenders. The *Kights of the Honey Fly*, who also called themselves the *Breton Brothers*, made up a veritable secret army, the leaders of which, Messieurs de Pontcallec, de Talhoët, de Rohan-Polduc and a few others, were beheaded in Nantes in 1718.

It was a rude blow and the organization seemingly disbanded.

But the League of the Breton Brothers, which had predated the Conspiracy, even though it had lost its political purpose, still carried on its secret operations.

It is in the nature of such secret organizations to thrive underground. The Breton Brothers first refused to pay taxes, taking up arms, then ostensibly laying them down. But while they lived, they continued plotting.

Twenty years after the events we are about to recount, and which form the prologue to our story, we shall find traces of their on-going secret existence, for mystery is the very essence of man, and secret societies die a hundred times, only to be reborn anew.

In the year 1719, almost all the nobility had withdrawn openly from the association; but the principles of the Brotherhood still existed, indestructible, in full vigor

---

Prince of Cellamare. The plan was strongly supported by some of Philippe d'Orléans' most notorious enemies, namely the duke and duchess du Maine, Louis Auguste de Bourbon and his wife, Louise Bénédicte de Bourbon, who had entered into correspondence with the Spanish Prime Minister Giulio Alberoni. The correspondence between the duchess of Maine and Alberoni was intercepted by the police and thus reported to the Regent, who acted swiftly; on 9 December, the Prince of Cellamare was arrested and sent back to Spain; Alberoni was arrested on 5 December 1718 at Poitiers; the duchess was exiled to Dijon, while her husband was imprisoned in the fortress of Doullens in Picardy.

amongst the citizens of the towns and the sturdy peasants of the forests.

The noble *Brothers* who remained were icons.

The castles of these redoubtable champions of independence became sacred altars around which the grievances of the oppressed were grimly muttered. A tacit but powerless resistance was organized, incapable of acting on a larger scale, but able to protest in all impunity.

It would have cost a sea of blood to suppress them, so many were their family connections throughout the region.

After what we have said about the Forest of Rennes, one might be justified in thinking that it was the very hotbed of this stern opposition; for its population consisted, without exception, of hardy, uncultivated men, accustomed to dangers and privations of every kind, and therefore singularly fitted for resistance to the royal will, inspired by powerful combined feelings of negativity and inertia. Sufficiently numerous to fight, if it should become necessary to have recourse to arms, the sons of the forest, at first, simply refused to comply with the mandates of the Intendant, confident in the inaccessible retreats the landscape afforded them, and relying upon their knowledge of its labyrinths, its gloomy coverts which bordered the meadows about Rennes, and extended almost to the suburbs of Vitré and Fougères.

They had many staunch adherents in these three towns; the first musket-shot fired, or the first saber that drank blood, would have called forth numbers of stout citizens of Rennes, the plebeians of Vitré—who still wore hauberks, brassards, iron head-pieces, and cuisses like men-at-arms of the 15th century—and the rough predatory legions of poachers of Fougères. With such resistance, one could reasonably hope that the troops dispatched by Monsieur de Pontchartrain might not find their task an easy one.

At the time of our tale, there was a gentleman in Brittany to whom the remnants of the old party looked up with the greatest veneration; so much so that if he had said, "pay your taxes to the King of France," they might have done so.

But that man was unlikely to issue such a proclamation, for he was one of the noblest-born, and the most determined of the Breton brotherhood.

Ever since its disbanding, he had never ceased to raise his voice in the Hall of the Estates, to protest against the invasion of the ancient lands of the Dukes by the armed men of the King of France.

This gentleman was Nicolas Treml de La Tremlays, Seigneur of Boüexis-in-the-forest, who possessed in the neighborhood of the small town of Liffré, a domain of such an extent that it made him lord paramount of the region.

His castle of La Tremlays was one of the most ancient and most striking in Upper Brittany, and his manor-house at Boüexis-in-the-Forest was no less magnificent; indeed, it took two hours to ride from one residence to the other, and during the transit, the cavalier never left the estates of Treml.

Monsieur Nicolas, as he was called, was a man of great stature and austere visage. His long white locks fell in thick clusters upon his well-worn, stained buff-coat; the snows of many winters had not sufficed to tame the heady current of his blood; and whilst his gallant war-horse bore him lightly through the forest, seated like a statue in his saddle, the peasants would doff their hats to the stern old man, and, turning to each other, say:

"So long as the brave old lord is still with us, there will be a true Breton left, and let the French bloodsuckers beware!"

And they spoke truly. The love of Nicolas Treml for his country was invincible. The gradual falling-off of the members of the independent party, instead of being a lesson to him, had only confirmed his obstinacy. Year after year, his colleagues in the Estates listened to his energetic protestations with less patience; but he continued, and, with his hand upon the cross of his good sword, he never ceased to fulminate his denunciations against the representatives of the King of France.

One day, as he was declaiming, as usual, in the Hall of the Estates, some members burst into fits of laughter, and others observed audibly that Monsieur Treml de La Tremlays must have lost his wits.

On which the brave old man stopped suddenly in his harangue; a deathly pallor overspread his face, and his eyes flashed fire as he took up his ample hat and stalked majestically to the door.

Arrived at the entrance of the Hall, he turned slowly round, crossed his arms upon his breast, and threw a look of withering contempt upon his fellows on the benches, as he emphatically said, in a heavily accented voice that rang loudly throughout the Hall:

"I thank God, Messieurs, that I have only lost my wits, when I see that you have lost your hearts."

In an instant, the noblemen sprang furiously from their seats, and twenty rapiers glittered before the eyes of Nicolas Treml, who stood unmoved.

"Sheathe your swords," he said. "It is I who am insulted, but the blood of a Breton will not appease my wrath. Fare ye well, gentlemen. I trust your children may someday forget their fathers, and think only of the brave deeds of their noble ancestors. I renounce you, and I quit you, now and forever. You have helped to place poor Brittany in her grave, but I will not leave its tomb unbloodied. The time for fighting for our rights and liberties is now past, but vengeance will yet come—and yes, death."

Nicolas Treml left his comrades abashed and astounded, mounted his fine horse, and directed his steps towards his castle.

Those who passed him on the road that day could not guess the turmoil that occupied his mind. Tough of body and soul, he knew how to repress his rightful wrath. His brow remained uncreased and his eyes passed indifferently over the flat countryside of the neighborhood of Rennes.

As he entered the outskirts of the forest, the sun was setting upon the horizon. Monsieur Treml de La Tremlays scanned with a practiced military eye, the natural entrenchments and admirable defensive positions of the land, and involuntarily counted up the numbers of hardy, daring men who would shed their heart's blood for his banner, should it once again float in the air.

He reined in his horse, and a smile lit up his features as he thought:

In such a country and with such soldiers, war would indeed be glorious!

Then a sudden idea seemed to flit across his mind. He drew himself up in the saddle, his lip curled and his eye sparkled as the exclamation involuntarily broke from him:

"No! Not a war! A single combat on my good horse, and with my faithful sword in my hand. One blow well struck, and one death will suffice!"

Having uttered these ominous words, Nicolas Treml put spurs to his steed, and, as he galloped along the woodland road, concocted a scheme at once madly audacious and chivalrous, but impossible; an idea which could only have sprung from the brain of an old world, country nobleman, profoundly ignorant of the manners of the day, and gauging the feelings of the present age by those which had forever flown hither.

But although the scheme of Nicolas Treml exceeded the bounds of possibility, it must not be supposed that he had become mad, and was not aware of the danger the attempt, and its execution, would involve. The excess of his enthusiasm did not conceal from him the depth of the abyss before him.

Yet, the gaping chasm would not deter him from plunging into it, if by so doing he thought he should preserve his native land.

One circumstance alone tended to shake his proud determination; and that was that the house of La Tremlays now had only one direct heir, Georges Treml, a child, five years-old, the grandson of the noble old man. What would become of young Georges, without a natural supporter, if his grandfather was struck dead? Nicolas Treml could scarcely brook that this obstacle should interfere with the execution of his plan.

"Should I succeed," he murmured, "I shall leave the boy a rich heritage of glory. If I fail, my cousin De Vaunoy will guard his patrimony. Yes: it shall be so—Monsieur de Vaunoy is a good Christian and an honorable man!"

The words had hardly issued from his lips, when he was surprised to hear a harsh voice near him singing a song common to that portion of the kingdom; a slow, melancholy, wailing lament, upon the piteous fate of young Arthur of Brittany, foully done to death by his cruel uncle, John Lackland, the recreant King of England.

Monsieur Treml de La Tremlays shuddered as a terrible idea rushed into his thoughts.

"Impossible!" he cried. "De Vaunoy could not be such a villain!"

Still the harsh croak of the voice came nearer, and seemed, in Nicolas's excited state, to take on a tone of irony.

"No, no!" he said, "it must be done, come of it what may. My little Georges is a Breton, and if necessary, his happiness, like his blood, belongs to Brittany!"

For a few seconds, the mysterious voice was hushed, and then it broke out vigorously, immediately above Nicolas Treml's head. Bringing his horse to a dead stand, Nicolas looked up in amazement, and beheld in the foliage of a tall chestnut tree, whose head was brightly tinged by the beams of the setting sun, a being of savage, strange, uncouth, and almost diabolical appearance, his features of ashy hue, clothed in white skins, and jumping with marvelous agility from branch to branch. If an explorer had met him in the forests of the New World, he certainly would not have labeled him "human," and Monsieur de Buffon's volume on Natural History [4] would contain one more creature: the white

---

[4] Buffon's *Histoire naturelle, générale et particulière* (1749–1788: in 36 volumes; an additional volume based on his notes appeared in 1789) was originally intended to cover all three "kingdoms" of nature, but the *Histoire naturelle* ended up being limited to the animal and mineral kingdoms, and the animals covered were only the birds and quadrupeds. Written

baboon; for the character indeed resembled a large white monkey, jumping from branch to branch with wonderful agility, and with each jump, dropping a small bunch of reeds.

His song continued undisturbed.

Indeed, this was not the first time Monsieur Treml de La Tremlays had seen the creature; for on his whistling—as a sportsman calls his dog—the song ceased.

The creature swung itself from branch to branch of the tree, until, when he was only a few feet from the ground, he dropped lightly down, and with an amicable gesture, threw himself respectfully upon one knee before the horse.

The appearance of this man—for such he was—was more extraordinary when viewed near than from afar. His long, bare, sinewy legs, covered with white hair, supported a muscular, deformed, short body, his brawny neck served as a pedestal to a face with high-boned cheeks, covered with a white substance nearly allied to down; his eyebrows, hair, and nascent beard, were like the driven snow; and his whole countenance was not at all embellished by a pair of fiery-red eyes.

There was no appearance in his person that could precisely indicate his age.

Perhaps he might be young, or middle-aged, or old.

But the dexterity he evidenced in descending from the tree, gave lie to the two latter suppositions.

Youth alone could inhabit this unnatural exterior.

His lowly reverence being made, the Albino raised himself with one bound, and stood firmly before Nicolas, in the middle of the road.

---

in a brilliant style, this work was read by every educated person in Europe.

"How goes it with your father, Jean Blanc?" Monsieur Treml de La Tremlays inquired, in a kindly tone.

"How goes it with your son, Nicolas Treml?" the Albino replied, cutting a fantastic cabriole.

A black cloud lowered upon the Baron's brow; for the abrupt question corresponded in a singular manner with the subject of his reverie.

"You become insolent, lad," he answered. "I am too complaisant towards you, woodsmen, and you abuse my kindness. Get out my way, varlet, and let me not hear you speak in that impudent tone again."

Far from obeying this peremptory command, Jean Blanc seized the bridle of the nobleman's horse, and smiled as he said:

"You are deceived, Monsieur Nicolas. It is not to us poor folks that you are too good; but to others whom you love, but who despise you."

"Let go of the bridle, you fool!" Monsieur Treml de La Tremlays shouted.

But the Albino kept his hold, and continued:

"Jean Blanc's father goes on bravely. Jean Blanc watched over him last night, and will watch over him tomorrow; but who will watch over Georges Treml? Will you do so tomorrow, Monsieur Nicolas?"

"What do you mean?"

"There is an old song about young Arthur of Brittany. Listen: I can glide through a covert as well as climb the chestnuts and the elms. I watched your steps as you came through the forest; you were talking with your conscience. I heard you, and so I sang the *Lament for Arthur*."

"What!" cried Monsieur Treml de La Tremlays. "You heard me? You know all?"

"No, not all; you said too much, and spoke too low for me to hear all. But, believe me, do not leave young Georges to the mercy of his cousin. If you are going on a journey far away, take him on the saddle with you; if you cannot, then kill him at once; but do not abandon him. And now, I must away and cut some wood for hoops. May God forever bless you, Monsieur Nicolas!"

So saying, the extraordinary creature dropped the bridle, sprang across the road, and climbed a chestnut tree with the speed and fearlessness of a wild cat, as his dress of white rabbit-skins glimmered palely in the increasing darkness of the night.

Silently and thoughtfully, Monsieur Treml de La Tremlays resumed his route, pondering over the words Jean Blanc had uttered.

"Bah! He's nothing but a half-wit!" he said to himself.

But his heart sank within his breast, and as the mournful notes of the *Lament* were wafted to his ears by the breeze, the stout-hearted noble trembled, and the name of his beloved grandson issued slowly from his lips.

CHAPTER II
The Iron Chest

Night had fallen when Nicolas Treml de La Tremlays reached his castle gate; he threw the horse's bridle to one of the grooms without uttering a word, ascended the great staircase with an abstracted air, and proceeded to the chamber where young Georges rested.

He was, in truth, a lovely boy; his fair hair was scattered in silken curls upon the pillow as he lay, and at the moment that his grandfather approached, some pleasant dream must have had possession of his mind, for he smiled sweetly, and stretched out his little hands as if to woo a parent's fond embrace.

When children smile in their sleep in Brittany, the gossips say they are *laughing with the angels*, a charming and poetic notion.

But in Brittany, everything charming and poetic quickly turns to melancholy, and such a circumstance is invariably held to be a mournful augur, for the child is thought to laugh because he sees the angels by his bed, ready to bear away his spirit to the skies.

Nicolas Treml leaned gently over the couch, and his mustachioed lips touched the infant's satin cheek without awakening him from his slumber.

"Arthur of Brittany!" he murmured, for Jean Blanc's words had made a deep impression on him. "What if the last hope of my family were to be sacrificed? But no; I cannot think so! The poor fellow is half-crazed, and my cousin De Vaunoy does not resemble that accursed English king John Lackland anymore than a faithful dog does turn into a wolf."

He sat beside Georges and his mind wandered back to his original scheme.

Monsieur Treml de La Tremlays, rich and powerful as we have noted, had lost his only son two years before the events we now relate. This son, named Jacques Treml, was Georges' father and had been a good and brave man during the period he was permitted to remain on earth. He had inherited his father's love for Brittany, and deep hatred towards France, two things in which he believed passionately.

So much so that with the noble Jacques' death, his father's hopes for his bleeding country were buried in his son's tomb.

Nicolas Treml felt himself growing old. Would he have time to teach Georges such love and hatred?

Potent monarchs from whom Destiny tears the son they fondly prayed would succeed them in their regal honors, and carry out their mighty projects, weep tears of blood as they survey the cradles of their grandchildren.

That child would not become a man for twenty years, and a dynasty could crumble in a day!

Nicolas Treml was no king, but he looked upon himself as the last personification of a defeated race, which might yet someday prove victorious. His dear son Jacques had been his right arm, his successor, his other self, whilst Georges was but a puling infant.

And now that the strife was at his door and threatened to deluge Brittany with blood, instead of a proven sword, Nicolas held but a slender rose twig in his hand.

There was a poor family of obscure origin in Brittany, who had proclaimed themselves to be a minor branch of the Tremls, and had had the impertinence to add that honored name to their own proper designation. Before Jacques' death, Nicolas Treml had initiated a lawsuit against this family, the De Vaunoys, to compel them to desist from appropriating his family name.

The suit was still pending, but according to reliable sources, the Parliament at Rennes was about to rule in favor of Nicolas Treml and against the De Vaunoys when Jacques had passed away. That sad event produced an immediate change of heart in the conduct of Monsieur Treml de La Tremlays. He withdrew the suit and instead invited Hervé de Vaunoy, the eldest of the family, to come and see him—an invitation with which that astute gentleman hastened to comply.

On the following morning he crossed the forest, on a heavy horse taken from the plough, and when he arrived at the boundary of the domain of Treml, and the coverts of Boüexis, he removed his hat and respectfully saluted the rich lands, whilst a leer curled the corners of his thin lips, and elevated the tips of his moustache.

Hervé de Vaunoy, at that time, might have been forty years of age: a profusion of reddish hair fell upon and surrounded a lively countenance; his small grey eyes were scarcely visible beneath the lashes that heavily fringed their lids, but so much of them as could be seen corresponded with the debonair expression of his features.

In a word, he seemed a perfectly frank-hearted fellow, and those who saw him for the first time were delighted with him.

The second time they would suspend that judgment.

On the third meeting, they would suspect he was far less good than he initially appeared.

As he plodded along upon his cart-horse, he carefully noted the wealth of the Manor of Boüexis, finding the fields, the orchards, and the farms pleasing, and admiring the vast swath of woodland, seeing in his mind's eye the trees bending and tottering beneath the laborer's stroke. During that time, his triumphant leer continued to twist his mouth, as if the little man thought that someday soon, all this would be his.

But what he most admired was the antique castle of La Tremlays, and as he slowly paced along the avenue of stately elms that led up to its portcullised and escutcheoned gate, he could hardly refrain from giving vent to the malignant joy that grew in his heart.

"Holy Virgin!" he ejaculated, "our whole residence at Vaunoy, stables, dove-cotes, gardens, outhouses, and all, would be lost inside the great hall of this castle. The soul of my good cousin Nicolas Treml would have to be harder than stone for him not to give me a foot's length within this paradise! And then, the Devil will help me to take the rest."

Then crossing the lowered drawbridge, and lifting the ponderous iron hammer that served as a knocker to the folding gates, he removed his smile, and instead assumed a humble, and submissive air.

When Hervé de Vaunoy was announced, he found Nicolas Treml seated before the capacious fireplace of the great hall, whilst a dog of noble breed slumbered on the hearth, and little four-year-old Georges played about the room with his nurse.

The old nobleman turned to survey the newcomer, but his hound, gaining his feet, uttered a menacing, loud growl.

"Quiet, Wolf!" said Nicolas Treml.

The dog crouched down again at his master's bidding, but kept his glaring eyes steadfastly fixed upon De Vaunoy, who stood respectfully in the center of the hall, waiting for his cue.

Monsieur Treml de La Tremlays continued to silently examine him minutely for five minutes.

Then, seeming to make an effort, he got up and exclaimed with brusque courtesy:

"Approach, cousin; you are welcome beneath the ancient roof of our common ancestors."

De Vaunoy absolutely trembled with delight as he found the long-coveted relationship—about which he, himself, felt dubious—so suddenly and easily acknowledged. In obedience to the lord's request, he seated himself next to the fireplace.

The following conversation, brief and to the point, ensued:

"I hope, Monsieur de Vaunoy," said Nicolas Treml, "that I find you a true Breton?"

"Heaven knows, my good cousin, that I am so, to the death."

"Determined to shed your blood, if necessary, for the welfare of the duchy?"

"Body and soul, cousin—blood and bone. I hate the French oppressors! May the foul fiend seize me if I do not curse them all! I'm ready to eat them alive when the day comes."

"'Tis good!" Nicolas Treml exclaimed, pleased. "There is my hand, Vaunoy, my friend. We understand each other perfectly, and that child there, my grandson Georges, will never want for a parent should any accident befall me."

That very evening, Hervé de Vaunoy was installed in the castle, and never left it, up to the commencement of this tale. Young Georges was especially confided to his care, and to all appearances, the cunning villain was lovingly devoted to the little boy.

For the next eighteen months, Hervé rose daily in Nicolas Treml's opinion, and began to enjoy his total confidence. The grooms, valets and female domestics—taking the cue of their master—treated him obsequiously and with consideration.

There were only two beings on the estate who did not exhibit any reverence towards him: Wolf, Nicolas Treml's noble dog, and the Albino, Jean Blanc.

Every time that Vaunoy entered a room where the dog would be, the faithful, sensible, animal fixed his large round eyes upon him, and growled incessantly, until Monsieur Treml de La Tremlays ordered him to stop. All of De Vaunoy's coaxings were in vain. Wolf, as a good Breton, was just as stubborn as his human masters and did not easily change his mind.

Nicolas Treml was often puzzled by Wolf's aversion to his cousin; as he considered the dog to be a perspicacious, intelligent animal, whose opinions were by no means to be ignored; but then De Vaunoy was so respectful, so truly humble, so serviceable, and so devoted!

And he detested France so completely!

How was it possible to entertain suspicions of a man who hated the Regent Philippe d'Orléans with all his heart and soul, just as much as he did?

As for Jean Blanc, his aversion was less dangerous than Wolf's, seeing that he held a lower position in the social scale than even the poor dog. It was true that he made barrel-hoops to gain a living, but he passed for an idiot, and most assuredly would not have been able to maintain his bedridden father without the charitable assistance of Monsieur Treml de La Tremlays. He was received in the kitchen and the buttery of the castle because the indiscriminate hospitality of Brittany was extended alike to beggars, wanderers, and even animals; but nevertheless Jean encountered many difficulties in making good his corner by the fire, and was obliged to play innumerable fantastic tricks in order to disarm the hostility of the grim house steward when he made his daily distribution to the poor.

"Back, you nasty white mongrel!" spat the chief steward of Treml. "Aren't you ashamed, you devil cur, to take food away from good Christians?"

Jean—as the humor took him—would sometimes shake his head woefully and retire, or burst into a fit of laughter; but if, by chance, a gleam of reason found its way to his benighted brain, the inflamed scarlet bordering of his eyes glowed like lit charcoal, and a deep red flush was seen upon his cheeks. This, however, endured but for an instant, and the idiot then recovered his serenity.

On all these occasions Jude, Nicolas Treml's most trusted squire, took the poor Albino's part, after Jean's natural apathy had won over his brief burst of anger.

"A little more charity, Master Alain," Jude would say to the pompous steward. "Jean Blanc is the son of his brave sire, who was a staunch servitor of the House of Treml. Our good lord will not hear that the stout sons of the forest should be treated in this manner."

Jude told the truth. Nicolas Treml always behaved kindly towards his vassals. But no matter how generous the master, insolence, that plague of sour servants, always found room in their hearts.

Then Alain, the steward, would swear a Breton oath, and hand Jean Blanc his soup and bread with a contemptuous sneer. The Albino would consume it without making a remark, and, having finished it, would receive another portion, which he would immediately take to his aged parent, Mathieu Blanc, the well-known basket maker of the dark Wolf's Pit.

Great doubt existed amongst the inhabitants of the castle as to whether Jean's imperturbable tranquility was assumed or real. Those who knew him best affirmed that his brain did not contain that intelligence which Providence has assigned to the majority of mankind, but neither was he absolutely idiotic.

Whilst daylight lasted, he would sit perched in the high trees, cutting the branches best suited to his occupation, and singing all sorts of ancient ballads; when evening came and he repaired to vespers, his extraordinary face would force a smile from vergers, choristers, and beadle, which appeared to afford him exquisite delight.

And yet, he prayed devoutly.

And yet, he attended his afflicted father with the affectionate devotion of a daughter. When old Mathieu was worse than usual, Jean worked twice as hard to buy him medicines at the pharmacy of Rennes; and more than one peasant would testify that they had seen him on his knees, praying by the bedside of the sick old man.

Moreover, he was known to be capable of sentiments of gratitude that knew no limits; he had thrown himself, unarmed, in the way of a wild boar that had attacked his protector, Jude; and he had been known thrice to scale the high walls that surrounded the castle for nothing more than the gratification of kissing the tiny hands of young Georges, his benefactor's grandson.

His affection for the infant was beyond belief; and those who did not hold with the idea of idiocy, said that his hatred of Hervé de Vaunoy was caused by his regarding him as an interloper, out to steal the hereditary wealth and titles that rightfully belonged to the lovely little boy.

It must, however, be understood that Jean Blanc was only a secondary subject of conversation, when, in fact, the retainers, male and female, had nothing else to talk about. Indeed, with the exception of De Vaunoy, who feared him, and Jude, and Monsieur Treml de La Tremlays, who didn't mind having an occasional chat with him, no one ever wasted a thought upon the poor Albino.

All admired his wonderful dexterity in bodily exercises, precisely in the same degree as they would a squirrel gamboling amid the branches of a tree; but the half-suspicion that his idiocy was affected, served to divest him of that respect which, in ignorant, pastoral countries, is paid to beings whom the Almighty has deprived of reason; the foresters also, for their own reasons, had their doubts upon the subject, and distrusted him.

As for the women, poor Jean was to them an object of unmitigated horror and contempt. They would laugh at his countenance, seemingly plastered as it were with flour; but at night, they trembled and hastened away when, in temporary anger, they beheld the phosphorescent flashing of his red eyes.

But let us return to Nicolas Treml, whom we left meditating by his grandson's bed.

Doubtless, the subject of his thoughts must have been momentous, for he remained there motionless for long hours, indeed for so long that one might have mistaken him for one of the stone sculptures that are often used to adorn gravesites.

The sound of the castle bell, tolling the hour of midnight, recalled him to himself.

Starting from his reverie, he regained his feet. He took up a lamp, and with a slow step and melancholy visage, walked across the chamber to the door, subduing the clinking of his spurs as much as possible, for fear of disturbing the slumbers of the child.

"Vaunoy," he said, "is incapable of betraying me. Upon my soul, I believe so. But faith must not drive out prudence; for only Heaven can sound the depths of a man's heart. I must take precautions…"

Shading with his hand the flame of the lamp, which the night winds threatened to extinguish at every moment, Monsieur Treml de La Tremlays traversed several corridors, descended the great staircase, and repaired to the armory where Jude Leker, his squire, slept.

He woke him up gently and motioned him to follow him.

Jude silently obeyed his master.

Nicolas Treml reascended the staircase with rapid step, and traversing other corridors, entered an octagonal room located on the first floor of one of the castle's towers, to which he always retired when he wished to be alone.

After his squire had joined him, Monsieur Treml de La Tremlays locked the door behind them.

The honest squire never presumed to ask his master the reason for any of his actions; if Nicolas commanded, Jude listened with the deepest respect, and obeyed implicitly.

But now the old Lord's conduct seemed so strange, the expression on his face so solemn, that he forgot his habitual caution, and could not help exclaiming:

"My good and noble master, what is wrong?"

Nicolas Treml made an imperative gesture requesting his silence, and opened the lock of an iron cabinet sunk into the masonry of the wall.

He took out a small iron chest which he placed, perfectly empty, in Jude's hands.

Next, he produced several bags of gold pieces from a secret compartment of the cabinet, and counted them one by one as he placed them in the empty chest.

It took quite some time for him to reach the amount of one hundred thousand *livres tournois*.[5]

After that, Nicolas Treml double-locked the chest.

"Tomorrow morning," he said in a low but calm voice, "before daybreak, my trusty Jude, you will harness your best horse; take this chest with you, and await my coming at the Wolf's Pit in the forest."

Jude inclined his head, in token of obedience.

"Before you leave," Monsieur Treml de La Tremlays continued, "please go to Monsieur de Vaunoy's chamber, and request him to come to me at once. Now, go!"

---

[5] One of numerous currencies used in France in the Middle Ages, initially minted by the abbey of Saint Martin in the Touraine region of France. Soon after Philip II of France seized the counties of Anjou and Touraine in 1203 and standardized the use of the *livre tournois* there, it began to supersede the *livre parisis* which had been up to that point the official currency of the Capetian dynasty. The *livre tournois* was divided into 20 sols (*sous* after 1715), each of which was divided into 12 *deniers*. Between 1360 and 1641, coins worth one *livre tournois* were minted, known as *francs*. The first French paper money, issued between 1701 and 1720, was denominated in *livres tournois*. This was the last time the name was used, as later notes and coins were denominated simply in *livres*, the *livre parisis* having finally been abolished in 1667.

Jude was already moving towards the door, when Nicolas Treml added:

"Wait! You must dress and arm yourself for a long journey. Take your weapons, as one who is about to do battle to the death; and before you depart, make sure to say good-bye to all of those thou love. Have you drawn up your will?"

"No, my lord."

"Then do it now."

Again the squire bowed, and left the room, carefully carrying the iron chest in his hands.

CHAPTER III
The Confidant

Nicolas Treml did not sleep that night. Before the first grey streak of dawn was visible, he heard the tramp of Jude's charger in the castle yard, and almost at the same moment, Hervé de Vaunoy appeared in the open doorway, no longer with the humble air he had assumed, when first introduced, but with upright figure, a complacent smile, and familiarity of address, scarcely compatible with affectionate respect.

"Holy Mother!" he exclaimed, as he advanced sedately across the room, "you are early, my dear cousin. I was but in my first sleep, when they came to wake me on your behalf—"

He stopped suddenly, as he beheld the pale countenance of the fine old nobleman, and saw that his stern eye was fixed upon him, as if he would read his heart.

Then, with an involuntary shudder, he stammered:

"Is anything the matter?"

Nicolas Treml pointed to a chair, and De Vaunoy sat down.

"Hervé," said the old gentleman in a slow and resigned tone, "when it pleased the Almighty, in His infinite wisdom, to take my dear son from me, you were only a poor man, sustaining an unequal, useless contest with me..."

"But you were generous, my good cousin," interrupted De Vaunoy who started to feel concerned.

"Will you be now grateful for my leniency?" asked the old man.

De Vaunoy rose, seized Nicolas's hand, carried it to his lips, and said solemnly:

"Heavens! I am yours, my cousin, body and soul!"

Nicolas Treml marked a pause, during which he still scanned his crafty cousin narrowly.

"I would believe you," he said at last. "I do believe you. So there is no more time for hesitation, and my determination cannot be altered. Listen to me!"

Drawing his chair towards De Vaunoy, the Baron said:

"I am about to depart from this castle, perhaps never to return... Please, do not interrupt me... My journey will be long and tedious; and at the end, there is a perilous abyss. Providence may aid me to surmount this danger—but does it still shield a Breton, or protect what is good in Brittany? My hopes are faint, and my firm belief is that I go to certain death."

"To certain death?" De Vaunoy repeated, without in the least comprehending what his cousin meant.

"To certain death!" exclaimed the old man, a sublime enthusiasm suddenly lighting up his whole countenance. "Did you ever feel a strong, innate, uncontrollable desire to die for Brittany, Monsieur de Vaunoy?"

"By the Holy Virgin, my cousin, perhaps such an idea may have crossed my mind at times."

"To die for Brittany, to perish for our oppressed, downtrodden mother! Is not that the duty of a loyal Breton gentleman?"

"Well, yes, no doubt, my lord, but—"

"Time presses," interrupted Nicolas Treml, "and it will not allow me to enter into long explanations. When I am gone from my domains, my grandson Georges will need support..."

"He shall have mine."

"Will you be to him as a father—even as I have been?"

"Do I not owe you, sir, the gratitude and reverence of a son?" replied the hypocrite pathetically.

"Will you swear to love this infant whom I leave with you? Will you replace me, teach him to love our dear Brittany, and hate the French? Will you stand in my stead?"

De Vaunoy pretended to wipe away a tear.

"Yes, yes," the old man said, repressing his emotions. "You are grateful, good, and honorable. I will trust you, and my last moments will be happy."

He rose, crossed the room, and opened a cabinet. From it, he drew forth a written parchment, sealed with his coat of arms.

"Here is a deed which I drew out myself this night, by which the ownership of the whole of the domains of Treml are transferred to you."

Hervé was well nigh overcome by the welcome, but unexpected, statement; his eyes were dazzled, and a thousand meteoric lights seemed to dance before them; a tremor shook his frame, and the blood rushed tumultuously to his cheeks; but Monsieur Treml de La Tremlays was so intent upon unrolling the document, that he failed to notice the reaction of his cousin.

"Without confiding to you the whole of my secret, which belongs to Brittany," he continued, "I may state, that my enterprise may expose me to the charge of treason and *lèse-majesté*; and that crime—such the fools may call it—will not only bring certain death, but the confiscation of all my land and goods. The inheritance of Georges Treml must therefore be placed above this risk; and therefore, cousin, I have selected you to be the guardian of my grandson's rights."

The accomplished hypocrite contented himself with again lifting up his eyes, and again laying his hand upon his breast.

"Do you accept this sacred trust, Hervé de Vaunoy?" asked Nicolas Treml.

"Do I?" De Vaunoy replied, recovering his voice precisely at the proper moment. "Holy Mother, how can you ask me such a question? Is not this the very time, the best occasion, to prove my unlimited devotion to you?

Taking the old man's hands in his, he added:

"Thank you! Thank you, my noble cousin! I will prove to you that your confidence is not misplaced."

As he spoke, Wolf, Monsieur Treml de La Tremlays' favorite dog, which had been lying quietly before the fire, growled audibly, rose up and, placing himself between his master and De Vaunoy, kept his glowing eyes fixed upon the latter, who trembled and recoiled instinctively.

Wolf and Jean Blanc, thought the old man, for, like a true Breton, he was susceptible to superstition. *It is strange that both the dog and the idiot instinctively hate my cousin...*

He hesitated for an instant and was perhaps tempted to keep the deed, but the voice of what he thought was his patriotic duty compelled him to carry on with his plan. He pushed the dog away from him and handed the parchment to De Vaunoy.

"God sees you, and He will punish traitors. You are now sole master of the destinies of Treml."

A long, plaintive howl was uttered by the dog, as if he understood these fatal words.

"And now, Monsieur de Vaunoy, not from any distrust of you, but merely because man is mortal, and none of us know when we may be called upon to die, I must

44

ask you for some guarantee that these lands will not pass from me or mine altogether."

"Anything—everything you desire, cousin."

"Write then," said the Baron, pointing to a table and the necessary materials.

De Vaunoy sat down and Treml dictated the following:

"*I, Hervé de Vaunoy, swear to restore the domains of La Tremlays and Boüexis-in-the Forest, with all their dependencies, to any direct descendant of Nicolas Treml de la Tremlays who shall present this document to me…*"

"My good cousin," Hervé interrupted, "this may put arms into the hands of the King's Prosecutors. If you are condemned for *lèse-majesté*, this document may be deemed suspect."

"Go on," said the Baron, "write further as I shall dictate to you: …*Along with the sum of one hundred thousand livres, representing the price paid by me for said domains and dependencies.* The Prosecutor will not be able to question the sale; one hundred thousand livres is a considerable sum, even though it is still less than the real value of the estates."

De Vaunoy remained silent for several minutes; then, taking the parchment from Monsieur Treml de La Tremlays, he saw that it was a regular deed of sale, properly and legally drawn up. The frown disappeared from his face.

"Well, well," he said at length, "since you will have it, it must be so! But Heaven is my witness that I wish that these papers may be rendered useless by your safe return."

"Wish it, my cousin," said the old man, "but do not mislead yourself by believing it. And now, sign and seal the papers."

De Vaunoy did so in due form; each of the contracting parties took possession of the document that belonged to him by the arrangements.

A death-like calm ensued. Monsieur Treml de La Tremlays seemed plunged in a reverie, which his cousin for some time respected;

"These preparations, my cousin," said De Vaunoy finally, "do not indicate your immediate departure, do they?"

But in his heart, he knew otherwise—and was not wrong.

His voice awoke Monsieur Treml de La Tremlays. Rising quickly from his seat, he murmured:

"It is time! You have recalled me to my duty, cousin. I must go."

"Already?"

"Yes. I have lingered too long already, and am late. See that my horse is saddled, Vaunoy, whilst I bid adieu to the home of my noble ancestors, and embrace my son's child, probably for the last time."

De Vaunoy drooped his head, with every indication of deep grief, and withdrew to carry out his cousin's mandate.

Nicolas Treml drew himself up to the full of his majestic height, took from the wall, and girded round himself, the good sword that had descended to him from a long line of ancestors—a tried Damascus blade that had cloven many an English skull in the days of the old wars. Next, he slung his mantle over his shoulders and placed a broad-brimmed hat on the thick meshes of his snow-white hair.

The grand reception hall used on state days and holidays was located between Nicolas Treml's private apartment and the room where young Georges slept. It was a spacious chamber, the walls were lined with black oak paneling, relieved by pillars of variegated walnut, with gilded flourishes and cornices.

From each panel hung a portrait of some member of the family, surmounted by an escutcheon with the full quarterings of their arms.

Nicolas Treml de La Tremlays, entering the hall with slow step and melancholy look, and dropped on his knees before two portraits at the upper end.

"Adieu! dear mother!" he exclaimed. "And farewell to you, my father. I go to die—as you both lived— for Brittany."

As the devoted patriot rose, an oblique ray of the morning sun pierced through a pane of one of the large painted windows, brightening the gilding and casting a momentary appearance of life upon the countenances of those feudal chiefs and hardy knights. It seemed for an instant that the starched, noble dames smiled and inhaled the odors of the bouquets of roses they all held; whilst the good knights laid their gauntleted hands upon their mailed hips or trusty swords, as they heard the voice of the last true Breton about to stake his life for his native land.

Before he left the hall, Nicolas Treml took off his hat and saluted one last time the twenty generations of ancestors who applauded his sacrifice.

Young Georges slept soundly until the rough beard of his grandsire aroused him from his dream, and as he awoke, he stretched his little arms round the old man's neck.

Monsieur Treml de La Tremlays had bade adieu to the resemblances of his great ancestors without a sigh; but his strength of mind forsook him, a deep groan escaped his Herculean breast, and a tear stood trembling in his eyes as he gazed upon the last scion of his race, soon, possibly, to be an orphan, and who now smiled upon him bright as a summer's morn.

"May God for ever bless you, my beloved child!" he murmured. "May He make you a gentleman and a true Breton! May you resemble your progenitors, who were valiant, good, and—free!"

Taking the child into his arms, he kissed him frantically replaced the wondering infant in his bed, and hurried from a sight that rent his heart in twain.

When Monsieur Treml de La Tremlays reached the castle yard he found his cousin holding the horse saddled and bridled for the road. Wolf, too, was there, and was chained up to prevent him from following his master.

Nicolas Treml mounted and rode forth with De Vaunoy at his side until they arrived at the end of the long avenue of trees. There he said:

"Return to the castle, cousin. None must know where I direct my steps."

"Farewell, my excellent friend," said De Vaunoy, with many sobs and sighs, "although my heart is breaking as I say the word."

"Farewell!"replied the old man. "Keep your oath in mind, and pray to Heaven for my soul."

Nicolas Treml struck the noble horse with both spurs. The animal bounded along the causeway, and speedily the clatter of his hoofs was lost on the soft moss of the wood.

Hervé de Vaunoy listened intently till the sounds died gradually away; and then, striking his clenched fist into the open palm of the other hand, he chuckled as he said:

"Just as I planned! I was given a foot's length within this paradise, and the Devil helped me to the rest! A pleasant journey to you, most noble cousin, and a happy and quick death at the close of it. I will certainly keep all my fine promises, and your domains shall pass into the best of hands."

Turning on his heel, with a fiendish smile upon his face, and his hat cocked fiercely on one ear, he passed by the kennel where the dog, Wolf, was lying, and when within reach, he commenced his career of tyranny and crime by striking the faithful animal severely with his pommel of his undrawn sword.

"Thus, thus!" he shouted, "will I treat all who do not bend the knee before me, and obey my will!"

On that day, the menials of Treml forgot to lighten their labor with their songs; a dark cloud obscured the minds and depressed the spirits of the good servants, and all anticipated some fearful catastrophe.

As for the brave old Nicolas Treml, he soon left the narrow beaten track through the forest, struck into the tortuous bye-paths, and plunged through a thicket of underwood.

The further he went, the more rough and savage the aspect of the land became; gigantic brambles reared their thorny heads on high from tree to tree, interlaced as the in the primeval forests of the New World.

Here and there, where a clearing permitted the hardy broom to spring, the smoke from the chimney of a miserable hut showed that some human beings inhabited the waste.

After the old gentleman had accomplished half-a-league, he was compelled to slacken his rapid pace; for the forest had become almost impassable.

Pulling up as he perceived Jude's charger attached by the bridle to a tree, he dismounted, fastened his own horse near his stable mate, and made his way through the ragged covert.

Soon, he found his trusty squire, seated upon the little iron chest.

CHAPTER IV
The Wolf's Pit

About a half-hour's journey from the eastern edge of the Forest of Rennes, situated in the clearest portion of the wood, and far from any habitation, there was a deep ravine, the steep and rocky sides of which were covered with stunted trees springing up amidst holly bushes and tangled under-wood, attaining an extraordinary height.

A slender stream ran through the bottom of the ravine in the rainy season, but in the summer it completely disappeared, and the bed of the rivulet was traced only by a small green line of grass that crossed the yellow, arid soil.

The course of this ravine ran due north and south; on the eastern side there were a number of dark oaks, and the western rose almost perpendicularly, woody at its base, and then bare rock up to the very top and in the center. Several deep gorges pierced the steep scarped wall fringed with yellow cypresses and sepulchral yew.

In 1719, the appearance of this ravine was even more somber. On the summit, the remains of two short towers of masonry—which had formerly been windmills—could be seen, their moldering, cracked walls seemingly about to be precipitated to the earth by every gust of wind, and all around the soil had given way, covered with the ruins, which had already fallen.

Some few paces off, on the right-hand side of these towers, the land showed signs of having been explored at some very early period; here and there the eye of the inquisitive traveler would discover the remains of trenches, excavations, and galleries, similar to those in stone quarries and mines, and portions of dismantled habitations proved that extensive buildings must have once been built there.

All these remains of ancient edifices long predated the windmills, which nevertheless crumbled from old age. To identify their origins and their purpose—obviously, some kind of industrial enterprise—one would have had to not only go through the entire Middle-Ages but perhaps even further back in time, to the days of the Roman occupation.

However, since we could state with near-certainty that the number of archeologists in the Forest of Rennes in the 18th century was virtually nil, no one ever questioned those ancient ruins.

Immediately in front of and below the ancient mills, the ravine suddenly became so extremely narrow that the tall trees on each side mingled their verdant branches and formed a vault that was almost impenetrable to the light of day. This solitary, dark, savage gorge was called *the Wolf's Pit* by the local inhabitants.

No need to explain to our readers the obvious origins of that name.

A lost traveler who would have unwittingly come across that wild location—the gloomy colors of which, transposed onto a painting, would have marvelously served as a background for one of our popular Boulevard melodramas—would have found no traces there of the neighborly presence of Man. A solemn silence reigned throughout the ravine and the adjacent forest, broken only by the sylvan sounds which never fail to exist where Nature is left completely to herself.

One could have believed himself to be in the midst of an impenetrable jungle.

Nevertheless, after careful survey, the eye would light upon a hut half-concealed amongst a thicket of hazels, constructed of wood and mud, plastered with lime, and having only one aperture, where patches of coarse cloth and slips of paper performed the offices of glass. That wretched dwelling was leaning against one of the towers and projected upon its surroundings a feeling of distress and abandon.

It was in the Wolf's Pit, close to this secluded spot, that Nicolas Treml de La Tremlays had ordered his squire Jude to await his coming. The loyal servant had arrived there before daybreak.

While he sits there patiently upon the iron chest with its hundred thousand livres that represented, at that point in time, the estimated value of the entire estates of Treml, let us lift the cloth door of the hut, and see what was happening within.

The interior consisted of a single chamber; the scanty furniture being a rudely-framed table, a truckle bed, and two small three-legged stools. The damp earth served the occupants for flooring, poles stretching from the sides and crossing at intervals formed the rafters, and being lined with rushes, and plastered likewise with mud and lime, constituted a tolerable roof. In one corner, there was a quantity of straw, and on it lay a young man fast asleep.

An aged peasant, reduced by long illness to a skeleton, occupied the bed, and seemed, whilst he pressed both his hands convulsively upon his breast, as if he desired to stifle the expression of acute pain in order not to wake his younger companion.

There was a remarkable resemblance between the two men; both were as pallid as corpses, and their hair was like the winter's snow, but Time had heaped the frost upon the head of one, whilst the other had borne this stamp of old age from his birth.

They were Mathieu Blanc, an ancient retainer of Treml, and his son, Jean Blanc the Albino.

When a sharper pang than usual drew a cry of pain from the older man, Jean was on his feet in an instant; then, bounding to the bedside, he took his father's hand affectionately, and pressed it to his heart.

"My son," said Mathieu, "I am thirsty."

Jean took from the ground a cracked bowl which contained some drops of liquid, and held it to his father's mouth. The old man drank with avidity.

"I'm still thirsty," muttered the old man, asking for more. "So very thirsty."

Jean quickly searched the hut with his eyes, but there was nothing more to drink.

"There is no more, father," Jean answered. "But I will go to work, and bring you back some food and medicine."

The sick man moved upon his ragged couch, evidently in great agony, and groaned aloud; but as Jean stood with his hatchet on his shoulder at the doorway, he called him back in plaintive accents:

"Please, stay," he said. "I suffer most when I'm alone."

Jean laid down his hatchet, and again approached the bed.

"I will stay with you, father," he replied, "and when you're asleep, I will go to the castle and ask for what you want from Nicolas Treml. He never refuses a poor man."

"Never!" said Mathieu solemnly. "Monsieur Nicolas is a true nobleman, heart and soul, and does not forget his old servant, who now has not the strength to work or fight for him. And he does not despise you, my poor boy, because your hair and skin are not like that of other men. May the Almighty bless him!"

"God save his soul!" the Albino reverently uttered.

Then, the old man, raising himself with difficulty to a sitting posture, looked his son steadily in the face, and said:

"Jean, my son, my memory is feeble because I am so very old; but I think I heard you say that the son of Nicolas Treml is in great danger?"

"He died two years back, father."

"It's true. You told me. Ah, I cannot recollect as I once did! His grandson, then? The last heir of Treml?"

"Yes, it's as I told you, father."

"What danger, my son—what danger threatens him? Can't we help him?"

Jean looked sadly at his father's old and exhausted form.

"Pray for the noble child, father. I will act. Yesterday, as I was working in a chestnut tree, cutting hoops, I saw Nicolas Treml returning from Rennes, where the Estates had gathered—"

"It is a noble and gallant assembly, Jean."

"It was so once, father. Anyway, I slipped down from the tree to make my humble salute to our good lord, as is my custom; but he was so taken up with his thoughts that he did not see me, and as I followed in the covert by his side, I overheard some words that he spoke aloud."

"What did he say, my boy?"

The features of the Albino contracted; then every muscle of his countenance worked in an agitated manner, and he burst into a fit of laughter.

"What did he say, Jean?" the old man repeated.

But instead of answering, the youth began to gambol around the room, chanting a harvest-song peculiar to the province.

His father made a gesture of despair, fell back upon the bed, and with a sigh, turned his face towards the wall, as if he was used to the fits of madness.

It was ever so. Jean Blanc, without being a confirmed idiot, as he was generally held to be by the woodcutters and charcoal-burners of the forest, was subject to frequent fits, which deranged his intellect for the moment, and left him in a state of great depression. His physical defects and mental affliction made him a thing apart from his fellow creatures. He knew this, and as a result, felt himself inferior in this fashion to the robust denizens of the wood, over whom, when in full possession of his faculties, he easily towered intellectually.

He frequently affected strange manners to use this weakness as a shield between himself and the world, especially when he had some concealed purpose.

He became half-maniac, half-misanthrope; sometimes a deliberate jester, but at other times, a true lunatic.

To his father, who was dying from the conjoint effects of old age and the want of proper nourishment, he alone appeared as he really was, and on him he lavished all the filial tenderness that glowed within his heart.

There was one other man for whom Jean Blanc's devotion knew no bounds, and he was Nicolas Treml de La Tremlays. But the humble woodcutter, to whom Providence had denied the usual attributes of the human form, possessed indomitable pride. Contenting himself with just the miserable alms doled out to him by the steward of the Castle, he kept his distance. And Monsieur Treml de La Tremlays, permanently preoccupied by his ideas of resistance to the French King, knew not that his ancient servitor, Mathieu, was destitute of the absolute necessaries of existence and dying from want. He had once given orders to the steward that Jean should have all that he required, and relied upon that man to follow them.

However, Alain, the steward, detested Jean Blanc and purposefully thwarted his master's generous intentions; but Jean Blanc never complained of his hard lot. When Jean met Monsieur Nicolas accidentally in the forest, he spoke with fervor of the affection he felt for the boy Georges, and uttered in cryptic words his suspicions against Hervé de Vaunoy.

Their conversations were always of a singular complexion; the feudal Lord and the vassal stood on a footing of equality: the former, pitying the infirmities of the latter, addressed him with the freedom and kindness of a friend; and the latter, devoted, but proud beyond measure, enveloped himself in his idiocy, as with a mantle, that permitted him to throw all deference aside.

On the present occasion, Jean remained for half-an hour prey to the frenzy that had seized upon him; bounding from side to side, and muttering between his firmly-closed teeth:

"I am the white rabbit… the white rabbit…"

And he laughed bitterly, full of irony and pain.

But when the paroxysm seemed to be at its height, the fire in his eyes died and and his fit subsided. He cast his eyes out the window, and looked feverishly in the direction of the Wolf's Pit.

At that moment, Nicolas Treml and his squire Jude were coming up the glen, hastily proceeding towards the Pit. Jean rushed through the door, but by the time he got out and up the ravine, the nobleman and his servant had already disappeared amongst the tall trees.

We shall now recount what had taken place between the two of them.

CHAPTER V
The Hollow Oak

In the center of the Wolf's Pit, a colossal oak had buried its sinewy roots into the scanty soil along the steep side of the rock, and its mighty limbs, radiating on all sides, created the shade that covered that side of the cleft.

There were numerous legends in the forest about this monarch of the woods and the two neighboring towers. It was believed that this giant oak grew directly above a vast cave, the entrance of which existed in the foundation of one of the towers, or amidst the excavations or ruins of the ancient buildings on the opposite side of the ravine.

No one, in the characteristic manner of Breton apathy, had ever bothered to look for such a concealed entrance, and because of that, everyone was convinced that such a thing did, indeed, exist.

The superstition of the peasants, and the evil reputation of the Pit itself effectually precluded any attempt.

The opinions of the rustics were so divided on the origins of these supposed subterranean passages that no one, in the memory of living men, had ever even attempted to explore the area. Some asserted that they were merely ancient mine galleries, whence iron ore had once been extracted; whilst others, rejecting this common sense hypothesis, maintained that the passages and spacious caverns spread beneath the forest in every direction, all the way to the neighboring manor of Boüexis, which, according to tradition, had been the focus of resistance to the hateful Edict of Union signed in the days of the good Duchess Anne, the popular Breton noblewoman whose actions were hated, but whose memory is still cherished.

According to this last hypothesis, the caves and passages served as convenient retreats for those resistants who first assumed the name of Breton Brothers under the reign of Louis XII.

However that may be, anyone who ventured to question the existence of these caves was deemed a fool or ignorant.

There were certainly no visible indications of any caverns in the vicinity of the giant oak that sprang from the bottom of the gorge, the roots of which dug deep into the soil.

Its circumference was enormous; and although it was completely hollow and apparently held together by the strong-fibred bark, it showed no signs of decrepitude or ultimate decay.

Two huge apertures formed entrances into a chamber, wherein ten men might have sat with ease.

It was at the foot of this marvelous tree that the Monsieur Treml de La Tremlays rejoined his squire.

Nicolas Treml was concerned; and the emotions that weighed on his heart were reflected on his austere face. Jude was armed to the teeth, dressed and prepared for a long journey. As he heard the heavy tread of his master coming up the glen, he rose, and silently pointed to the iron chest.

"Good," said Nicolas Treml.

Then he dropped upon one knee, unlocked the chest, and deposited the paper De Vaunoy had signed beneath the gold it contained.

"Thus," said he, as he reclosed the lid, and turned the key twice in the lock, "rich or poor, the sons of Treml will be able to reclaim their heritage, and treachery be defeated, if any there should be."

Jude remained motionless, marveling at the strange proceeding but not comprehending it in the least, ready to obey his master's next command, but not wishing to anticipate it.

Jude Leker was a stalwart, hard-featured man; his high cheek bones, standing prominently out from the rounded shape of his face, gave to it the characteristic of a genuine Breton.

His hair fell to his broad shoulders in massive locks; his grey beard descended low upon his breast.

His costume, like that of his master, was at least one hundred years out of date; and with their steel head-pieces and long swords with plain crossguards, one would have thought that the days of the errant knights of yore had returned.

In Brittany, time does not fly, it crawls, its wings made heavy from the contact with the damp and misty Armorican air. Local customs follow this pattern, remaining unchanged. As we write this, there is still between Paris and some towns of the county of Léon, Cornwall, or the Bishopric of Rennes, the same distance that exists between the Middle-Ages and today, between wood and gas, coaches and steam; but also between belief and doubt, poetry and prose, the spires of yesterday's cathedrals and the bastardized rooftops of today's temples of Mammon.

In character, Jude was one of those honest, simple men, raised in the doctrine of passive obedience to their masters. Jude obeyed because it was his pleasure, as well as his vocation; but in him, submission assumed the as-

61

pect of devotion untainted by servility. Nowadays, it is hard to conceive of those social contracts, both tacitly implied and irrevocable, which turned master and servant into a single unit, in possession of the strength of two men at the service of a single will.

Today, the notion of domestic servants carries the aura of subservience and, whether that be true or false, that concept weighs heavily upon an entire segment of our society. But in those times, when the social classes were rigorously organized from serf to sovereign, through a thorough system of ranks, a servant was to his master what the latter was to his king. There was a sense of mutual and comparable reciprocity, which therefore excluded contempt from one to the other.

In even older times, when chivalry was still the order of the land, the sons of knights seldom became knights in turn, and could inscribe a motto on their shield, before they learned to carry another knight's lance. It was only by submitting themselves to the trials of domesticity that they earned the right to call themselves by the most glorious title of all times: that of chevalier.

As we said, social customs had hardly changed in Brittany, and memories endured. At the beginning of the eighteenth century, when Voltaire was put on a pedestal and work began on the great *Encyclopedia*, feudal laws were not yet extinct in Brittany, the land of stones and sea. The great landed proprietors, who seldom lost sight of the smoke that curled about their hospitable roofs, sternly rejected all innovation and new ideas; their servants, or retainers, were to them vassals in the strictest sense of the word, that is to say, one small cog within the great feudal machine.

Their valets were nothing but "little vassals."[6]

Therefore, we must not be surprised that we make a difference between Jude and an ordinary salaried employee of today. Doing so is to be true to the then state of Breton society. Jude, although disposed to obey implicitly, did not lose his dignity as a man. His obedience rose from the same source, and stood in the same relation to his master, as did that feudal noble to his liege, lord and king.

When Monsieur Treml de La Tremlays had re-locked the iron chest, he cast a searching, uneasy glance around him.

"Are we alone?" he asked the squire. "Are we truly alone?"

Jude examined the adjacent brush and underwood thoroughly, and replied in the affirmative:

"We are."

"I am asking," the old man said, laying his hand upon the chest, "because the fortune, and perhaps the life, of the heir of Treml are confined within this chest, my good man. It is my secret, the hope of my descendents, the price of my sacrifice, and my very best friend would risk the loss of his life were he to behold what I am doing now."

"Should I retire?" Jude asked.

"No, my faithful friend; you are mine own. I know, by every tie, that you would perish rather than betray me."

Jude laid his hand upon his heart by way of answer.

"You are alone," he repeated.

---

[6] Valet derives from *vasslet* or *vasselet*. (Note from the Author)

Monsieur Treml de La Tremlays again looked furtively around, his eyes drifting towards the edge of the ravine.

"What's that?" he inquired, finally noticing Mathieu Blanc's hut behind the ruins of the mills.

"Nothing," replied Jude. "That's where the White Rabbit sleeps. His father is dying."

A cloud passed over the old man's brow.

"Jean Blanc!" he muttered.

His thoughts reverted to his encounter with the Albino on the preceding day, which he interpreted as a bad omen.

"The poor boy has incurred the enmity of Master Alain, your steward. It might fare ill for him after we are gone."

Nicolas Treml took out a purse of gold, and handed it to Jude, who understood immediately. He threw it over the low trees so that it fell immediately in front of Mathieu's cabin-door.

"And now, to work!" said the old gentleman.

With Jude's help, he carried the iron chest into the hollow oak, which Jean used as a general magazine, and contained his working tools with several chestnut branches which he had cut for hoops.

At a sign from his master, the squire took a pickaxe and commenced making a large hole in the ground at the bottom of the oak.

After an hour's labor, rendered onerous by the nature of the soil and the spreading roots of the surrounding trees, the chest was placed in the hole, covered carefully with earth, and the tools and chestnut branches were replaced in their original positions, so that without a minute investigation, no one would have supposed the ground had been disturbed.

The sun was high above the horizon when Monsieur Treml de La Tremlays and Jude issued from the oak.

"Let's go!" said Nicolas Treml. "The road ahead of us is long, and I am in a hurry!"

The master and his servant went rapidly down the glen as fast as they could walk.

It was at that precise moment that Jean Blanc sprang from the hut. Gifted with wonderful agility and supernatural speed, he dashed into the covert; but when he emerged from the tangled underwood, he found that both had disappeared. However, he heard the echoing sounds of the coursers' hoofs as the horsemen galloped away.

He dashed out again, but the horses were moving like the wind; all attempts to catch up with the travelers would be in vain. Then, with a sudden inspiration, he climbed a tall elm with the rapidity of a squirrel, and caught sight of them hastening towards Fougères.

"Monsieur Nicolas!" he shouted in despair.

The old gentleman turned briefly around, but did not stop.

Jean then placed a hand on each side of his mouth to concentrate his powerful voice, and began to intone the *Lament* with all his might.

For one moment, he thought his expedient had succeeded.

Monsieur Treml de La Tremlays suddenly drew up and appeared undecided about what to do next. But the next instant, passing his hand across his brow, as if to chase away a last hesitation, he struck his gallant steed with both his spurs, and again thundered down the road.

Slowly and sadly, Jean descended from the tree, and silently returned to the Wolf's pit.

When he reached the hut, he saw, by the sun's glittering rays, the purse that Nicolas had left.

Tears came to his eyes.

"May the Almighty forever bless him. He is kind. He thinks he is about to do good..."

He sat down on the threshold and remained there, lost in his thoughts.

"Poor, poor Monsieur Georges! Alone in the keeping of that villain Hervé de Vaunoy, who does not believe in God!"

He paused, then continued:

"They call me the White Rabbit, but if I am a rabbit, he is a wolf... It is an unequal fight, because the Wolf has teeth that can rend and bite... But what if I grew teeth, too? The rabbit could then turn into a wolf to protect or avenge those whom he loves! I will try—yes, I will..."

CHAPTER VI
The Journey

The last voice which Nicolas Treml heard upon his vast domains was that of Jean Blanc, whose mournful chant seemed to him an evil omen. It required all his strength of mind, and that dogged obstinacy which is one of the characteristics of a Breton, to overcome the melancholy thoughts that pressed upon his soul.

However, making a mighty effort, he thrust the image of his grandson from his mind, and continued on his way.

As he was desirous that no one should know the direction, after traveling for two leagues towards Couesnon and the sea, he suddenly made a turn at Vitré, a black citadel now lit by the meridian sun, took the high road to Laval, leaving to his right the many meadows through which the tranquil Vilaine pursued its quiet course.

Between Laval and Vitré, a little beyond the town of Ernée, which eighty years afterwards played such an important part in the bloody wars against the *Chouans*,[7] two stumps of posts were seen upon a rising ground.

Between these were the worm-eaten remains of a barrier, which had been destroyed many years before.

---

[7] The *Chouans* were a royalist uprising or counter-revolution in twelve of the western *départements* of France, particularly in the provinces of Brittany and Maine, against the French First Republic during the French Revolution. It played out in three phases and lasted from the spring of 1794 until 1800.

Reaching the spot, Nicolas Treml stopped his horse and took off his hat, an act which Jude Leker imitated.

"A few more paces," said Nicolas Treml, "and we shall be on hostile ground, the land of our eternal enemy, the hated France. Whilst we are still upon the soil of our own native land, join with me in an *Ave* to our Lady of the Forest."

Both piously recited the Latin orison.

"In days of old, Jude," the nobleman continued, "these stumps were uncut and each bore two emblazoned shields—on this side, escutcheons of ermine, surmounted by a ducal coronet, and on that side, three golden lilies upon an azure field. On this side of the barrier, there was a Breton man-at-arms, and on the other side, a French soldier. They looked at each other, at a lance's length apart, for France and Brittany, Dreux and Valois, were on an equal footing."

"Those were glorious days, Monsieur Nicolas," Jude sighed.

"The great house of Dreux is no more," continued Treml in a trembling voice. "Brittany is but a province of France. But Heaven is just, and no doubt, it will strengthen my arm. Onward, Jude, onward!"

They rode through the ancient borders of the two States, and silently continued on their way.

The journey was long and tedious.

First, they reached Laval, the ancient fief of De La Tremoille; then Mayenne, which gave its name to the one of the main Leaguers.[8]

---

[8]Charles of Lorraine, Duke of Mayenne (1554-1611), a.k.a. Charles de Guise, a military leader of the Catholic League during the French Wars of Religion. Following the assassina-

And finally, they arrived at Alençon, which was the legacy of the royal Sons of France.[9]

In each of these towns, they were obliged to stop and rest their horses and themselves. They then quickly left again.

Where are we going? Jude often wondered

But he never asked this aloud. If it pleased Nicolas Treml to remain silent as to the purpose of their journey, it didn't behoove him, Jude, to inquire about it.

His uncertainty and curiosity, however, were not doomed to remain long unsatisfied; for after passing through Mortagne, Verneuil, and Dreux, on the morning of the sixth day, they crossed the gilded gates of the palace of Versailles.

The palace was, at that time, somewhat abandoned by the Court; but its white marble pillars still shone in all their former glory.

Statues, antique vases, colonnades and pediments still contained the remnants of their former splendor. It had only been a short time since the royal city was in mourning. The gravel of the spacious walks still bore the imprint of the ladies' satin slippers, and the lords' ver-million-colored high-heeled shoes.

Weren't there still flowers in the vases, verses of amorous swains graven upon the trees, and didn't the bronze Naiads still spout forth their crystal streams?

Alas! The period of mourning had gone on for too long. The flowers had withered, bronze and marble had acquired the austere beauty of antiques; the songs were

_____

tion of his brothers at Blois in 1588, he fought King Henri IV, but eventually made peace with him in 1596.

[9]Alençon became the seat of a dukedom in 1415, belonging to the sons of the King of France until the French Revolution.

gone, and with them all their joy; and all that was left was to weep over the lost grandeurs of the monarchy, like the poet who wrote:

> *Oh! que Versailles était superbe*
> *Dans ces jours purs de tout affront*
> *Où les prospérités en gerbe*
> *S'épanouissaient sur son front!*
> *Là, tout faste était sans mesure.*
> *Là, tout arbre avait sa parure.*
> *Là, tout homme avait sa dorure.*
> *Tout du maître suivait la loi.*
> *Comme au même but vont cent routes,*
> *Là les grandeurs abondaient toutes.*
> *L'olympe ne pendait aux voûtes*
> *Que pour compléter le grand roi!* [10]

Nicolas Treml de La Tremlays and his trusty squire were not men to think much of sculptured marble and magnificent water spouts. They cast mere passing glances at all the bronze divinities who simpered, played upon the flute, or danced with wreaths of grapes and vine-leaves on their heads and continued on their way.

After a few more hours, they reached the banks of the Seine.

---

[10] Féval is quoting Victor Hugo's *Les Voix Intérieures, Sunt Lacrymae Rerum*. Translation: "Oh! How superb was Versailles / In these days devoid of all affronts / When bouquets of prosperity / Blossomed on its forehead! / There, splendor was without measure. / There, every tree had its finery. / There, every man had his gilding. / Everything followed the law of its master. / Like a hundred roads go to the same destination. / There, all grandeurs abounded. / Olympus only hung from its ceilings, / Only to complete the great king!"

"Is Paris still far?" asked Nicolas Treml to a bourgeois mounted on a donkey who was traveling in the opposite direction.

The man turned around and pointed to the east. Nicolas Treml, looking in that direction, perceived a glittering point. It was the bright dome of the Invalides which shone in the bright rays of the rising sun.[11]

"Courage, my friend," the old man said. "This is the end of our pilgrimage."

"Good!" was Jude's reply.

If the horses could have spoken, they might have expressed their satisfaction in a more explicit manner.

On entering the city, Nicolas Treml de La Tremlays inquired where the Regent, Philippe d'Orléans,[12] resided, and pressed his horse to get there faster. A fever seemed to be burning in his veins. Jude followed him step by step. The trusty squire's face now reflected a powerful curiosity. What could Monsieur Treml de La Tremlays want with the Regent of France?

---

[11] Its construction (designed by Mansard) was completed on 28 August 1706.

[12] Philippe II, Duke of Orléans (1674-1723), member of the royal family who served as Regent of the Kingdom from 1715 to 1723. His father was Louis XIV's younger brother, Philippe I; his mother was Elizabeth Charlotte of the Palatinate. Named regent for Louis XV until the young man attained his majority on 15 February 1723, the period of his *de facto* rule was known as the Regency. On the majority of the king, the Duke stepped down. At the death of Cardinal Dubois on 10 August, the young king offered the Duke the position of prime minister, and he remained in that office until his death a few months later. He died in Versailles on 2 December 1723 in the arms of his mistress. Louis XV mourned him greatly.

At length, the nobleman pulled up his exhausted horse before the Palais Royal. Dismounting, he sought entrance, but the valets and porters barred his passage.

"Go, tell Philippe d'Orléans," said the old man, "that Nicolas Treml would speak with him."

But the valets, seeing his antique costume, now literally covered in dust, turned their backs on him or laughed in his face.

One, more courteous than the rest, said diffidently:

"His Royal Highness is at his castle at Villers-Cotterets."

The Breton nobleman remounted.

"Will one of you," he asked, "show me the way to that castle?"

The Regent's lackeys redoubled their impertinent laughs.

"Such as you, mine ancient friend, are not admitted at Villers-Cotterets," said one.

"'Tis but a peasant from the Danube," said one man.

"Or rather," said another," the Wandering Jew who stole a nag and a servant on his way!"

"It's Don Quixote!"

"No! Monsieur de La Palisse!"[13]

Jude laid his hand on his sword, and half drew it, but his master stopped him with a gesture. An insult that comes from such lower depths dies on its way and cannot be heard.

Monsieur Treml de La Tremlays stopped at a nearby hotel that bore the arms of Brittany. Without even

---

[13] The reason for this sarcasm in that context seems obscure. This nobleman and brave military officer is only remembered, rather inaccurately, for a tautology inscribed on his tomb.

taking the time to remove his boots, he asked the inn-keeper to find him a guide that could take him to Villers-Cotterets immediately.

Jude's astonishment was now so great that he could no longer keep his curiosity in check. Unable to remain silent, he finally asked humbly:

"Monsieur Nicolas, you must have a great desire to see this Philippe d'Orléans?"

"And you're asking me why?" replied Nicolas Treml, energetically.

That answer only increased Jude's surprise.

"On my life," he said, "I have no idea what Monsieur wants with the Regent!"

Nicolas Treml heard the truth in his squire's voice. He grabbed his arm and replied:

"I want to kill him!"

Jude reproached himself for not having guessed so simple a design,

"I understand," he said. "Good."

And he fell back to his usual tranquility.

The innkeeper then returned with a guide.

CHAPTER VII
The Forest of Villers-Cotterets

The magnificent castle of the Regent, Philippe d'Orléans, on that morning presented an unusually joyous aspect. Superbly appointed carriages were being readied in the great courtyard, surrounded by busy lackeys; saddle-horses stamped and pawed the ground, and seemed to call their masters; and an army of pages, foresters, and grooms lounged upon the broad flight of steps that led to the entrance of the palace.

Philippe was still in the breakfast room. As the meal ended, crowds of courtiers and noble women, bedecked in satin and lace, descended the great steps to the courtyard. At once, the carriages were filled with graceful faces, the horses plunged and reared beneath their owners, and the great gates were opened for the brilliant cortège to pass through.[14]

---

[14] There a section here that was removed by Féval for the publication in book form:

"Although the day was far advanced, Philippe was still in the breakfast room, where he regaled himself with a few of the chosen favorites of his Court; for this Prince possessed none of the fine tastes of the elder Bourbons; rejecting the pompous, magnificent voluptuousness of Louis XIV, he confined himself to the worship of the god of wine and the goddess of the fair, and generally divided his time with his *bon-vivants* between the table and the ladies' bower.

"The Regency was a happy period for the wildlife in the royal forests. Too indolent to hunt or shoot, Philippe preferred the silken downy cushions of a coach to the hard, uneasy saddle; and, indeed, as his excursions generally took place after a

As a singular occurrence, the Regent had not chosen to sit in his own carriage, preferring instead to ride a high-bred English courser that had been sent him by Queen Anne; it was a gift which he especially enjoyed because of its provenance, for the Regent was a true Anglophile at heart.

Historians agree that Philippe d'Orléans was a handsome man, and the portraits that have come down to us bear out the assertion. When it pleased him to throw

---

hearty meal, he had great need of pillows upon which to repose.

"But all things here below must have a termination; so the *déjeuner* being at an end, crowds of courtiers and noble women, bedecked with satin and lace, descended the great steps to the palace yard, redolent of generous wine.

"All were in admirable humor: there was not a rosy mouth that was not graced with a most enchanting smile—not a powdered wig that did not oscillate as its wearer attempted a smart retort, or lisped an amorous declaration, whilst mumbling into a perfumed minion's glove. It was a delightful, hearty hubbub of marquises and dukes, crammed with pastries, truffles, and Madeira, and countesses saturated with jellies and champagne. Shirt-frills were tumbled, coiffures rumpled, and ladies' fichus somewhat disarranged; but, nevertheless, morality was preserved intact, for the Right Reverend Father Guillaume Dubois, incumbent of a hundred abbeys, and expectant of a cardinal's red hat, sanctified the royal orgies with his pious and patronizing presence.

"Madame de Carnavalet, who had enjoyed the honor of being distinguished by the Regent for the last twenty-four hours, gave the signal for departure by stepping into the carriage prepared for her especial use; in a few minutes the rest were filled with graceful forms and sparkling eyes, the horses plunged and reared beneath their owners, and the great gates were opened for the brilliant cortège to pass through."

off his libertinism and assume a stately presence, he was recognized as a true descendant of the kings of France, and he looked princely indeed.

That day, being in good spirits, he reined his steed with ease, sat firmly and gracefully upon his back, and the cortege left the castle.

There was a marked difference between the wild beauties of the Forest of Rennes and those of Villers-Cotterets. In the latter, there were, undoubtedly, somber groups of trees, broad oaks, tall elms, and chestnuts that might have shaded a whole army; but the hand of man was everywhere to be seen.

It is good for a land to belong to a prince. When the hand of its master need not spare the gold, nature can be shaped and embellished without losing any of its august splendor. Now, extensive paths wound through the wood in a thousand serpentine meanders, or swept away in one long line until the limits of the arcades were lost to view, whilst the double rows of trees met overhead, and seemed, with their slender pillars, to support roofs of everlasting verdure.

Between the two forests, one was forced to concede that the the advantage did not lie with Brittany.

The forest of Villers-Cotterets was truly filled with admirable features. When walking along the shrouded paths that led to the valley, one was often reminded of the Garden of Eden. And when one climbed to the tops of the hills, the horizon suddenly opened widely onto the azure sky, and gained that expanse that is all too often missing from the Breton countryside.

Besides, that poor Forest of Rennes could only boast some obscure gentleman's retreat or the steeple of a village church to compare to the magnificent castle built by the Valois, or the noble Abbey of Prémontré.

It had only been an hour since the cortège had left the castle. They passed slowly through the forest. The cavaliers caracoled by the carriages, which rolled noiselessly along the mossy paths. All the while, the Regent chatted pleasantly through the carriage door with Madame de Carnavalet, who kept looking longingly at the handsome Monsieur de Nancré through the other door.

Suddenly, as the princely train turned a corner, two horsemen appeared in the center of the road, barring the passage of the cavalcade.

They were two tall men of athletic build, whose antique vestments were covered with dust.

The elder of the two strangers inquired aloud of a peasant mounted on a donkey who was their guide and kept a respectful distance:

"Which of these men is the Duc d'Orléans?"

The peasant pointed to the Prince, then trotted away.

The man spurred his horse towards the Regent, who, recoiling instinctively, laid his hand upon his sword. The courtiers, who had remained paralyzed with surprise for a brief instant, threw themselves in front of their master.

Some of the ladies thought about fainting, but changed their minds, because the incident promised to be interesting.

"Who are you?" the Regent asked, after the first moments of silence.

"I am Nicolas Treml de La Tremlays, Seigneur of Boüexis-in-the-forest," the stranger replied.

"What do you seek here?"

"To fight the Regent of France in single combat."

These words were uttered calmly and firmly, without a hint of bluster.

The courtiers looked at each other, fleeting smiles appearing on their lips. The ladies were mightily captivated; they watched the scene as intently as if they'd been in a theater.

It was, indeed, a singular and amazing sight to behold these two men, steel-clad remains of the past century, but vigorous, collected, and intrepid, in the midst of a host of mincing, powdered, gaudy butterflies; see their iron scabbards, and long swords, with a simple guard, among the golden-hilted rapiers and the flaunting sheaths; to contrast their buff-coats, corslets, headpieces, and heavy gloves with the ribbons, fringes, velvets, and plumed beavers of the Court.

It was as if a Breton knight of the fifteenth century had risen from the tomb and challenged the descendants of his country's conquerors to mortal combat.

At first, Philippe d'Orléans had felt a brief concern, but now that ten courtiers stood between him and the old Breton, he forgot all about his momentary fear.

"The poor man is mad," he said, "and will frighten our ladies. Remove him!"

The order was explicit, but Monsieur Nicolas' rapier was long, and no one rushed to execute it.

He old gentleman then removed his ox-skin glove, which must have weighed half-a-pound.

"We must end this," said the Regent, impatiently.

"Yes, we must," repeated Nicolas Treml, gravely. "I was told that the Bourbons boasted heroic blood; but that report must have been a lie, or its valor died with the elder branch. Philippe d'Orléans, Regent of France, I, for the second time, challenge you to mortal combat!"

Upon saying so, Monsieur Treml de La Tremlays drew his sword.

The courtiers did likewise. The ladies thought the spectacle was unfolding marvelously.

"Ladies and Gentlemen, hear me, and bear testimony to all I say," Monsieur Treml de La Tremlays added solemnly, "Your king, being an infant, in the eye of the law, is not liable to the charge; but I accuse the Regent of France of holding Brittany in bondage, a province which, by express stipulation and inalienable right, is free, and here I am to make good my words with my body in single combat without quarter, and to the death! If God wills it that I should fall, Brittany will have lost but one more son; if I survive, however, my country will have regained her ancient rights and privileges."

" A single combat to the death," whispered one of the courtier who found the incident rather amusing. "A Divine Judgment between His Royal Highness and Monsieur Nicolas. What a novel idea!"

The Regent was no longer laughing.

The ladies, enchanted by the Romanesque aspects of the incident, now admired the older man's austere face and grey beard, and some even began to support him.

Madame la Duchesse de Berry whispered in the ear of Monsieur de Riom, who stood by the door of her carriage:

"What a magnificent madman!"

"So, Regent of France," said Nicolas Treml, his eyes burning with righteous indignation, "what say you?"

A profound silence followed these extraordinary words, and a presentiment that some disaster was about to happen filled each heart. As the Regent was about to repeat his previous command to remove the old Breton,

the latter anticipated him and, turning to his squire, coolly said:

"Jude, move those men aside!"

The faithful squire dashed his ponderous war-horse
into the midst of the courtiers, who were driven back on
all sides by the rudeness of the shock.

For an instant—one instant only—Philippe
d'Orléans and Nicolas Treml met face-to-face, but that
instant sufficed for the old man to take his glove and
strike the Regent of France on the cheek, as he shouted:

"For Brittany!"

Thirty swords flew from their sheaths and the owners pressed towards him to avenge this insult to their
Prince. The ladies at last felt free to faint.

Under the blow, Philippe d'Orléans had grown pale.
Then, he drew forth his sword, like his men, and stepped
towards the aggressor.

But the next moment, he stopped. Anger held little
sway on this man whose head easily overrode the commands of his heart. He turned back towards Madame de
Carnavalet, who had simulated a faint, in order to pretend to assuage her fears.

Meanwhile, an unequal combat, the issue of which
left no room for doubts, had begun between the two
Bretons and His Royal Highness' courtiers. Those gentlemen who, despite being part of the Regent's festive
coterie, had nevertheless preserved their sense of honor,
endeavored to take the hardy Bretons prisoner without
wounding them. After several minutes, Nicolas Treml
was thrown off his horse, seized, and tied to a tree.

He remained silent, his head held high, before his
conqueror.

Jude still retained his weapon and, although surrounded by his foes, was not yet beaten.

Monsieur Treml de La Tremlays, seeing that no resistance could avail, made a sign to him to yield. Jude, obedient to the last, threw down his sword, and gave himself up.

At that moment, a bitter smile passed across the old man's face which, until then, had simply exhibited a stoic calm. A memory had just sprung into his mind: that of the boy Georges, smiling in his cradle.

Until then, his hope had sustained him. He had believed he could force the Regent to dismount and fight in single combat for the destiny of Brittany.

It was a simple and natural plan. He had never even imagined that he would be forced to compel Philippe by an outrageous insult. Now, he understood its folly. The delirium had passed.

As is often the case after a bitter defeat, a thousand sinister forebodings rushed upon his mind like a flood; fearful doubts sprung up about the honor of Hervé de Vaunoy. Suddenly these doubts resolved themselves into certainties, and he thought he heard the lugubrious tones of the Albino chanting the *Lament*, the requiem for the last scion of his race.

He cast a discouraged look at Jude, and repented of having made the squire give up his sword.

"Jude!" he shouted, "break through these minions, mount, spur for Brittany and watch over the boy."

Jude obeyed as always. He made a desperate attempt to free himself, but was overpowered, as valets and stable boys had now rejoined the cortege. As he fell, he cast a last glace at his master, his eyes full of respectful sadness.

"I tried—but I could not," he said., as if excusing himself for disobeying an order.

Nicolas Treml lowered his head.

"Poor Georges," he said. "May the Almighty punish only myself and take the child into His mercy!"

By this time Madame de Carnavalet had regained her senses—if ever they had fled. The Regent gave the signal to return to Villers-Cotterets.

On the way back, he chatted to the ladies as if nothing extraordinary had occurred. He did not bear a grudge. But while ascending the flight of steps into the castle, he leaned towards Father Dubois, and whispered the word "*Bastille*." The councilor nodded.

It was the warrant for the incarceration of Nicolas Treml and his honest squire, Jude.

.

CHAPTER VIII
Guardianship

A few hours after the strange battle, Nicolas Treml de La Tremlays and his squire were locked inside the dreaded Bastille.

One might well believe that the old Breton's mind was full of dark thoughts as he stepped over the threshold of the prison. As for Jude, he thought nothing at all. With the true stoicism of his people, he worried about nothing, so long as he was permitted to remain with his beloved master.

Whatever his secret misery might be, Nicolas Treml was too proud to show it outwardly, and, ascending the dark stairs, he entered the solitary cell head high, as calmly as he would the great saloon in his own castle.

But when the old man was alone, he gave full way to all his bitter grief. He accused himself of having abandoned his grandchild, and almost cursed his insane enterprise, which now appeared to him in its true light. The sight of the Court had removed the veil from his eyes, and he saw, now that it was too late, that an attempt which would have been fraught with the greatest dangers even in the great days of chivalry, had become, in the eighteenth century, nothing less than madness.

"I did it for Brittany!" he said, trying to console himself.

But he did not feel consoled.

His anguish and regrets would have increased a hundred-fold if he could have seen what was happening at the castle de La Tremlays. Hervé de Vaunoy was not a man who did things by halves: from a few words dropped by Nicolas Treml during their last conversation, he had divined the object of the old man's journey, and, knowing his cousin's fierce feelings towards France, it enabled him to predict the rest.

He quietly allowed things to go on in their usual course for a fortnight, and, after that time, foresaw that the nobleman would never return. He then began to put a well-laid scheme into operation, his first step being to discharge all the old and loyal servants from the castle, retaining only those he had won over, especially Alain, the morose house steward, who had become his confidant.

De Vaunoy's character began to change. During the last two years, he had pondered night and day how he could attain the full, uncontrolled possession of the wealthy domain of Treml; and now his wishes were accomplished. Poor, before Nicolas had plucked him out of obscurity, owning nothing, so to speak, but his rapier and his cloak, he had now become one of the most opulent of all the old nobility of Brittany.

There was enough there to send any ambitious man over the edge, and Hervé de Vaunoy fell deeply.

It was true, nevertheless, that his newly-acquired fortune was not altogether his own. At present, the castle of La Tremlays and its dependencies were merely held in trust for the boy Georges,

But for a trustee who knows his business, the sky is the limit. Men are but mortal. The infant was always subject to a host of these same ills that constantly threaten our poor species. Children die of measles, fevers, small-pox, whooping cough, and other juvenile ailments; because they eat too much., or not enough; they're ambushed by wolves, like in one of Perrault's tales, or

84

drown from imprudently venturing out in boats; and who knows what else!

At a more advanced age, boys fall from trees and horses, and later still, dangers are incurred in chasing the stag and the wild boar; and above all, jealousies and duels will arise from that same passion which caused the fall of Troy.

Because of all this, the ward of an experienced guardian rarely reaches his or her majority, especially if the size of the estate is large enough.

Monsieur de Vaunoy knew all this; yet, as he was eager to enjoy the pleasure of his newfound wealth without restraint, and as there was always the chance that his youthful ward might still escape all the perils we have just enumerated, he decided he would not trust to the hazard of the die.

Bretons are generally good and kind, but when they are bad, the arch-villains of the worst melodramas are as angels compared to them. They let nothing stand in their way and the means they're prepared to use are of diabolical brutishness.

Our readers will be able to judge soon enough for themselves.

So Monsieur de Vaunoy continued to treat Georges as the cherished and respected grandson of his legitimate lord, ostensibly with great affection, wishing to create warmth in his heart in case Nicolas Treml de La Tremlays returned. One month, two months passed. Hervé had discharged all those who had served the blood of Treml. Yet, there were one faithful servant he hadn't been able to dismiss: Wolf, Monsieur Nicolas' beloved dog.

It was in vain that the valets, acting under his orders, had driven the dog with their whips from the castle and into the forest, he always came back. Just when Hervé thought him far away, he found him in the evening laying by the cradle of the sleeping child. The noble animal kept his nightly watch, and we cannot affirm that, without his vigilance, the heir of Treml would have spent his nights peacefully and undisturbed, for Hervé often cast malignant, meaningful glances at his youthful cousin as he lay.

Wolf wasn't the only one to keep an eye on little Georges. Another figure was watching, protecting the boy with his vigilance as with a shield. With the contents of the purse that Nicolas had thrown him, Jean Blanc had been able to relieve his father's suffering. Now, he no longer worked. By day, he slept or wandered the castle grounds; at night, he mounted a tree whose branches shaded the window of the room wherein the infant slept, and, gazing in, kept watch over him until the morning.

Hervé had threatened him, even hinting that he might be mistaken for a marauder and shot; but the Albino could run through the foliage of the trees like a sailor amongst the masts of his ship. He did not fear bullets, but had to stay alive because he had sworn to defend the boy.

He forever muttered:

"The rabbit may yet turn into a wolf!"

CHAPTER IX
The Lake of La Tremlays

Six months after Nicolas Treml de La Tremlays had left, no one in Brittany knew what had become of him. The foresters mourned his loss deeply, and prayed to Heaven for his soul.

One autumn evening, Hervé de Vaunoy threw his wild fowl long gun upon his shoulders, and took young Georges by the hand. Followed by the dog Wolf, he directed his steps towards a somber pool. The dark, ominous glances he cast towards the dog were indicative of his sinister thoughts.

The boy ran in the fields, picking flowers. His blond hair shimmered under the evening breeze. His grace and charm embodied all the delights of childhood.

The lake of La Tremlays was located about half a league to the west of the castle. Its form was that of an oblong square, three sides of which were bordered to the water's edge by willows backed by underbrush and trees, whilst the fourth rose slantingly, and was crowned with a copse of holly, hazel, and poplar trees.

In the centre of this thicket, the rough, stout trunk of an oak tree, partially undermined by the action of the water washing away the earth, had fallen from its perpendicular position, and now hung angularly above the pool, covering that portion of it with its mighty branches.

Immediately in front of, and a few paces from it, the water was transparent, and attained its greatest depth, whilst all the remainder of its surface was covered with rushes, sedge, and weeds, frequented in the winter by thousands of widgeons, divers, wild ducks, teal, and other migratory aquatic birds.

Today, there is a small village and a mill on the western shore of the lake; but at the time of our story, the place was completely deserted, and it was exceedingly rare that a passer-by came to disturb the frolicking of the fish.

When De Vaunoy reached the banks of the little lake, he unlocked the moorings of a small boat which was tied to a pontoon, and placed Georges inside it. He then took the oars, and was about to leave the bank, when the dog, uninvited, jumped into the boat and sat down by the young boy's side,

A few powerful strokes sufficed to bring the boat into the deepest portion of the pool. There, De Vaunoy, laying down the oars, cocked his long gun, looked around, and, seeing a diver among the reeds, far out of the reach of shot, fired in the direction of the bird.

The noise of the discharge disturbed the dog, and he raised himself swiftly to his feet; the smell of the powder excited his olfactory nerves, his natural instincts returned with the rapidity of lightning, and he looked towards the reeds.

"Seek it, Wolf—good fellow—seek it," De Vaunoy said in his most insinuating tone:

We all know the fable of the cat which turned into a lady. Seeing a mouse, Minette jumped on all fours and started chasing her. Wolf, excited by the sight, jumped overboard, and swam vigorously towards the reeds, leaving his startled ward sitting upon the bench.

"Find it, Wolf! find it!" De Vaunoy repeated, recharging his gun as quickly as he could.

The dog kept looking, but couldn't find a prey, which never had been hit by the first shot.

Monsieur de Vaunoy took aim.

"Look at the mighty oak, Georges," he said.

While the child's attention was diverted, he fired. A loud report was heard, and, with a plaintive howl, the faithful animal sank dead beneath the reeds.

"I saw something tall and white move within the branches of the oak," young Georges exclaimed.

De Vaunoy looked hurriedly, but could discover nothing.

"Look again," he said. "You must be mistaken."

Then he muttered between his teeth:

"And now, I shall no longer be thwarted by that accursed dog!"

"See! There's the white shape again!"

At that moment, Hervé de Vaunoy's bosom heaved, and he felt almost afraid of his own shadow. Night was falling quickly and he peered at the foliage of the dark oak, but saw nothing. He thought the child might have been hallucinating.

But his hands were trembling as he dropped the gun on the flooring of the boat, and his whole frame quivered as he took the oars and pulled out further into deep water, but still immediately in front of the large oak. There, he stopped rowing. Again the boat was brought to a dead stand. De Vaunoy leaned his head upon his hand in deep, agitated thought, as cold drops of sweat trickled from his forehead down his face.

Night had completely fallen when De Vaunoy raised his head; three times, he extended his hands towards the boy, whose attention was still riveted upon the oak, but each time those hands fell back, nerveless. At length, he made a violent effort upon himself and asked the child:

"Well, boy, do you still see the white shape?"

Without turning his head, Georges Treml de La Tremlays replied:

"Yes, he is looking at us right now!"

Before he could finish his sentence, De Vaunoy grabbed the unsuspecting child by the neck, held him for an instant high in the air, then hurled him into the deep waters of the lake.

At the same instant, by the pale light of the rising moon, a white figure could indeed be seen, but De Vaunoy did not notice it, so busy was he rowing away from the spot with the energy of desperation, all hell raging in his heart. The rising moon disclosed the pale features of the Albino, Jean Blanc.

As De Vaunoy reached the bank, the Albino glided like a snake on one of the great arms of the tree that hung above the lake. Joining his hands together, and springing from the branch, he plunged into the water and swam desperately towards the spot where Georges had disappeared.

De Vaunoy doubtless heard the plunge, but the kind of superstitious terror that often follows a criminal after his crime had too great a hold on him to permit him to ascertain its cause. Plugging his ears with his fingers, he ran to the castle as fast as his legs could carry him, breathless and haggard.

Meanwhile, near the reeds, Jean Blanc reappeared a few seconds later, holding the senseless child with one hand above his head, whilst he swam to the shore with the other.

His cadaverous visage assumed an air of joy as he again stood on the bank, and then, clutching the child convulsively to his breast, he started off at the top of his wondrous speed, and did not relax in his exertion until he had placed a considerable distance between himself and the castle of La Tremlays.

At intervals, whilst he ran, he murmured as he smiled:

"I knew it would be so, I knew that evil deeds would be done upon the young lord, but I was there. He is mine, now—mine! I was there so that the strong should not slay the weak, like poor Arthur in the *Lament*!"

Those who best knew the unfortunate young man could have foretold to a certainty that the fit would soon be on him; even he himself seemed to feel the approach of the temporary madness, for suddenly he came to a halt in one of the tracks through the forest, and placed the infant gently upon a sloping bank.

The night was cold and damp, and a heavy dew, mingled with small sleet, begun to fall as young Georges remained pale, rigid and motionless, on the sward.

"Wake up, little one, wake up!" Jean cried, rubbing the child's breast, and chafing his ice-cold hands. "Holy Mother of Heaven, please wake him up!

Tearing the tunic of white skins from his own body he enveloped the still senseless boy in it; his bosom heaved, his eyes glowed like fire, and the foam stood upon his lips, as he struggled manfully against the mental storm.

"Holy Virgin Mary, give me only time to wake him up, and I swear—"

An irresistible paroxysm of laughter stopped the invocation; with the last glimmer of intelligence Jean took off a copper medal of Our Lady of the Forest, and hung it round Georges' neck. Then, with shrill cries, the hapless man, jumping, dancing, laughing, shouting, "The White Rabbit, I am the White Rabbit!" plunged, like a wild deer, into the recesses of the forest.

The poor child, still unconscious, remained within the Holy Virgin's protection.

The frenzy lasted for a full hour, because the emotions that had triggered it were powerful, but at the end of that period, the young man became calm again, and the remembrance of the poor boy rushed across his mind.

Casting a glance around him, he saw where he was, for the depths of the forest were as well-known to him by night as by day; and immediately he dashed off towards the spot where he had left the child. No obstacle that intervened could bar his passage; he ran across the open paths like lightning, bounded over the low shrubs, and pierced through the coverts like a hunted boar; and in a few minutes his heart leaped with joy as a ray of the dim moon showed him his own white coat.

"Georges! Georges!" he shouted.

Alas! the child did not reply.

Two energetic bounds brought him to the side of the white skin; then, as it remained immovable, his heart sank within him; he raised it tenderly and carefully, but—

The child was gone!

CHAPTER X
A Night Vigil

Twenty years weigh heavily upon the head of man; but for the material world, save for man—Nature's greatest achievement—it passes as the breeze, which touches things, but does not destroy them.

A lapse of twenty years had changed the chief actors of our tale almost beyond recognition. The child had become a man; the once strong man had become an old man; and the patriarch had ceased to be alive.

But the time-honored castle of La Tremlays still reared its head on high, stern and enduring as of old, at the end of its avenue of stately elms. If some trees had perished in the mighty forest, others had sprung from the soil, and, full of sap, wooed the sun that gilded their verdant heads.

The Wolf's Pit preserved its somber aspect, and the colossal oak still bore its arms untouched; the two mills rocked and tottered as of old, but the hut of Mathieu Blanc was almost level with the ground—an almost insignificant detail.

As for the lake, the same still waters reposed in their deep, peaceful bed, and wild rushes still concealed the whitened bones of Wolf, Nicolas Treml's faithful dog.

It was the autumn of the year 1740, and a night vigil was taking place in the kitchens of Monsieur Hervé de Vaunoy de La Tremlays, Seigneur of Boüexis-in-the-forest.

The kitchen was a large, square room, lit by four large windows—one on each side—and a massive oaken door opened its panes immediately opposite a vast fireplace. It was sufficiently capacious to accommodate twenty guests with ease. The dried trunks of four or five trees burned upon the hearth, mingling the lurid light of the denser portion of the wood with the bright sparkles of the exuding resin. On a long, roughly-hewn table in the centre of the hall, a number of pitchers, filled with cider, were ranged, with drinking-horns and a few mugs. Huge quantities of potatoes were roasting in the wood-ashes on the hearth; several sides of bacon were placed on racks, suspended from the roof; and saucepans, ladles, spits, skimmers, and other culinary utensils, were seen on every side.

About twenty servants and domestics warmed themselves before the ample fire, with a few strangers who were receiving the hospitality of the castle.

In the place of honor, on a three-legged stool, so close to the fire that the ashes singed her wooden shoes, was seated Dame Goton Réhon, the confidential housekeeper. The chronicles of the forest recorded that she had had an exuberant youth, but was now a comely matron; as forty-one years had flown since the former period. She was smoking a short, clay pipe, black with age, with the gravity consonant to a person of her great importance in the household.

Near to her, but on one side, and slightly in the rear, were to be seen the cook, the chambermaids, the pigeon-tender, the scullions, and the milkmaids, and even the favorite chambermaid of the fair Mademoiselle Alix de Vaunoy. The presence of the young lady was an unexpected honor—but time does hang heavily, and Yvon, the lord's huntsman, was a young, courteous, and especially handsome man.

On the other side of the chimney, the men were ranged according to their estimated rank: first, Simonnet, the master of the presses, André the gatekeeper; and Corentin, the ploughman; as well as many laborers, who do not merit any particular remarks.

Right next to the fireplace and directly opposite Dame Goton Réhon, a guest of La Tremlays, who deserves a more detailed description, had been seated for some hours,.

No one could possibly take Pelo Rouan[15] for other than a charcoal-burner; a thick veil of smut and dirt covered his face and throat, and the inflamed lids of his fiery eyes seemed to be irritated by the ruddy glare of light, as he shaded them with his broad, soot-blackened hand. His costume was that generally adopted by the foresters; namely, a party-colored worsted cap, now blackened by the smoke; a long, close-fitting jacket with sleeves; knee-breeches of the same coarse cloth; blue worsted stockings and hob-nailed shoes, with large, heavy, iron buckles.

The most singular thing about this man was his confusing stature; whilst seated, he would have been reckoned considerably below the middle height; but when he rose, it was perceived that his legs were of extraordinary length, sinewy, and the muscles elastic, to a very unusual degree. His age was as questionable as his height; no one was acquainted with his origin or birth-place; it was merely known that he had first been seen in the Forest of Rennes about fifteen years before, and as he appeared then, so did he now.

---

[15] Pelo is a Breton variation of Pierre, i.e.: Peter.

Thus were the servants disposed in the hall, and thus were they occupied. We shall now spy on them, in this castle into which we have not set foot for twenty years.

Renée, Mademoiselle Alix's chambermaid, chatted with Yvon, the comely huntsman, as he fitted a new lash to his whip for the edification of the hounds, Mirault, Gerfault, Renaud, etc., who would babble, hunt, heel, or run riot in the pack. André the gate-keeper was oiling the lock of his flint gun. Corentin was gallantly making a goad for Annette, the pretty superintendent of the milkmaids.

Up to six o'clock, the conversation was anything but general; but as soon as that hour rang on the great clock in the belfry, old Simonnet, the master of the presses, screeched out some verses of the *Angelus* evening hymn, and then silence ensued, during which all the servants prayed, or pretended to pray.

When the silence had lasted sufficiently long in Dame Goton's opinion, she made a final sign of the cross, and took up her pipe again, noting:

"Time passes quickly."

That acute observation was met with unanimous assent.

"Come the end of the month," she continued, "and we shall be obliged to have candles for the *Angelus*."

"True, true," Simonnet added.

All joined in the chorus:

"Yes, time passes quickly—there is no denying it."

Dame Goton listened with delight to the approbation which her intelligent remark had caused.

"Master Simonnet," she then asked, "will you hand me a tankard from the table, if you please? My throat is parched."

Instead of a single tankard, ten were passed around and everybody drank their fill.

"Sound, and of right good flavor," she said, after imbibing a copious draught, smacking her lips with the air of a connoisseur. "It is to be hoped that this year's cider will be as good as the last. Eh, friends?"

Now, as this was a proposition not admitting to the slightest doubt, all her hearers agreed in the affirmative, and Simonnet took another drink, just to prove the sincerity of his opinions.

"We all know what last year's wood and cider was," he proceeded to moralize in a sententious manner, "but who can tell what this year's may be. We shall want much timber in the winter, and my lord says the times in which we live make felling it too dangerous."

Renée, the chambermaid, stopped chatting with Yvon, raised her head with a slight show of anxiety, and asked:

"Does our lord fear an attack by the Wolves?"

The charcoal-burner started slightly, half-closed his eyes and cast a furtive look around.

"The Wolves!" said Simonnet, striking his clenched fist upon the table. "If I were only the king's Intendant, I would soon exterminate those damned villains! After what they did to by best press! Burned it, they did!"

"And they stole my best cows!" exclaimed the dairy-woman.

"And destroyed my dog kennels!"

"Poached more game than could be shot fairly in six months!"

"Netted my pigeons!" "Broken my espaliers!" "Broken up my fallows!" cried all the servants of the castle, and then there uprose another chorus of "Oh the infernal thieves!"

97

Meanwhile, Dame Goton lit her pipe carefully, ejected three tremendous puffs from her mouth, and Pelo Rouan seemed to be fast asleep, leaning his back against the wall.

After a lapse of a few minutes Dame Goton made another tremendous puff of smoke, shook her head ominously, and said:

"Twenty years ago, the lord of this castle was named Nicolas Treml, and in the days of that brave old man, the poor folks you now call *Wolves* were as quiet as young lambs. Ah! Misery has since sharpened their teeth, poor things!"

This observation did not meet with as much approbation as the good old woman's former ones.

"The Tremls were good masters," Simonnet ventured, with the embarrassment of a courtier speaking of the virtues of a deceased monarch before the adulators of the reigning king. "No one can deny it, but the Wolves are damned robbers, for all that. There is nobody but you, Dame Goton, who defends them."

The old woman raised her palsied head with dignity, and answered:

"Master Simonnet, I do not defend the Wolves; they can do that well enough themselves. I only say that they are Bretons, that is all, and that some folks are braver by the fireside than in the forest."

This was an unexpected accusation, a galling taunt. An acute observer might have detected a derisive smile cross the swarthy features of the charcoal-burner.

"Patience! patience!" Simonnet replied. "A brave officer of the king is supposed to soon come down from Paris and take command of the troops at Rennes, and protect the collection of the royal taxes through the forest. These damned Wolves killed the last captain, but—"

"Let the new one beware!" Dame Goton interrupted.

"Why, one would think you wished the brave gentleman some misfortune," Renée uttered peevishly.

"No, no, my pretty lambkin," the housekeeper retorted with stinging sarcasm. "I am old now, and merely regret the good old days, but don't you meddle with what you don't understand: resume your chat with Yvon, and remind him that before you two roam together in the forest, it would be better to first have a few words pass between you in presence of the worthy curate in the parish church at Liffré."

The chambermaid blushed deeply, but did not dare reply. The subject would have fallen into silence had not Pelo Rouan, who likely had some personal motives, appeared to wake up, rubbed his eyes and said:

"Did I dream it, Master Simonnet, or did I hear you say there was a new captain coming down from Paris to chastise these scoundrel Wolves, whom I pray our Lady of the Forest to confound?"

"I did say so, my man, and it is no more than the truth. So long as these brigands contented themselves with pillaging Monsieur de Vaunoy, the Government did not care one denier about it; but since the atrocious vagabonds went in broad daylight to the residence of the Intendant in Rennes, and robbed him, His Majesty has sworn to destroy them, root and branch."

"What a pity!" said the incorrigible Dame Goton, with a sarcastic smile.

"In truth, they are a set of insolent, plundering varlets," the charcoal-burner continued. "But when will this new officer arrive?"

"He is expected any hour."

Pelo Rouan rose from the settle, took up a horn of cider, lifted it to his lips, and quaffed it.

"To the health of the brave captain!" he toasted, with an enthusiasm in which Dame Goton thought she saw a smidgen of irony.

"To his health!" echoed all the servants of La Tremlays.

CHAPTER XI
Blossom-of-the-Broom

Before putting his tankard back on the table, Pelo Rouan added a complement to his toast:

"And to the confusion of the Wolves and all their cubs!"

All drank the toast with enthusiasm, except the rebellious housekeeper, who chose to express her sympathy for the oppressed, downtrodden men of Brittany.

"Well! Well!" she exclaimed, "it is mighty courageous of Pelo, a poor son of the forest, to set himself up against the White Wolf, who has a thousand daring men to execute his orders. I suppose he will soon take up his holly cudgel and beard him in his own Pit. However, I wish the man no harm."

"Thank you kindly, Dame," Pelo replied. "I, for one, only wish you the best."

In fact, Pelo Rouan was altogether a mysterious individual. While he spoke thus, his eyes were fixed upon Dame Goton, while the red lines of his eyelids twitched in the light of the fire. There was in his eyes a gratitude for the interest she had expressed for his welfare more ardent than that passing observation seemed to warrant; but it was always difficult to understand the reasons for most of his actions. Occasionally, those who saw him would think they perceived the means by which he was proceeding slowly but surely to some explicit yet mysterious goal, but then all traces of him would be lost, and the most sagacious and determined spies were thrown off his track. Besides, no one would have seriously considered spying on him. Why would they? His frequent visits to Monsieur de Vaunoy, the sworn enemy of the Wolves, totally belied the supposition of his having foreknowledge of their schemes, and only some kind of association with them could have raised him in the social order of the times.

About fifteen or sixteen years had passed since Pelo Rouan had come to reside in the Forest of Rennes, bringing with him a female infant in her cradle. Morose in temper, and appearing to shun the society of his fellow men, he had built a humble cottage in one of the most solitary recesses of the forest, dug a pit for a charcoal kiln, and burned as much wood as sufficed to purchase necessities for himself and the child.

But while Pelo worked, Marie, the lovely girl, had grown up to womanhood, and was at this moment *"Thoughtless of beauty, she was beauty's self."*[16] Nurtured in solitude, she feared the sight of men. When she heard the sounds of the horn ringing through the forest, like the timid hind, she only plunged the deeper into the woods.

Never had one of the gallant gentlemen who partook in these hunts been able to be close enough to her to take her chin and call her *pretty*—as all gentlemen have done since the farthest antiquity. Never did she place cheese in a wicker basket and take it to the castle, with apples, eggs and cream, as is regularly shown in the plays performed at the *Opéra Comique*. She never danced in the glades, nor sang by the streams. She was neither a ward of Madame de Genlis,[17] nor an ingénue

---

[16] From *Lavinia*, a poem by James Thomson (c.1700-1748).

[17] Stéphanie Félicité du Crest de Saint-Aubin, Comtesse de Genlis (1746-1830) was Governess of the Children of France,

from one of Monsieur de Marmontel's[18] comic operas, contemplating God, Nature, and everything else under the sky. In fact, she was a pure, simple, rustic maid, but bearing in herself the elements of everything that was graceful, kind, and good.

The usual expression of her face was one of exquisite kindness and exalted sensibility. She had large blue eyes and a sweet smile, which warmed the soul as a ray of sunshine. Her pale cheeks were framed by a twin cascade of soft and curly golden hair that waved with each of her movements. The shade of her hair would have irritated a painter because the colors that are available to human artists were inadequate to acceptably capture it. Her nuances in a painting would have seemed dull; her bright reflections would have faded in the eye of the beholder, never contrasting enough with the whiteness of her skin. A human artist could only steal but half of the heavenly palette.

In Marie, this was but an excess of charm; her fine but bold features appeared sweet and veiled under this misty halo. It was the same mystical effect, so naively rendered, that the painters of the middle ages employed as an ornament on the divine forehead of the mother of God.

Marie, like her father, loved solitude. When she did not stay in their cottage weaving wicker baskets, which her father sold at the market of Saint Aubin du Cormier,

---

an office at the royal French court during Pre-Revolutionary France charged with the education of the children and grandchildren of the monarch. The holder of the office was taken from the highest ranking nobility.

[18] Jean-François Marmontel (1723-1799).

she would often wander through the tangled paths of the wild wood.

Often, a plodding wayfarer would stop to listen to a voice, melodious as an angel's, singing the *Lament for Arthur*, which we mentioned earlier in our tale. Those of mature age who remembered Jean Blanc would think for a moment of the hapless young Albino, but the majority of those who heard the unseen minstrel would merely recognize the melancholy chant with which hundreds of Breton mothers still lulled their babes to sleep. Besides, one always hear the nightingale, but rarely sees her.

Nevertheless, some strangers had chanced to see young Marie, and the report of her beauty had traveled through the region. Her name was utterly unknown, for her father bore no idle questions, especially about his daughter, and Marie became mute the moment she was in the presence of a stranger; and thus it happened— because of the innate poetry that has flourished so long in Brittany—the young sons of the forest, who had seen the maid, vied with each other in devising names for the mysterious object of their admiration, until, by common consent, one only of all these remained, and Marie, the dark charcoal-burner's child, was called, from the golden color of her locks *Fleur des Genêts*—Blossom-of-the-Broom.

Pelo Rouan left Marie in total liberty, and she employed her leisure to the full, not realizing it could have been otherwise; indeed, it would have been impossible for Pelo to have kept a strict watch upon his daughter, for his journeys from the forest were long and frequent; the cause of them was a secret even to his beloved Marie, and week after week, his wood remained unburned, but when he did return, the kiln smoked again, and he worked night and day to make up for the time that had been lost.

No one had ever seen the interior of his cottage. If someone wanted to see the charcoal-burner during the night, which was frequently the case, for reasons we can't yet elucidate, they knocked at the door in a peculiar fashion, Pelo Rouan would go out to meet him, and sometimes accompany him some distance on his road. Marie paid no attention to these interruptions.

One day, however, during his absence, a young and handsome stranger entered the inhospitable hut. For the first time in her life, Marie was not frightened at the sight of a man; her heart beat more rapidly, and a burning blush suffused her cheek; the miserable cottage suddenly seemed less murky, as if it had been touched by an enchanter's wand, the trees and shrubs assumed a livelier green, the heavens wore a deeper azure in their hue, and she felt a rapturous, new existence bounding through her heart.

From that day, the wanderings of the beauteous girl had a defined object—to meet the handsome stranger, to sit for hours by his side at the foot of some old oak, and to receive from him the thrilling, fond embraces of honorable love. Only deer or a spying fox could have reported on the topics of their long conversation, but La Fontaine [19] was dead and the animals no longer spoke.

This blissful state of affairs lasted for some months, but the young man was eventually compelled to depart, leaving the maid as pure as the first day he had crossed

---

[19] Jean de La Fontaine (1621-1695), French poet of the 17th century. He is known above all for his Fables, many starring animals, which provided a model for subsequent fabulists across Europe.

the threshold of her father's cottage; and after he was gone, the sons of the forest again beheld Blossom-of-the-Broom roaming through the wood with lowered head, and restless eyes, mournfully singing the sad *Lament*.

Pelo Rouan refrained from asking the cause of her distress, because he had already guessed it.

But let us return to the night vigil in the kitchens of La Tremlays. After the toast of the "Captain's health" had been drunk with uproarious honors, the charcoal-burner took up his holly staff, lit his short pipe, and said in a careless manner to Master Simonnet:

"By the bye, what did you say was his name?"

"Whose name?"

"This bold Captain's."

"Our master may tell you, Pelo, but I cannot.

"He must be one of the King's most loyal servants, that's all that matters. Will he be lodged here?"

"Perhaps. Or maybe at the Intendant's house in Rennes."

Pelo Rouan hesitated for a second as to whether it would be prudent to ask another question.

"You're right," he said at last. "Who will be lucky enough to accommodate this excellent officer and the brave soldiers of His Majesty."

Then, he walked towards the door, pressing Yvon's hand as he passed, and furtively exchanging a glance of intelligence with Corentin.

"Good night to you, Master Simonnet, and to you all."

As as he placed his hand upon the knob, the sound of the heavy hammer on the great front gates was heard, and he paused.

A few minutes later, two strangers were ushered in. Their broad-brimmed beavers and capacious cloaks effectively concealed their features; but as one of them moved across the floor, and the light of the fire fell upon his face, Pelo Rouan started, and glided, unobserved, into an embrasure formed by one of the deep windows of the room.

CHAPTER XII
In the Forest

The newcomers were both tall, robust men, the younger in the flower of his youth, the other with a grey head, which had felt the weight of sixty years.

"Whoever you may be, sires," Simonnet said with a low bow, using the well-known hospitable Breton salutation, "you are welcome to this roof. What would you have?"

Dropping his mantle from his shoulders, and letting it fall carelessly over his left arm, thereby showing the uniform of a Captain of the Maréchaussée, the light cavalry employed to scour the high-roads and kill or arrest robbers, the handsome, well-dressed officer replied:

"I would like to speak with Monsieur Hervé de Vaunoy."

"'Tis the new Captain," whispered the servants.

Renée, Mademoiselle Alix's pretty chambermaid, arranged a side-curl with her fingers, and smoothed down the plaits of her apron. The rest of the women—less instructed in the manners of high life—smirked and blushed to the eyes; the housekeeper rose and made a reverential curtsey; the laborers ducked their heads and scraped one leg backwards.

And Pelo Rouan—watching his moment—passed from the window to the door, exchanging one last glance with Yvon and Corentin.

"So, this is our new Captain..." he murmured pensively.

Then he walked swiftly to the forest.

On hearing the words of the gallant Captain, Master Simonnet again bowed respectfully, throwing into the action all the dignity and importance he deemed necessary to discharge the duties of a reception that ought to have been performed by Master Alain, the house steward, who, by this time in the evening, was always asleep from drinking hard brandy. Cap in hand, he conducted the strangers across the vestibule to the salon where Hervé de Vaunoy and his family spent their evenings.

Meanwhile, let us go back in time a few hours and make the acquaintance of the Captain and his comrade at the moment they left the town of Vitré to enter the dangerous forest of Rennes. It is not only the simplest way of doing so, but this will also enable us to witness several incidents that should be disclosed to our readers.

The grey-beard, a stout, hardy-looking man, of austere visage, and slightly bowed by age, but with unwrinkled forehead and firm step, acted as valet to the officer, The serenity of his gaze expressed the perfect tranquility of his soul.

It would have been difficult to find a better looking, and more perfectly formed, man than the young Captain. His hair was turned back from his high forehead in one large roll, powdered according to the custom of the times; careless, indomitable courage sparkled in his eyes; a silken dark moustache curled upwards from each corner of his good-humored mouth; he wore his gray uniform without the slightest affectation or constraint; sat his blooded charger like a Centaur; and was between twenty-five to twenty-seven years of age.

The servitor was Jude Leker: his master, simply Captain Didier.

Twenty years of suffering and imprisonment had made but slight alterations to the devoted servant of Nicolas Treml; he still sat upright as a statue on his horse, and the thin, sharp-pointed rapier he now bore at his side was as dangerous as his former broadsword with the simple iron guard.

At about two o'clock in the afternoon, when Didier and Jude pushed their horses through the outskirts of the forest, a pale autumn sun played languidly amongst the sere and yellow foliage, and the tramp of the noble beasts was scarcely heard upon the leafy covering, with which, in that season, Nature strews the woods. Jude drank in the old-accustomed atmosphere with intense delight, he could scarcely refrain from embracing some notorious, well-remembered tree. It had been twenty years since Jude had seen the Forest of Rennes.

The Captain smiled at the enthusiasm of his man, and the following dialogue took place between them:

"Your Nicolas Treml must have been a worthy and gallant old man," said the Captain, interrupting Jude in a long detail of their journey up to Paris, and the defiance to the Regent. "I love the bit about that glove of his that weighed so much, and I would have loved to be there to look at the Regent's discomfited face!"

"Aye, Captain, he was that; but then he clapped us both up in the Bastille."

"Really, my good fellow, I do not see what else he could have done in good conscience."

"Well, sir, Nicolas Treml—Heaven, save his soul!—was an old man when he was first imprisoned; and so, what with the grief of having failed to free Brittany, and thinking continually about the boy…"

"What boy?" the Captain interrupted.

"Young Georges Treml, sir, who, by this time, must be a valiant soldier, if he has a drop of the blood of his ancestors in his veins."

Didier yawned, but Jude went on to say:

"So, Captain, the old nobleman thought day and night of his dear grandson, left without any protector, except Monsieur de Vaunoy, until three years ago when he died, quite worn out by despair, leaving the child—with his last breath—to my care."

"And what has become of this boy, Georges?"

"Heaven only knows, sir! As for myself, they gave me my liberty two years after my poor master's death; but I was destitute of money, and without the means of returning to my dear native land, if Providence had not thrown you in my way, wanting a guide to conduct you to Brittany."

"You are a noble fellow, Jude," the Captain exclaimed, holding out his hand. "I respect you for your attachment to your good old lord, and your native country. It shall be your own choice, my man, if you ever quit my service."

Jude touched the Captain's offered hand respectfully, as he answered:

"I could well wish it to be so, Captain—upon my soul, I could—for there is something in you that reminds me of the frank honesty of the Tremls. But first and above all, I remain loyal to the child—and Brittany. But did I not hear you say, sir, that you have been sent here to destroy the remnants of resistance to the King?"

"Yes; I am informed they are but a handful of gallant fools who still rebel against his rule; and when rebels become weak, they degenerate into robbers. I am here to punish these brigands."

Jude muttered, with a frown of anger:

"In the olden times, they did not deserve that term... Excuse me, Captain, but I am a staunch Breton, as you know."

"You are correct, Jude, but those who once were *The Frères Breton* have now become *The Wolves*."

"The Wolves?" said Jude, without appearing to comprehend the designation.

"Yes. They have chosen that savage appellation for themselves. It is not against Brittany, but against the Wolves that I have come to fight, by the King's command."

Jude was not altogether convinced of the truth of the distinction, for he said:

"I do not know who these Wolves may be, but in any case, they are Bretons-born, while you are French!"

Didier, seeing that the conversation was taking a tone that threatened to disturb the good understanding that subsisted between his servant and himself, handed his gourd of wine to Jude, saying:

"Let us talk no more about it, my good fellow; drink, drink, and drown all care; for whether I am French or not is quite beyond my power to tell. And now let us find our route through the forest. This by-path, I think, will take you to Saint Aubin-du-Cormier."

"Yes, sir, and here we separate; for that other road will conduct you to Rennes, whither I suppose you are proceeding?"

"Not so," was the unexpected answer. "I go to the castle of La Tremlays."

Jude started suddenly, and then was lost in thought for several minutes. At length he said:

"You have evidently been in these parts before, Captain, for I have observed whilst we were in the forest, you were never at a loss, and know every inch of it, as well as I do. Perhaps, sir, this is not the first time that you have been to the castle of La Tremlays?"

"Perhaps not!" Didier replied carelessly, avoiding an explicit answer.

"And if you have been there before, sir," Jude exclaimed, in the greatest agitation, with a tear in his eyes, "you must have seen a young gentleman—a fine, handsome gentleman, the inheritor of these wide domains, the last scion of a noble stock, as old as Brittany itself."

"His name, my friend?"

"Georges Treml."

It was the Captain's turn to be surprised. For the first time, he associated the name of Treml with that of the chateau and he understood that the old gentleman whose sad story he had just heard was the former Lord of La Tremlays.

"No, I have never met the man," he replied.

CHAPTER XIII
Captain Didier

The affectionate squire was astounded.

My God! What have they done to the young lord? he wondered.

The young Captain looked on him kindly, pitying his intense devotion to the noble house he had so long served. Perhaps he knew enough about Monsieur de Vaunoy to not entertain any illusions about the boy's fate.

Jude sat upright on his horse.

"My task is clear," said the squire, "and I must perform it. Captain, I beg you, as you are of noble blood, to lend me your assistance."

A sad smile crossed the young man's face.

"Am I of noble blood?" he murmured.

"By she who bore you!" said Jude.

"My mother, you mean? By my faith, Jude, you have made a sad mistake. However, I am an officer of the king, and that is as good a title as any nobleman's throughout the land—you shall have my aid."

"A thousand thanks, sir; and let me tell you that your generosity has bound me to your heart and soul. And now, I pray you, turn your horse's head this way, and accompany me for half-an-hour, and then we will go together to the castle."

The Captain made a sign of acquiescence, and for the next quarter of an hour followed Jude along the route to Saint Aubin du Cormier; and then as his servant, turning short to the left, entered a dense thicket, the Captain asked him whither they were going.

"To the spot," Jude answered solemnly, "where my lord, Nicolas Treml, before leaving for the French Court, deposited the hope and the fortune of his family."

"You have great confidence in me then?"

Jude hesitated, gazed at him steadfastly for a few seconds, and then said:

"Captain, I would trust my life in your hands without one moment's hesitation; but you're correct; the secret of the treasure of Treml is not mine to share. It were better I should be alone."

"Aye, Jude; and better for me that I should not wander too deeply in this dense forest, which is the chosen retreat of the Wolves. They might chance to bite me. Go where you will, do what you must, and at the end of it, you will find me here."

Jude gave his thanks; then dismounting, he led his horse into the thick trees and underwood which we once saw Nicolas Treml traversing when he carried the paper signed by Hervé de Vaunoy with him.

As soon as the gallant young officer was left alone, he dismounted likewise, fastened the horse's bridle to a tree, extended his handsome form upon the grass, and gave himself up to a pleasant reverie. An orphan, without a name, devoid of influence, raised by his merit only to a post which others did not attain until their moustaches became grey and age had thinned the locks upon their head, he beheld before him a lengthened, honorable, bright career. His mission to Brittany was not without importance; but he hoped easily to subdue a mere handful of rebellious men, who still obstinately resisted the levying of the royal taxes, and occasionally had the audacity to seize the moneys collected in the monarch's name.

But his arrival in Brittany had a peculiar personal interest apart from all political considerations. The previous year, he had spent six months at Rennes in the retinue of the Comte de Toulouse, the then-governor of the province, who subsequently had obtained for him a commission in the Musketeers, where he had so distinguished himself that he had been rewarded by his present grade of Captain in the Maréchaussée.

Being a pleasant person, and naturally susceptible to tender passions, he had not failed to make numerous conquests in the capital of Brittany, whose ladies were held to be as kind and complaisant as beautiful; roving from the blonde to the brunette, fluttering from flower to flower, and living a life which agreed entirely with his frank, happy, joyous disposition.

For the year that had passed since he had left the town of Rennes, he had only retained the remembrance of two of his tender liaisons with mistresses whose virtue he had scrupulously respected. The first of these was Mademoiselle Alix de Vaunoy de La Tremlays, a noble creature, whose lovely face was less perfect than her mind, and whose mind responded to the goodness of her heart. Didier had met her at the residence of Monseigneur de Toulouse, who had maintained a regal court in the Breton capital, and with the ardor of his temperament, thought he loved her; she, with the simplicity of her country, did not endeavor to conceal the strength of her affection for him, and their mutual feeling, without ever passing the boundaries of strict propriety, had become a matter of public notoriety.

At first, her father, Hervé de Vaunoy, either did not perceive his daughter's passion, or secretly gave way to it, which much surprised the gossips of the city, as it was known that De Vaunoy aspired to a powerful alliance for his only child, and had in his eye no less a personage than Monsieur Béchamel, Marquis de Nointel, the royal Intendant in charge of the taxes, one of the most opulent financiers in Europe; but when he made as much of the fortunate young officer as of the heirs of the most noble families, their surprise and curiosity knew no bounds. It was also remarked that this change in Hervé de Vaunoy's behavior to Didier dated from the day on which one Lapierre, a valet of Monseigneur de Toulouse, had passed from his service into that of De Vaunoy. But it was deemed unlikely that this little ante-chamber revolution could have had any influence on the subsequent conduct of Monsieur de Vaunoy.

It happened soon after this mysterious occurrence, that one night when Didier left the house of his inamorata's father, and was sauntering to his quarters, thinking only of his mistress, he was suddenly attacked by three ruffians, who received nothing but hard blows for their pains, and sundry thrusts from the Captain's walking rapier. He himself was slightly wounded in the neck, but as he left Rennes soon afterwards in the Comte's retinue, no notice was taken of the murderous attempt.

The second remembrance—far less transitory than that of the proud Alix—was that of a simple daughter of the forest, whose soft image appeared before him nightly in his dreams—with the countenance of a bright angel, placed upon the airy figure of a sylph.

Even now as he lay upon the grass beneath an elm, wrapped in his meditations, his thoughts reverted to the woodland nymph; the name of Marie chased that of Alix from his lips, and as in his waking dream, he beheld the exquisite form and thousand graces of she who was nicknamed the "Blossom-of-the-Broom."

Taxes, bloodshed, Wolves, and the expected contests, vanished from his mind.

If only she came here, he thought, desperately searching the dense foliage with avid eyes.

It was in this very wood he had first seen Marie, and now hope whispered to his heart that she might possibly return there. As he had thrown off his cloak, and his glittering uniform was quite exposed, it was more likely that a bullet from a Wolf's musket would be the first arrival; but the God of Love watched over him that day, and when he had reposed for about half-an-hour, a soft voice in the distance, responding to his wish, was heard singing *The Lament*.

Didier deliciously savored this known voice and melody. But by a kind of sentimental refinement, like a gourmet who does not hasten to bring a sweet meat to his mouth, he felt that the wait also had its joys

Starting at the sounds, the soldier raised himself upon one arm, and listened intently as the dulcet strains drew nigh; every instant the voice came nearer, and the words were more distinct; she sang this passage of the popular lament, where Constance de Bretagne begins to despair of seeing her unfortunate son again. We translate it here from the patois of the peasants of the Ille-et-Vilaine:

> *Elle attendait, car pauvre mère,*
> *Longtemps espère.*
> *Elle attendait, le cœur marri,*
> *Son fils chéri.*
> *Elle mettait son âme entière*
> *Dans la prière.*

118

Elle disait à Dieu tout puissant
Mon doux enfant ![20]

Marie was no more than a few steps from Didier but they did not yet see each other because of the thickness of the bush. The Captain held his breath that he might not lose one syllable of her sweet tones. Marie went on singing the last two verses, according to the usage:

Elle disait à Dieu tout puissant
Mon doux enfant
Arthur ! Arthur ! Hélas absence
Brise espérance
Et bien souvent son œil d'azur
Pleurait Arthur ![21]

The nature of this song is so melancholy, tender and profound that the singer who sings it to a rustic public is certain in advance of a tearful success. But poor Marie was singing only to herself and the last stanza of the song issued from her soft lips in a harmonious fading.

"The Blossom-of-the-Broom," murmured Didier, unable to contain himself any longer.

Slight as was that whisper, the quick ear of the maiden caught it; with the lightness of the roe she

---

[20] She was waiting because, poor mother, so long she hoped. She was waiting her heart wounded for her dear son. She put her whole soul in her prayer. She said to God Almighty: My sweet child!

[21] She said to God Almighty: My sweet child! Arthur! Arthur! Alas absence destroys hope, and often her azure eye wept for her Arthur.

bounded through the under wood towards him, and, uttering a piercing cry, fell senseless in his arms.

CHAPTER XIV
The White Wolf Shows His Muzzle

Didier took the girl in his arms and laid her on the grass near him. The poor child could not speak because she was too happy. She looked silently at the handsome captain who was gently smoothing the locks of golden hair on her forehead. Their soft eyes met and shyly smiled at each other. The thick cradle of leaves that hid the sky enveloped them in its shadow, and occasionally, when the wind shook the branches, a fleeting ray of sunlight touching their faces. It was a tableau, such as painters rarely have the opportunity to depict, and that poets only dream of when bursts of inspiration settle into their hearts.

After a few minutes of silence, the Blossom-of-the-Broom suddenly shook her long golden hair and began to look with joy on Didier's uniform.

"You are so handsome," she said "and I love you."

Didier took her small white hand and raised it to his lips.

"You grew up," he replied, "and you are more beautiful than ever."

She did not conceal her joy.

"Yet, I have cried often," she said, "and they say tears make young girls ugly."

"Why did you cry, Marie?" he asked.

"Because all the wild paths of the forest spoke of you, Didier, and of your absence; because the grass had grown back over the places where you used to sit; and because my father had told me you would never return."

"Your father!' Didier exclaimed. "So he knew…?"

"He knows all," the girl replied in a mournful tone. "Think not you can escape the eyes of Pelo Rouan! He knows everything."

Didier remained silent for a minute, then said:

"He must have watched us then?"

"Who can tell what Pelo Rouan does!" replied Marie. "He knew of our love, dearest, because nothing is hidden from him. After you left, he called me to him, and, kissing my forehead tenderly, said: 'My child, you must forget him; he is a hated Frenchman, and the villains always lie.'"

A dark cloud spread over the proud Captain's brow as Marie uttered these ominous words, but she did not observe it, and continued:

"Pelo Rouan knows not what it is to lie. I was frightened; but now that you are here again, I see that he was wrong. So, Didier, will you love me still?"

By way of answer, Didier pressed her passionately to his breast, and after the first gush of happiness had subsided, the youthful pair sat down upon the bank, and formed a thousand schemes of future joys and never ending love.

Whilst they were thus engaged uttering those vows of eternal constancy, which are so charming to the lover's ear, but would look ridiculous upon paper, Jude Leker was experiencing great difficulties in making a passage through the forest; for, on first entering the thicket, he could not discover any clearing, but after working his way about a hundred yards on he saw, with surprise, a number of narrow tracks coming from all points of the compass, and tending to one common centre.

Following one of them at hazard, he soon reached the edge of the ravine, known as the Wolf's Pit, and then he reflected that these small paths, which formerly did not exist, denoted the proximity of a rendezvous of men in numbers. With this exception no change had taken place in the savage aspect of the glen, and unbroken silence reigned, the same as ever.

Aiding himself with the branches and the bare knotty roots of the trees that projected from the sides of the ravine, Jude scrambled to the bottom, where the hollow oak reared its massive trunk. As he drew breath after his perilous descent, his face assumed a somber, melancholy expression, when he recollected that the last time he had stood there was in the company of his beloved master; and he heaved a bitter sigh as he thought that someone might have disinterred the fortune of Treml.

Before entering the cavity of the tree, Jude carefully examined every bush around, in order to ascertain that he was quite alone.

As his searching eye fell upon one of the traces of the mills, he perceived the ruins of what had once been the hut of Mathieu Blanc.

"They were ever staunch and brave retainers of Treml," he said, and reverently uncovering himself, added: "Heaven save their souls!"

Having replaced his hat upon his head, he stepped into the tree, where he found some remains of barrel hoops, and many of the tools of the Albino, Jean Blanc, nearly eaten through with rust, showing that they could not have been used for a considerable period.

Seizing a pick-axe, he proceeded at once to remove the earth, below which the iron chest, buried by his Lord, reposed.

He was so intent upon his work that he did not perceive a rustling movement in the underwood around, nor
human heads that peered above it, two masked with
pieces of wolf's skin, and a third hidden under a white
mask, almost touching the branches of the oak.

At a signal from the individual with the white mask,
the others sank down noiselessly into the covert, whilst
he, throwing himself gently flat upon the ground, wound
his way along silently, like a snake, until he reached the
oak.

He then raised himself so as to peep through the top
of one of the apertures that time had made, and, taking
off his mask to obtain a clearer view, he showed, be-
grimed with soot and smoke, the harsh features of Pelo
Rouan, the mysterious charcoal burner.

Jude worked on stoutly, not dreaming that a watch-
ful eye was surveying his proceedings.

After a few minutes, the pick-axe struck against
some hard substance. He grabbed a spade, hastily removed the earth, and saw the iron chest that his master
and himself had buried in that spot twenty years before.

The charcoal burner caught sight of it at the same
moment, and, returning in the same manner as he had
advanced, regained the shelter of the thicket unseen.

When Jude had examined the chest for a few seconds, and ascertained that it had not been disturbed during his long absence, he came forth from the oak, and
again looked cautiously around on every side of the tree,
then re-entered it, took a small key from his vest, opened
the lock with a trembling hand, and saw, with delight,
that its valuable contents, both the writing and the gold,
remained untouched.

Here, he thought, as a smile passed across his rugged features, *is the wherewithal to give Georges Treml*

his fair domains again, even if he be begging his bread from door to door.

But instantly the joyous expression died away as he thought:

But where can he be?

Jude couldn't wait to arrive at the castle to find out the fate of George Treml.

Then, replacing the little chest, recovering it with earth, and replacing the tools, hoops, and dead branches over the treasure, he left the tree and walked pensively back to the spot where he had left Captain Didier.

Pelo Rouan followed him with his eyes as the old squire walked away.

"That was Jude Leker," he murmured. "That was really the squire of Treml. But he didn't take that chest away. I'll return tonight and see what's inside. In the meantime, my men shouldn't get any wind of this, because they could betray me."

As soon as Jude Leker had entirely disappeared, the men with the wolf skin masks rushed towards the hollow oak, followed more slowly by the charcoal-burner.

"Master," they asked, raising their fur caps respectfully, "what did you see the old fellow do in this old tree?"

"Ah, my good fellows!" Pelo replied. "'Tis a pity you do not live in Vitré, for you are as curious as old women, and would make excellent gossip. If you must know, I saw an old man dig up, maybe, a half-dozen gold coins he had buried there."

"Six gold pieces?" one of the Wolves growled. "Perhaps there may be more!"

"Search, then, if you like," Pelo answered with great indifference; then he added fiercely: "Whilst I keep watch for you."

The Wolves hesitated for one moment, noting Pelo's anger, then bowed as a mark of obedience and returned to their posts.

Pelo said to them:

"There! Now you are yourselves again. But bear this in mind: when I am on the spot, my eyes watch with yours, and I can afford to pass over some slight neglect. But when I am away, negligence becomes treason, and you both know how I punish traitors. Soldiers of the Maréchaussée have been seen in the forest, and perhaps at this very hour, they may be searching for some of our lairs. The least imprudence could betray us. Return to your watch, and be careful.

The charcoal burner pronounced these words in a short and imperious voice. The two Wolves answered humbly:

"Yes, Master, we will keep watch."

Pelo Rouan then removed the two pistols that hung from his belt and hid them under his clothes.

"I must go to the castle, to see how the land lies there."

Uttering these last words, he stalked away, leaving his wondering companions muttering:

"The White Wolf is like the Devil. Only the two of them can run and disappear like this. What do you think, Guyot?"

"I think that I would have liked to see what's in the hollow of that oak, François."

"Me too. But you heard him. He spoke the truth."

"Yes, he did, and that was enough."

And the two Wolves resigned themselves to return to their watch.

Meanwhile, Jude Leker was returning with a much lighter heart than when he had set out, for one of his great fears had been relieved; the heir of Treml, if still alive, now possessed the means of repurchasing his inheritance.

Marie and Didier heard his heavy tramp approaching. They had been together for a little more than two hours, but the time had seemed short.

It was with great regret that the girl got up to leave:

"Goodbye," she said. "You won't leave me again, will you?"

"Never," replied the captain with a kiss.

The thicket opened and Jude appeared. Didier was alone.

"You didn't waste any time, my friend," said the young captain cheerfully. "I did not expect you back so soon."

Jude interpreted the remark as a reproach addressed to his slowness and apologized profusely.

"Let's go," said the captain, who jumped into his saddle without touching the stirrup, "I was asleep and must have had a wonderful dream, for I was in no hurry to see you back. So, what happened to the treasure of Treml?"

"Heaven still has it in its care."

"So much the better! And now on to the castle, unless you have some other mysterious mission to accomplish?"

Jude shook his head, and the horsemen cantered off in the direction of the old castle.

It rarely happens that a Breton of the true old strain sympathizes completely with the careless gaiety that forms the basis of the French character; so in the present instance, as the Captain pressed on to make up for the two hours lost so rapturously in the forest, Jude felt uncomfortable at the scraps of songs, then in vogue, hummed by his new master, and after following him for half an-hour without uttering a word, he rode up to his side, and respectfully reminded him of his promised aid:

"Monsieur," he said, "my duty lies heavy on my soul, and my limited mind now relies on the help you promised me."

"And you shall have it," Didier answered, reining in his horse, and bringing him to a walking pace. "But what is it that you expect me to do exactly?"

"In the first place, Monsieur," said Jude, "it is important I should not be discovered, and although it is twenty years since I have been in the castle, there might be some old servitors who may recollect me. So, I pray you, let us not enter before dark."

"Certainly! The air is not cold this fine evening, and night will soon set in. We can wait in the forest. But you have forgotten, my old friend, that there are torches and candles in Monsieur de Vaunoy's residence…"

"True, true," murmured Jude. "I hadn't thought of that."

The captain continued, smiling:

"However, do not despair; we will wrap ourselves in our cloaks, and trust me to find some clever way to conceal you from all prying eyes. What's next?"

"What's next?" the faithful fellow stammered, with a sigh. "Well, I must endeavor to find out if young Lord Georges still lives."

"Let's proceed, then."

Thus it was, as we have seen, that the Captain and the old man-at-arms obtained admission to the castle, and were ushered into the great reception room, under the guidance of good Master Simonnet.

When the Captain entered the salon, he found there Hervé de Vaunoy, his daughter Alix, Mademoiselle Olive de Vaunoy, Hervé's younger sister, and Monsieur Béchamel, Marquis de Nointel, the French King's Intendant and tax collector.

The new royal officer had been expected for some days, but as no one was acquainted with his name, when Simonnet merely announced, "the new Captain," all eyes turned with the greatest curiosity towards the door.

Didier entered, while Jude remained with his large hat covering the upper, and his horseman's cloak shading the lower portion of his face, standing motionless beside the door.

Didier stepped forward, his hat underneath his arm, his head erect, with that easy, chivalrous manner that had prepossessed so many ladies in his favor before.

His presence caused various effects, which he could read legibly on the faces of the four persons in the room:

Mademoiselle Olivia pursed up her mouth and played nervously with her enormous fan;

Alix turned pale and leaned back against the armrest of her chair;

A twitch of bitter disappointment shone through Hervé's habitual fawning smile;

Finally, Monsieur Béchamel, Marquis de Nointel, made the most awful grimace that was ever seen on the face of a surprised financier.

CHAPTER XV
Sketches of the Family

The gallant Captain bowed his head almost to the ground before the ladies, saluted Hervé de Vaunoy less profoundly, scarcely noticing Monsieur Béchamel, and before his courtesies were completely at an end, his astute host, recovering from his astonishment, advanced to meet him with his usual smile, and cried:

"Good Heavens, my young friend, you are thrice welcome to my humble roof. Something told me that the next time I saw you, you would wear these epaulettes, and I am right glad to see such decorations on your shoulders. Your hand, my brave young friend! Your hand!"

Didier took this affectionate greeting in good part; passing on to the ladies, he kissed Alix's hand without a word, that of Mademoiselle Olive de Vaunoy with a gallant compliment, and then, turning to Hervé, said:

"His Majesty's commands permitted me to choose between your hospitality, Monsieur, and that of Monsieur Béchamel, and I trust that it will not displease you to accommodate me for a few days."

"Displease me! Out with the graceless word, my young friend; nothing can afford me greater pleasure."

"I thank you; and to put your good will to the test, I will ask you to let my servant be shown to the room you have reserved for me."

Mademoiselle Olive rang a small silver bell that stood upon the mantel-piece.

"The good fellow should drink a grace cup before he retires, with my steward, Master Alain," De Vaunoy observed.

Hearing that name caused a thrill throughout Jude's frame.

"I'm afraid my servant is greatly fatigued," replied the Captain, "and requires an early bed and rest."

"As you wish, my friend."

A servant entered, having answered Mademoiselle Olive's bell.

"Prepare a bed for this good man," instructed De Vaunoy, "and treat him as the servant of a man whom I love and admire."

And Jude, still enveloped in his mantle, was escorted from the room by the domestic who, despite his curiosity, was unable to see his face.

We are already familiar with Hervé de Vaunoy, now Lord of La Tremlays and Boüexis-in-the-Forest. The twenty years that had elapsed had not in the least altered his round, self-complacent, sleek, and smirking countenance.

His sister, Mademoiselle Olive, had, in her youth, been remarkable for nothing but her ugliness. Age cannot embellish but at least erases the excessive differences that separate beauty from ugliness. At fifty, what remains of an ugly woman is very close to what remains of a courtesan. Only the expression on one's face can restore categories. That on Mademoiselle Olive expressed nothing, except a sense of self-importance, a stubborn delusion of kindness, and incomparable prudery. She was dressed in the latest style of Parisian fashion, with a long-waisted satin robe, open and laced up the front, showing a white muslin bodice trimmed with the finest Mechlin lace, with an enormous hoop, her head powdered and frizzed to an inconceivable degree, Morocco leather slippers, sewed with golden thread and without heels, and a fan of extraordinary dimensions in her hand. Her cheeks were dotted here and there with patches of court-plaster, two lines of Indian ink gave her the semblance of well-arched eyebrows, whilst rouge unsparingly applied added the glow of youth to either cheek, and a skillful cosmetic conveyed an unnatural brilliancy to her lips.

The youthful Alix in no ways resembled her father or her aunt. Her tall, exquisitely-proportioned figure wore the stamp of nature's own nobility; her raven hair, undisguised with powder, was simply turned back from a high forehead, the proud majesty of which was relieved by the softness of two deep-blue eyes; the general expression of her face was pensive, but not austere, and defined lines of her mouth indicated firmness and resolution unmixed with obstinacy. She was, in fact, a perfect ideal of what a woman should be—beautiful in countenance, and graceful in form—joining energy to softness—enduring suffering without a murmur—and capable of loving unto death.

Hervé de Vaunoy had married a year after the departure of Nicolas Treml. His wife had passed away eighteen months later. Alix was his only daughter and she had now attained her eighteenth year.

As for Monsieur Antinoüs Béchamel, Marquis de Nointel, he was a corpulent man, about forty to forty-five years of age, with fresh-colored, chubby cheeks; round, grey eyes; a double chin; and undeniable calves to his legs. His court-dress on high days and holidays was garnished with diamond buttons each worth twenty thousand *livres*; his ruffles and shirt-frill were of the most costly point-lace that could be procured. He offered snuff to the ladies out of a box of the finest tortoise shell, richly carved, set with emeralds and lined with gold; and, as his memory was tolerably good, he retold several *bon-mots*—not more than six months-old—which he retailed as his own whenever he found a fitting opportunity. To complete his portrait, he possessed an admirable appetite, to which he sacrificed one-third of his income, and a digestion exceeding all belief.

In summary, this grotesque, gastronomic, wealthy nobleman was not too different from most of the noble financiers of the times.

Monsieur Béchamel had a number of important occupations in Brittany. First of all, he was desperately in love with Alix de Vaunoy, and wanted to make her his wife at all costs. Monsieur de Vaunoy was not hostile to the notion, but Mademoiselle Alix's opinion on the matter was diametrically opposed to his, and, consequently, all his gallantry, the excellent dainties of his table, and his well-remembered impromptus, were lost upon the haughty Breton maiden. However, Monsieur Béchamel was not discouraged and every day redoubled his incessant and useless efforts.

Secondly, as has been stated, he was the royal Intendant, collector-general of the taxes—an employment that required much personal activity, for the population of the ancient Duchy lacked both money and the will to pay the heavy taxes that ground them to the earth.

Thirdly, Béchamel had a certain class of the small claimants to nobility beneath his thumb. By the "Pact of Union," the nobles of the Duchy were exempt from fiscal contributions, and therefore many persons endeavored to substantiate that right by assuming a nobility of birth to which they were by no means entitled. Béchamel took upon himself the strict investigation of these assumptions; and thus it was that not only was he the cause of large additional annual sums being paid into the royal treasury, but he profited largely by fines imposed by the Breton Parliament at Rennes upon those who put forth false claims to nobility.

As a result, he had a vested interest in finding usurpers. In so doing, he did not fail to upset the local gentry and was so greedy that even the local lords loyal to the French King loathed him. It would be difficult to say whether this overactive collector was more feared or hated.

In fact, in such a patriarchal province as Brittany, a country of proverbial simplicity, honor, and good faith, where noblemen, known as such from time immemorial, took no heed of preserving title-deeds, the power of the Intendant was almost omnipotent. Avaricious, narrow-minded, haughty and supercilious to the humble, but submissive to his superiors, he was a tyrant in the fullest sense of the word. Money was the sole thing that could bend him; did a man come to him with the amount of the usual fine in his hands, and a few hundred crowns to boot, he might rest assured that he would never be disturbed, however ridiculous his pretensions to nobility might be: for ten thousand *écus*, he would have left the descendant of a scullion in the possession of the title of Duke; but if money were not forthcoming, he exacted the strictest proofs, and put many gentlemen to a fearful, abominable expense, in defending their undoubted rights, and substantiating their long-descended claims. The memoirs of the times relate several instances of noble gentlemen driven to ruin by his machinations.[22]

---

[22] Authentic. (*Note from the Author.*)

Under these circumstances it can readily be conceived that Hervé de Vaunoy, whose title to nobility was at best doubtful, would tremble before such a man, and evil slanderous tongues did not scruple to assert that he had approached the financier with the never-failing sedative of gold. Indeed, the position that De Vaunoy now held in the province was one which required the greatest skill and address for him to retain. As his right to bear the arms of Treml, and the actual possession of the hereditary domains of that noble family, depended only on a mysterious sale, which could not be very well proved, he had early on sought every means of propitiating the Intendant. Luckily for him, Monsieur Béchamel had met him more than half-way on that road, esteeming him, outwardly, as his most excellent good friend, and making no concealment of his passion for his fair daughter, Alix.

De Vaunoy, with his usual ability, had not failed to profit by this lucky stroke of fortune, and as the Intendant had done all he could to induce the father to exert his influence with his child, the adroit parvenu speedily became high in favor and influence.

De Vaunoy promised the royal officer that he soon would have Alix for his wife, although at the same time, he deemed it expedient to play off against him the intimacy which had existed formerly at Rennes between his daughter and young Didier.

During Didier's stay in Rennes, Monsieur Béchamel had not failed to notice the romance between the two young people, which explained his somber face when he saw Didier's return.

As for Mademoiselle Olive, she played with her fan, giving herself all the pretty airs of a youthful miss.

Dinner being the most important part of Breton hospitality, a few minutes after the arrival of the Captain, Master Alain, the majordomo, appeared, wearing his gold chain of office, his eyes still red from his drunken nap, and throwing open the folding doors of an adjoining room, announced that supper was served.

"Tomorrow, we shall discuss business," said De Vaunoy, "but now, let's dine."

"Yes, let's," said Monsieur Béchamel, who seemed to have recovered some of his composure.

Alix rose, and instinctively held out her hand to Didier, but it was the Intendant who seized it much to her disgust. The Captain was obliged to content himself with the bony fingers of Mademoiselle Olive, who simpered.

The supper passed in an unusually heavy manner. De Vaunoy did all he could to promote hilarity, but was not successful in the attempt. Monsieur Béchamel ate and drank voraciously, paying his accustomed attentions to Alix, who heeded him not, for her eyes were fixed with a melancholy expression upon her former lover, who did not vouchsafe her one look, but was taken up entirely with her dear old coquette of an aunt.

Twice De Vaunoy in drinking toast with the young Captain exchanged sinister glances with his steward; and about the end of the repast, having whispered something to him, Alain transmitted the order to a truculent-looking lackey, named Lapierre, whom Hervé had lately inveigled from the service of the governor of the province.

At the conclusion of the supper, De Vaunoy personally escorted his new guest to his chamber, and, shaking his hand warmly, wished him "good-night" with every demonstration of cordiality.

Jude was still up, pacing across the room with pensive steps, plunged in deep thought.

"Well," asked his master, "are you happy with me? I spared you from their prying eyes."

"Monsieur, I thank you," replied Jude.

"Did you find anything of interest?"

"Nothing about the child, which is a sad omen, but I now know that Dame Goton, who was the nurse of the little gentleman, is now a housekeeper at the castle."

"Ah. She may have news."

"I also know that it will be difficult for me to remain unnoticed for long, for I saw an old, determined enemy: Alain, the steward of Treml."

"And I, too, good Jude," the Captain added. "I caught a glimpse of the face of a scoundrel who was in the service of Monseigneur de Toulouse, and whom I suspect was involved in the nocturnal assault of last year in Rennes that cost me a sword thrust in the neck. But let us sleep, my old friend, and with the new day we will see what can be done."

"Go ahead, my Lord, sleep."

The Captain fell on his bed, but Jude continued to keep watch.

CHAPTER XVI
The Private Council of Monsieur de Vaunoy

The Captain slept the sound sleep of health and youth, dreaming alternately of the noble Alix and the humble daughter of the forest, for, desperately in love as he now was with the "Blossom-of-the-Broom," he had not seen the former again without mixed emotions.

Jude walked slowly and quietly to and fro in the chamber, taxing his tortured brain to devise some mode of discovering the lost heir of Treml.

Monsieur Antinoüs Béchamel, Marquis de Nointel, was enjoying the delights of a superb vol-au-vent pastry; the ancient demoiselle Olivia was occupied building a castle in the air, in which she saw herself as the mistress or wife of a handsome gallant officer in the service of King Louis XV; and the fair Alix strove to combat the fever that boiled her blood, and vainly sought relief in sleep. She dared not inquire of her heart the cause of the tumult that possessed it; but yet—despite herself—that heart would speak, and tell her it was Love.

Up to that evening, the only obstacle she had perceived to a union between her and Didier had been the desire of her father for her marriage to the Marquis de Nointel; but now hope had almost fled, and an abyss yawned beneath her feet, for Didier loved her not.

Let us leave the poor girl for a while in the depth of her distress, and see what was happening in the chamber of Hervé de Vaunoy.

Three men were seated there—himself, Alain, the Steward, and the valet, Lapierre.

Alain was now an old man. His rough countenance, upon which a state of daily intoxication had left deep markings, bore no other expression than stupid and pitiless hardness.

Lapierre was a man of about forty-five, without any distinguishing traces of Breton lineage in his countenance— indeed, he was from southern Anjou, a province proverbially fertile in vagabonds and every kind of adventurer. Up to his twenty-fifth year, he had followed the respectable triple profession of quack doctor, sword swallower, and tight-rope dancer. Then, as he told it, becoming tired of his wandering life, he had entered the service of the great Comte de Toulouse, who was not yet Governor of Brittany. He had brought with him a lovely child, whom he used to exhibit on his stage, and whose beauty never failed to attract spectators to the show. The Comte, having taken a fancy to this boy, made him first his page, taking care of his education, and then, after a few years, promoted him to gentleman of his household. It was then that Lapierre had conceived an unconquerable aversion toward his former dependant, now so immeasurably his superior.

One day, when the Comte was in residence as Governor of Brittany, Lapierre had requested the honor of a private audience with Monsieur de Vaunoy, which, being granted to him, lasted for a great length of time. It was said that De Vaunoy's face more than once paled or became rubicund during that conference. The result was that Lapierre received a heavy purse of gold on the spot, and soon afterwards, the mountebank left the service of Monseigneur de Toulouse for that of Hervé de Vaunoy.

From that day, the new Lord of La Tremlays made much of the young man, Didier—for it was he!—thereby vehemently exciting the jealousy of the Marquis de

Nointel. And, as we explained, a few weeks afterwards, Didier was treacherously attacked in the streets of Rennes, on his return from a ball.

Silence had lasted for several minutes in Monsieur de Vaunoy's room, but as midnight struck, he rose from his seat, and walked up and down with hurried steps and glaring eye, whilst the two servants remained quietly by the fire, Lapierre balancing his chair on one leg, with the dexterity of his ancient occupation, and Alain nursing a flat bottle, underneath his jacket, containing good Calvados brandy, to which he paid his respects every now and then when his master's back was turned.

"Holy Mother! Holy Mother! Holy Mother!" Hervé de Vaunoy spat out three times, stopping suddenly before the men and stamping violently on the floor.

Alain shook a little before his master's fury, but Lapierre did not lose his balance.

"You were three against one! And at night too! Three stout swords against a toasting-fork, a dress-rapier, and yet you could not succeed!"

"You should have been there yourself, my lord," Alain grumbled, "and seen how the young fellow fought back. May I be hanged if I did not feel the wind of his rapier ten times close to my throat!"

"And I have a pretty remembrance of him," Lapierre said, turning back his collar and showing a triangular scar on the shoulder. "Joachim, our lamented comrade, saw rather too much of him, since he was left dead upon the spot. Heaven save his soul!"

"Amen!" grumbled Alain.

"May the Devil take both of yours! You were a coward, Alain, and you, Lapierre, are no better, you rascally mountebank, to run away with only that paltry scratch."

"Aye!" said Alain, in a surly voice. "You would have liked us to have remained with Joachim. Dead men tell no tales, eh, my lord?"

"Shut up!" Hervé shouted.

He resumed his angry walk, swearing loudly. As he did so, Lapierre leaned over to the steward and whispered:

"This shall cost him a Louis d'Or for each of us."

Alain seized this opportunity to swallow a swig from his flask and nodded. Both men exchanged a sly grin of profound intelligence, sure of their hold over the nobleman.

After few moments, De Vaunoy saw that he had been playing a false game, and an ingratiating smile returned to his face. Almost gliding up to the two servants, he placed his hand in his pocket and said:

"Holy Mother! I believe I have been out of temper. Anger is a sin, my friends, and must be expiated by a penitence. Take these two Louis, and let there be peace between us!"

The gold coins were happily accepted.

"Now," Monsieur de Vaunoy continued, "let us think what can be done—how we shall get over this misfortune!"

"When I was a doctor," Lapierre suggested, "if one dose of my elixir did not do, I always doubled it.

"That's it!" added Alain, whose imagination was being stimulated by the brandy. "Last time, three men weren't insufficient. Let's use six instead!"

"And this time, I guarantee the cure will take," concluded the former mountebank.

De Vaunoy shook his head.

"Impossible," he said.

"Why not, my lord?"

"In the first place, I see that he distrusts us. Secondly, circumstances have changed. When he was a hotheaded youth, running about the streets and getting into scrapes at all hours of the night, his assassination would have been a simple thing, and not excited the least suspicion. But now he is my guest, here in trust as an officer of the King. His stay at La Tremlays is somewhat official. The laws of hospitality, my good friends, prevent a man from murdering his guest—that is, unless it can be done quite quietly, so as to obviate any subsequent inquiry."

Alain and Lapierre laughed at the joke.

"We need to devise another method to be rid of him," said the nobleman.

The two servants seemed to reflect deeply.

"So?" asked Hervé de Vaunoy after a few minutes.

"I can't think of anything," replied Alain.

"Neither can I," added Lapierre, after a short pause. "Unless… what about poison? Would you prefer that to a dagger, My Lord?"

"Under my roof? Worse, Lapierre! It always leaves some traces behind. Holy Mother! How unfortunate it is! Every day may reveal to him who he is. And the Devil only knows if he doesn't already know! Where is he lodged?"

"In the old nursemaid's chamber," answered Alain. "You escorted him to the door."

"The nursemaid's chamber," repeated De Vaunoy. whose face suddenly grew pale. "Where he was rocked in his cradle! I didn't think about that! He may remember it!"

"It's hardly likely!" said Lapierre. "An infant cannot distinguish one room from another.

"Indeed," said Alain who now seemed barely able to stay awake.

But this assurance did not appease Hervé de Vaunoy's agitation.

"And what about his sick servant?" he said in a worried voice. "He obviously wished to conceal himself That augurs no good. What sort of a man is he?"

"That, I cannot answer," Lapierre replied. "He held his cloak so high up on his face that I could not see one feature."

"It is strange—so very strange... I like not this mystery," said De Vaunoy, now compelled to see something sinister behind even the most ordinary event. "I want to know who this man is."

"Tomorrow will be soon enough, My Lord," said Lapierre, calmly.

"No, tonight, Lapierre, this very night," replied De Vaunoy in a fevered tone. "Something whispers to me that this man's presence is too dangerous. Come, follow me!"

Lapierre was tempted to reply, that, in all probability, the Captain and his man were in bed and fast asleep; but De Vaunoy had spoken with so much determination and authority that he did not dare to disobey.

Both he and Alain, having left their seats, went out softly into a long corridor that reached from one wing of the castle to the other.

Hervé preceded them, but, after having taken a few steps, he pointed to a light glimmering from underneath the door of the chamber where the Captain and his attendant lay.

"They are not asleep!" he muttered to himself. "What can they be doing at this ungodly hour? Perhaps they talk of his former prospects—and of me! This uncertainty is unbearable! I must know; and, if my suspicions are correct, by all the powers of Hell, his royal mission shall not save him!"

Stepping softly along, the confederates reached the chamber door. Alain—now fully awake—knelt down and applied his eye to the key-hole.

Jude was on his knees praying at the foot of his master's bed, but the steward could not see his face. After a few seconds, the old squire rose to his feet, and, as the light of a lamp fell full upon his face, Alain started back.

"I know this man," he said in a whisper.

As quick at thought, Hervé was on his knees, and his eye was at the key-hole, but, at the moment he applied it, Jude blew out the light, and the guilty villain saw nothing but the red wick of the lamp, and then heard the old squire throw himself upon the bed.

"Holy Mother!" he said. "You said you know this man. Who is he then?" he asked Alain in a frenzy.

"I cannot recollect just now," replied the servant, is brow creased under the effort of trying hard to call. "It must have been many years ago…"

De Vaunoy stopped himself from from uttering a blasphemous oath, while Lapierre repeated calmly;

"Tomorrow will be soon enough, My Lord."

CHAPTER XVII
The Early Visit

Long before daybreak, Jude Leker left his bed, dressed himself quietly without disturbing Captain Didier, who slept soundly as one does when one is twenty-five years-old, especially after a long and tiring journey.

Although not one ray of dawn shed its early light upon the corridor, Jude found his way along it, without stopping for a second to orient himself, for he had been born in that castle, and had lived there for more than forty years.

Ignoring the grand staircase with its double banisters, he entered a narrow passage and series of stairs that led to the servants' quarters. Luckily for him, in all the marvelous changes of the castle, no alterations had been made to the interior arrangements, otherwise his memories of long ago might not have been as helpful.

He counted three doors in the main corridor that crossed the servants' quarters and tapped, without hesitation, on the fourth.

It was obvious that Dame Goton, the main housekeeper, was not used to receiving visits nor entertaining visitors at such an unexpected hour. The good woman was sixty years and at that age, she was only afraid of thieves. She also slept very soundly and Jude had to knock again more loudly to wake her up.

"Holy Virgin!" said the old woman, her voice choked up. "Is the castle on fire?!"

"No, Dame Goton," Jude replied, still tapping. "It is I–Jude Leker!"

The housekeeper still had a stout heart in her old age, and scrambling out of bed, she put on a petticoat and disposed herself to open the door. She also grabbed a heavy poker, as she was somewhat deaf, and had not understood one word Jude had said.

"Coming! Coming! If you're the Wolves, why, I'll tell you stories about old Nicolas Treml, and you'll be too embarrassed to set fire to even a speck of dust of what was once his home. And if you're ghosts, well..."

She crossed herself and stopped.

"Open the door, Dame Goton," said Jude.

"Who are you?" the old woman repeated. "If you're a ghost," she repeated. "Well, all things considered, I'd rather you be the Wolves!"

She held firm to her poker and opened the door. She raised her poker, which Jude gently pushed to one side.

"Who are you?" she repeated.

"Hush, Dame! Silence—in the name of Heaven!"

"Who are you?" she asked for a third time.

This time, Jude grabbed the poker from her hands, went in, and closed the door behind him.

"A man, whose name must not be uttered, except as a last resource, in the hereditary house of Treml," he replied.

"The House of Treml," said the old woman, her heart beating more rapidly as she heard the unaccustomed words. "Thank you, whoever you may be. It's been twenty years since I have heard its true name given to the house now inhabited by Hervé de Vaunoy."

Then, taking the squire's hand, but trembling with curiosity and anxiety, she led him in the dark as safely as if it had been day, to a stool beside the hearth. She did not need to see him; it was like a secret and mysterious greeting between the two faithful servants.

"But who are you again, you who remembers Treml?" she asked again.

Jude whispered in her ear.

"Jude!" she cried aloud—forgetting all prudence in the intensity of her astonishment. "Jude Leker! Our good Lord's squire! Oh, let me see you once more, my man, let me behold your honest face."

Trembling far more than she had previously done, Dame Goton groped for her lighter, then struck the flint and steel, and having lit a small bit of pinewood, held it up to Jude's face.

She shook her head as she saw the ravages that time and imprisonment had made. Then her thoughts reverting to Nicolas Treml, she asked:

"And *him*, Jude, shall we see *him* again?"

The squire turned away his head, and pronounced solemnly the one sad word:

"Dead!"

The housekeeper dropped upon her knees, the tears ran down her wrinkled cheeks, and she recited a *De Profundis* for the repose of the old nobleman's soul. Anyone who might have seen her then would have felt powerfully moved because nothing moves one's soul like tears rolling down on a wrinkled face, and anyone who might pass smiling in front of two beautiful tear-filled eyes will grow pale when he sees the eyes of an elderly person fill with the same tears.

Jude held his peace whilst the good woman prayed; and even when her prayer was over, he seemed afraid to put an end to his uncertainty by asking news of the boy. But recollecting that time was passing fast, that the household would soon be afoot, and he should not then be able to regain the Captain's room unseen, he made a mighty effort and simply said:

"What about the child?"

"Georges Treml?" she replied. "Twenty years have passed since my poor eyes saw that sweet boy, smiling and holding up his little arms to me in his cradle."

"Is he… dead too?"

Jude covered his eyes with his hands, his broad, manly chest heaved as if it would burst, and a gasp escaped from his mouth.

"I did not say so, Jude. No, I did not say so. I cannot believe it—he may yet live. Alas! I have thought so for twenty-years, and now every day my hopes grow less."

Jude fixed his eyes on hers. He did not understand.

"Yes," she said, "I hope… I tell myself that someday I might see our little boy return, tall and strong, his head held up proud, a shining sword at his side. Alas, alas, I've been telling myself this for so long…"

"But then, what became of him?" asked Jude. "Tell me, Dame, quickly—for mercy's sake, do not keep me in suspense any longer."

"I know—and yet I know nothing. One evening—come closer to me, Jude, for this must not be said aloud—one evening, the boy had left the castle with Hervé de Vaunoy to take a walk in the fields. Then De Vaunoy came running back, pale, with haggard face, and staring eyes, looking like the pictures of the first murderer in the great Church at Rennes, and said that Master Georges had fallen into the pool of La Tremlays, and had drowned. Well, every one ran to the lake, the water was searched inch by inch, but the body of the babe could not be found."

The squire's eye had dilated, as the old dame spoke, but now it resumed its gloomy expression.

"And is that your only hope?" he asked despondently.

"No! Do you recollect the hapless idiot whom we'd nicknamed the White Hare?"

"I remember Jean Blanc."

"Well, what of him? What had he to do with the boy?"

"The poor creature!" said the dame. "He loved the Tremls almost as much as we did."

"But Georges—Georges!" Jude interrupted.

"Jean Blanc was in the habit of telling strange tales of the forest, and he swore he'd seen Hervé throw the child into the lake."

"He said that!" said Jude, his eyes fiery with anger.

"By my faith, he did; and though sometimes he was thought mad, everybody believed every word he said about Treml. But that was not all. Jean insisted that he'd dived into the water, and brought up Master Georges, and placed him on the bank…"

"Ah!" said the loyal squire, with deep sigh of relief.

"…but then, Dame Goton continued, "one of his fits came over him and he ran off, and when he came back, the child was not there, where he had left him."

"Ah!" said Jude.

All of his hopes were scattered to the winds, and he remained spell-bound beside the hearth.

"And that was twenty years ago," concluded Dame Goton.

"Where is Jean Blanc?" Jude asked. "I want to talk to him."

"Alas!" the Dame replied, shaking her head slowly, "it is impossible for the poor to withstand the rich and powerful. Hervé de Vaunoy soon heard of the tales that were whispered through the forest, and immediately afterwards, the soldiers came down upon Mathieu Blanc for the accursed taxes. So the old man died, and Jean fled. No one knows what has become of him, but it is suspected he is now a Wolf."

"I have heard that word before, Dame. Who are these men?"

"Bretons, Jude, who know how to defend themselves, aye, and to avenge themselves too, when an opportunity occurs. The name has been given to them because their hidden retreats are somewhere near the Wolf's Pit, although no one cares to ascertain the particulars. They wear masks made of wolf's skin, and their chief wears a white one."

"I must see these Wolves," Jude said, after reflecting a few moments.

Dame Goton thought for a moment.

"Listen, there is one person in the forest, who, I think, might give you some information regarding Jean Blanc—if he is still alive. This man is a Breton, though sometimes he pretends to be French in his heart, and about the time he came here bringing an infant with him, all the foresters said the girl had the features of poor Jean Blanc."

"And where shall I find this man?"

"His cabin is about a hundred yards from the Cross of our Lady of the Forest."

"His name is—?"

"Pelo Rouan, the charcoal-burner."

The light of the dawn now began to make all things distinct.

"Farewell, then, Dame," said Jude. "I shall see this man within the hour."

He then shook the housekeeper's hand warmly, and prepared to regain the room where he had passed the night.

"May God be with you, my good man," said the old housekeeper, watching him as he crossed the long corridor, until he turned the corner and disappeared. "It has been a long time since my poor heart has felt such joy. May God be with you, and return the legitimate heir of Treml to his domains."

But in her heart, Dame Goton felt more desire than hope because she shook her head sadly while pronouncing these last words

CHAPTER XVIII
Dreams

When Jude reentered the bedroom, he found Didier still sleeping soundly, his calm, almost smiling face announcing the presence of a happy dream. The old squire looked at him attentively.

He is loyal and handsome, he thought. *His countenance reminds me of Nicolas Treml, before time had tinged his thick moustaches with grey. He looks happy! Oh! What I wouldn't give to see young Georges in that same position.*

By this time, the rays of the rising sun were tingeing the silken curtains of the room with gold. Just as Jude had placed his large cloak upon his shoulders and girded on his sword, the Captain moved slightly.

"Alix," he whispered softly.

Jude looked through the window, and saw most of the servants were assembling in the great courtyard

It's going to be hard to slip by unnoticed, he thought.

"Marie," Didier now murmured.

"Bravo!" said the squire, smiling to himself, "Perhaps I shall now hear another of his loves."

"Blossom-of-the-Broom!" said Didier, as if meeting the challenge.

Then, waking completely, he sat upright in his bed.

"Oh, it's you, friend Jude," he said after looking all around the room, as if he had expected to see someone else. "I think I was dreaming."

"You can say that again, young Master, and joyfully so," replied Jude,

Didier's eyes lighted upon the antique draperies of the chamber, his smile became more joyous.

"The poets are right," he murmured, as if he spoke to himself, "in praising the delights of returning to the ancestral roof. In my dreams, friend Jude, I felt that I, a man of unknown family, was wont to be cradled in such a room as this; and at this very moment the delusion comes upon me strongly. It seems to me that in my childhood I have seen the sun playing upon curtains like these; it seems to me that in just such another chamber, I—a child whose lineage is utterly unknown—have basked in the smile of tender parents who have almost smothered me with their affectionate caresses. It is a strange feeling…"

"Monsieur," the squire broke in, "forgive me, but I must leave you for the present to accomplish the vow I have undertaken."

"Stop yet a moment, Jude, stop, I beseech you. These new sensations are so overwhelming… I feel that I could weep..."

"Are you ill, Monsieur?"

Didier placed his hand in the old man's grasp and fell back on the bed.

"No, Jude, quite the contrary; but I would not lose these feelings. Happy, indeed, must they be whose recollections of their infancy are not vain delusions!"

"There are some," Jude replied in a melancholy tone, "to whom it is not given to behold the roof of a long line of ancestors. It must be a bitter pang for a child to die unknown and friendless, far from his native home."

153

"You are thinking still, my honest friend, of Georges Treml?"

"I am, Monsieur."

"Then lose not sight of your good work, since it is one of Christian charity. Now I see a cloud passing over the bright sun, and with it, the enchantment vanishes and I become Captain Didier again, and ready to swear that, as a child, I saw more canvas tents than silken curtains. Go, my friend, I will not detain you longer."

Didier, shaking himself, jumped out of bed. Before leaving the room, Jude looked down again into the courtyard, and drew back instinctively as he saw Alain, the house steward, talking with Lapierre.

"I fear, Captain," he said, "it is too late now for me to go forth unseen; I see there below a man who will recognize me immediately."

"Which one?" said the young soldier, approaching close to the window. "Do you mean Lapierre?"

"I know not whether he has changed his name, but in my time, he was called Master Alain. It is the older of the two."

"I see. Is he the one you named as your sworn enemy yesterday?"

"Yes."

"Well, then! As for the other fellow, my good friend, I have reason to believe he is mine."

"A common lackey, your enemy?"

"Are you surprised, Jude? How many times must I repeat to you that I am not a nobleman? That lackey is the sole person upon earth who knows the secret of my birth. He wants to keep it to himself, and that is his right. He boasts of having been my protector in my early days…

154

"Look here," he continued, baring his shoulder and showing a scar upon one of his blade-bones.

"It looks like a wound, one given treacherously," said Jude, frowning.

"Yes, and I have every reason to believe that it was that fellow down there who struck that blow; but if I am not a born gentleman, I am still the King's officer, and cannot condescend to chastise such a paltry scum as he."

"If it be your will, Monsieur, just say the word, and I will do so on the instant."

"Ah! Ah! Brave Jude! All ready to forget about young Georges now! I see the spirit of chivalry still thrives in that heart of yours, fine old Breton. But think of your young lord, my good fellow! Now, let's go down together. Monsieur de Vaunoy is too devoted and loyal a subject of the king to permit his servants to examine too closely a domestic of a Captain of the Maréchaussée."

Didier put on his cloak and followed Jude downstairs.

When the Captain and his attendant reached the courtyard, Alain and Lapierre bowed respectfully to the former, who returned the salute by touching the brim of his hat with his finger.

"Have my servant's horse saddled on the instant," ordered Didier.

While Lapierre hastened to see the order executed, Alain stayed, trying to peep under Jude's cloak,

"My friend, is your sickness so bad that you must remain wrapped inside your cloak?" he asked Jude.

But Didier cut the steward short, by asking":

"What is thought about these insurgent Wolves in the country?"

"That they are fearful brutes, Captain," Alain answered, and then turning to Jude again: "Will you share a friendly cup of Calvados with me?"

"And what do the good folks in the forest do about it?" the Captain again interrupted.

"Make hoops, and wooden shoes, and bowls, Captain," grumbled Alain with bad grace. "Well, comrade," he added for Jude's benefit, showing off his *vademecum*, that is to say, his tin flask, "would you like a drop of Calvados?"

But all necessity for further colloquy was avoided when Lapierre returned with Jude's horse. The squire was in the saddle in a moment. But as he got into the stirrups, his cloak slid off a little, and the cunning steward was able to see a portion of his face.

"The Devil take me if I haven't seen that face somewhere before," he grumbled. "But where? Ah! I am getting old!"

"Meet me at Rennes tonight," instructed Didier. "Now, good luck! Go!"

The trusty Breton did not wait for the order to be repeated and left the courtyard at a sharp trot.

Then Didier turned around, directing his attention to de Vaunoy's servants.

"Restrain your curiosity, fellow," he told Alain in a menacing accent. "It is a bad character trait that only brings bad luck." And then, to Lapierre: "And you, you had better beware."

As the officer walked away, the two men looked at each other significantly, and when he was out of hearing, Lapierre said with a mocking sneer:

"Beware! What say you of this, Master Alain?"

"The cockerel crows loudly, and thinks he is a chick of the game, but his comb may be cut for all that. However, Beware—is good counsel, even from an enemy!"

Meanwhile, Didier—without knowing where he was going—had taken the direction of the garden. He soon found himself surrounded by high hedges cut in the fantastic fashion prevalent at the close of the seventeenth century. At times, he came upon statues of white marble shining through the labyrinth of green.

As he looked vaguely around him, his mind reverted involuntarily to the subject of his dream and the thoughts that engrossed him, when he first awoke. The illusion came back upon him in full force; the massive walls of verdure appeared to him like old acquaintances; he wandered into the maze and found his way out of it with as much facility as if he had possessed the thread of Ariadne; and then the idea came to him that he must have been there before.

"It is strange! It is wonderful!" he said. "Well, let me solve this enigma, and see whether my memory is correct, or whether my imagination misleads me. One or the other tells me that at the end of this alley on the right, there is a bower, and in it a statue of a nymph."

Impatient and much disturbed, he walked quickly towards the spot; and when he arrived at a sharp turn in the walk, he stopped suddenly, rubbed his hands across his eyes, became pale, pressed his throbbing heart, and uttered a short cry, for there were both the bower and the nymph, with the exception that the statue, a living maiden, started as she heard the noise, and turned her head towards the spot where Didier remained lost in mute astonishment.

CHAPTER XIX
In the Bower

A moment sufficed to scatter the illusion to the winds: Didier had half expected to behold an arbor and a statue, and his expectations were doomed to be half realized, for the arbor most undoubtedly was there, but the nymph was a charming girl of flesh and blood; no other than Alix de Vaunoy de La Tremlays. In fact nothing could be more excusable than the mistake, as the young lady was simply habited in white muslin that morning, and as Didier advanced, she stood attentively, reading a crumpled letter which she had just taken from her bosom, and which she dropped inadvertently, as she heard the Captain's exclamation.

Her first impulse was to fly; but on reflection she controlled her emotion, and advanced a few steps towards the spot where Didier stood, for with the quickness of affection, she had recognized his voice at once. The paleness of her lovely countenance showed that she had passed the night devoid of rest; her look was fixed and grave as she saw Didier approach, when she stopped in her turn, and allowed him to come so near as to stoop and pick up the letter she had dropped. Casting his eye upon the writing, he saw it was from himself, and his imagination at once brought the rich color to his mantling cheeks.

Alix could scarcely restrain her agitation, and said without lifting up her eyes:

"It is the letter you thought it was your duty to write to me when last you left Rennes; it is fortunate that it has fallen into your hands, Monsieur, for it was my intention to return it to you."

These words were few and insignificant, but while Alix spoke, her compressed lips showed that she forbore making any complaint, and her whole demeanor proved that, from some hidden cause, she was strenuously combating a deep, sincere, but hopeless passion. Didier gazed upon her with respect, regret, and tenderness; the feelings he had once entertained for her, and which he had deemed love, he thought were gone—for though in that age morality was not of a too high and noble character, his frank, honorable disposition would not permit him to pay attention to two women at one time.

But he was only twenty-five years-old and his heart spoke louder than his conscience; so, kneeling at her feet in admiration, he took her hand, and lifting it to his lips, murmured:

"What I wrote then, I still feel. Is it you then, Alix, who have changed?"

"I, change?" she replied in evident surprise. "You know full well it is not I!"

His eyes were again cast upon the ground as she continued with a melancholy smile:

"Listen, Didier, it is far better that it should be so, for what we thought affection for each other was nothing other than madness; and when I found you yesterday indifferent and forgetful, I thanked Heaven, and deemed that coldness a blessing for us both."

"Alix, I don't understand This affected calmness…"

"Was all too real—I believe so, and I hope so."

"You hope so?" said the young man, with a note of bitterness.

"Yes," she said with the utmost composure, although her heart was breaking inside. "I sincerely do."

These words—destitute of coquetry—sank to the bottom of the Captain's heart, and momentarily relit the ashes of his almost extinct love. He turned on her a look of mingled wonder, anger, and disappointment. But Mademoiselle de Vaunoy, who could be duplicitous at times, was not, in this instance, playing a role.

"This letter," she continued, pointing to the writing which he still held in his hand, "ought never to have been written. We were children then, but some years have passed since, and Time breaks every tie. No, do not interrupt me, Didier, I know all too well what you want to say—the sight of me has caused a chord to vibrate that had not been struck for many months—you are much moved, you mistake that emotion for enduring love, and are ready to renew those vows you made to me long ago; but I neither can nor will hear them."

"But Alix, hear me, my dear Alix, for Heaven's sake! I swear I am not changed."

"She is a lovely girl," Mademoiselle de Vaunoy continued, without noticing his fervent protestation, "and her face is that of an angel; she loves you to distraction, and if you do not respond to that love, she will be miserable."

Again the poor girl stopped, whilst her features worked convulsively for a few seconds, and then she went on as calmly as before:

"But you do love her, Didier, and passionately too."

The Captain was now crunching the letter in his hand, his face surly and sad.

"Who are you talking about?" he uttered faintly, beginning now to get a glimmer of the truth.

"You know whom I mean; her name is always on your lips; and her image never leaves your heart."

"I can't tell, Alix, whence this supposition comes?"

"It is no supposition, for I have the strongest proofs. There is a feeling of almost sisterhood between us Daughters of the Forest, rich and noble as well as poor and humble; as children, we were frequently together in the woods, and we played together often beneath the great oaks that canopy the pillar to our Lady of the Forest. But while she remained in her native innocence, amid the verdant coverts, I went out into the world and became acquainted with what are called the duties of my station; I learned to clothe myself in rich attire, to speak carelessly to all mankind, to smile and to deceive. Strange it is, Didier, that the same fate befell us both, I in the high society of Rennes and she alone in the forest, and that she gave her heart to the same man whom I once—once thought I loved."

"What, Alix? Do you not love me still?"

"What does it matter now? We will speak no more of it. One day, Monsieur, when you had been absent about two months, I was walking alone in the forest, thinking of the brilliant fêtes of Monseigneur le Comte de Toulouse where we first met, and perhaps a little of yourself, when I heard a sweet, sad voice in the bushes singing *The Lament* of Arthur of Brittany…"

"Blossom-of-the-Broom!" the Captain involuntarily exclaimed.

"Blossom-of-the-Broom," repeated Alix, shuddering. "At least, you now know of whom I speak, Didier. Well, it had been a long time since I had seen her, and when she came to me with open arms, she first threw herself upon my breast, and then she spoke to me of you."

"Of me!" Didier repeated.

"Yes. She did not name you, but I knew from her description that it could be no one else. I was foolish then, and must confess that when she avowed her love, I felt my heart sink within my breast."

Didier took the hand of Alix gently as she wiped away an unwilling tear that would obtrude itself into her eyes, and said:

"Alix, dearest, I fear I have been guilty towards you both."

"Towards her only, Monsieur, if you say another word," she answered with an effort. "Do not forget that you love her—and that she loves you."

"But what about you, Alix?"

There was no vanity in that question that had come straight from his heart

"Fear not for me—presently I will inform you of the brilliant destiny provided for me; but first, one more word about her. Have you resolved to marry her?"

Didier had never put this question seriously to himself, and now, coming so suddenly upon him, he remained silent, not knowing what to answer.

"You must marry her," Alix said in a firm tone, frowning. "It is your duty—you must and will. She is poor, but you have your sword, and happily for both of you the prejudices of birth and rank do not enslave either of you."

In saying these last words, Alix had managed to strip all of her melancholy expression. She had spoken, in a firm and convinced tone.

"I am not a nobleman, I am well aware of this, Alix," he exclaimed somewhat harshly. "And perhaps there was no reason for you to recall the distance that exists between us. You despise my attachment, Alix, it is clear, and I will endeavor not to think of you in that way any longer: but do not plead for Marie, for when you do, and I behold you so noble, so generous, so disinterested..."

"But I have forgotten you, Didier," Alix added, with a forced smile, whilst a dagger went through her heart.

The young officer bit his lips, and every moment his position became more embarrassing: he saw that love, powerful love, was still shining through Alix's coldness, and felt that her feelings towards him were entrenching themselves behind the barriers of her rank. Too proud and too strong-minded to become a forsaken woman, she took the initiative, and in dismissing her faithless lover, affected to tear him from her breast.

On the other hand, his recollected memories of Blossom-of-the-Broom pleaded eloquently. He saw her sweet smile behind Alix's haughty manner. Maybe he might have remained cold before Alix weeping, but she was asking mercy for her rival. The human soul is weak against such surprises.

"No, Alix," Didier said after a short pause. "You cannot have forgotten our love—it is impossible!"

"Must you have further proof of it?" she added, repressing the tears that almost blinded her. "Didier, if I loved you still, I would not be here with you now. I shall speak plainly to you, Monsieur, and tell you that I have the ancient prejudices of my caste. I am a Vaunoy de La Tremlays, and when I marry—if ever—the name my husband has to offer must at least, be equal to my own."

"Can this be true, Mademoiselle?"

"Indeed it is, Monsieur, but let us quit that subject."

"Oh, yes, let's quit it, Mademoiselle. I wish to God that we had never broached it. I would have kept my entire admiration for you, for I thought you superior to other women."

Alix could not hold back a sigh, but in a second she resumed in a cheerful tone:

"Let us rather speak as two old friends who have met after a long separation. Did you know that my father wishes me to marry?"

"Ah?" replied Didier, suspiciously.

Then he added with a note of sarcasm:

"That is undoubtedly the reason for your behavior."

"No," she said, "for the man for whom my hand is destined could not offend you, if you were for me anything other than a friend. I will never be his wife."

"Isn't his name equal to yours, at least?" asked Didier, still sarcastic.

"It is Monsieur Béchamel, Marquis de Nointel, the Royal Intendant."

Didier burst out laughing.

As if there had been an echo under the bower, another fat, loud laugh sounded at about twenty paces.

"It is them!" exclaimed Alix. "My God, I did not have time to tell you everything I had to say. Farewell, Didier, we shall meet again."

She fled hurriedly down a bye-path leading back to the house, leaving the captain dizzy with her sudden disappearance.

"Does she still love me?" he said to himself.

As for Mademoiselle de Vaunoy, as soon as she was alone, tears fell from her eyes.

"My God, my God," she murmured. "Shall I love him always?"

The burst of laughter sounded again under the bower. A cacophony of voices joined it and soon appeared from behind a corner Messieurs de Vaunoy and Béchamel.

CHAPTER XX
Before and After Breakfast

Monsieur de Vaunoy and the royal Intendant seemed happy. They stepped eagerly forward toward Didier, who was having a hard time keeping himself from looking embarrassed.

"We came here, my dear guest," said De Vaunoy, "guided by your laughter. I gather that this solitary promenade amused you?"

"Did I laugh?"asked Didier, mechanically.

"Why, yes, by God, you laughed," replied Monsieur de Vaunoy.

"You did indeed laugh," said Béchamel, adding: "I have the honor of saying good morning to you, Monsieur."

"I do not remember laughing," said Didier.

"Eh," said De Vaunoy, noticing the letter that the young man still clutched in his hand. "Perhaps this is what caused your morning hilarity?"

"That must be it," said Béchamel. "Please tell us how you fare?"

Didier crumpled the letter and tore it into tiny pieces. That done, he replied to the Intendant's salute, adding a few banal courtesies.

Monsieur Béchamel's mood had greatly improved since the previous day because Monsieur de Vaunoy had convinced him that he had nothing to fear from the rivalry of Captain Didier, and that Alix's hand was guaranteed to him. So that morning, he felt an unusual benevolence towards the young man. As for De Vaunoy, he had not yet decided to remove his mask of bonhomie. He looked like a kind uncle approaching his favorite nephew.

"Messieurs," said the captain, whose coldness contrasted strongly with the cordiality of the two gentlemen, "would it please you that we now speak about His Majesty's business?"

"Certainly," replied Monsieur de Vaunoy.

And Béchamel repeated:

"Definitely."

After reflection, however, he added:

"But perhaps it would be more suitable to have breakfast first?"

"Fie, Monsieur Béchamel! Fie!" said De Vaunoy smiling.

"In that case, my friend, forget that I spoke! Obviously, I prefer the service of the King to breakfast—or even lunch! Still, a cold breakfast is a mighty sad thing... We are all ears, Captain!"

Didier drew from his pocket a scroll, sealed with the Royal Arms—which Béchamel saluted humbly by taking off his hat—and then read:

"At the instigation of His Highness Monseigneur de Toulouse, Governor of Brittany, His Majesty has been graciously pleased to select me for the office of safely escorting the royal collector through this province, which at the moment is reported to be in a state of disaffection, if not of actual rebellion."

"This is sadly the case," said De Vaunoy.

"Most woefully so," added the collector.

"The King has charged me, moreover, to superintend the collection of his revenue with an armed force, and, if necessary, to chase and destroy by all possible means the handful of rebels who call themselves the Wolves."

"God be your shield!" said Hervé de Vaunoy. "It is an honorable mission!"

And one that I don't envy you at all, my young master, thought the Marquis, adding out loud:

"May Heaven help you, gallant Captain!"

"I thank you both, Messieurs. Heaven shall protect France, and I trust its aid will not be wanting in my present task. Your own assistance too, I presume?"

De Vaunoy replied to this sudden and frank appeal with another bow and an obsequious smile; but the Marquis remained silent. The epicurean Monsieur Béchamel was lacking in diplomatic skills.

"I can confidently rely upon your aid?" Didier, again asked.

"On more than one account, my young friend," Hervé de Vaunoy quickly responded. "From my loyalty to the King, and my attachment to yourself."

"I stand entirely united with my friend in this matter," said the Marquis.

"Thank you, Messieurs. I expected no less from two such loyal and devoted subjects of the Crown. I must warn you that I shall not spare your best offices in the approaching strife, and I pray you now to give your earnest attention to me."

Monsieur Béchamel took out his watch and noted painfully that the hour fixed for breakfast had passed. He let out a heavy sigh, not daring to complain more openly.

"Messieurs," Didier continued, "I have not journeyed this far without laying down a plan for my campaign. I have already initiated certain actions. I instructed the Maréchaussée of Rennes to hold themselves at the ready to obey my orders night and day; those of Laval

167

are on the march at this very moment, and the armed police of Vitré, of Fougères, and of Louvigné-du-Désert stand in reserve should I need them."

"By mine honor," said the Intendant. "All these forces will form a pretty little army."

"About three hundred men, Monsieur."

"They will not be enough," Monsieur de Vaunoy observed. "The Wolves are said to have four times that number."

"Oh! I had heard they were more numerous," said Didier coldly. "So we shall be one against four—we are too many!"

"I do not understand," said Béchamel.

"I said we are too many, because all the advantages are on our side. You cannot think that it is my intention to attack them in their stronghold at the Wolf's Pit?"

Hervé started, as if a snake had stung him.

"Do not be surprised, my worthy host. I know the name of their lair; for, thanks to circumstances, which are not necessary to mention now, I am as intimately acquainted with the forest as if I had been born in its immediate locality."

Upon hearing these words, Monsieur de Vaunoy turned so deathly pale, and trembled so violently, that his friend the Marquis noticed his sudden indisposition, and moved forward to give him support.

"What ails you, my friend?" asked the Intendant.

"Nothing," stammered Monsieur de Vaunoy. "It is nothing."

"On the contrary! I am sure you need to eat something, for it is a fact that we have missed our usual breakfast hour by more than thirty-five minutes."

Monsieur de Vaunoy, with a sudden effort, recovered his composure and rejected Monsieur Béchamel's help.

"Captain," he said, "I beg you to excuse me… A sudden bout of light-headedness… I am subject to this infirmity… Please continue!"

"In your own interest, my friend," insisted heroically Monsieur Béchamel, "I encourage you to eat something. The Captain and I will join you…"

But Monsieur de Vaunoy made an impatient gesture and the Intendant recognized with deep sorrow that breakfast would now be delayed indefinitely.

"As I told you," continued Didier, who had only paid mediocre attention to this incident, "every inch of the forest of Rennes is well known to me, and I am aware that the position of these rebels at the Wolf's Pit is considered impregnable. Therefore, I shall not attack them in their natural fortress—at least, until the convoy of the king's taxes has left the region safely. But it is absolutely necessary that I should have support and headquarters locally, and therefore, Monsieur de Vaunoy, I respectfully ask you for the use of your castle, and you, Monsieur le Marquis, for your mansion at La Cour-Rose!"

"My mansion!" Monsieur Béchamel said with great surprise. "What, may I ask, do you intend to do there?"

"I scarcely know as yet; most probably convert it into a temporary arsenal for guns and powder."

"Guns and powder! But there are carpets in every room, Monsieur, splendid carpets from Tournay, that cost me twenty-thousand écus!"

"Fie! Monsieur Béchamel, fie!" Monsieur de Vaunoy exclaimed.

But this time, the epicurean Intendant had been touched on a tender point, and would not be silenced.

"There is carved, veneered, inlaid, and gilded furniture; exquisite lacquer-work from Japan, sculptured marbles from Italy, porphyry statuettes from Sweden, English mirrors, and Bohemian glass! Thirty thousands écus, Monsieur!"

"Fie! Monsieur Béchamel, fie!" Monsieur de Vaunoy repeated.

"My stoves, ovens, and kitchen vessels cost me no less than fourteen thousand five hundred livres, Monsieur, and you would subject all these precious things to pillage. Why, your brutal soldiers would destroy my furniture, empty my cellars—the best supplied in all of France and Navarre—ruin my carpets, break my porcelain and my glass, and I know not what besides. Mon Dieu, Monsieur, do you think I had this mansion built for no other purpose than to harbor your rude, uncouth men!"

"Fie Monsieur Béchamel, fie!" De Vaunoy repeated the third time. "For the love of God!"

The selfish financier paused for want of breath; and Didier, as if he had not heard the furious tirade, calmly replied:

"In all probability, an arsenal; but at any rate, I shall give you two hours' notice."

"That will be fine," said Monsieur de Vaunoy, who seemed determined to approve of everything the officer proposed.

"My friend, I do not understand you," said Monsieur Béchamel, exasperated. "Why…"

As Marquis was about to break forth again, Monsieur de Vaunoy pressed his hand significantly—a universal message to shut up—and gave him a look of intel-

ligence which reduced the exasperated nobleman to silence.

"Am I right in thinking, my honored guest," Hervé
de Vaunoy continued in his blandest tone, "that the
measures you speak of will form the last portion of your
scheme, and that you will endeavor first to escort the
treasure safely from Rennes before you think of fortify-
ing yourself in our respective mansions? For it is ru-
mored that the King's coffers are empty—or nearly so."

"Such is my plan indeed, Monsieur."

"In that case, then, Captain, allow me to offer you
the castle of La Tremlays as a resting place for the escort."

"And I, my mansion, too!" added the Marquis de
Nointel. "For a resting place, well and good, but for an
arsenal…"

"Since the King's treasure," Didier interrupted,
"remains under the care and responsibility of the Royal
Intendant while it remains on this side of the border of
Brittany, it is you, Monsieur, who will choose the places
where the escort shall spend the night."

An expression of great uneasiness became instantly
visible upon the face of Monsieur de Vaunoy—an uneasiness that must have been intense indeed to betray itself
on the features of a man in general so completely in con-
trol of his emotions, and practiced in their concealment.

Didier and the Intendant both noticed the fact. The
former did not pay much attention to it, He thought he
already knew Monsieur de Vaunoy, whom he despised
but without suspecting him guilty of treason. In his
haughty indifference, he did not deign to concern himself with such a slight incident.

The Marquis, on the other hand, interpreted it in his
own way, thinking it must have been avarice, fear of the

expense that would be incurred by lodging and feeding so many troops.

"My friend," he hastened to tell Monsieur de Vaunoy, "as the chief officer in charge of the convoy, I shall naturally defray all charges...:

But his proposition was only received by De Vaunoy with increased paleness and a scowling brow.

"I said, I shall pay for everything," repeated Monsieur Béchamel. "For me, hospitality is a sacred duty and..."

"You are proposing to accommodate the king's troops in your mansion at La Cour Rose?" asked Hervé de Vaunoy, whose anxiety appeared to be increasing.

"No, not at all," replied Monsieur Béchamel at once. "That is not what..."

Suddenly, the red color came back to Hervé de Vaunoy's cheeks, his eyes brightened, and he breathed more easily.

This change was so powerful and marked that Didier could not help but notice it. But it only lasted for a moment, and as composure returned to Monsieur de Vaunoy's face, the young Captain's doubts dissipated. But for an attentive and disinterested spectator, it would have been obvious that a bold design had just arisen in the brain of the nobleman, a design greatly favored by Monsieur Béchamel's choice of La Tremlays for the escort's resting place.

The Marquis de Nointel could not understand how or why his decision could possibly please Hervé de Vaunoy, so he took it upon himself to excuse himself further:

"I repeat to you, my friend," he said, "that you will have nothing—absolutely nothing—to disburse..."

"It doesn't matter," interrupted Monsieur de Vaunoy.

"Please! I am—as I am sure you make me the honor of believing—a loyal and devoted subject of his Majesty. My modest mansion is, of course, entirely at the King's service, from the foundations to the attic, including of course all the floors in between, but we are talking about five hundred thousand livres tournois that have been collected…

"Five hundred thousand livres tournois," slowly repeated the master of La Tremlays.

"Yes, that much, my friend… With even a few more écus… If this sum was taken away, my own solvency, which is adequate, would be dreadfully impacted. My mansion is not suited to sustain a siege, and if the Wolves…"

Monsieur de Vaunoy shrugged with affectation.

"Monsieur the Intendant is correct," said the Captain, who, for the last few minutes, had only paid very limited attention to the discussion.

"Please, allow me," said Monsieur Béchamel responding to Monsieur de Vaunoy's gesture. "I would be mortified if you believed that…"

"Say no more, my friend, my castle can be rendered proof against any force that may be gathered together by these rebels; and now let us in to breakfast!"

The word had a magical effect upon the Marquis; he turned joyously upon his heel, his nostrils dilated, and he snuffed up the savory odors that emanated from the kitchen, as a hound sniffs the air tainted by the game.

Monsieur de Vaunoy leaned on Didier's arm with familiarity. While the trio traversed the small space that intervened between the garden and the breakfast, it was decided that the rich convoy should leave Rennes the following day, and the escort, under the command of the Captain, should guard it during the night in the castle of La Tremlays. From the city to the castle, the distance was short, but in 1740, the roads of Brittany were traced so as to quadruple it.

Notwithstanding the prominence of his fair, round, belly, the gourmand Marquis mounted the broad flight of steps that led from the garden with the agility of youth. Two minutes sufficed to tie his table napkin round his neck, and the next he was deeply engaged in the delights of a *salmis* of woodcocks' wings and legs, which he declared to be without parallel.

The Captain's feelings were too much hurt by his recent interview with Alix, to allow him to indulge his usual youthful appetite.

Hervé de Vaunoy scarcely touched a morsel. The repast was hardly at an end before the Marquis laid down upon a couch to digest the enormous quantity he had consumed. Monsieur de Vaunoy, making a polite excuse to Didier for leaving him alone, left the room, and meeting a lackey in the corridor, ordered him to bring Lapierre and Alain the steward immediately to his own apartment.

The man bowed and hastened to obey. Monsieur de Vaunoy continued leisurely walking towards his room, but casting his eyes by chance through one of the windows that looked into the garden, he perceived his daughter, with bended head and eyes upon the ground, walking pensively along.

"Still deep in melancholy!" he muttered, with unaccustomed sensitivity. "Poor girl! However, she is not being sensible... Béchamel will make her the most kind and obedient of husbands, and she will only have to mould him to her will."

Whilst he gazed through the window at his daughter, he saw Didier walking down another path, and the fire of all hell suddenly gleamed in his malignant eyes.

"She was about to forget all about him," he whispered. "I was sure of it! Another month, and that childish love of hers would have been only one of those melancholic remembrances that amuse women, but do not stand in the way of a good and strong marriage. Now he is back, and his presence here inevitably disturbs all my plans... And what if, by some infernal chance, he came to discover the truth..."

Monsieur de Vaunoy stopped. The two alleys that Alix and Didier followed were going to intersect. Each step brought them closer to each other and they would meet in a few seconds.

"And even if he doesn't find out, his star seems to cross my path at every step! It matters not—the deed must be done, even in self-defense, for if I do not destroy him, assuredly he will cause my ruin!"

Whilst he gazed through the window at his daughter, he saw Didier advancing towards her. He lifted up his dog whistle to his lips, and blew shrilly through it. Alix raised her face towards the quarter whence the sounds originated, and Hervé beckoned to her to come back. Curtseying to Didier, she retraced her steps toward the castle.

"It is sure, they had planned this meeting," the villain muttered. "Twice already he has escaped me, but the third time will be the charm. This time, I will make sure, aye, sure!"

He entered his apartment, where his two servants, Alain and Lapierre, soon joined him.

Almost at the same moment Alix opened the door.

"You called me, father?" she inquired.

Monsieur de Vaunoy, who was about to give orders to his two acolytes, hesitated a little and almost dismissed his daughter, but he suddenly changed his mind.

"Stay here," he said to the valets. "I'll need you in a moment."

Then he took Alix's arm and gently led her back into the corridor.

In the meantime, Master Alain and Lapierre stayed alone in his private room. The former, whose intelligence had considerably weakened under the weight of age and drunkenness, pulled his tin flask from a pocket and drank a large swig of brandy.

"Wilt thou take a sup, friend?" he asked, presenting his constant companion to the valet, his worthy mate.

"No, Alain. There is a time for all things; I never drink when I am to have an interview with our lord."

"But I do—double."

"And see so too. Why, yesterday you could not recollect where you had known the Captain's servant!"

"I'm getting old," replied Alain taking yet another sip. "The fact is that my poor memory isn't what it used to be. But if I see him again I'll recognize him—maybe."

"And what if he doesn't show up again?"

Instead of replying, Alain took another draught and soon dropped fast asleep. Meanwhile, Lapierre softly made the tour of the chamber, and appropriated to himself all the stray coins he found lying carelessly about. Fortunately for Monsieur de Vaunoy, his drawers were locked.

This piece of characteristic ingenuity being successfully accomplished, the ex-mountebank leaned upon the sill of the window that looked into the garden, where Didier was still strolling, and then soliloquized in the following manner:

"Ah! There he goes! I thought I'd hate him more... He's a handsome lad... And De Vaunoy is a bad pay-master, who asks so much for his money... If I–well, we shall see..."

"Another sip?" muttered Alain, who was toasting in his dreams.

Lapierre looked at the old steward with contempt.

"And that's what working for that close-fisted sneak leads to... A man who never leaves any of his drawers or cabinets open... Only a few paltry bits of gold for so much labor... Upon my honor it's a burning shame for a gentleman to damn himself for such a paltry pittance!"

CHAPTER XXI
Mademoiselle de Vaunoy

While Alain and Lapierre waited, Hervé de Vaunoy walked slowly up and down the corridor arm-in-arm with Alix, affectionately patting the fair, cold, hand she had abandoned to him.

After taking two or three turns, he said to her in his blandest tone:

"My dearest Alix, I really must scold you for being deficient in courtesy to Captain Didier."

He looked covertly at her as he pronounced the name, but no emotion showed itself in her calm, pale face.

"You must not overshoot the mark, my child," he went on. "The Captain is a brave officer of the King who is entitled to all our respect, and when one does not love such a man, it is good to force oneself a little."

"And what if I love him?" she replied.

Monsieur de Vaunoy flinched and could not restrain a grimace of discomfort, but he recovered immediately.

"Folly! my darling, folly! A year ago I recollect we spoke together about that childish romance and you promised me...."

"I promised to try to forget him, father; but Heaven knows that I could not."

"Alix, you then promised me still more."

"True," she said in a tone of the greatest de-spondency. "I also promised you to renounce all hope of ever being his."

Then, after a short pause, she added in as very sad voice:

"Father, I have kept that promise: I no longer have any hope."

Monsieur de Vaunoy kissed his daughter's hand, coughed slightly, and made some common place observation; but the tone in which Alix had uttered the last words had thrown a chill upon his assumed gaiety, for he loved his child and that was the only honorable feeling that crime, excited by ambition and cupidity, had left within his heart.

As she had grown towards womanhood, he had desired to make her happiness, but now events pressed him and he no longer had any choice. A word from Monsieur Béchamel, Marquis de Nointel, could endanger his fortune, his title, and even his life. He had to use the Marquis' passion for the lovely girl to secure his support.

Moreover, Monsieur de Vaunoy's paternal tenderness was influenced by his own inclinations and habits. He was quite sincere when he treated love with a certain amount of indifference. He had once been young, but never in his heart. Happiness, for him, was only land and gold; therefore, for a young woman, according to him, it should be gold too, and the luxury that comes from attending lavish parties, humiliating rivals, and consorting with a crowd of likeminded young women. To say the truth, the astute nobleman was not far wrong in his estimate of the then state of women in France's high society.

In marrying Alix to Monsieur Béchamel, she would have all that in abundance, and more. The memory of Didier would be just another trinket, because it is good that a woman keeps in the depths of her mind a string that tenderly vibrates during her hours of migraine or vapors. Still according to that old thief, Monsieur de Vaunoy, a woman, even with the clothes of a queen and the diamonds of a sultan, did not have all that she needed if she lacked this melancholy token of an unfortunate and distant love that would bring tears to her eyes at times when the brain needed her to cry

At this moment, Monsieur de Vaunoy felt embarrassed. Alix dominated him from the height of her frankness, For the thousandth time perhaps, he repented of having used cunning with her, recognizing but too late that all his ruses were powerless against her candor. Too dishonest to feel in his fatherly heart the anguish that he should have felt, surprised to have been caught by his own child in an act of deception, he felt humiliated and made an effort to cast that mask away.

"Alix!" he continued, "my own sweet child, I was wrong to doubt your obedience for even a moment, but you know the dearest wish of my heart: say it, will you—will you disappoint my hopes?"

"Father," she replied, "I will do all that I have promised, nothing more and nothing less."

"That will be enough, my child. Time is the great remedy for all capricious girls' fantasies. But I think at present you had better not meet Captain Didier alone."

"Father, I have already done so."

"Ah! And spoken to him?"

"Yes."

"So your affected submission was nothing but a lie, a performance?"

Alix did not throw herself with a start and a jerk into that conventional attitude by which our actresses invariably deem it fit to illustrate outraged virtue; she did not lift up her eyes to heaven as they do theirs to the cen-

180

ter chandelier—taking the luster above the pit as the great witness of their innocence, but she gently said:

"My actions, Monsieur, deceive you no more than my words. I have kept my promise, and if it cause my death, which is most probable, I will still keep it sacredly. Besides, father…" here, her voice failed her, she blushed and continued in trembling accents, "…my promise is not the only guarantee, for Captain Didier no longer loves me."

"Really?" exclaimed Monsieur de Vaunoy with a brutal joy that was careless of the pain it might inflict upon his child. "That is excellent news! My good child, why did not you tell me at once? Ha! This Captain, this impertinent soldier of fortune…!"

He uttered these last words in a tone of ironical pity that would have deeply hurt a vulgar heart, but Alix was above this gross manifestation. Her forehead remained serene and it was with a melancholy but quiet smile that she spoke again:

"I share your opinion, father," she said. "I believe everything is for the best."

Monsieur de Vaunoy knew his daughter, and even though he did not understand her much, he had for her a kind of respect. Nevertheless, her resignation seemed so extraordinary to him that he could hardly believe it, and, following his old habit, he resumed his act of moral pomposity.

"By God!" he said after a silence, "you are the paragon of daughters, Alix, and I'd wager that one might search all the way from Rennes to Nantes to find your like. Not a regret, not a complaint! It is hard to believe and it gives me hope for the chances of our good Monsieur Béchamel who is dying of love for you!"

Alix remained silent.

"But let's no longer talk about this," continued the master of La Tremlays. "I've won this battle and it is not good to ask too many favors of Heaven at one time. And I, who almost lost my sleep over it! Now I no longer fear him! I know you are too proud to approach him. Has anyone ever seen such presumption! And I am ready to swear that this encounter, of which we were speaking earlier, will be the last one, and you will no longer have anything to do with him. Is that not so?"

That last sentence was the most important part of Hervé de Vaunoy's little speech. All the rest was only in preparation of it. So he waited with anxiety for an answer, trying to guess what Alix would say.

But he was again forgetting that his concern was superfluous. Alix's words defied his interpretations and needed no explanations.

She left the support of the window against which arm had been pressed and, with her extended hand, pointed toward Didier who was crossing the last section of the park, almost disappearing under the cover of the trees.

"I must await his return," she said.

"His return?" Hervé de Vaunoy exclaimed in great amazement.

"Yes, his return! I promised Captain Didier to see him once again. Ask me not to refrain from doing so, it is a sacred duty. Father, I implore you to throw no obstacles in my way."

"But…" started Monsieur de Vaunoy, surprised and intrigued.

"Do not refuse me, father," Alix said in a burst of feeling. "I have never disobeyed you, and, Heaven is my witness, it would grieve me much to do so!"

"And yet, it seems to me, Mademoiselle, that if I should forbid your keeping this unseemly rendezvous with that insolent soldier, you would be prepared to disobey me?"

Alix bowed her head in silence.

"Holy Mother!" Monsieur de Vaunoy exclaimed, stamping furiously, looking nothing like an offended father. "This is beyond all belief. But at least, I stand forewarned. May I ask what is the nature of the all-important business that demands a *tête-à-tête* between this base-born Didier, and the noble Alix de Vaunoy?"

"Father, I may not tell you."

"Better and better! God grant me patience! Know you not that should it be my will, you will be confined to your chamber?"

"Father!" Alix replied to this implied threat, drawing herself up to her full height, "I hope you will not have the cruelty to do so."

"And what if I did?" shouted the nobleman, truly angry.

Alix spoke with a firmness and dignity that left no doubt of the sincerity of her intention:

"Hear me, once and for all. I respect you and I love you; and that love is what has impelled me for so long to deceive Monsieur Béchamel. But if I spoke…"

She stopped, ashamed of threatening her own father. But Monsieur de Vaunoy had understood the ramifications of what she had just said. His anger subsided instantly. He called on his face to make one of these sudden changes of expression, this time adopting a look of cheerfulness.

"You are a naughty child, Alix," he said, kissing her loudly on the forehead. "You know that I cannot refuse you anything, and you abuse that power that is quickly becoming tyrannical. You mad child, what I said was only motivated by curiosity. I wanted to learn this great secret of yours, but you have won, and I shall no longer engage with you in a battle of words. Next time, I will set my worthy sister against you, and then, you had better watch out!"

Alix did not mistake this sudden gaiety. Monsieur de Vaunoy was correct in feeling that, despite his long experience at intrigue, he was not strong enough to match his daughter's haughty uprightness. The Lord of La Tremlays was wasting his diplomacy skills in vain.

"I'm happy to hear you say this," replied Alix.

"Excellent! Then be kind and show some compassion for poor Monsieur Béchamel... But that will come, and we will have time to discuss it later."

Then, taking out his watch, Monsieur de Vaunoy observed:

"Eleven o'clock, already. I'll leave you alone, and give you carte blanche. I know my confidence is well placed. Goodbye."

He made a familiar and caressing gesture, to which Alix responded with respectful reverence, and hastened back to his apartment where his two servants were waiting for him, one philosophizing, as typical of a mountebank, the other snoring in the manner of the righteous drunk.

When Alix was alone, her face lost its calm, dignified expression, and melancholy at once regained possession of her features, as she murmured:

"Must I then see him again? Listen to those commonplace phrases of regard, with which he tries to console me; read pity in his eyes, and not raise my own to his, except in pleading for my rival!"

Without being in the least aware of what she was doing, Alix had descended an interior staircase and the great steps that led into the garden; when there, she dropped upon a mossy bank, completely concealed from the house, and buried her head within her hands.

She remained like this for a long while. When she looked up, her dry eyes seemed to make an effort to cry After a few minutes, she drew from her bosom a small coarsely-graven copper medal suspended by a ribbon round her neck, gazed at it with swimming eyes, kissed it passionately, and sobbed audibly as she gasped out:

"My God! How much I love him!"

Then, a ray of enthusiasm flickered under her tears and, pressing with force the copper medal against her heart, she added:

"It will break my heart to see him again, but it must be done—to save him!"

CHAPTER XXII
Two Faithful Servants

Conversations such as the one in the foregoing chapter were unusual occurrences between Monsieur de Vaunoy and his daughter. Alix was thoroughly acquainted with the reasons her father had for pressing her union with Monsieur Béchamel, as she was aware of the precarious tenure by which Monsieur de Vaunoy held both his nobility and the broad acres of the Treml estates; but she never abused this knowledge, although, in no way wishing to become her father's judge, the cunning meanness of his character had been a constant source of distress to her since she had attained the power of discriminating between right and wrong.

Her serious and loyal spirit was accustomed to sadness, and her brief love with Didier had been the only moments of pure joy she had tasted in her life.

To be sure, she only perceived in the usurpation of the domains by Monsieur de Vaunoy, danger but not crime, because she could not be aware of the fate of the rightful owner, and Nicolas had not left any known heir in direct succession. It is even possible that if she had never met Captain Didier, she might have sacrificed herself to secure her father's happiness and safety—for her enthusiasm was devoid of limit; but the few weeks in which she had exchanged vows of eternal love with the young soldier, had been the only joyous ones she had ever known, and the contrast between him and Monsieur Béchamel was too great to permit such a sacrifice ever to be made.

The ridiculous personal appearance, pompous manners, insufferable pride, and filthy gastronomic propensities of the Intendant inspired her with such invincible aversion, that it required all her devotion to her father, and all his untiring assiduity to prevent her from openly dismissing the Marquis de Nointel's odious suit.

Certainly Monsieur de Vaunoy did not tire of importuning her with every inducement with which the daughters of Eve are ordinarily tempted; but he made no progress with his scheme, merely buying time.

That day, he would not have found leisure to pester Alix in his usual manner, but Didier's arrival had placed him in instant and imminent danger; the presence of the Captain threatened to destroy all his projects, and therefore he interposed the barriers of his will between his daughter and her former lover: however, as frequently is the case, chance had served him far better than his own well-laid schemes.

Without losing an instant after leaving Alix, Monsieur de Vaunoy rejoined his two servants in his own room, and forthwith devoted his energies to carrying that daring design which had entered his mind when standing in the bower before breakfast with the Marquis and Didier. During the meal he had calculated all his chances of succeeding with impunity, and was determined to stand the perilous hazard of the die.

He spoke for a half-hour without interruption to his acolytes. Master Alain had shaken his somnolence and Lapierre was sitting attentively in an excellent armchair.

When at last Monsieur de Vaunoy held his tongue, and looked earnestly at them for a reply, Alain answered with a meaningless gesture, while Lapierre, turning half round, balanced the armchair upon one of its legs.

"Did not you hear me?" Monsieur de Vaunoy inquired, regarding them steadfastly.

"I most certainly did," said Lapierre.

"As did I," added Alain.

"And what do you say to my proposal?"

The old steward would have liked to have recourse to his usual flask for inspiration, but dared not in his master's presence; so, with great prudence, he left the reply for both to Lapierre, who continued balancing himself upon the chair.

"What say you, then?" Monsieur de Vaunoy again asked, with a furrowed brow.

"Hum" said Lapierre, trying to sound as if he was thinking deeply.

"Hum indeed," added Alain, emphatically.

"What?" Monsieur de Vaunoy cried in a rage. "Don't you understand that his death will be considered a natural, uncontrollable occurrence? That all suspicions will be effectively turned away from me, and that nothing but bad faith or madness could possibly accuse me of being the cause of such an accident?"

"Oh, yes, Monsieur," replied Lapierre, "That, I understand perfectly."

Master Alain signified his endorsement by nodding vigorously.

"Well, then?" Hervé de Vaunoy asked again.

"Hum" repeated Lapierre.

Monsieur de Vaunoy's face grew redder and he muttered a fearful oath between his teeth.

"Yes," said the ex-mountebank without being moved in the slightest way. "Of course, he would not be able to escape. If we were there, I would not give six sous for his life, but…"

"But what?"

"Well, we are not there!"

"Don't you think that the temptation of five hundred livres is strong enough?"

"They'd do it for a tenth of that sum."

"For a twentieth," added Master Alain sotto voce. "For that, I'd sell my soul to the Devil, and I'm an old man and a loyal subject of the King."

"Where, then, rests the difficulty?" Monsieur de Vaunoy asked Lapierre.

Master Alain listened so that he could later steal his colleague's opinion. Lapierre let the chair settle on all its legs, then turned his face towards his master with a look of consummate impudence, and said coolly:

"You have, no doubt, my lord, heard about the fables of Monsieur de La Fontaine, I suppose? No, no, if you get angry, I shall become dumb... This La Fontaine is a poet of very good advice, which is rare, and I remember one of his fables..."

"Holy God!" interrupted Monsieur de Vaunoy. "I would give ten louis to beat you soundly with my cane!"

"By all means, if you have the money," replied Lapierre unperturbed. "As for the fable of which I speak, you cannot judge it before having heard it. Not knowing it by heart, I will not recite it to you..."

"By all the saints in Heaven! Get to the point, you insufferable rascal!

"I beg you to excuse my failing memory," continued Lapierre, "for the lack of the actual text, but the tale itself will suffice. Here, then, is what it is all about: The rats take advice and seek a way to kill a very formidable cat..."

"Now I understand!" cried Monsieur de Vaunoy, violently.

He rose and ran up and down the room.

"I don't," said Master Alain.

I understand you," repeated Monsieur de Vaunoy. "You are afraid of the young man, you coward."

"You are incorrect," replied Lapierre. "It would be better for your project if I were afraid. But I am not, and I am determined to do like the rats of the fable."

"You'd defy my orders, you miserable scum?"

"Attempting to attach the bell would be a piece of tomfoolery quite apart from my principles and practice. Let another undertake that portion of the job, and he shall enjoy the benefit of my advice and assistance."

"What is he talking about?" asked Master Alain. "And why are talking about rats?"

Monsieur de Vaunoy strode up and down the room again hand on the hilt of his sword. Once or twice, he was in a tempest of ungovernable anger. His face, ordinarily so pleasant, was absolutely purple with rage, and his lips moved convulsively.

"Awake, awake, the storm will be a rough one," Lapierre whispered to Alain.

"By the grace of God, what is this all about?" whispered the old steward.

Lapierre leaned over and slowly communicated some more intelligence, which made the old man tremble and mutter:

"By our Lady of the Forest! I would rather go to Hell at once!"

"You have no choice, my ancient comrade—for, believe me, there is already a place reserved for you there by the Devil himself; but if you wish to defer making that journey as long as possible, follow my example, do as I do, and be firm."

"Holy Virgin, Saint Joseph save me!" whispered the old man, shaking.

"Take a sup, for the enemy has halted, and the grand attack will soon begin."

The steward was not the kind of man to neglect such counsel; he glanced towards his master, saw that he was standing with his back to them, applied the bottle to his lips, and kept it there until compelled to remove it for sheer want of breath.

"He is going to be enraged," Lapierre continued, "because for him, it is only a move in his game, but for us, we can be hanged and, worse, we will be roasted alive down there."

"At the very least," sighed Master Alain with conviction. "I would like to get out of here, even if I must swear to not drink again for a whole day."

Monsieur de Vaunoy suddenly stopped and walked quietly towards the two men, with a sparkling eye, determined brow, and resolute expression on his lips; the usual caution stamped upon his physiognomy was gone, and he was an altered man.

Alain closed his eyes and drew back in fear at this inexplicable change, but Lapierre threw himself back in the armchair, coolly crossed his legs, and remained in an easy attitude of attention. The terror of the one, and the calmness of the other, were equally lost in the present instance on the nobleman, who, contrary his usual custom of first bursting into a fit of anger if someone refused to obey his orders, and then falling back upon wheedling, flattery, and bribery, went straight back to his own armchair. He then looked at them one after the other in a manner that compelled attention even from Lapierre.

"Within an hour," he said, dwelling upon each word with almost syllabic articulation, "one of us three must be in the saddle."

"With all my heart," Lapierre said, "provided it is not I."

"Silence! I repeat that within an hour, one of us three must mount. It is necessary. I could use force to compel you, since I am the master here; but force might fail against your apathy, Alain, or against your stubbornness, Lapierre. And time is too precious for me to waste it in punishing you I prefer to buy your obedience. Which of you two will earn a thousand livres tournois?"

Avarice sparkled in the old steward's eyes, and he repeated mechanically:

"A thousand livres tournois!"

Monsieur de Vaunoy kept silent, leaving the proposition to sink into the hearts of the two men. He thought for a moment that the old man might be dazzled by its magnificence; however such was not the case with Lapierre, who appeared to reflect for a minute, and then coolly said:

"A thousand livres is a large and comfortable sum; but dead men never come back to collect their wages, and, unfortunately for me, I have not any heirs."

Alain scratched his ear, and kept muttering:

"Holy Virgin... A thousand livres!"

"Two thousand livres!" Monsieur de Vaunoy reiterated. "I will pay two thousand livres upon the instant to him who will obey my wishes."

But the bribe had lost its attractions: Lapierre waved his dissent with his hand; Alain shook his head negatively, taking his cue from his comrade; and, as their master turned from them in a fury, he again paced up and down the room, big drops of sweat rolled down his cheeks, and fell upon his chest.

"Holy Mother!" he ejaculated, stopping again, and wringing his hands in the extremity of his distress. "I tell you it must be done. Whichever way I turn, he is my rock ahead; he is a very serpent in my path! and, while he lives, danger remains before me!

"All as true as the Sword of Damocles," said Lapierre, who knew his classics. "This is the God-given truth."

"His presence here" continued Monsieur de Vaunoy, growing more emotional by the minute, "threatens my schemes for my daughter, my name, my fortune, and my life."

"Absolutely true," said Lapierre.

"And yet you would deny your aid, when, with it, and one good blow, he could be crushed at once. Say, what the sum should be—should I double it? Triple it? Quadruple it?"

"Eight thousand livres!" Master Alain muttered.

"Eight thousand, my good and faithful servant! Why, ten thousand, if you want! And my gratitude and—"

"A grass-green grave in some snug corner of the forest," Lapierre interrupted. "Tempting."

"Speak only for yourself," Hervé de Vaunoy said, catching hold of Lapierre's arm, "and do not attempt to influence our good old Alain. I will pay you, even for your silence."

"Good!" replied Lapierre. "Now, we're talking! How much?"

"Ten louis."

The ex-mountebank fell silent; but his last remark had had its full effect upon the steward, who had been dazzled for an instant by the glittering vision of ten thousand livres, but now recoiled at the thought of death.

He only answered the nobleman's renewed entreaties with a mournful shaking of his head.

"And so, you both refuse?" said the Lord of La Tremlays getting up.

"I do," replied Lapierre.

Master Alain said nothing.

"I might have expected it!" whispered De Vaunoy. "Often it happens, that the trusted blade will break in the soldier's hand when most he needs it, and then he must combat with his adversary in close quarters by mere bodily strength."

Then dashing his hand upon a table in the center of the room, he said sternly:

"Alain, get out my riding coat and cloak: see to the flints of my pistols, that the locks are in good order, and that they are properly loaded. And you Lapierre, see that my horse, saddled and bridled, be brought round to the door; look, too, that the girths are sound, for, peradventure, I may have to gallop hard."

Alain left the room quickly, but Lapierre, looking in his master's face with wonder, asked:

"Did I comprehend you thoroughly, Monsieur? Are you planning to take this risk upon yourself?"

"Order my horse, I say."

"In your place, I should not be in such a desperate hurry. But a willful man shall have his way; and if you return alive, why, I shall think the gallant Captain rests upon the cold turf."

Shrugging, he walked towards the door, but turned as his hand was on the handle of the lock, and said:

"Monsieur de Vaunoy, you are a far bolder man than I thought. The Devil owes you a lift, and perhaps he may help you at a pinch: however, the game is dangerous, and I had much rather you played the cards than I."

The moment Monsieur de Vaunoy was left alone, the excitement that had sustained him vanished, and he

194

sank into a chair, where he remained almost motionless, until Alain returned with the riding boots and coat, which he put on mechanically, and descended to the great courtyard. His normally rubicund face had grown extremely pale.

He mounted the horse without uttering one word, and paced slowly down the avenue of elms that led to the castle.

As his horse passed through the gateway, Lapierre said to Alain satirically:

"A safe journey to our master!"

"Will you have a drink?" replied Alain, tendering his flask.

"Willingly, comrade; soldiers may carouse when the day is won; but my head is weak, and had I availed myself of your offer earlier, instead of being here, I might be on the high road right now, on my way to an early grave—like Monsieur de Vaunoy. *Santé!*"

"*Requiescat in pace*!" replied the steward.

CHAPTER XXIII
Jude Leker's Journey

Hervé de Vaunoy was not what the world might call a daring, or even simply a courageous, man, although in the present instance, the risk he ran, in his mysterious expedition, was similar to that of a man who fights a duel, without quarter, and to the death.

In fact, he had staked his existence against that of Didier; it might be, that his thirst for the young man's life had blinded him to a portion of the imminent peril he ran; it might be that he counted upon extraneous aid, that he had not mentioned to his two acolytes; but whatever the real truth of the case might be, when once on the road, his heart sank within him, and those who had seen him riding, pale and trembling towards the forest, would never have recognized him for the energetic, determined individual they had seen in the castle half an hour before.

Long before Monsieur de Vaunoy had left the castle that had been his own for so many years, Jude Leker, Nicolas Treml's loyal squire, had gone to seek the cottage of Pelo Rouan, the charcoal-burner.

The evening before, the faithful squire had arrived in his native province, uneasy certainly, but full of hope; for if he should discover Georges Treml, his lord's grandson, despoiled of his heritage, at least he knew where to find the means of buying his estate back again.

But now his uneasiness had increased to anguish, and hope failed him, for the young lord was nowhere to be found, and it would have been a thousand times better that he should be alive, brave and strong, with even only his sword to sustain his quarrel, than that he should be lost, and the chest of gold, buried by his grandfather, remain in its old place. Georges alive, would be a tower of strength; but, dead or absent, the iron chest—that was, in effect, the fortune of Treml—was without a legitimate owner, and Jude's devoted mission had become purposeless.

There was still vengeance, some might say, the last resource, the sole enjoyment of those devoid of hope; but Jude was old, his blood did not now run so briskly through his veins, his honest nature had more of love than hatred in its constituent parts, and he viewed revenge as an inefficient consolation.

"No!" the faithful squire murmured to himself. "I will seek him long and carefully throughout every inch of the forest; I pray to Heaven to spare me the misery of hearing he is dead; but if he is so, and foully murdered too—as Dame Goton insinuated—then I will find out his assassin, and in the name of my old dear master Nicolas Treml, I will pass my rapier through his heart."

As he walked his horse through those somber paths, so often traversed by him, a remembrance of some past incident met him at every step. Through this alley it was, that the old lord used to canter, when he went with his infant grandson to the manor of Boüexis; there it was, in that covert, that Job, the noble, faithful dog, had killed a wolf, after a desperate struggle; and in that path, so narrow that a deer could scarcely pass it, which led directly to the lake of La Tremlays, which might be—though he knew it not for certain—the final resting place of the whitened bones of the last of the Tremls.

His heart broke; tears came to his eyes as other mournful considerations rushed across his mind. He now remembered, the cheerful smoke issuing from the roofs of the cabins occupied by the charcoal-burners, the hoop-makers, the basket manufacturers, and other woodsmen, but where was it now?

The cottages themselves—or their remains—were there; some still standing entire, others half-ruined, but all silent and forsaken, resounding no longer with the glad songs of joy that never failed to accompany the sounds of the mallet, the hammer, and the saw.

What scourge had passed over the blithe forest of Rennes? What pestilence had depopulated these clearings, and given the hue of death to spots once so redolent of life?

Jude pursued his way with moistened eyes, sadder even than all those sad places, crossing himself through habit at crossroads where hung pious crosses, now without the offerings of the pious dwellers in the wood; and at times he pronounced certain names before some well-remembered hut, but no well-known voice responded to his call.

At times, he would discern a human form at the angle of a path or standing in a clearing, but the person would disappear instantly upon seeing him; and at the same time, with the sagacity of an old, thorough huntsman, he saw, by the agitation of the underwood, that his solitude was not so perfect in reality as in appearance, and that many keen eyes were fixed upon him behind the massive, verdant walls.

When he arrived at the cross of Our Lady of the Forest, in the center of the wood, the landscape became, if possible, even more desolate than before. In this place, where all the main roads through the forest met, the clearings were more open, and the sides of the roads had been covered with an unusual number of huts and cottages, the majority plastered with lime, and inhabited by industrious foresters. All along the wide and beautiful paths that cut into the woods, from the foot of the cross, were a series of cottages with thatch roofs where coopers, basket makers and cloggers worked. However, Jude found most of them burned or otherwise destroyed, and those which yet remained upright, showed evident traces of having been pillaged by the devastating hands of man.

Pulling up his horse before these mournful ruins, Jude's memory reverted to the good old days when Nicolas Treml was Lord of this land, and all these cottages were inhabited and their residents happy.

"The accursed Frenchmen have been here! Under the pretext of collecting taxes, they have demanded men's purses, or their lives. As the sons of the forest had no purses, they have all perished."

Jude was right: these ruins were the work of the agents of the Crown, aided, it must be granted, by a few recreant Breton noblemen, amongst whom Hervé de Vaunoy was pre-eminent.

Monsieur de Pontchartrain, the first collector-general, and after him, the Marquis de Nointel, having put in charge of collecting the Breton taxes, and having a personal stake in the proceeds of their efforts, it became their interest to not allow any portion of the province to be exempted from their payment, and therefore, they did not shrink from any violent means in order to coerce the inhabitants of the forest to pay their share. That was what Jude had called, demanding "their purses or their lives."

As for the noblemen, their interests lay elsewhere, but were no less real. The sons of the forest, as they were called, spread over so many of their holdings, claiming exemption from the payment of local taxes on prescriptive rights, and thus burdened them with duties, but no rewards.

While Nicolas Treml had lived, since he owned the majority of the land, all the other noblemen had modeled their attitudes after him in all things; and since the old man was a true Seigneur, gentle with the weak, firm with the strong, he had been more disposed to add to their comforts than to take from the hard-earned means of their existence.

But after he had unfortunately left Brittany, and Hervé de Vaunoy had replaced him, the latter had not hesitated to use every sort of base methods to increase his income, and the neighboring lords had imitated his example. There speedily ensued a system of vigorous attack, and dogged resistance, upon and by the hardy foresters.

Thus, with the royal tax collector on the one hand, and the feudal landlords on the other, the poor men of the forest soon lost all their means of subsistence.

But the sons of the forest partook more of the wild boar than of the hare. In the beginning, tracked, pursued, and hunted like wild beasts, they sought safety in flight, and hid themselves in the natural, dark recesses of the woods. But their warlike temperament ill brooked this pusillanimous submission. They reflected that union is strength, and banded together in resistance. At the first cry from a leader, they rose en masse. The murky glens spewed forth hundreds of determined men, and they took deep, bloody revenge both upon the tax collectors of the French King and the parsimonious noblemen who had summoned this storm.

Many corpses covered the mossy lanes, legions of bones whitened, unseen, beneath the coverts; and in the dark, long nights, more than one landholder, attacked unawares, paid for his lord's avarice with his life.

Soldiers were dispatched from Rennes and the adjacent towns to quell the insurrection, but as the attempts to levy the various taxes became more cruel and oppressive, the resistance, too, became more violent and obstinate. It was soon seen that the insurgents—who refused to be labeled "bandits"—were under the command of a resolute and skilful chief, whose orders were executed with blind obedience.

The moment came at last when the parts in this bloody drama were exchanged; the defense was converted into a series of daring attacks, the oppressed became the aggressors. Armed parties beset every avenue of the forest, threw themselves upon isolated convoys, and murdered agents of the Maréchaussée when and wherever they could intercept them. Finally, one morning, five thousand stalwart men, whose faces were concealed in wolves' skins, headed by a man in a white mask, marched boldly to Rennes, and looted the house of the collector-general in open daylight.

From that moment, terror seized upon the citizens of the neighboring towns, and the insurrection acquired that importance which is always attached to a first successful onslaught. The chief of the Wolves, as they were now designated, was enshrouded in an inscrutable mystery. Every one could narrate some of his seemingly miraculous exploits, and his followers became popular amongst the peasantry, who never failed to aid them when they could do so with impunity. They had even their own historian amongst the wild literati, and their complete organization was traced in direct descent from the celebrated political association of the *Frères Bretons*, who, in the middle of the previous century, had failed just short of dividing Brittany from the French Crown.

At the start of this armed rising, the leaders of the revolt had enrolled themselves in a secret society, under the orders of the redoubtable chief, who speedily attached such terror to his cognomen.

Men of the Forest—natural allies of this Association—had all to fear if they should be recognized, and therefore, they never sallied from their retreats upon an expedition without disguising their appearances and covering their faces with a mask composed simply of a piece of wolf's-skin, whence they acquired their designation, which from being, in the first instance, a term of contemptuous reproach, was a few months afterwards never pronounced without a shudder, throughout the vicinity of Rennes.

Affairs lasted in this state for a period of fifteen years, with varied successes and reverses on the part of the insurgents, but without the royal forces ever being able to discover their retreats.

For a long while, the neighboring noblemen had entered into a tacit truce with these foresters, and the collector-general, disheartened by his numerous defeats, had discontinued his efforts to reduce the woodsmen to submission; but six months before Captain Didier's arrival, Monsieur Béchamel had determined to again enforce the collection of the taxes. In pursuance of this resolution, he secretly ordered the troops at Rennes to hold themselves in readiness, dispatched them into the forest with a forced march, killed, burned, and ravaged ruthlessly, and in one day, almost every hut and cottage was in ruins.

Charcoal-burners, hoop-makers, and others, taken completely unawares by this sudden, sweeping inroad, retired to the stronghold at the Wolf's Pit, the seat of their brotherhood; there they found a magazine of arms under their famous chief, and on the following day, in their turn, they carried fire and slaughter to the gates of Rennes, looting again the residence of the Royal Intendant.

A war of reprisals—without quarter, immediately ensued: the king's soldiers, day-by-day, entered the forest and destroyed every habitation they could find; killing every man who had the misfortune to fall into their hands; and, on the other side, the Wolves, driven from their homes and not allowed to gain a scanty subsistence by their labor, seized upon all comers, and largely indemnified themselves for the losses and the persecution sustained.

Next to the collector-general, Hervé de Vaunoy was the individual who suffered most severely from their rancor. From time to time, the Wolves would make a descent upon his domains, driving off every living animal, destroying his growing crops, setting fire to his ricks and barns, and damaging his implements of labor.

It was true that the hated possessor of the estate of their old feudal lord—whose memory they still cherished with adoration—was foremost in counseling the harsh measures undertaken by Monsieur Béchamel, Marquis de Nointel, notwithstanding that he studiously concealed his agency. Yet every reprisal on his property followed so instantly upon every fresh scheme of aggression, that it was surmised that the leader of the Wolves must have the most correct intelligence from spies in the castle of La Tremlays.

Only recently, and since Monsieur Béchamel had been in the castle, when Hervé had proposed to him to attack the Wolf's pit with an overwhelming force, and crush the Wolves in their stronghold, within a day afterward, his manor-house at Boüexis was sacked from the foundations to the roof.

In a word, the Wolves had no more deadly enemy than Hervé de Vaunoy, and, truth to say, they returned him hate for hate.

Knowing the proceedings on one side of the civil war, and expecting soon to become thoroughly acquainted with the other, Jude Leker's choice could not be doubted for a moment. His devoted attachment to the memory of his master, and all his ancient sympathies, drew him forcibly towards the Wolves—who were true *Bretons*, as Dame Goton had said, but he had neither will nor leisure to allow him to espouse their quarrel at present, or to lend them the powerful assistance of his mighty arm. His mission was distinct; the last words of the dying Nicolas Treml still resounded in his ears, and he would have considered it a crime to hesitate on the route traced for him by his beloved master, or even to deviate from it for one moment.

It was about eight o'clock in the morning when Jude came in sight of the Pillar of Our Lady of the Forest. This spot was held in the greatest veneration by the woodsmen, and all of them had a holy regard for a small figure of the Madonna placed in a niche, roughly hewn in the body of the cross. It was at this station of the Virgin, that Nicolas Treml—as we have seen in the early part of this narrative—had said his last *Ave* before leaving Brittany, to which he was never to return.

Now, Jude dismounted before the rustic cross, dropped to his knees, and reverently uttered a sincere prayer. Then, rising, he beheld across the topmost branches of trees the smoke ascending from the cabin of Pelo Rouan, the charcoal-burner.

His cabin was almost hidden in a clump growing on a rising ground covered with underwood and elms. At the foot of the little mound, Pelo had dug his ovens; but although situated so deep in the forest, a small garden, in which flowers bloomed, cultivated by the hand of Marie, the "Blossom-of-the-Broom," gave a smiling aspect to the otherwise uncouth, rugged scene.

As Jude passed through the intervening trees he beheld Marie seated before the cabin's door making a wicker basket, without appearing particularly conscious of what she was about, and he who knew her secret would have had no difficulty in guessing that her thoughts at that moment were fixed on Didier.

She sang as her small fingers twined the reed twigs; but her strain was not one joyous, uninterrupted chant; her thrilling voice swelled, then fell, and then broke forth again, and anon would wander through the softest tones of *The Lament*. In truth, she was recalling to her. mind the delight she had experienced the preceding evening; she had seen Didier again, more tender, more loving, and more handsome than ever, more tender than her dreams had painted him during his long absence from her, and she was happy; dwelling on her joy, she would not lose one atom of it, and chased far from her all ideas of doubt or fear.

Why, she thought, should she doubt or fear? Was he not as noble in his heart as in his person? He had never lied—and then he had told her that he loved her, yes; he had told her with his lips, his eyes, and with his soul; and thus it was that the girl's song was a hymn of thankfulness and praise, rising sweetly from her pure heart to the skies.

The Blossom-of-the-Broom was dressed that morning with some coquetry as if she had almost thought she would soon see her lover; a few wild azure autumn flowers were seen at intervals amidst her golden hair; the open corset worn by the daughters of the forest was laced with sky-blue ribbons, and her little feet were cased in the neatest boots that the town of Rennes could furnish; but of all these charms the most enchanting one of them was the calm joy that radiated from her heart and spoke through her soft eyes.

Those lustrous orbs were turned towards heaven as she sang, and as she sat she well deserved the name the young men of the forest had conferred upon her, for she was as brilliant, fresh, and perfumed as the broom.

The instant that Jude saw the girl, a paternal smile passed across his honest countenance, and then, as he advanced towards her, his heavy step disturbed her reverie, she started blushing and would have run away, but the kindly features of the stout squire reassured her, and she rose to receive him with the respect that youth, when properly nurtured, always yields to age.

"My pretty maiden," were the squire's first words, "can you direct me to the cabin of Pelo Rouan, the charcoal-burner?"

"He is my father, Monsieur," the girl replied.

"Then Providence has blessed him with a lovely child; and since, as I suppose, this is his cottage, I will ask you to let me enter it."

Suiting the action to the word, Jude was about to pass towards the doorstep, when Marie bounded lightly between him and the entrance.

"No one, Monsieur, enters the house of Pelo Rouan," she exclaimed. "Rest yourself here, and welcome, but no one passes our threshold. Such are my father's orders."

"But…"

"Such are my father's orders," she repeated.

The squire's object in seeking Pelo Rouan was of too serious a nature to be satisfied with the petty obstacle now thrown in his way. He persisted, saying that he should go in, but Marie was determined, like a faithful guardian, to defend the entrance of the cabin as best she might, when, luckily, a voice was heard to say from the depths of the cabin:

"Daughter, give way. Look well at this man's face, that you may never again refuse him entrance to my home."

Blossom-of-the-Broom turned her eyes in silent wonder to the spot where her father stood, and at the same moment the charcoal-burner said:

"Enter, Jude Leker, good and faithful servant of Treml. I have long awaited you."

CHAPTER XXIV
The Cabin

Obedient to her father's orders, Blossom-of-the-Broom stepped aside, and no impediment was offered to Jude's entrance into the cabin. However, he did not immediately avail himself of the permission accorded, but instead remained stationary, for he feared falling into some trap, and asked himself who this man could be who spoke of the Tremls with so much affection and respect.

In such a situation, and in those perilous times, that suspicion was fully justifiable. Although the door was now open, Jude's eyes could not penetrate the interior of the cabin, for smoke issued through the single aperture which served for both light and entrance, and as he gazed earnestly inside, it seemed to him that if he entered, the first thing that would meet his sight would be the glaring eyes of some wild beast.

Moreover, Jude had arrived in Brittany only the previous evening; twenty long years of captivity had changed his countenance materially, and yet, here was a person who recognized him at once, who knew his name, and said he had been waiting for him. Was he friend or foe? And in this inhospitable cabin that opened its doors to him alone, might there not be some treachery concealed beneath this sudden show of courtesy?

Jude was brave, even to rashness, but he had vowed his life to his late master, and he feared to die before Nicolas's last wish could be carried out; nevertheless his uncertainty was not of long duration, for casting a glance at Marie, her angelic features removed all doubt from his heart. He felt that treachery could not exist where that fair girl dwelt, and he stepped into the cabin.

At first, he could not distinguish any object in the interior, and stopped motionless upon the threshold.

"This way," cried a rough voice from the far end of the cabin.

As the squire's vision became more accustomed to the darkness, he perceived two glaring eyes a few short paces from him; and, advancing resolutely towards them, a powerful hand caught hold of his, and pulled him gently down upon a wooden bench, where he sat, with his back turned to the bright ray of light that streamed in through the aperture.

Looking around, Jude saw that he was in a large square room without windows, or else they were blocked—the ceiling was so low that he was astonished that he had not touched it as he stood upright. In one of the corners, two or three planks were roughly joined together and covered with straw to serve as a bed for one of the occupants of this miserable retreat, and the rest of the furniture—if such it could be called—consisted of two benches, some stools, and a wooden table.

Marie's chamber, he thought, must have been in some other portion of the hovel.

Between himself and the door, Jude saw the black profile of a man, seated beside him upon the bench, of whom he immediately asked:

"Are you Pelo Rouan, the charcoal-burner?"

"I am, indeed, the person who is so called. Welcome again, comrade. I have long awaited you."

"You do know me then?" Jude asked in great surprise.

"Tolerably well, my friend."

"But I cannot say that I know you, since I cannot see your face."

Pelo Rouan rose, took Jude by the hand, and, leading him to the door, bade him look upon his face as he exposed it fully to the light. Jude examined it attentively, and then said, with a sigh:

"I do not recollect you."

The charcoal-burner took the squire's hand again, and led him back to the bench; both men resumed their seats.

"You are right, Jude," Pelo said. "This cabin was not built until long after the departure of Nicolas Treml; but let that pass, and tell me what has brought you here—it was not for nothing that you sought me."

"That's true. I looked for you because…"

"You did the right thing," interrupted the charcoal-burner. "As you have always done, Jude Leker, because your heart has been always faithful and honest, and I can guess the purpose of your visit…"

"You can?" said Jude, surprised.

"Yes. You came here to ask me what happened to the poor idiot who used to be called Jean Blanc."

"Is he dead?"

"No!" the charcoal-burner answered. "He is not, and you wish to know this because he can tell you what became of the heir of all these lands—young Georges Treml."

"That is true, all true!" Jude exclaimed in the utmost astonishment. "But who are you, mysterious man, who seem to know the secrets of my soul? In the name of Heaven, who are you?"

"I am Pelo Rouan, the charcoal-burner, a poor man whose life has been cruelly outraged, and who still has some injuries to avenge."

210

"And what—what do you know of our little Monsieur Georges?"

The voice of the charcoal-burner quivered as he answered:

"Nothing, absolutely nothing more than you yourself already know. Would to Heaven that the castle of La Tremlays had been as true a guardian of its treasure as the hollow oak at the Wolf's Pit."

Jude bounded up from the bench, his eyes lightened, and his whole frame trembled with astonishment and rage as he ejaculated:

"The hollow oak at the Wolf's Pit!"

"Yes. The hollow oak at the Wolf's Pit!" was the calm reply.

If the darkness had been less dense, one could have seen Jude's face change colors twice or three times in the space of a second. He grasped Rouan's arm, and said in a low, determined, tone:

"Whoever you may be, you know too much."

The small arm of the charcoal-burner appeared but a trifling obstacle to the iron strength of such a man as Jude; but, notwithstanding the dreadful threat, Pelo's countenance was as calm as that of a sleeping babe.

"Who told you of the hollow oak?" continued Jude. "You know the secret of Treml, of which I believed myself the sole depository, and now, you must say your prayers to Heaven, for you must die!"

But before the single-minded squire could carry his hand to the dagger at his belt, the charcoal-burner suddenly wrenched his arm from Leker's grip.

He reached the other end of the long room with one bound, like a hunted deer, and there he stood, awaiting the attack, his eyes glittering fiercely like those of a wild cat.

Jude, unsheathing his dagger, rushed impetuously towards the spot, caring nothing for a brace of pistols that he heard the charcoal-burner cock. However, in the darkness, he tripped over a stool, falling heavily to the ground.

In another second, Pelo's knee was on his chest, one hand firmly grasped his throat, and a loaded pistol was pointed at his head.

"Stir not, my man," said Pelo, calmly, to the prostrate squire, "for if you rise, you may kill me; and if you attempt to do so, you will die."

Jude remained still.

"I see that your brave heart is still unchanged; alas, so is your hot brained head," continued Pelo. "Your old age still contains the qualities of your youth. Let there be a truce between us, honest Jude. What use do you think I have for your secret? If the hundred thousand livres had tempted me, do you suppose they would be in the old oak still?"

"That's true!" Jude muttered for the third time. "I am at your mercy, and must yield; but I do not know who you are."

"And perhaps you never will," replied the charcoal-burner. "But I have shown you that I am a friend of the Tremls, and Heaven knows, living or dead, they have too few of them that they should not think of cutting each other's throats when Providence brings them together."

"True, again. Let me rise; I swear I will not try to harm you."

Pelo let go his grip, and assisted his antagonist in getting up.

"Take up your dagger, and replace it in your belt," he said. "I will have confidence in you, and take you at your word—although you now serve a Frenchman."

"He is a good, gallant young man."

"But no less an enemy of Brittany, and therefore of me," said Pelo, with some bitterness. "But let this pass as well. His time shall come. Let us now return to the subject of Treml…"

The two men sat down again, side by side, without the least distrust, and Jude resumed the conversation:

"You are generous, Pelo Rouan, for I attacked you savagely and rashly. Therefore, I will not ask you how you became acquainted with my secret, for I feel that it is safe in your keeping. There is my hand. Take it freely, in token of our friendship."

"Willingly, my man; Jean Blanc—who is, as I may say, my other self, has often talked to me about you. You were always kind to the poor Albino, and he has not forgotten. Perhaps someday, he may be able to repay you for all the kindness you showed him."

"Let him rather repay Treml, the poor man."

"He has done all he could for Treml," Pelo said solemnly.

"No doubt, my friend, but the poor creature could not do very much."

"Once, Jude, it was so, because Jean could only repay good with good; but now, he has learned to render injury for injury—and he has become powerful."

"Is he not still mad?" asked Jude.

"Heaven sometimes tries men so sorely that some of sound mind go mad under the shock, but sometimes misery and ill-treatment will drive insane men back to their senses. Today, Jean Blanc is no longer mad."

"Can he recollect what took place many years ago?"asked Jude.

"He remembers everything."

"Then I must see him!" Jude exclaimed.

Pelo's eyes glistened, and a tear seemed to stand in them, as he replied:

"It has been a long time since anyone could boast of having met Jean Blanc face to face in the forest... Be content with asking me what you want to know, and do not think of seeking out Jean Blanc."

"But perhaps he might tell me..."

"Not more than I can tell you."

"Still..." Jude persisted.

"Be satisfied: Jean has often opened his whole soul to me. Would you like me to recount to you the particulars of the villainous murder of young Georges, in the lake of La Tremlays? I know all, even the most minute details... Yes, at this very moment, I think I can see Hervé de Vaunoy as he acted on that accursed night."

"Tell me! Tell me," Jude cried eagerly. "I already hate that man, but I feel that I can hate him even more!"

Pelo Rouan then proceeded to give a complete, detailed accounting of all that had taken place at the lake of La Tremlays, when Hervé de Vaunoy had attempted to destroy the child Georges, then only five years-old, the grandson of his benefactor.

Jude did not lose one word of the recital. When he heard the story of the death of Job, the noble dog, a tear dropped from the squire's eye; and when the charcoal-burner described Jean Blanc's arrival, he could barely restrain his enthusiasm.

"So? So?" he asked. "May Heaven reward the faithful fool! What happened next?"

Pelo continued his story until he came to the renewal of Jean's frenzy in the forest, and then his voice failed him, and he sobbed like a child.

"Jean left the boy," he stammered, "and when he came back, in his right mind, the child was no longer there. Nothing remained on the bank, but the garment of white skins, which formed the poor creature's usual dress. Then, he fell to his knees, prayed to the Almighty, and wept."

Jude shrugged his shoulders, gnashed his teeth, and uttered an exclamation of furious disappointment.

"Yes! Poor Jean wept tears of blood," the charcoal-burner went on to say, as a convulsive sob escaped from his broad chest. "And he does so every time he speaks of the event, for the remembrance of it pierces him to the heart."

"Why did he not search for the boy further in the forest?"

"Jean's reason—as you know—was weak at that time. He remained all night groveling on the damp earth, and, in the morning, he ran everywhere that he thought of, but could not find the child."

"Were there no traces of him—no signs of which way he must have wandered?"

"None, none!" Pelo said, in a tone of deep dejection.

Jude, who had listened with agitated, feverish attention to every word the charcoal-burner had said, let his head drop upon his chest.

"Then, there is no hope," he said at last.

"Jean long ago lost all hope; but God is merciful, and the race of Treml has only produced good and God-fearing men. It is possible that some passer-by may have seen the boy and picked him up. In that case, with the help of Providence, we may recognize him if we should chance to meet him."

"How so?" Jude asked.

"Jean Blanc, you see, possessed one of those copper medals, struck many years ago at Vitré, in honor of our

Lady of the Forest. It was the only keepsake his dear mother had left him. On that dreadful evening, when he felt the madness coming upon him, he took it from his neck, and put it on the boy's, thinking in his pious simplicity he was placing Lord Georges under the protection of the Virgin."

"But there are many of those medals!" Jude interrupted.

"Jean Blanc's had a cross roughly engraved on its back, and Mathieu Blanc, his father, was the only person who possessed one just like it. It is at this moment on Marie's neck."

"That lovely girl I saw outside?"

"Yes. She is the child of Jean Blanc, the Albino."

Marie, who had continued singing the *Lament* in a low tone as she weaved her basket, hearing her name, rose and looked into the hut over the half-door.

"The daughter of…"

"Hush!" said Pelo to the squire. "She believes she is my own daughter:"

Then to the girl:

"Come in, my love."

The Blossom-of-the-Broom obeyed, and Pelo, taking the medal from her neck, placed it in Jude's hands, who turned it over and over, and examined it thoroughly, murmuring:

"May Heaven send that I find another such! I'll recognize it now, but it's a poor clue."

Marie resumed her seat at the cabin door and her song.

"She is singing the poor Albino's favorite air," remarked Jude. "It is singular that so repulsive a man should have been blessed with such a lovely child."

"He was repulsive, it is true," Pelo replied, "nay, almost disgusting, and yet the Almighty was gracious, and allowed an angel to look upon him without horror and detestation. For you see, my friend, Marie is the very image of her mother. But I have not told you," he said, altering his tone, "that there is still a chance of your finding the lost heir of Treml. It is a very precarious one, to be sure; but with the aid of Jean Blanc…"

"That name again!" the impatient squire muttered. "Forever and ever, nothing but Jean Blanc! What can that poor devil do, when men of sense and strength have failed?"

"You do not know him, Jude," said Pelo Rouan, with a note of mystery in his voice. "Hark you, and I will tell you all that he has done. Then, you may judge what he can do for the heir of Treml."

CHAPTER XXV
Eight Men and a Tax Collector

The last words uttered by the charcoal-burner went straight to the old squire's heart. Hope returns quickly when it is vehemently desired; the simple possibility of success restored courage to Jude Leker's soul, and he approached more closely to Pelo Rouan that he might not lose one word.

But his host appeared to have fallen into a reverie, from which he did not seem likely to awaken.

"So? By which means could we find the boy?"

"Which means?" Pelo Rouan said, shuddering slightly. "I did not say means—I spoke merely of a precarious chance—if there had been means, do you not think Jean Blanc would not have used them?"

Again this Jean Blanc, Jude thought.

His curiosity combined with his sense of duty to fuel his impatience.

What miracle can have made the idiot the solid arch on which the destinies of Treml rest?

"Listen Jude: it happened twenty years ago," said Pelo slowly, as if he was speaking to himself, "but there are some things that men remember until the day they die. Attend to what I say, and at the conclusion of my tale, you will understand Jean Blanc as intimately as I do myself... A few months after the mysterious disappearance of the child, Monsieur de Pontchartrain—whom God confound!—was still the collector-general of the taxes, but his agents had not yet dared to penetrate the recesses of the forest. One morning, Jean Blanc was cutting wood for hoops in a tall chestnut tree in that part which leads from Rennes to Boüexis, when he saw a number of armed men approaching through the wood.

"They were soldiers in full marching costume, and amongst them, two bloodsuckers clad in black cloth—whose occupation Jean did not then know, but was soon to learn in a most fearful manner, and two noblemen rode at their head.

"The Albino thought at first they were a cavalcade of burgesses, soldiers, and seigneurs traveling to France, but soon, he recognized the cowardly Hervé de Vaunoy at their head as the men drew near; for ever since his attempt to drown the boy, Hervé hated Jean Blanc because he would not hold his tongue."

"He was right," Jude interrupted. "The lad ought to have made that foul crime known throughout Brittany."

"When certain things are said, good Jude, men must not speak too loudly. At that time, Jean Blanc was less thought of than Job, the faithful dog of La Tremlays, had been. And when Job, barked, he was shot dead, the poor creature! Jean would have done better to hold his tongue, but he had not, and Hervé de Vaunoy was not the kind of man willing to forget the gossip that had spread throughout the region. So when Jean saw the villain at the head of the armed men, he became afraid. He thought of his father, who lay alone in their hut at the Wolf's Pit, and, gliding down the trunk of the chestnut tree, he crept after them cautiously through the coverts.

"The cavalcade halted not far from the cross of Our Lady of the Forest. The soldiers dismounted, threw themselves upon the ground, and gourds of wine and liquors passed from hand to hand. The two noblemen and the men in black held a conference apart.

"Jean wound himself, like a snake, as close to them as he could—so close that the soldiers of the French King could have seen his white whiskers if they had been paying attention. He realized that he had not been mistaken: he could see the duplicitous face of Hervé de Vaunoy just as I would see yours, if there were more lights in here. He listened attentively, but they spoke so low that he could only hear one word they uttered—and that was his father's name!

"A chill seized upon poor Jean's heart. The name of Mathieu Blanc on the lips of Hervé de Vaunoy here, in the forest, could augur nothing but ill—nothing but the most horrible disaster. So he drew himself closer through the underwood, crawling like a snake in the briar wood, without anyone noticing him until he could hear every word.

"He then ascertained that the men in black were tax collectors who had come into the forest to rob and harass the poor folk in the name of the French King, and that the soldiers accompanied them to destroy the huts, and shoot all those who should resist. They were agents, deputies of the collector general, who had agreed to share the plunder with him.

"It appeared from their conversation that the name of Mathieu Blanc had been pronounced because the officers in black did not want to trouble themselves with so poor a man. But Hervé de Vaunoy assured them otherwise:

" 'He has gold, I know it for a fact!' he exclaimed. 'He is a false indigent; his misery is but an act. Holy Mother! I will go with you into his den; but recollect this: he has gold! And a few strokes with the flat of a sword will force him to show you where it is concealed.'

" 'Fine! We will go there,' the men in black said.

"And Jean, retiring as he had advanced, regained his legs when out of the covert, and ran back swiftly to his father's hut at the Wolf's Pit.

"For once Hervé de Vaunoy had not lied, for, by the merest chance, there was some in Mathieu's cabin—the few coins that Nicolas Treml had given him when he was leaving Brittany..."

"Yes, I remember!" Jude exclaimed. "Our good lord had not forgotten his old retainer when he went away. It was I who picked up that purse from the ground and threw it across the threshold of his hut!"

The charcoal-burner did not notice the interruption, and continued:

"When Jean reached his father's hut, he was so overcome with exertion that he could scarcely stand, and his heart completely failed him. You knew Mathieu Blanc, good Jude. Formerly, he was a brave, bold man-at-arms, but age and poverty had pressed too heavily upon him in the last days of his life, and at the time of which I am speaking, he lay night and day on his miserable pallet, worn out with illness and the approach of certain death too long delayed.

"Jean, when he had partly recovered breath, kissed his father's forehead, and then the old man said in a feeble tone:

" 'I am not in so much pain now...'

"On any other occasion, Jean would have rejoiced, for he loved his father with all his heart, but he remembered that the men he had seen in the forest were, no doubt, coming to the hut, and he trembled both with rage and fear.

"The purse with the few pieces of gold that remained was on the table. Jean did not think of concealing it, as he might have done, but grabbed an old musket which his father had used in his campaigns, a piece that carried far and true, and threw it, with a horn of powder and a box of balls, into the thicket nearest to the hut.

"Then, he sat down and remained by his father's bed.

"After a few minutes, Jean heard a dull tramp upon the soft moss in the forest, from which he knew that the cavaliers had dismounted on the outside of the ravine and were coming up on foot. Looking through the window and the lowest branches of the trees, he spied ten men advancing: eight soldiers, one tax collectors, and Hervé de Vaunoy.

"They reached the top of the bank, and the man in black struck the door until the oak-boards creaked and rattled. Just as Jean was opening the door, the man in black called out:

" 'Let us in—in the name of the King!'

"The soldiers entered tumultuously. Hervé de Vaunoy prudently kept close to the door. The collector, taking a slip of parchment from his pocket, read something that Jean did not understand. When he had finished, he said:

" 'Mathieu Blanc, I order you to pay one hundred livres tournois for taxes and arrears—for ten years back.'

"Old Mathieu turned himself painfully in his bed, and looked uncomprehendingly at the man in black with haggard face.

"The collector repeated his summons, and the soldiers struck the table violently with the hilts of their swords.

" 'Jean, I am thirsty,' the old man murmured. 'Give me to drink, my son.'

"Agony was painted on the face of the dying man, and on Jean's too, when, on reaching his hand to take up a pitcher on the table, one of the soldiers shattered it with his sword, crying out with a jeering laugh:

" 'Let him pay first, and drink afterwards!'

"Hervé de Vaunoy, who was still on the threshold, smiled with ill-concealed glee.

"Poor Jean, who could do nothing, ground his teeth, held hard his breath, and vowed a full and deep revenge as he pointed out the purse to the collector, who grabbed it.

" 'I told you he had gold,' Hervé chuckled.

"The man in black counted out four louis, and demanded the remaining four livres.

" 'Jean, child, my lips are parched,' the old man said with the death-rattle in his throat.

"Alas! There was not one drop of liquid left in the hut with which to allay his burning thirst. Jean threw himself upon his knees before one of the soldiers, who had a gourd, and the trooper, having compassion on the dying man, was handing it to the youth, when Hervé de Vaunoy thrust the Albino away rudely, shouting:

" 'Let Mathieu pay first!'

" 'We have no more!' cried Jean. 'I swear it upon my soul! Kill me if you will, but take pity on my father!'

" Mathieu Blanc made an effort to get up. It was horrible

" 'Water, Jean—water, my son!' issued almost inaudibly from the old man's lips.

"Then he fell back, a corpse upon the couch."

Gradually as the charcoal-burner had reached this part of his story, his voice had become fainter. Now it ceased at once, and Jude felt tears falling upon his hand.

In fact the stout squire was not less moved than Pelo.

"The poor boy!" said the squire, clenching his fists. "The poor boy! To see his father murdered in that cruel way… And that villain Hervé de Vaunoy! What did Jean do next, my man? What next?"

"Jean Blanc," the woodman replied, as if he were choking, "when he dies will not suffer so sharp a pang as he experienced at that dreadful moment. He dropped at once upon his knees beside his father's body and covered the dead man's face, but the ten men who were mocking his pain did not give him an instant's rest, for the collector growled:

" 'Come, fellow! Where are the four livres you still owe the King?'

"Jean jumped up and stood face to face with the men who had just killed his father. For a moment, one single moment only, he thought his weak brain would give way to the madness; he felt the delirium coming over him, but he repelled it with a mighty effort. Then a miracle happened: his brain suddenly became sound, and he was every inch a man. It was as if one ray of Heavenly light now irradiated the dark night in which he had so long groveled.

"He shouted, in a voice of thunder:

" 'Out!'

"The men placed themselves between Jean and the door; but he had not lost his wonderful agility. With a mighty leap, he jumped through the tattered cloth curtain that covered the window and, quickly alighting upon his feet, before the soldiers could recover from their surprise, he had already lost himself in the coverts of the wood.

" 'Fire!' Hervé shouted. 'Fire upon him as you would on a wild beast! Or else he'll have his revenge!'

"Some shots were fired at random, but the Albino was not hit. He had successfully concealed himself in the brushwood, while still remaining within sight of the dwelling.

"And then commenced a deed without a name.

"Hervé de Vaunoy, the man with the soft, smiling face, who murders while he smiles, furious that one of his intended victims had escaped from his vengeance, ordered the men to set fire to the cabin. Some dry wood was soon piled against it, a light was obtained by snapping a pistol-flint, the wood was lit, and soon the flames surrounded the dead body of the faithful servitor of Treml."

"The villains!" Jude muttered between his teeth. "And what did Jean Blanc do?"

"Wait," Pelo said, with his teeth hard set too. "Jean did not stir so long as the soldiers remained near the hut, blaspheming and laughing like demons. The moment they were out of sight, however, he came forth from his hiding place, rushed into the hut, and bore the blackened body of his father out of it, in order to give him a Christian burial later. He could not pray, for his brain was on fire, and there was other work to be done, but he kissed the forehead of the corpse and laid it reverently upon the ground.

"Then, he darted to the spot where he had concealed the gun. He primed and loaded it, descended the ravine like lightning, mounted the opposite bank with a few vigorous bounds, sprung along a path and pursued his father's murderers, who by this time were some distance in advance. But the wind was not as swift as Jean was on that bloody day…"

"Very good," said Jude. "Very good!"

"Wait! Before the men had reached the clearing where they had left their horses, a musket-shot was heard. The tax collector fell, never to rise again."

Jude clapped his hands in ecstasy.

"And De Vaunoy?" he cried. "What about De Vaunoy?"

"The moment he heard the shot, he had become paler than the corpse of Mathieu Blanc, and his teeth chattered in his head as he cried:

" 'Haste, my men, haste, haste, away!'

"They did hasten, but just as they reached the horses, another shot was heard, and the soldier who had broken the pitcher Jean would have handed to his father, bit the dust."

"But De Vaunoy... What about Hervé de Vaunoy?"

"Wait, I said! They climbed on their horses. Terror and despair were now painted on the faces of those insolent soldiers. They dashed their spurs into the sides of the poor beasts, and galloped off, thinking, no doubt, that they should be outside the range of the unseen deadly gun. The fools! Jean Blanc was acquainted with every nook and corner of the forest! He knew a turn of the road which they must come round, and how, by making a shortcut to abridge the distance they must traverse, he could easily catch up with them, He plunged fearlessly forward. No tangled brake, no thorny thicket, no sharp-pointed briar, no stunted holly, checked his impetuous course.

"The road was sinuous, at every corner, the good weapon did its duty, and a man fell dead at every discharge, for Jean shot ever with unerring aim. Jean hunted them from point to point, and not once did he fire in vain.

"Occasionally, the soldiers tried to beat the wood to unearth the invisible avenger. More than one ball whistled past Jean as he recharged the musket behind the friendly shelter of a massive oak, but these useless efforts to destroy their enemy only served to delay their flight, and as soon as they returned to the traveled path, another shot was heard, and another man fell dead."

Jude's blood rose at every sentence the charcoal-burner uttered.

"By the bones of Nicolas Treml!" he cried, "I did not think our White Hare was capable of such a daring deed. By the holy Virgin, Pelo, he was a gallant youth! But did he not try to slay that miscreant Hervé de Vaunoy?"

"Wait! Jean had not forgotten that villain, but he kept him for the last—like the gourmands who save the best for last.

"The moment came when the last soldier had fallen, and De Vaunoy was left alone. Jean Blanc had killed eight men, and a tax collector. The villain, more dead than alive, was madly urging on his tired horse with whip and spur. Jean rammed down two balls in the barrel, and waited for him behind a tree at the last angle of the road upon the outskirts of the forest…"

"At last!" said Jude, rubbing his hands.

The good squire was like those folks who become passionately involved in the melodramatic twists and turns of a stage play. He had seen Hervé de Vaunoy alive and well only the day before, and yet he hoped that he was going to be killed in Pelo Rouan's story!

But the charcoal-burner shook his head:

"When Hervé de Vaunoy appeared, Jean Blanc leveled the musket full upon him. His eye was clear, revenge was in his heart, and no power on Earth could have saved the miscreant, but..."

"But? But?" Jude shouted, seeing that Pelo Rouan hesitated.

"But," the charcoal-burner said slowly, "Hervé de Vaunoy reached the castle unharmed."

"How? Did Jean Blanc miss the murderer?"

"No! He did not fire at all."

Every nerve in Jude's body quivered with agitation and he let out a cry of despair.

"Jean Blanc did not fire," the charcoal-burner said slowly, "because thoughts of Treml crossed his mind then, and he understood that, even to avenge his father, he should not destroy the last chance of discovering the fate of little Georges."

CHAPTER XXVI
An Epileptic Fit

The voice of the charcoal-burner. was hoarse as the raven's croak, whilst he described Jean's bloody pursuit in the forest. His words issued with difficulty from his lips, his bosom heaved, and his eyes brightened with the ferocity of a tiger's; but when he spoke of the boy, his voice became choked, and his manner lost all the savage energy with which he had described the deadly chase.

When the silence had lasted some short time, and both the men had become somewhat calmer, the squire broke it by saying:

"If the life of Hervé de Vaunoy might be of any use in discovering what happened to Georges, Jean did well in sparing him; but just now ,I cannot see how this dastardly traitor can ever prove of any value to the Tremls."

"When he shall be far away from help, with a loaded pistol held to his forehead by the strong arm of a determined man."

"There may be some sense in that," Jude rejoined, but after a slight pause, he added: "That is, if he knows more about the child than we do."

"Maybe. But the hour is at hand when he must answer some questions truly, or die upon the spot. But to return to my tale. Jean did as I have told you, honest Jude, and spared his father's murderer. But the sentiment of gratitude which had predominated over vengeance soon passed away. The burning cinders of the hut rekindled the feelings in his heart. He soon regretted having forgotten his father in favor of a stranger's son."

"A stranger!" Jude exclaimed, quite angry at the epithet. "It was the only heir of his lord and master!"

"Jean Blanc never had a master," Pelo replied haughtily, "even in the days of his affliction. So, he immediately regretted having let de Vaunoy go, and would have gone after him again, but it was too late, for the murderer was now spurring up the main avenue of his castle with the fear of death in every feature of his face.

"I can't tell if it was a good thing or a bad thing," muttered Jude.

"There will be opportunities enough, my good fellow, to chastise that consummate villain. It is an easy thing to get him within gunshot—and Heaven knows, that since that fatal day, Jean Blanc could have killed Hervé a hundred times, even in his own hall, surrounded by domestics—but the real difficulty is to find him alone, defenseless, and say to him, 'Speak—or die.' But Jean Blanc shall try."

"And, by Heaven, Pelo, I shall assist him!"

The charcoal-burner grasped Jude's hand warmly, and asked:

"What about your duty to the French Captain?"

"My service to Treml takes precedence over it; it has been so agreed between us."

"Beware, Jude," said Pelo Rouan, with severity, "how you make known a Breton secret to a Frenchman."

"He is brave, and true as steel. I shall answer for him with my life."

"Brave and true, but after the fashion of the French," replied the charcoal-burner, bitterly. "Just enough to not be ashamed of betraying an innocent, young girl. However, my quarrel with him does not concern you; you have enough on your head. Let me proceed.

"When Jean Blanc returned to the Wolf's Pit, he forgot everything but his dead father. So he cut wood, and made hoops for two nights and days incessantly, sold them at Vitré, and with the money, gave old Mathieu Blanc a Christian burial, and had masses said for the repose of his soul.

"When that sacred filial duty was accomplished, he did not wish to return to the ruins of their hut, filled as it was with dreadful memories. Instead, he crossed the forest, and took up his abode in a cabin near Saint Aubin-du-Cormier. He remained there, alone in the woods, exercising his trade but only enough to purchase the necessities of life. He was still suffering under the hand of the Most High, for though his insanity had passed entirely away, he was now subject to terrible epileptic fits.

"In the midst of his calamity, when he was devoid of all hope of consolation on this earth, Heaven, in its mercy, sent a pitying angel to his cabin, who conferred upon him a degree of happiness beyond any of his wildest dreams could have conceived; a happiness, alas! too short, and which, when passed, only plunged him deeper into despair.

"A gentle, lovely, young, amiable girl—more beauteous even than the generality of her sex—took pity on the rejected of his fellow men. Her name was Sainte and—Heaven bless her!—it was well deserved. The first time she beheld the poor Albino, she did not put her hands before her eyes and escape from the sight of him as most young women did. No! She permitted the tired man to sit by her fire and gave him milk to drink. Aye, my friend, I see that this surprises you… And yet, the angelic creature did still more. The soul of Jean Blanc was that of a man, although encrusted in a miserable case. One day, when seated by the fair girl's side, his full soul and daring heart prompted him to say, 'I love you!'"

"I'll be..." said Jude, slightly ironic.

"The result was that, a year later, Marie was born—Marie, the girl outside—the very image of her mother—Marie, whom the men of the forest, with their poetic imaginations, have nicknamed The Blossom-of-the-Broom, because the golden flower of that wild shrub is the brightest that grows in untamed Brittany. Marie, who is the daughter of Jean Blanc and Sainte."

"She must have been a good girl, this Sainte," murmured Jude whom the story now only amused poorly.

"She was an angel, a merciful spirit, faithful Jude. The two short years that Jean passed with her were the one sweet honey-drop in the gall and wormwood of the cup he had been doomed to drain to the very dregs, the only green oasis in the arid desert of his life, the single glittering star of his long, lonely, dark night. He was intoxicated with his felicity, to forget the deep wounds in his heart—he had no wish nor fear, nor hope, and for two years he was happy..."

Pelo Rouan stopped and wiped his brow with his hand, before continuing:

"But at the end of that period, French soldiers and collectors again showed their detested faces in the forest. The evil De Vaunoy had discovered Jean Blanc's retreat, and his cottage was attacked. The first time, he drove the men away, for Hervé well remembered the old gun, and none cared to come within its deadly range; but he was watched night and day, and when he was known to be away from his home, the men came back, and one villain, Jude, wearing the livery of France, outraged his

232

poor wife, whose only defense was of her sleeping child...

"I will not tell you what followed... Nay, I cannot, because my blood is boiling just as I speak to you of it, and it takes both my hands to contain the beats of my heart...

"The angelic Sainte died that day, praying to God for the salvation of Jean Blanc and their daughter."

Pelo's voice failed him again, at this point.

"By my faith, Pelo," Jude growled, "I can well understand why the lad does not like very much the soldiers of France."

"He hates them!" shouted the charcoal-burner. "Words cannot express his detestation, nor mine either. Even now, if one of them would try to do to Marie what that other soldier did her mother... Let him be warned, friend Jude, there is an old musket that guards the purity of The Blossom-of-the-Broom' a weapon, my friend, that carries far and true. Since you serve Captain Didier, tell him to limit his desires to the daughter of his present host, and to forget the paths that lead to Marie's heart."

"He has not made me the confidant of his secrets, but I know he is generous and brave, and if any one attacks him, in ambush or face-to-face, he shall have my aid—save if it conflicts with my oath to Treml."

"As you will, Jude, but do not interrupt me, for my tale is drawing to a close. Jean Blanc took his young child upon one shoulder, and his musket on the other, and thus he traversed the forest, despair in his heart, and vengeance in his brain. The sight of the spot where his father had been murdered increased his animosity, and a deep, deadly, inextinguishable hatred of the French boiled within his breast.

233

"It happened that at that time, the honest, industrious woodsmen, hunted both by the tax collectors and the landlords, who, stirred up by Hervé de Vaunoy, wished to drive them entirely from the forest, had become desperate, and were determined to oppose force with force. They remained in their cottages during the day, but at night, they assembled in the vast subterraneous caverns under the Wolf's Pit, with which one man had made them acquainted in their hour of need.

"That man was Jean Blanc, who had once discovered the entrance that led to the caverns not more than twenty paces from his father's hut, behind the ruins of the two old mills.

"Jean had once told himself that the hare could strike as a wolf and bite and rend to protect those it loved. Now, there were none left to protect, as all those he had loved had died, so Jean Blanc became a wolf."

"They said something to that effect," interrupted Jude.

"It was also about that time I built this hut, and for certain reasons, which it is not necessary I should detail to you, I took Jean's daughter with me, and have brought her up. When she was very young, she had the white hair of the Albino, with her mother's lovely face and figure, but time has tinged her flowing locks with gold; all traces of her wretched father have disappeared, and she is—as you see her—lovely, kind, and good, The Blossom-of-the-Broom.

"I have nothing more to tell you. You arrived at the castle last night, and must have heard some mention the brave Wolves, for it is the first word the stranger hears when he comes upon this land, and the last when he departs. The avaricious, beggarly small land-holders, who, for the sake of cutting down a few more trees, have snatched the bread from the mouths of five hundred families, now tremble behind the fortified walls of their crumbling manor houses, and not only do the French King's troops fear to show themselves within the confines of the forest, but that fat, luxurious glutton, Monsieur Béchamel, Marquis de Nointel, dreads to send the produce of his rapacity to Paris, because the forest lies between Rennes and the French capital."

"Your Wolves are true Bretons, and, no doubt, good men and true," said Jude, becoming rather impatient, "but I should prefer leaving them at rest for the present, and return to the subject of young Georges Treml."

"My friend," Pelo replied, "there is a greater connection between the Wolves and Treml than you suppose. Monsieur Nicolas—Lord rest his soul —was the last Breton nobleman, and the Wolves are the last Breton men. As for Hervé de Vaunoy, you, true-hearted, faithful Jude, cannot hate him worse than I do. Mathieu Blanc and Sainte are not yet avenged, and the day on which De Vaunoy shall have given the last information he can respecting the fate of Georges, that day, Jean Blanc will reload his old musket, and renew the chase that was interrupted eighteen years ago at the last turning in the forest. But until now, the villain has always escaped. I will tell you that the recent attack upon Castle Boüexis was undertaken solely to get him alive into our hands, but he had left the same night, and those who reached his rooms found only the still warm remains of his supper on the table."

"Hervé de Vaunoy is an experienced, wily fox," said Jude, shaking his head doubtfully.

"But Jean Blanc a patient huntsman," Pelo rejoined. "And his pack numbers two thousand Wolves!"

"Ah!" said Jude, who now began to comprehend the mystery. "Is it so? Can the Albino be the dreaded, mysterious White Wolf?"

"My good friend, seek to know no more at present. Jean is a Wolf, and his hair is still white, but I do not know if it is of he whom the old housekeepers and the timid valets speak during the long evenings in the neighboring mansions. Jean Blanc can do much, but the hand of Heaven still weighs heavily upon him. He is increasingly subject to fearful fits of epilepsy. And most assuredly," added Pelo Rouan, whose voice suddenly cracked, "he could not have told you the story you just heard without suffering great pain, for Jean Blanc never faces his memories without paying the price."

After slowly and painfully uttering these last words, Pelo Rouan fell silent. Suddenly, Jude saw that his eyes had become dilated; the muscles of his face worked convulsively, and cold drops of sweat stood upon his forehead.

"Are you not well?" he cried.

"I pray you, leave me now, for I would be alone," replied the charcoal-burner, with visible effort. "You know all that I could tell you."

"But I cannot help you? What should I do? Should I help Jean Blanc?"

"Leave me!" the charcoal-burner again said in a faint voice. "In the name of God, go! When the time shall come, Jean Blanc will know where to find you."

Jude, surprised, rose and went to the door. Before he had crossed the threshold, Pelo slipped off the bench and fell to the ground, where he screamed with muffled groans. Jude turned around, but the day was waning. The interior of the cottage was growing gloomier, and he saw only a black mass thrashing about through the darkness.

"What ails you, my friend?" he asked again, softening his rough voice.

Only a cry of anguish answered him, then he heard the voice of Pelo Rouan, broken, unrecognizable saying for the third time:

"Go!"

Jude obeyed, as he was not accustomed to taking care of things he did not understand. He mounted his horse and soon forgot Pelo to think only of Jean Blanc and the Wolves, and some means of entrapping Hervé de Vaunoy alive.

While making these plans, he spurred on his horse and rode in the direction of Rennes, where his new master had ordered him to join him.

One could still hear the sounds of the squire's horse under the cover of the trees, and the door of the cabin had barely closed when the Blossom-of-the-Broom lit a lamp. Pelo Rouan lay on the ground in the grip of a furious epileptic fit.

Marie applied herself to relieving Pelo's agony, with the nature of which she was well conversant. She showed no other emotions but the pain she felt.

By the light of the lamp, the interior of the cabin felt more comfortable than it had seemed in the darkness. In one corner was a door leading to Marie's chamber; above the mantelpiece, a brace of pistols and a musket of old workmanship, were hanging against the wall. A clock, with a long pendulum and heavy leaden weights, common to Breton farms, ticked behind the door.

When Pelo's epileptic fit was at its height, a peculiar knock was heard at the door. Marie opened it without the slightest hesitation. A man, dressed in peasants' clothes, but wearing the so-often described mask of wolf-skin, entered.

"Where is the master?" he inquired abruptly.

The Blossom-of-the-Broom pointed to Pelo, then rolling on the earthen floor, churning the foam that gathered round his mouth.

The Wolf, swearing an oath of disappointment, sat down upon the bench, and waited patiently for an hour, hoping the fit would pass, but it did not.

"This is most unfortunate, girl," he said, stamping his foot on the ground. "Tell your father that Yaumi came and waited for him, and that Pelo Rouan will regret all his life not having been able to take advantage of the hour that we just lost."

Just as the Wolf prepared to leave, the charcoal-burner heaved a deep sigh, and extended his contorted limbs.

"He is coming to!" said Marie who held a phial to his lips.

After drinking its contents, Pelo passed his hand across his forehead, wiping off the heavy drops of sweat, shuddered slightly, and, with Marie's help, got back to his feet. Then perceiving the Wolf, he told the girl:

"Leave us!"

She obeyed, but moved slowly, obviously not wanting to leave her father alone after such a fit. Before she had left the room, Pelo asked the Wolf:

"What is it?"

Yaumi threw a defiant look at the girl, moved closer to Pelo, and whispered something in his ear.

"Do you speak the truth?" exclaimed the charcoal-burner. "Has Heaven finally put that man in our hands?"

He rushed towards the door, but Yaumi pulled him back.

"I knew it was of the utmost importance to you, master," he said. "Heaven condemned him a long time ago; you absolved him… But now, the time has come…"

Yaumi pointed at the clock.

"They only gave me two hours to find you, but one has already passed while I saw you suffer from the fits; but…"

Pelo Rouan clenched his fists violently and dropped down on the bench.

"What's the plan?" he inquired.

Yaumi whispered something more in his ear, just as Marie was pulling back the door of her room.

By chance, one word caught her ear. The pretty girl's face changed colors and she purposefully left the door ajar and put her ear to the opening

The word that she had heard was the name of her handsome Captain.

CHAPTER XXVII
The First Béchamel[23]

That same day, Antinoüs Béchamel, Marquis de Nointel, had resolved to launch a decisive attack upon the heart of the "cruel beauty," as he had nicknamed Mademoiselle de Vaunoy. He shortened his usual two-hour nap after lunch, and hastily went down to the kitchens of the castle of La Tremlays, where he loudly summoned the chef.

Béchamel was visiting Monsieur de Vaunoy only as a neighbor, without ceremony. This was damaging for his campaign plans on this important occasion, because it deprived him of the precious advice of his chef, Salomon Bador, who was mentioned with praise in the Memoirs of the times. So he had to rely only on the inspirations of his own genius. Fortunately, said genius was particularly fertile in all areas that concerned the kitchen, and even his most bitter enemies could not ignore the fact that nature had endowed him with a very

---

[23] Béchamel sauce has been considered, since the 17th century, as one of the main sauces of French cuisine. It was originally from Tuscany (the name derives from Balsamell or Besciamella) and was brought to France in 1533 by Catherine de Medici. In 1651, it was renamed after Louis de Béchamel (or Béchameil) (1630-1703) by the famous chef François Pierre La Varenne (1615-1678) in his best-selling book *Le Cuisinier François*. Béchamel was a wealthy tax collector, first for the Duke of Orléans, then from 1692 to his death in Brittany. In 1697, he bought the marquisat of Nointel. He is known for the revision of Breton nobility titles and the creation of new taxes.

special gift when it came to food preparation, and that this royal steward possessed all that the qualities required to have made an excellent *marmiton*.

There is no one who does not wish to show himself to his best advantage in the eyes of the one he loves. Unlike Zeus, Béchamel had no thunder to set his would-be mistresses on fire; his very ordinary plumage did not allow him to parade like a peacock; and he readily acknowledged his mediocrity when it came to the art of eloquence. Because of this, he had undertaken to leave behind the usual, well-worn means of seduction and resolved to charm Mademoiselle de Vaunoy once and for all with the aid of a white sauce of the most perfect and exquisite nature; an original sauce which Alix would be the first to taste, and which he would name after her to immortalize her beauty throughout the centuries to come.

Ovid, Raphael, Petrarch, Titian, Leonardo da Vinci and many other famous lovers had rendered similar honors to their respective mistresses.

We must not think that Monsieur Béchamel had gone down to the kitchens of La Tremlays with only a vague plan. On the contrary, he carried in his head a complete recipe, with the exact quantities of nutmeg, clove and cinnamon. No dramatic epic poem—even the best of them—had ever been more carefully planned and more artfully coordinated than Monsieur Béchamel's supreme achievement. And let us say now that the dish served that day by the royal Intendant lived on for many more years than the comedies or tragedies of today, which expire in a matter of days. It became a universal sauce, immortal, glorious, one that the chefs of five continents shall proudly include on their menus until the end of times.

The chef of La Tremlays put at the disposal of his illustrious and noble colleague all his spices and pans. Monsieur Béchamel gathered his wits about him for ten minutes; then, with the necessary precision, resolutely set to work

Old Goton Réhon, the housekeeper, who was smoking her pipe in a corner of the kitchen, and watched the royal Intendant throughout, was later heard to say that, in all of her life, she had never seen a cook so dedicated to his task.

The royal Intendant paid no attention to the old woman. He had rolled up the sleeves of his coat, pulled back the lace of his shirt, and pushed back his wig. His pink face had become a peculiar shade of royal purple—a color the secret of which was lost with the Romans. His eyes were bright, shining, full of thoughts. His white hands, ringed with diamonds, were handling the saucepan with an indescribable grace. Any impartial observer would have said that he was there, more than anywhere else, in his rightful place.

"O, divine Alix," he murmured tenderly, as the sweet-smelling smoke rose towards the sooty ceiling. "You, who are perfection incarnate, must be gifted with the most delicate of tastes... How could you resist this turbot... Let's add a soupcon of ginger... I would have no choice but to expire at your feet..."

It was the turn of phrase consecrated in that century when lovers spoke in deplorable madrigals, and not otherwise.

Monsieur Béchamel added a pinch of ginger and breathed in to better judge its delicious effect.

"Delicious! Heavenly! Alix, you shall be mine, my cruel beauty! One would have to be a complete savage to resist such an aroma!"

"'Tis true that it smells good," grumbled Dame Goton in her corner.

Monsieur Béchamel put on his monocle and looked at the old woman sitting by the fireplace with an air of modesty and self-satisfaction.

"You are right, old crone! This is a meal worthy of an Empress!"

"It will make a proud stew, true enough," answered Dame Goton while relighting her pipe with gravity, "but, beg your pardon, if I were a man, and a marquis to boot, I think that I would rather handle a sword than a saucepan."

Monsieur Béchamel dropped his monocle and contemptuously turned away from Dame Goton and returned to his task, thinking only of Alix.

Meanwhile, the young woman was not thinking of the royal Intendant in any way; she was seated beside her aunt, Mademoiselle Olive de Vaunoy, in the small salon of La Tremlays, working distractedly at her embroidery. Mademoiselle Olive was occupied in the same manner, but the aging maiden had taken care to place herself in such a way in the room that she was reflected in three mirrors, so that, whichever way she turned her head, she caught a glimpse of her own sweet, smirking self, and the imposing majesty of her coiffure. Every time she drew out her needle, she looked towards the glass; but, as the shining plate was mute, the old lady found the occupation rather tedious, and soon became tired of the ridiculous show.

Several times she endeavored to begin a conversation with her niece on her favorite subjects, namely the defects in the persons, tempers, and dress of all her acquaintances and friends; the relative merits and demerits of the last fashions from Rennes, and Mademoiselle

Scudery's newest romances, which were then still greatly in vogue in Brittany.

Alix replied in monosyllables, without any refer-
ence to the three delightful subjects. Not only had she
not given the proper answers, but she was not listening
at all, which was something even more cruelly mortify-
ing for any interlocutor, and especially overwhelming
for a lady of a certain age in desperate need of gossiping.

"My God, child!" said the aunt, after having made a
tremendous effort to remain silent for almost a minute.
"This is intolerable! I must ask you to tell me where
your mind has been wandering for the past hour."

Alix slowly raised her head and looked at her aunt
with distracted eyes.

"But I agree with you," she said, more or less randomly.

"Again! This is pure reverie, child! Have you fallen
prey to...?"

The day before, Mademoiselle Olive had read in
Clélie [24] that sweet reverie and similar symptoms were
the heralds of true love. She wanted to question her
niece more directly, but did not dare. Alix's firm and
dignified character imposed a sense of reserve on the old
woman. Then Olive commenced a fierce attack upon her
niece's former attachment to Captain Didier, who, she
now firmly believed, had transferred his affections to
herself.

---

[24] *Clélie, Histoire Romaine* is a novel by Madeleine de
Scudéry (1607-1701), published in ten volumes from 1654 to
1660. In it, she invented the famous *Carte du Tendre*, a map of
Arcadia where the geography is based around the theme of
love: the river of Inclination flows past the villages of *Billet
Doux* (love letter), *Petits Soins* (Little Trinkets), etc.

"My darling," she resumed diplomatically. "Don't you think he is a handsome young man?"

"I must see him!" answered Alix resolutely.

"See him, my darling? What do you mean by it, please? There are several ways of 'seeing' someone: a simple conversation, the kind of ordinary encounter that anyone can have; the private conversation, where two people talk while being surrounded by others—that is already more suspicious—and finally, the *tête-à-tête*, which is to be entertained with only the greatest reserve, and to which a young girl must never submit... Did you grant him a *tête-à-tête*, my love?"

When Mademoiselle Olive spoke, usually her niece listened to her, often with heroic patience, But that day, Alix was overwhelmingly preoccupied and her aunt's long tirade passed by her without having any more effect than a background buzz.

"I must ask you again, my love—were you imprudent to grant that man a *tête-à-tête*?" repeated Mademoiselle Olive, with some sourness.

Alix appeared to wake up and looked at her aunt with astonishment.

"I ask you, child," said Olive, barely repressing her bad mood, "to do me the grace of answering my question, if only by a yes or no."

"Of course, auntie."

"So, what is it?"

"Yes, auntie."

Mademoiselle Miss Olive fidgeted uncomfortably on her chair, Alix stood up, curtsied duteously, and left the room.

"At least, she is frank about it," exclaimed Olive, looking at the mirror, which, this time, instead of a smile, reflected an ugly grimace. "'Yes, Auntie' she said, without the least emotion and not the slightest regret. 'Yes, auntie," as if it were the most ordinary thing in the world. 'Yes, auntie,' a secret rendezvous, a lover's plot, like in the novels, and no mystery, all in broad daylight... 'Yes, auntie,' Ah! If ever Cupid had wounded me with one of his burning arrows, what veils wouldn't I have used to cover such weaknesses! I would have murmured the name of my beloved only in the evening breeze. I would have wandered at midnight under the bower, and spent delightful hours contemplating the moon..."

And Mademoiselle Olive de Vaunoy continued to mutter a multitude of delightful poetic things that we regretfully must omit here.

Meanwhile, Alix did not suspect the storm she had just created. Truthfully, she had other things in mind.

She quickly proceeded along the corridor and reached her own chamber where she began to pace back and forth.

"I want to see him," she said again after a few minutes of restless silence.

She took a silk purse from a bedside casket and rang a small silver bell. This bell was to call Mademoiselle Renée, her chambermaid.

Mademoiselle Renée hastily put an end to her own *tête-à-tête* which she was having in a closet with the handsome Yvon, the master of the hunt of La Tremlays, and ran to her mistress's room, passing her fingers through her disordered hair and smoothing her rumpled apron as she went along.

When she made her appearance with the face of simplicity itself, Alix said:

"Go and tell Lapierre that I wish to speak to him at once."

Renée immediately went out and, a few minutes later, Lapierre was ushered into Mademoiselle de Vaunoy's chamber. At his sight, Alix could not repress a small gesture of violent disgust.

Lapierre took off his hat but kept that air of indifferent effrontery, which was natural to him, on his face.

"Mademoiselle asked for me?" he said.

Alix sat down and made a sign to Renée to leave. For a moment, she remained silent and looked down as if she was hesitating to speak.

"Do you wish to stay in the service of Monsieur de Vaunoy" she asked at last with some abruptness.

Another man may have been surprised by this question, but Lapierre was made of sterner mettle.

"Of course, I do, Mademoiselle," he answered.

"Ah. That's unfortunate because I have decided to send you away."

"You, Mademoiselle?"

"Yes, I."

"And am I allowed to ask the reason why?"

"No."

Lapierre lowered his head but smiled under her breath. Alix saw this and blushed.

"You will leave La Tremlays" she continued, repressing an outburst of anger and contempt. "I desire it. It shall be so."

"Damn!" said Lapierre, ironically.

"You shall leave La Tremlays today, right now."

"So soon?"

"Silence! If you go willingly, I will reward you for your obedience."

Alix shook the gold coins inside the silk purse.

"But if you resist, I will have my father throw you out," she concluded.

247

"Really?" said Lapierre, appearing not to care.

"Do you want this gold?"

"Yes, of course, but I want to stay too... Unless, of course," he added with irony, "Mademoiselle deigns to tell me how a poor devil like myself was able to attract the hatred of such a noble lady... I am quite curious to find out."

"Hatred?" repeated Alix, whose traits expressed only more contempt. "You're mad. But I will tell you why your stay at the castle has become impossible. It is because you are a murderer, Lapierre."

"So?" he said, without being moved in the least.

"I do not know what there could be in common between a man like you and Captain Didier," continued Alix.

"Ah, ah! There it is!" interrupted Lapierre, loudly enough to be heard.

"Silence! Or I will have you whipped for your insolence. I do not know what compelled you to commit this crime, but it was you who last year savagely attacked Captain Didier in the streets of Rennes."

"Ah, but you're wrong, Mademoiselle."

Alix pulled the copper medal that the reader already knows from her bodice.

"It is useless to lie," she continued. "It was I who bandaged your wounds when you were brought back to the castle, and I found this very medal, which I knew belonged to Captain Didier, on you. You stole it from him, probably believing it was made of gold."

"And you, Mademoiselle," said Lapierre smiling, "have kept it precious since then, even though it is only made of copper."

"Do you still deny it?" asked Alix, without deigning to answer.

248

"What good would it do?"

"Then you no longer refuse to leave the castle?"

"I'm afraid I still do," replied the villain.

"Are you insane, you miserable wretch?" exclaimed Mademoiselle de Vaunoy. "I shall denounce you to my father!"

Lapierre burst out laughing. Alix arose indignant.

"This is too much!" she said. "As soon as my father returns…"

"Who knows if he even will, Mademoiselle," said Lapierre in a low voice

"What do you mean?" asked Alix, now with a sense of worry.

Lapierre opened his mouth to speak, but held back. His smile of reckless irony returned to his lips.

"We are all mortal," he said, "and man is exposed to die seven times in a single day. That's all I meant to say, Mademoiselle. As for your threat, you made it; let's not speak of it again. But I will beg you, in the future, please refrain from issuing threats. It is humiliating to threaten a servant in vain."

"On my mother's grave!" exclaimed Alix, exasperated by this latest provocation. "I do not threaten in vain! Monsieur de Vaunoy shall know everything!"

"You should change the tense. I know a little grammar, Instead of the future tense, speak in the present, and you will tell the truth, Mademoiselle,"

"I… I do not understand," stammered Alix, who became suddenly very pale.

"I think you do, Mademoiselle, and very clearly. Believe me, it is better if you do not force me to dot the i."

"Explain yourself," said Alix with great effort.

"As you will. The exquisite common sense which which you are gifted made you realize at once that there could be no enmity between a honest lad like myself and a fatherless child like Captain Didier. This enmity indeed did not exist. But fate was unfair to me; I am only a servant, and therefore the hatred of others may become my own, and to earn my wages, I may be compelled to draw my sword just as if I really hated someone…"

"You're lying," interrupted the young girl in distress.

"You know full well that I am not. I only tried to kill him because I was ordered to do so."

"Oh! So you dare to accuse my father you unspeakable villain!"

"I? Did I utter the name of the very respected Monsieur Hervé de Vaunoy? I don't think so. But a word to the wise is enough. Good day, Mademoiselle."

"You're lying, you're lying," repeated Alix whose mind was reeling.

"Let's pretend that I did, Mademoiselle, if that makes you happy. But whether I lied or not, if, as I believe, you exhibit some interest in Captain Didier, do not waste your time threatening a man who cannot fear you… A man who, by the way, is only a mere weapon. You must either stop the arm who brandishes that weapon, or muzzle your own heart."

He stopped and added in a lower voice:

"And when your father returns—if he does—you must act without wasting a minute."

After uttering these words, Lapierre bowed deeply and took his leave with all the appearance of the most perfect calm.

Alix had not heard his last words, but she had heard enough. As soon as the servant had left, she collapsed in her seat and took her head in her hands. A storm of heartbreaking thoughts ran through her brain.

"My father... my father..." she whispered through her sobs. "I do not want to believe it... This miserable liar..."

A fearful suspicion that would sometimes cross her mind was almost confirmed: it was her father who had ordered the assassination of Didier.

But why?

She got up and staggering to the mantel piece, she rang the bell again. She wanted to tell Didier to flee from this castle where his life was threatened; she wanted to tell him... But what could she tell him without accusing her father?

Renée, responding to the call, found her young mistress lying in a swoon upon the floor. Alix had succumbed to her emotions.

As a result of her fainting, a terrible fever took hold of her, she suffered from delirium, and the physician who came from Rennes to attend to her saw in it the symptoms of a serious—possibly even fatal—illness.

Meanwhile, the hour of dinner came as if nothing had happened. Monsieur Béchamel left the kitchens and entered the living room, followed by his incomparable, new white sauce.

The worthy Intendant had an air both modest and yet proud. He seemed to savor in advance the unanimous praise with which his masterpiece of culinary art would be welcomed, and was already preparing a madrigal with which he intended to offer to Mademoiselle de Vaunoy the honor of attaching her name to this newborn dish. Certainly, it was not a small boon for the beautiful Alix. It was immortality itself, for the dish was nothing less than a turbot fish in béchamel sauce, the first of all future *Béchamelles*.

Unfortunately, fate is entirely random and quickly negates the designs of men. The virginity of this precious new dish was to be despoiled only by the poorly educated palates of two infamous servants.

When he entered the dining-room, Monsieur Béchamel smiled his most brilliant smile to greet his hosts, but it was a pure waste for there were none.

Hervé de Vaunoy had still not returned, Alix was in the grip of atrocious suffering, Mademoiselle Olive was looking after her, no one knew where Captain Didier was.

Realizing this, Monsieur Béchamel, normally so calm, became violently angry. Insulted to have no one there to savor the merits of his new dish, he asked for his coach to be readied forthwith. Then, he left and galloped back to his mansion of La Cour Rose.

The exquisite turbot in béchamel sauce remained untouched on the table.

An hour after, Alain the steward and Lapierre entered the dining room by chance and saw the dish.

"He won't be back," said Lapierre.

"You're a bird of ill-omen" said old Alain. "He will be back."

They were talking about Hervé de Vaunoy.

The two servants eventually ate the turbot without further ceremony. One must believe that the new sauce proved to be to their liking because, ten minutes later, there was not a single drop of it left.

"He still isn't back," repeated Lapierre, throwing himself back in his seat like a man who has eaten more than he should.

"He will be," repeated Alain, who put the neck of a square bottle into his wide mouth. "Do you want any?"

"Gladly! If he does not return, we might not lose anything. The little soldier, Captain Didier, has a generous heart and his hand is always open... He will buy what we have to sell at a good price."

"What if he hangs us instead?"

"Come on!"

Then they heard three hard knocks on the outside door. The two servants jumped off their seats.

"It's Monsieur de Vaunoy!" said the old steward.

"Or Captain Didier," said Lapierre. "I have an idea. If it's Didier, why don't we tell him everything? De Vaunoy is a miser. We're rotting away serving him."

Alain hesitated and took a swill from his bottle. After he had drunk, he no longer hesitated.

"Let's shake on it!" he said cheerfully. "If it's Didier, we will talk... And if De Vaunoy returns, he'll be too late. But what if it's De Vaunoy?"

"Then it clear to me for that Satan has him under his protection, and may God save the soul of Captain Didier!"

"*Amen!*" replied Master Alain.

They heard footsteps in the antechamber.

The two servants got up; their eyes were fixated on the door.

"Something tells me that it's the Captain," murmured Lapierre.

"I think it's De Vaunoy," countered the steward.

"Shall we bet on it?" asked Lapierre.

"Yes!"

"One écu if it's the Captain."

"And one if it's De Vaunoy."

CHAPTER XXVIII
Amongst the Wolves

During the time the charcoal-burner was narrating Jean Blanc's sad history to Jude Leker, a man wrapped up closely in a large cloak was seen carefully and painfully descending one of the steep banks of the Wolf's Pit. At every other moment, as he paused in the descent, he cast uneasy, wary glances round him, but kept continually in motion, although he seemed convinced he was incurring extraordinary danger.

When he reached the bottom of the ravine, in front of the hollow oak where Nicolas Treml had buried the iron chest, he stopped to take breath.

"I hope they haven't spotted me yet," he murmured, his teeth chattering with fright.

The hope was a vain one, and probably the emotion that made all his limbs tremble so violently had partially impeded the clearness of his vision, or he would, undoubtedly, have seen that several men, with wolf skin masks upon their faces, had been closely watching him as he descended.

At the moment he attempted to renew his course towards the spot where the hut of Mathieu Blanc had once stood, four of them started from their hide outs, threw themselves upon him, and hurled him to the ground.

"Who the Devil are you?" one of the Wolves cried, putting his foot upon the breast of the prostrate man.

The stranger did not lose his presence of mind at that awful moment, and tried to hide his face.

"Friends," he shouted in a trembling voice, "do not ill-treat me! I have come for a good reason..."

"He's a spy from the collector-general!" cried one of the Wolves.

"Let's hang him from the first convenient tree," shouted another.

"Holy mother, my friends!" the man exclaimed in an agony of fright, "do not think of committing such an crime, my friends! As I told you, I've come here for your special interest..."

"He's lying!"

"Upon my soul, I'm not! Bandage my eyes, if you will, so that I cannot see anything you wish to keep concealed, and then take me to your chief, whom I much desire to meet."

The Wolves held counsel apart. One of them, a sturdy cobbler named Simon Lion, said:

"We can always hang him later."

The others loudly approved.

However, a basket-weaver named Livaudré added:

"But we should see his face first!"

Simon Lion then snatched the cloak from the man's ashy face, which was drooping upon his chest, and all exclaimed in amazement:

"The Lord of La Tremlays!"

Hervé de Vaunoy—for it was he!—tried to smile, but only produced a convulsive twitching of the mouth.

"Yes, my good friends," he said, "it is I, the Lord of La Tremlays."

"We are not your friends," growled Livaudré, in a threatening voice. "Could you have, by chance, stumbled on the one path in the forest that had led you to your certain death?"

"Come, come," stuttered Hervé de Vaunoy. "You jest, my good comrade. One never talks of hanging a man who brings a fortune in his pocket."

The Wolves exchanged meaningful glances, and Simon tapped the prisoner's empty pockets.

"You lie, you villain, as you have always have done," he said, "but by the Devil, you won't escape us now."

De Vaunoy's terror reached its apex and increased the danger he was in for it cost him his common sense and speech.

By way of proving the sincerity of the last statement, Livaudré undid a cord that was wound like a girdle around his waist, tied one end fast to a stout branch of an oak tree, and made a slip knot in the other, bringing the noose so as to dangle immediately before the nobleman's eyes.

It must not be supposed that when Monsieur de Vaunoy had left the castle, he had not calculated the chances of his perilous enterprise; but he had calculated them without reflecting on his own cowardice, and now his pusillanimity and terror were well nigh his undoing.

He had left La Tremlays in a moment of desperate resolution, which sometimes makes brave men of cowards; his hate of Didier—or rather his intense, overwhelming desire to get rid of the obstacle that was forever in his way—had obscured the magnitude of the danger from him, and made the chances of success appear much greater than they really were.

He could do nothing of himself against the Captain's life, as he was both the King's officer and his own personal guest; but it was necessary that the young officer should disappear forever, because, for Hervé, it was a matter of fortune and position, and would become soon one of life and death.

By a strange destiny, Didier was opposed to Hervé de Vaunoy on three points at once: the love Alix entertained for him, and her consequent dislike of Monsieur Béchamel, were, in themselves, sufficient causes of enmity, because at that moment when the Parliament of Rennes were incessantly occupied with searching into the numerous assumptions of titles of nobility that were put forward in the province, it was imperative that the Intendant should remain his friend, for it was most probable that if he were not, the usurper would lose his title, and the rich heritage of Treml. Apart from those powerful motives, there was one even more potent still; it was impossible that Didier and himself could both coexist in harmony.

Thus, the intelligent reader will have divined, if we have not completely failed in depicting the idiosyncrasy of Hervé de Vaunoy's character, that he must have had some very extraordinary motive in proceeding to the Wolf's Pit, the lair of those whom he had hunted and persecuted for so long, and braving, as it were, the lion in his den.

A truly resolute, brave man, after making such a determination, would have laid down a definite form of action, and carried the greatest coolness with him to its execution; but the present Lord of La Tremlays was a man of another mould. In traversing the forest, he had been alternately the sport of the most abject terror and the wildest hopes. Now, when acuteness, readiness of thought and action, and presence of mind were requisite to snatch him from the jaws of death, his knees knocked together, and he was already half dead with fear, like those unfortunates who, after being thrown from the top of tower, are believed to have died before hitting the ground.

Without saying another word, Simon Lion took Hervé de Vaunoy in his stalwart arms, and placed him, like an infant, beneath the fatal tree, where the dastardly coward remained motionless, whilst Livaudré passed the loop of the cord over his head and gave it a sharp jerk round his throat, making his eyes stare more wildly still.

"Pull!" ordered Livaudré.

Two ready and willing hands caught the slack of the rope, and Hervé's feet just about left the ground.

As we can see, Lapierre's presentments were not without some foundation.

But just as the rope drove purple blood into Hervé de Vaunoy's pale cheeks, another Wolf rushed through the brush wood.

"Come, L'il Yaumi," said one of the executioners pausing for a moment. "Come and say a last farewell to a very dear friend of ours!"

L'il Yaumi, whom we met earlier when he had come to fetch Pelo Rouan, was a strapping fellow, above six feet tall. He recognized Hervé de Vaunoy at once, despite the hideous contraction of his features.

"Stupid fools," he muttered. "They are going to kill him."

He drew a long sharp wood knife from his pocket, and severed the cord with one blow, thereby letting the half-inanimate body fall heavily upon the grass.

"A pretty piece of work you would have done, you fools," Yaumi exclaimed. "Don't you remember what the Master's orders are, if this fellow, for whom simple hanging is too good, should ever be captured—that he was to be brought to him alive? Is the Master near at hand?"

"The Devil knows where the Master is," Livaudré replied in a surly tone, "but this villain shall not get off that easily. We shall see whether the Council of Elders will decide or not that he should swing."

"The Elders must obey the Master, just as you and I, comrade," said Yaumi in a sententious tone. "They will do what he decides."

Meanwhile, Hervé de Vaunoy was twisting on the grass.

"Get up, brute!" Lion said, giving him a hearty kick.

De Vaunoy, who, in fact, was more frightened than hurt, rubbing his neck where the cord had galled it, raised himself to a sitting position on the sward. By some strange reaction, having narrowly escaped death had given him a new vigor.

"Do not let your Wolves ill-treat me," he told Yaumi in a firmer voice. "That bit of rope almost cost you half a million livres."

Yaumi's only reply was a shrug of disbelief, but the other Wolves muttered among themselves:

"Half a million livres!"

De Vaunoy breathed easier; the seed had been planted.

"Take me to your chief!" he repeated, in an imperious tone.

"Now," muttered Yaumi, shrugging his broad shoulders, "they're going to let him go. Ah! I'd give an écu for the Master to be here."

Simon the Lion bound De Vaunoy's eyes with a checkered handkerchief, and the confederates partly led, partly dragged, him to the western side of the ravine, on the top of which the ruins of the mills were situated.

Gradually, De Vaunoy felt the air become more damp; the glimmering of the light that pierced through the handkerchief disappeared entirely; occasionally, he was made to descend what, in his partial blindness, seemed almost perpendicular precipices; sometimes he was supported by the robust arms of the Wolves over uneven, broken ground.

After about ten minutes, he heard the confused noise of several voices, smelled the odor of brandy and tobacco, and then the handkerchief was removed roughly from his eyes.

He was in the great cave of the Wolves—just in time for dessert.

The red light of many torches at first pained his eyes, accustomed so long to darkness: he receded involuntarily from their glare, and his heart again sank when he heard the universal shout of gratified deep hatred with which his presence was hailed, and the hoarse clamor for his death which resounded on all sides.

But suddenly, comparative calm was restored when Simon Lion uttered three magic words: the noise subsided, and the deadly denunciations were turned into wondering exclamations of:

"Half a million livres!"

This whispering in some ways reassured Hervé de Vaunoy, and taking heart of grace, he determined to assume a high tone of protection, and act his part like a brave man.

However, the scene that met his view, when his eyes became accustomed to the smoky light, was not one that would convey an impression of complete security to a nervous man. He perceived that he was in an extensive cavern, the boundaries of which were not visible, and around him were groups of men, seated without the least regard to order, at tables, composed of roughly hewn, unplaned planks, supported upon thick stakes driven into the earth; and, as the torches were all fixed in one clump in the centre of the cave, the light became more feeble as it radiated into the remote portions of this cavern, and gave a dusky, unearthly appearance to the swarthy countenances that were seen on every side. It was impossible to give even a guess at the number of the band assembled in their subterranean hold; those farthest off in the deep shade, seemed prolonged indefinitely; and, on the other hand, when the torches would sparkle from the ignition of fresh resin, and cast forth new light, crowds of hardy faces seemed to spring from the dusky corners of the retreat.

All these drinkers and smokers were Wolves, honest sons of the forest, which, we are certain, exhibited during the day good-natured physiognomies. But the bloody glow of the torches put on their features an expression of savage ferocity. If they were good men, they did not look the part, and their gathering would have made a wonderful subject for a painting by the young graduates who produce bleak and melodramatic canvases for the so-called Spanish wing of the Louvre

Hervé de Vaunoy recognized several cobblers and weavers he had seen in the forest. Two or three men had put on their masks the moment they saw who he was; but despite the flittering play of the light and shadows, they could not disguise from him that they wore the livery of La Tremlays.

Precisely in the center of this vault, or cave, or cavern (since neither the walls nor the vault could be seen, it was difficult to assign a precise name to that place) was a table of rather better workmanship than the rest, around which nine old Wolves were seated—the "senators" of this strange republic.

But of the White Wolf, himself the great dictator, there were no signs of his dreaded mask. As no particular attention was paid to any individual, Hervé inferred that he was not present.

After a few minutes, one of the old men bade the rest be silent, and on his command being obeyed, he turned towards Hervé de Vaunoy, who was still struggling to regain his composure, and asked:

"What has brought you, vile oppressor, to the Wolf's Pit?"

"I came to seek what I have found," Hervé replied, gathering all of his courage. "I came to see the Wolves."

"It is a sight that may cost you much, Hervé de Vaunoy. Have you forgotten all the injuries you have done us?"

"No, but I relied upon your good sense, your own interest, and also upon your misery, which I thought," he added in a lower tone, "was greater than what I see here."

"We live in the best way we can," the old man continued. "The likes of you have tried to steal our black bread and our cider; but being thieves, we now eat white bread and drink brandy."

A scornful laugh from the Wolves accompanied these remarks, with shouts of:

"Bravo, bravo, Père Toussaint!"

"Peace, my sons, peace!" the old man replied. "As for our good sense, thank you for the compliment; but what is it that you want from our good sense, which tells us we should hang you, and from our misery, which you have made so grinding and complete?"

"I seek revenge!" Hervé de Vaunoy briefly exclaimed.

"Have you dismissed your liveried murderers from La Tremlays?"

"Enough! A truce, my friend," said Hervé de Vaunoy, with momentary impatience. "Let us talk like men, and come to business at once. Would you like to earn half a million livres?"

"Half a million livres!" burst from all the Wolves at once.

"Half a million lies, more like it!" shouted the rough voice of Little Yaumi, who came from out the crowd of Wolves, and stood upright before the table of the old men. "Père Toussaint, my friends," he continued, "don't believe one word this scoundrel says. Do you not know what an accomplished liar he is? Besides, in the Master's absence, nothing can be decided."

De Vaunoy pricked up his ears as the word "Master." That was a new contingence for which he had not planned.

Père Toussaint shook his head doubtfully and observed:

"The Master is the Master, no doubt, friend Yaumi, but we all count for something, and purses of half a million livres are not to be picked up in the forest every day; this fellow's proposition deserves consideration."

"But he is a liar," Yaumi reiterated.

A general murmur of disapprobation followed this observation, for the Wolves, to say the truth, were powerfully tempted by the prospect of earning half a million livres.

"Yaumi, my man," Père Toussaint continued, feeling himself supported by the crowd, "I pray you, let us manage our affairs in our own way; the Master will be satisfied with what we do."

"But what if he is not?"

No one said anything. The old man was visibly hesitating.

"He will be," he finally said after a long silence. "No one is more willing than I to obey the orders of the Master. But…"

"But will you run the risk of disobeying him, when you are told, as I tell you now, that he would give every drop of his heart's blood to have this man standing alive, a prisoner before him."

Hervé de Vaunoy trembled from head to foot as he heard this.

"I know that the Master has a long account to settle with this oppressor," continued Yaumi. "Detain him here whilst I go and seek him."

"Do you know where to find him?" Père Toussaint asked.

"Not exactly, but I think I know where it is most likely. Wait for me to return."

"You can't do this!" Hervé de Vaunoy cried impetuously, staking his life upon one throw. "All will be for nought if I am not back at La Tremlays in two hours."

"Two hours will be enough," said Yaumi.

The old men consulted. And so great was the authority of the Master—who was none other than the White Wolf himself—that despite their violent desire to earn half a million livres, the crowd came to Yaumi's assistance.

"Yes… He's right," murmured the Wolves on all sides. "The Master must be alerted."

"Go then," said Père Toussaint. "But if you haven't returned in two hour, we will decide without him."

However, Yaumi did not move.

"Before I go, I must know everything that this man wants."

"That is just," replied Père Toussaint. "Hervé de Vaunoy, tell us what you want from us."

"The half a million livres," started the villain, "represent the product of the taxes collected from the Bishopric of Dol, which the Intendant is sending up to Paris. They have planned to spend one night at La Tremlays. That should be enough time for you to act."

"More than enough!" said Père Toussaint.

"More than enough!" repeated the Wolves.

"As for the man I want you to kill, he is your enemy too; he is the new Captain of the Maréchaussée."

"Were he ten times worse than that, Hervé de Vaunoy," said Père Toussaint in a tone which was not without some regrets, "do not hope for our assistance in this matter. The Wolves are not assassins."

"Be it so, then, my friend: Let your Wolves attack the castle, seize the half million, and keep all the profits—I shall do the rest!"

Père Toussaint shook his head with satisfaction.

"We can agree to this," he said. "In good conscience, we can… Yaumi, do you know enough now?"

"Yes. I shall leave now."

Yaumi put on his wolf mask and started immediately on his quest, vanishing in the shadows.

Hervé de Vaunoy was unbound, invited to sit down, and refreshments were placed before him.

Two hours, he thought with anguish. *Two hours… And if if this "Master comes", what will be my fate?*

The wolves had resumed smoking and drinking, because these poor people, once honest and hard-working artisans, after having been thrown violently out of their ordinary lives, had embraced nearly all the vices that come from idleness and thievery.

Hervé de Vaunoy had put his watch in front of him and counted the minutes. From time to time, the voice of Père Toussaint asked some details in order to better plan their attack on the castle. It interrupted his painful reverie, but that was a good thing, because if the Lord of La Tremlays had not been thus distracted from his fear, it would have killed him.

An hour passed, then an hour and a half, then the hand in his watch passed the two-hour mark.

Hervé de Vaunoy took a long and deep breath, struck the oaken table violently with his hand, started up, and exclaimed joyously that he was free.

"By my faith, it is true," said Père Toussaint, secretly delighted that Yaumi had not returned, and now fully anticipating the possession of the money. "Honest men keep their words, the Wolves are honest fellows, and so their words must be kept."

"It is true," approved the Wolves.

"So you can leave," continued Père Toussaint. "Your life will be forfeit if you betray us Tomorrow, one hour after sunset, we shall be at the agreed-upon place."

"Tomorrow, then," said Hervé de Vaunoy who was already ahead of his guide on his way to the entrance of the cavern.

His eyes were bound again, and a quarter-of-an-hour later, he was on his start, galloping through the forest at the topmost of his horse's speed, plunging the spurs into his flanks at every stride.

"Oh my Good Lord! I made it! Oh my Good Lord!" he kept repeating foolishly

It was he, then, who knocked so heavily at the main door of the castle, and entered the dining room at the moment the bet between the old steward Alain and Lapierre was made.

He threw himself, with palpitating heart, into an armchair.

"He is mine—he is mine!" the villain muttered to himself. "I staked my life against his: I have won, and by all the powers of Hell, I will not spare him. But I swear to God, I shall never try something like this again!"

"Take your écu, Alain," said Lapierre. "You have won, and it is as I have said—may Heaven save the Captain's soul!"

CHAPTER XXIX
Before the Attack

The wagons containing the treasure left Rennes on the following morning, escorted by a troop of the Maréchaussée, and a company of the sergeants of the city, all armed to the teeth, and commanded by Captain Didier.

The distance between Rennes and the castle of La Tremlays was traveled over without the least obstruction, although, whilst the heavy wagons, laden with six livres coins, dragged their weary way through the mazes of the forest. An attack upon them would have been easily made, but no insurgents were seen upon the route. Jude's keen eyes, however, occasionally deduced from tiny motions in the underwood, that men, or at least some wild animals, were lurking in the coverts.

He thought that the Wolves did not care to confront the trusty guns and sabers of the Maréchaussée—unless they had another plan in mind.

The progress of the convoy was necessarily very slow, and the sun was sinking in the west, as it reached the long avenue of elms that led to the castle.

Jude rode up to the Captain, and whispered to him:

"Monsieur, it is not good for me to be at the castle. What I'm looking for is not there; and on the other hand, I might find there what I do not care to find."

"My good friend," the Captain replied, with a smile, "since last evening, you have dreamed of nothing but midnight assassins, and, yes, if all you have told me about Hervé de Vaunoy is true, he is indeed a scoundrel and a brazen murderer, but I cannot believe that he would… Who can even tell whether that charcoal-burner told you the truth!"

"Do you think Pelo Rouan lied, Monsieur? No, on my faith, he spoke the truth, for his whole behavior, and the tone of his voice, were those of an honest man. Dame Goton's story too, and the mysterious disappearance of the child! Every circumstance tends to confirm his tale."

"Well, you may be right. At any rate, I will dispense with your attendance tonight. If you have any friend in the forest, enjoy his hospitality for the night, and meet me tomorrow at Vitré."

"I shall see you tomorrow, then!" said Jude.

He was about to leave, but he turned back and whispered another word to his young master:

"Do not forget what I said, Monsieur. Pelo Rouan spoke of a terrible revenge, and he looked very grim when he said it."

But Didier smiled again and made a gesture of care-free bravado.

"See you tomorrow, my brave friend," he said.

Jude touched his hat respectfully, gave his horse to a soldier, and leisurely took his way down one of the by-paths.

Twilight was setting in, but it was already dark within the leafy wood, and the clearings alone retained some faint traces of the great orb of day which was now below the horizon.

As the stout squire walked slowly on, lost in dark thoughts, the high courage that had sustained him until then drooped, and he felt that all hope had fled. He thought it would be useless to search longer for the youthful heir, whom there was now, it seemed, no chance of finding, and he needed the remembrance of his dying master's charge, and all his devotion to the noble house he had so long served, to keep him on the path he had traced out for himself. Had there been personal peril to encounter, he would have met it and perished cheerfully; but now there was no death to brave, no danger to confront. If the House of Treml would not reap the benefit of the efforts, what then was the point of fighting?

Thinking thus, he roused himself from his reverie, and looking round him to ascertain where he was, took the direction of the charcoal-burner's hut.

"We will talk about Treml," he said, sighing. "Maybe he might have found something new since yesterday…"

He had scarcely proceeded twenty paces, when a sound familiar to an experienced soldier fell upon his ear.

He stopped, and listening attentively, heard the steps of a large number of men advancing through the forest, which could not be those of the military escort, for they came from the other side, and had not the regular, measured tread of troops.

Jude did not like to take a guess. He was still puzzling over this when the noise became louder. Stepping aside from the beaten path, he concealed himself behind the trunk of a massive tree.

A few minutes afterwards, under the murky light, he saw a hundred armed men issuing rapidly from the woods, marching in disorder on the path he had just left, and more were joining them all the time.

It was a terrifying sight because all wore a wolf's-skin mask, the rear being brought up by a man of sinewy frame, who, from his disguise, the squire guessed was the notorious White Wolf himself. This fantastic creature passed Jude's hiding-place some fifty yards behind the rest. The squire could see that his eyes glared like a panther's through the snow-white mask. He looked around for a few seconds, and then, with a few fantastic leaps, rejoined his men.

Jude remained for some time uncertain what to do. He was well aware that this irregular body of men were the Wolves, but he could not conceive what their purpose was in being abroad in such a number. He asked himself this question, but did not answer it right away, although the words of the Wolves whispering to each other as they passed by could have put him on the right track.

Then, he resumed his march to Pelo Rouan's cabin. As he walked through the forest's now deserted paths, his mind was working and now the vague words he had heard the Wolves whisper came back to him like so many threats...

The door of Pelo's cabin was closed when he reached it. He knocked loudly, but no one answered.

"It is surprising," he murmured, unknowingly intertwining his present disappointment and the object of his recent preoccupation. "This singular, white-masked figure whom I just saw walk by—the eyes I saw glaring through his white mask—they had the same expression as those that glistened in Pelo's head the other day, when he told me his tale in the obscurity of his cabin... Open up, my friend! Open to the Squire of Treml!"

There was response. But suddenly, he heard a series of knocks coming from the other side of the cabin, as if they intended to mock or imitate those he liberally made the door.

Jude went around to the other side and saw, by the faint light of the rising moon, the shutters of a window tremble and shake, evidently under the impetus of some-one from within trying to get out.

As he stood upon his guard, wondering what all this violence could mean, one of the shutters was dashed out and fell at his feet. A second later, he saw a young girl of exquisite proportions stand balancing herself upon the window sill, then jump to the ground with the lightness of a sylph, throw herself upon her knees, and raise her clasped hands in the attitude of prayer.

"Holy Virgin of the Forest!" she murmured, "pre-serve his life: in mercy, save him, and I vow to you a candle, a wreath of flowers, and my golden cross. Save him, and I swear to be your votary forever!"

The girl then rose from her knees—without seeing Jude—kissed a small copper medal suspended around her neck, and disappeared with the speed of the wind down the path that led to the castle.

"The Blossom-of-the-Broom!" the squire ex-claimed, totally bemused, after the girl was out of sight. "But whom does she wish to save? And the Wolves—what are they about to attack?"

As often, light broke out of the darkness. Pressing both his hands upon his forehead to concentrate his dis-ordered thought, a sudden idea came upon him, and he said, in a husky, broken voice:

"Captain Didier! She loves him, but Pelo hates him. He would kill him, but the daughter would save him: And the treasure, and the Wolves—by all the blood of Treml, there shall be one there to strike a blow in his defense!"

He turned hastily from the cabin, seeming to have recovered the agility and power of his youthful years, and retraced his way through the forest towards the cas-tle of La Tremlays with gigantic strides.

At that moment he felt, for the first time, the full force of the indefinable attachment which he felt for his young, new master. This honest and faithful nature needed a living man to whom to devote himself; the memory of Treml was not enough. Satisfying the eternal need to obey and love was everything to Jude, who was at heart a very moral man

When he arrived at the small iron gate that closed the home paddocks next the castle of La Tremlays, he felt an ever greater anguish, knowing as he did—because he was a child of the forest—that innumerable men were lying in close ambush near him. He felt instinctively that the castle was surrounded by a host of enemies.

But, as yet, all was quiet, and he hesitated to ring the bell there, for fear the steward should appear and recognize him. Should he enter by that gate or the main gate that opened directly into the castle's courtyard, the danger of discovery, he knew, would be equally as great. Jude had forgotten that the life that he had sworn to give to Treml no longer belonged to him, and only his zeal to save the Captain had made him forget his oath.

Fortunately, whilst he remained undecided what to do, he perceived the light of a lantern glimmering at some distance from him. Soon after, he saw the portly figure of Dame Goton, bearing an enormous bunch of keys, making her nightly rounds, by virtue of her office, to see that all the gates were closed.

Dame Goton and Jude were too good friends for the reader to have the slightest anxiety about the resolution of the old squire's embarrassing predicament. We shall let the good woman admit him inside the castle with all the required discretion, and instead we shall transport ourselves to the dining room where the guests were having supper with Monsieur Hervé de Vaunoy.

The repast was of the most sumptuous description, in order to do honor to the king's officers. Monsieur Béchamel, Marquis de Nointel, who had slept upon his anger, had thought it judicious to return to La Tremlays, and personally watch over the royal treasure until it passed the boundaries of the province over which his power extended. He had concocted a second and even more delicious version of his Béchamel sauce and, as usual, ate of every high-seasoned delicacy. The officer in command of the municipal force from Rennes found the wines excellent; and Didier was as frank and joyful as ever, not minding the obnoxious displays of hospitality manifested by Hervé de Vaunoy.

The presence of Alix was alone wanting, for she was still suffering in her room from the fever by which she was attacked the evening before, but her place was supplied by her aunt, Mademoiselle Olive de Vaunoy, who sat at the head of the table, and did the honors with a grace that she presumed internally was finding its way, at every second, straight to the Captain's heart.

The host was politely attentive to his guests, and poured the wine liberally. Once in a while, when he could do so perfectly unseen, he exchanged meaningful glances with Alain and Lapierre, who waited on the table, with the other servants gathered in the room for the occasion. While offering a thousand courtesies to the young Captain, the nobleman seemed to blame his two henchmen for the delay, and hardly contained his impatience.

After the first course was removed, the roast meats and entrées were placed upon the table, surrounded by a circle of fine pastries. De Vaunoy now called for rich wines of the south to be served, which gave the greatest satisfaction to Monsieur Béchamel and the officer from

Rennes. The claret was poured out by the men behind each chair, but at the moment that Didier held up his glass, he saw his host exchange a rapid glance with the servant, who stood immediately at his back, and turning suddenly around, he saw it was Lapierre.

The mountebank bore the fierce scrutiny unmoved, and as he retired in obedience to an imperious gesture from the youth, the latter openly threw the wine upon the floor. He then made an imperious gesture to Lapierre, ordering him to move away, which the servant immediately obeyed by bowing with feigned respect.

De Vaunoy became pale, as he said:

"Does my Guyenne not suit my young guest's palate?" he asked with a fawning smile.

"Do not say this, my friend," interrupted Monsieur Béchamel, who had been looking to say something clever since the soup, "or the good Captain will sue you for slander in front of our parliament."

That said, he felt the need to burst out laughing.

"Monsieur de Vaunoy," replied Didier with a formal bow, "excuse me if I request that that man," pointing to Lapierre, "does not come near me. I have good reasons for making the request."

"Of course!" said the nobleman. "You, leave!" he shouted at Lapierre.

Then, turning again towards Didier, he continued:

"Please, I beg you, select among my servants whosoever you wish to serve you, Would you like to be attended by my own steward?"

Now this was literally falling from Scylla into Charybdis; for Lapierre, before leaving the room in obedience to his master's order, had first secretly passed the bottle he held in his hand, to Alain the steward, who immediately had taken his place behind the Captain's chair.

Didier could not have any suspicion of a man whom he had never seen; so he held out his glass to the steward, who filled it to the brim.

"Let's drink to the King's health!" said Hervé de Vaunoy, standing up.

All the guests toasted, except Mademoiselle Olive who, being a woman, was not obliged to do so.

"To the King's health!" repeated Didier, emptying his glass.

Hervé de Vaunoy smiled almost imperceptibly and made an almost imperceptible sign to Alain, who quietly went to the window, and threw the empty flask into the yard.

No one noticed this incident and the supper continued as if nothing had happened.

A few minutes later, Captain Didier ceased to reply to the gracious compliments and attentions that Mademoiselle Olivia was heaping on him. His head began to droop involuntarily, and his eyes would close in spite of his persevering efforts to keep them open.

"Holy Mother!" said De Vaunoy, casting a malicious glance at Didier, "our young friend is by no means complaisant this evening; he spills our good wine upon the floor, and then goes fast asleep. Have you thrown a soporific spell around him, sister, with one of your old-world stories?"

Olivia did not deign to reply to this impertinent insinuation, and shot a dark glance at her brother.

"It is impossible to comprehend why he would not drink your marvelous Guyenne wine," said Monsieur Béchamel, candidly.

"Well, well," Hervé rejoined, "we will excuse this little defect in an honored officer of His Majesty, and he shall even be conveyed to his chamber in his chair, that we may not disturb his deep repose."

In obedience to a sign from their master, two servants lifted up the Captain's chair, and bore him to his room.

This greatly delighted Monsieur Béchamel and the officer from Rennes, who swore on his honor that Monsieur de Vaunoy knew how to extend his hospitality in all the proper forms.

Didier did not wake during the journey. The two servants laid him down on his bed, and retired.

An hour afterwards, a fierce attack was made on the castle by the assembled Wolves. All the gates were assailed at the same moment, and as there was no one to defend them—the troops of the Maréchaussée and the force from Rennes, being quartered in an extensive outbuilding, the door of which, by a strange fatality, was locked, they soon burst in, and the insurgents poured into the body of the place.

Dame Goton was the only person who made the least attempt to defend the castle. Having tried in vain to stimulate the courage of Master Simonnet, and the other servants, she seized a musket, and discharged it through the kitchen window.

At the moment the first sounds of the assault were heard, Monsieur de Vaunoy had left the dining room and was now whispering hurriedly to Alain, Lapierre, and two other armed lackeys:

"Now is your time," he said, with a tremor in his voice. "He sleeps, and there are four of you, For Heaven's sake, do not fail me this time!"

"I shall take care of him myself," Lapierre replied. "Candidly, that young fool has been daring me to kill him. Twice within the last twenty-four hours, he has spurned me, when I almost had it in my heart to do him a good turn; so now for my revenge."

"Enough words!" said Hervé de Vaunoy. "You take care of the Captain, I'll take care of the Wolves!"

The four men crept stealthily along the corridor until they reached the Captain's door. Lapierre walked ahead, a drawn sword in his right hand, a dagger in the other. Master Alain closed the march, which enabled him to take a swill from his flask without being seen by the others.

"On your guard," said Lapierre. "I'm going to knock. If by any chance he wakes up, you'll come to my assistance."

No one answered. They opened the door and went in. It was dark inside. Lapierre, walking softly, reached the bed and lifted up his sword to strike the sleeping victim.

But a strong arm parried the descending blow. The murderous villain started back, aghast.

"Raise your lantern, Jacques," ordered Lapierre, so that he might see who it was that stayed his arm.

Jacques obeyed and the assassins beheld, by the lantern's flame, a tall, powerful man, standing upright, with his naked blade in his hand, firmly on his guard beside the Captain's bed.

One look at this individual was enough for the drunken steward, who instantly cried out in alarm:

"May Providence preserve us all! Four to one will not be such great odds now, for by my soul, it is Jude Leker, Nicolas Treml's man-at-arms!"

CHAPTER XXX
Four Against One

When Jude had been furtively admitted by his old friend, the housekeeper, and found his way, unseen, to the Captain's room, he had thrown himself upon the camp bed in one corner, where he had remained in silence until he saw his master borne in by the men, much to his astonishment.

After they had departed, he had tried to awake Didier by every means in his power, but without effect, for a strong narcotic had been mixed with the wine that had been poured out for him by Alain the steward.

Quite out of patience with his fruitless efforts, the honest squire placed his hand upon the Captain's heart, to satisfy himself that he was a living man.

"He's asleep!" said Jude with a sigh of relief. "May God grant him a long and restful night."

But this wish was not to be fulfilled.

Just as he again sought his bed, he heard the sounds of the attack on the castle. Fearing for his young master's life, Jude resolved to be ready for anything.

After a few minutes, he heard footsteps in the corridor outside and overheard a few words from the conversation of the four would-be assassins.

"He must be awakened," he said to himself "Captain! Captain!"

So saying, he shook Didier sharply, but the young man remained totally inert. The brave squire wavered about what to do next, and finally decided to stand before the bed.

"If it's Pelo Rouan," he said to himself, "I will adjure him to spare Didier's life in the name of Treml. Besides, Pelo would not strike a sleeping man... But what if isn't him?"

In response to this embarrassing question, Jude drew his sword, and prepared to defend Didier's life.

At the same moment, the door opened to let him Monsieur de Vaunoy's assassins.

Although twenty years had passed, Jude Leker had lost none of the intimidating, martial presence that had caused the flunkies at the Regent's court to stand aside. In the dim light of the lantern, in the partial darkness, his unusual height and muscular proportions seemed even greater. His composure was firm. The point of his sharp sword was thrust forward with a steady arm. His quick eye comprehended the full danger of his position at a glance, and there dwelt upon his face the indomitable resolution of a brave man, prepared to dare all in the discharge of his duty, and, if need be, to die.

Hearing Jude's name, Lapierre recoiled a few paces and reflected rapidly on what course he should pursue. His subtle intellect perceived instantly, from the steward's exclamation, that Hervé de Vaunoy's situation had become one of infinitely greater peril. Jude's presence here rendered the death of the young man even more imperatively necessary—it gave additional reasons to De Vaunoy for ordering his death.

His first impulse was to order the attack to begin, but another look at the cool, intrepid, attitude of the old man-at-arms, stopped him, for he had heard much of the squire's valor from the older servants, and what he saw now did not tend to decrease the reputation Jude had gained. It was true that Jude was entirely alone—for the narcotic had rendered the gallant Captain no better than a statue—but of his three companions, two were men of whom he scarcely knew anything, and in whose courage he could put no trust. Master Alain, the house steward, was old and, as usual, two-thirds drunk. As for himself, although, if driven to desperation, he was no mean adversary, yet fighting was not at all his natural vocation, and only adopted as a last resource.

So that the contending parties were not so unequally matched, as, at first sight, they might have seemed.

Master Alain stood on Jude's flank, at a safe distance, however; Lapierre was facing the squire; and the two other servants were somewhere between him and the old steward.

After a few moments' hesitation, Lapierre replaced his dagger in the sheath, lowered the point of his sword, and called a parley.

"Comrade," he said to Jude, in his usual careless tone, "my friend here, the venerable steward, assumes to recognize you as an old servant of the castle; and, by that title and by your obedience to the present lord, may I request you to step on one side, and allow us to complete the little job we have in hand?"

Jude frowned darkly, but remained motionless, answering not a word.

"My good man," Lapierre continued, "we are four to one, and therefore your sagacity must perceive that your opposition cannot avail. Moreover, if you will give yourself the trouble to open your ears, they will tell you that we have a large body of friends in the castle."

In fact, the shouts and outcries were redoubled, for the Wolves had now penetrated into the interior of the castle. But still the Captain remained in his apathy, and Jude did not deign to answer.

"Friend," Lapierre said, in his most insinuating tone, looking, at the same time, at his companions, "it will grieve me much to resort to violence, but—"

The sentence was not finished: five swords flashed at once. Sparks flew from them for a second, then Alain the steward fell with a groan; one of the servants lay upon the floor in a pool of his own blood; and Jude, who had struck twice in quick succession, resumed his guard.

Lapierre and the second man quickly retreated to the door, much disconcerted by the failure of their treacherous attack, awed by the sight of his two accomplices having been so easily dispatched.

"*Vertudieu!*" he grumbled. "And I thought four might be too many! Raise your lantern, Jacques!"

The light fell full upon the squire, and Lapierre laughed scornfully as he saw the blood trickling down his chest from three wounds in his breast. Jude remained as straight and firm as ever, but their attack had not been the failure he had initially thought.

"Ah, ha!" the villain chuckled. "The Devil takes me if he'll last more than fifteen minutes on his legs with three such holes in him! Steady Jacques, my boy, let's keep still for a few minutes, and he will be ours. Keep close to the wall with your blade well forward, and when he falls, we will settle the Captain quite comfortably at our ease."

Jacques obeyed and he and Lapierre stood with their backs to the wall. Master Alain and the other servant now lay on the ground motionless, presumably dead according to all appearances.

Poor Jude knew his true position, but his determined courage was not one jot abated. He knew his situation was desperate. He felt that the fatal drain was diminishing his strength at every instant, and that he assuredly would die. But once he heard the sounds of the Wolves approaching the chamber, he had an idea and a faint hope arose in him.

"Pelo Rouan, help!" he shouted.

He preferred a loyal enemy to those contemptible hired assassins.

But the sounds of the retreating parties died away, and Pelo Rouan did not come.

"Oh, oh!" said Lapierre, with the sneer that had become a second nature to him. "The charcoal-burner, too, protects the orphan, does he? Happily, my sturdy friend, he is far enough off, and since you call for help, it appears we run no risk of being in the same plight as our poor dear friends upon the floor... Look, Jacques! He is staggering!"

The mountebank was right: Jude's knees trembled as his heart's blood ebbed away, but he made a Herculean effort, drew himself upright, and still maintained his guard.

"By my faith," Lapierre continued in the same jeering tone, "this doughty squire has the power of a bull. He has lost more blood already than I have in my whole body, and yet he will not fall. If this same Captain should finish his nap, you and I, Jacques, would find ourselves in quite a pickle!"

"Awake, my Captain, awake!" Jude murmured, pale and panting.

"Why not address him by his real name, my gallant friend?" said Lapierre, jeering. "Come on! Do it! That name might act as a spell within these walls!"

The dying squire did not comprehend the taunt. He placed his hand on one of the gaping wounds to repress the blood, but Lapierre made a feigned attack, which compelled him to resume a position of defense, and the blood welled out afresh.

"Rouse yourself, Captain Didier, awake!" Jude gasped, dropping his point, and sustaining himself with difficulty by the curtains of the bed.

But Didier still slept on.

Jude's strength had run out. His trusty sword dropped from his hand; his eyelids closed; his brain reeled; and he fell exhausted in a pool of his gore, murmuring with painful regret:

"Heaven has willed it that I should not die for Treml!"

"And for who else, then, my good fellow?" cried Lapierre, bursting with laughter. "Is it possible, by chance, that you do not know? It would be an excellent joke!"

A wicked smile clenched the lip of the mountebank as he spoke thus. He approached Jude who was breathing with effort and did not move anymore.

He knelt down by his side, and felt his low pulse, as he said:

"My good fellow, you have a few minutes yet to live, and if you will do me the favor to listen to me, I have a pretty little tale to tell you. Don't die just yet, my friend, for I am sure it will amuse you. One evening, you must know, about twenty years ago, when I was a travelling quack doctor, I happened to be very much in want of a good-looking child, and as I passed through the great forest of Rennes, I spied a pretty creature, wrapped in rabbit skins, left on a green bank by the roadside. Now, he was just the very thing for me, so I took him back with me to Paris—but I feel your pulse getting lower, so I must be quick. There, the boy grew up; his handsome face and gallant bearing attracted the notice of the Comte de Toulouse, who educated him, made him one of his pages, then gentleman of his chamber—Ah! Ah! Your pulse is getting stronger, and I see you are interested in my story—and next, a captain in the Maréchaussée. Do you guess now who he was—who he is?"

A slight flush came into Jude's cheeks, but still his eyes were closed.

"Well, if you cannot guess, I must be more explicit so that you may go happy into the afterlife. Now that will tell you the true reason for this night's work carried at the behest of the honorable Monsieur de Vaunoy. That child—your sleepy Captain here—was none other than Georges Treml!"

No sooner had Lapierre uttered this name than he let out a cry of anger and pain.

An immeasurable joy now filled Jude Leker's heart and acted like an electric current on his dying frame. The sound of the name of the adored son of his beloved master restored a semblance of life to him for a moment. Summoning up all his remaining energy, he suddenly grasped the villain's throat, as he leaned over him, tore his dagger from his belt, and plunged it deep in his heart.

"Jacques! Help me!" growled Lapierre.

Jacques stepped forward but he was not fast enough. Jude picked up his sword and plunged it with all his strength into Lapierre's chest.

Then, making one last gigantic effort, Jude raised himself to a sitting posture, with his back against the bed, and awaited the attack of the remaining servant.

But Jude was still a swordsman to be reckoned with, even at this, his final hour The servant was seriously injured during the first pass, threw down his sword, and ran away.

Finding himself alone, Jude dragged his body painfully along to where the lantern lay upon the floor, feebly illuminating the scene of carnage, and then, having trimmed it with his fingers, he crawled back to the bed where young Didier remained, still under the influence of the narcotic.

It was with infinite pain that the good squire, gathering all the strength that remained to him, by sheer force of will, managed to get up. He leaned with one hand on the mattress and, with the other, directed the light full upon Didier's face.

The Captain was still lying on his back, in the same position where Monsieur de Vaunoy's servant had left him. He had not moved since then. The light of the lantern fell on his bold, regular features.

Jude was dying, but his joy was delirious. He looked at Didier, asleep. An ecstatic delight illuminated his simple and honest features, while two burning tears slowly ran down his leathery cheeks.

"It is he, at last!" he murmured. "May God protect him and bless him! Here is the noble brow of Treml and those closed eyes, as I remember now, are the eyes of a brave and noble Breton. Oh, he is a handsome soldier, that last son of Treml! A worthy scion of this ancient stock. If only I had recognized him earlier!—and yet my heart was always drawn towards him with an affection for which I could not account…"

He took Didier's hand and leaned over it, unable to lift it to his lips.

"My lord, my son!" he continued him with such passion than the last drops of his loyal blood came back to his cheeks. "Awake, so that I may greet you with the valiant name of your forefathers! Awake, son of Treml! Your life will now be beautiful and glorious!"

He stopped and suddenly his gaze was filled with a deep terror.

"My God!" he said a dull voice. "He still sleeps and I'm about to die—taking with me forever the secret of his future happiness and everything else God made him to be…"

Deep despair succeeded to the transports he had felt, and he replaced both his hands upon his gaping wounds, as he found his life had almost ebbed away. Little did the faithful squire dream of remaining in this world, but the pang was a thousand times more agonizing than that of death to think that he should fail in his duty to the last Treml, at the very moment when one word would confer upon him happiness and nobility for life.

"I shall not to die," he resumed with great effort. "It would be treason, a base betrayal. I will live that I may love and serve him. Stop, stop, thou ebbing blood... I am going mad… Oh, my Lady of the Forest, holy mother of Christ, have pity! Let him awake, that I may speak one word, or give me but one more day to live! Blessed Virgin, the hand of Death is on me… I'm afraid…"

The unfortunate old man's agony grew worse; he needed both his hands to desperately hold on to the blankets. Another minute passed during which he suffered a martyrdom that we will not try to portray. Then his hands slowly slid along the covers.

"Awake—and listen—my dear, dear Lord. In the hollow-oak at the Wolf's Pit, there is an iron chest, and inside is gold, and a parchment. It is yours, Georges Treml, and it will restore your lands to you. Oh! Heaven! I am a bad servant… I die at the hour of your greatest need… When I should live… Please, forgive me—oh, for—"

His hands unclasped their hold, his head dropped upon his chest, his legs bent, and he fell heavily backwards, pronouncing one last time the idolized name of his young master.

Captain Didier, or rather Georges Treml, still slept.

A silence of death reigned in the room for several minutes. The lantern, left by Jude upon the bed, cast its pale light upon the scene of desolation.

Suddenly, one heard a long and resounding yawn. One of the corpses moved and began to stretch its limbs, as one does after a long sleep. This corpse was that of Master Alain the steward, who bore no other injury than a large hole made at Jude's expense in his shirt.

Half-fearful and half-drunk, the old man had fallen under the blow and not get up. And as we all know that a drunk poltroon could sleep next to a locomotive, Master Alain had, in fact, fallen asleep.

In waking, his first attention was to his flask. He remembered nothing of the tragic events that had occurred.

After taking a full swill, he got up on shaky legs, more drunk than ever.

"Where am I?" he wondered. "Why am I out of my bed?"

A glance thrown around refreshed his memories.

"Ho, ho," he said. "The battle is over. Here is my old friend Jude dead as I wanted him to be... And this young rascal, Georges Treml, asleep like the blessed dead... By my faith, I'm going to finish the job!"

He took his dagger and walked laboriously toward the bed without saying a word. On the way, he took another swig from his flask to give himself more courage.

In the middle of the room, he stumbled against Lapierre's body.

"Ah! He's asleep too!" he roared. "Come and help me, Lapierre, my boy! "

Lapierre failed to answer, so Master Alain leaned over and put the neck of his flask to his mouth.

"Do you want a drink?" he asked, after his custom.

But the alcohol just spilled on the floor. Master Alain got up.

"Hum. I guess he won't be drinking anymore," he said solemnly.

Just as he reached the bed, he stopped for a moment to listen to a soft, tearful voice singing the *Lament* of Arthur of Brittany in the courtyard.

"It's an odd time to sing," he murmured.

The curiosity of the drunken steward was so excited, that he could not refrain from going near the window to better hear the song.

The singer stopped and uttered a low tone with a desolate accent:

"Didier... My Didier!"

"Present and accounted for!" said Alain, laughing. "Let's have another couplet!"

The sweet voice of a young girl, as if she tried to obey that ironic command, resumed and sang the part of the *Lament* that tells of the pain of the Duchess Constance of Brittany, mourning her darling boy, in a voice full of tears

> *She sought in her distress*
> *The fortress*
> *Where the English kept locked up*
> *Her beloved*

Then, she said again:
"Didier, my Didier, where are you?"

The old steward reduced to a childlike curiosity by his drunkenness approached the window to see who it was who could be singing at that fearful time, just then, the door opened and a flood of light was poured throughout the room.

Master Alain turned around he saw Alix de Vaunoy, pale, haggard, holding a torch in her hand.

She also uttered in a muffled voice the same words as the singer's:

"Didier—my Didier, where are you?"

CHAPTER XXXI
Alix and Marie

The countenance of Alix de Vaunoy still bore the traces of deep suffering, and her eyes retained that appearance of lassitude which always accompanies the passing of a strong attack of fever.

At the moment that her father had ordered his assassins to Didier's chamber, Alix had been asleep in her room, attended by her aunt Olive, her chambermaid Renée, and another servant. The sounds of the attack on the castle had awakened her suddenly, and as the old maid and the girls fled in dismay at the discharge of the first guns, she had been left alone.

Slight and broken as her sleep had been, it had refreshed her exhausted body, and somewhat calmed her brain. The sound of the attack shaking her weakened brain caused a few vague thoughts to reemerge just like shaking the cloudy water of a basin might make a submerged body rise to the surface

Her mind reverted immediately to her conversation with Lapierre, her suspicions of her father's treachery were again aroused, and murmuring the Captain's name, she donned a white dressing gown, took up a lamp, and left her room.

Passing along the corridor, she met some of the Wolves, who were now masters of the castle, and were feeling quite at home. But seeing this pale figure wrapped in what looked like a shroud, they fled at once, thinking she was a ghost.

Thus she arrived in Georges' room in time to save him from certain death at the hands of old Alain.

It could not be said that Mademoiselle de Vaunoy was in a state of pure somnambulism, but neither did she possess her mental consciousness in all its clarity; she was awake, but her reason was enveloped in a temporary obscurity, and external things were viewed by her as through a misty veil.

As she opened the door of the Captain's bedroom, alone, and in the middle of the night, she did not perceive that she was exposing herself to imputations that might destroy her reputation for life, that she was committing an act opposed to every idea of female decency; she only knew that a chasm had opened between herself and Didier, rendered even more unfathomable by Lapierre's bold accusations. But, by some inexplicable presentiment, because of her tender feelings rather than cold, logical deductions based on what she had learned, she had sensed that the young officer's life was in the greatest danger, and she had come, instinctively, to save a man whom she loved deeply, but without hope.

The combat with the murderers, and the death of honest Jude, which took so long to relate in the previous chapter, had only lasted, in fact, for a few minutes, and was over when Alix de Vaunoy arrived.

She entered, as we have said, and involuntarily, perhaps without even realizing it, uttered the name which was constantly at the center of her heart..

The old steward, amazed at the sight of this strange apparition, remained motionless, and did not even have the strength to seek advice from his flask.

Alix, who had taken a few steps forward without seeing him, at last noticed his presence and, with her outstretched hand pointing regally at the door, ordered him to leave.

The half-drunken, half-frightened steward left as quickly as the bad condition of his sclerotic legs could carry him.

Placing the lamp upon a table, the unhappy girl sat down mechanically upon the bed, and passed her hands across her eyes, as for a few moments the fever again took possession of her brain.

"Whence comes this extraordinary smell?" she muttered after a few seconds, during which she had not noticed Didier's presence. "This faint, warm, suffocating odor... And these men, why are they sleeping here upon the floor? Oh! happy creatures that they can sleep at all, while I suffer, even in my dreams..."

Then she brushed her forehead with her hand and her lips were filled with a transient blush.

"Didier, do you remember those joyful, happy balls, given by Monseigneur the Comte de Toulouse? We danced together—always; and that other ball at my father's? You can't have forgotten it..."

She shivered violently.

"All night, we shared the joy in our hearts... And on the morning, when you left—ah! It is false, Didier; Lapierre lied! It wasn't my father who ordered the attack upon you by those ruffians—"

"Didier! Didier!" said a voice from the courtyard below—the young woman's voice we heard singing earlier.

"Didier, yes..." said Alix de Vaunoy, making an effort to marshal her thoughts. "I came to save him—where is he?"

293

Her eyes roamed wildly around the room, and as they fell upon the young man's form, her reason returned in all its force.

"Now, I remember," she said. "I remember... There was a terrible threat in the words of this miserable servant... Assassins may still be lurking ..."

She turned her frightened eyes upon the door and, as she did so, she was forced to take another look at the supposed sleepers on the floor. And at the same time, the odor of blood returned to assail her sense of smell.

"So they came! Was he hurt?... God be praised! He is just asleep... But then, who was here to defend him?"

Snatching up the light, she examined the corpses in succession; at a glance, she recognized Lapierre whose face, even in death, bore his carefree smile, and the other servant.

But then, despite not being acquainted with the squire, but thinking he had been attached to the Captain, and had died in his defense, she knelt down and imprinted a grateful kiss upon his still warm forehead.

"Heaven save his soul!" she stammered, with passionate gratitude. "Every night and morning—even if I to live to be a hundred—I shall pray to the Virgin for him. They were three to one against him—perhaps more! Oh, he was a gallant, faithful, friend!"

Then came the thought that more murderers might be dispatched to that fatal room to consummate the deed, and catching up Jude's sword, she sat again upon the bed, resolving, if need should be, like him, to die in Didier's defense.

"I shall stay here," she said, "until he wakes up. They will not dare to kill him in front of me!"

Whilst this strange scene was passing in the Captain's room, the Wolves were dispersed throughout the mansion, some pillaging, some drinking and shouting, as they celebrated their success. But, in the midst of the discordant sounds, Alix de Vaunoy could hear the plaintive voice in the courtyard, still singing *The Lament* in a low tone, and calling on the Captain to arise.

"He does not hear me," said the voice with great discouragement. "He no longer recognizes my song... O, Didier, it is I..."

Then, she sang despite her tears:

> *She sought in his distress*
> *The fortress*
> *Where the English had locked up*
> *His beloved*

Alix rushed to the window. The voice continued singing:

> *At night, she came in the shadows*
> *From the dark tower*
> *She said under the great wall*
> *Arthur, Arthur!*

A sudden light broke in upon the high-born maiden's mind as she recognized The Blossom' of the Broom's well-known strain.

"Marie! It's Marie!" said Alix, whose heart beat strongly. "Marie who loves him too, and who is loved in return. It's Marie who should be entitled to sit here in my place, and who will drive me away!"

"Didier, my Didier!" cried the exhausted voice.

"*Her* Didier," repeated Mademoiselle de Vaunoy with bitterness. "But it is true, he is hers... And I... Have I still the strength to suffer more?..."

She opened the window.

"Marie" she cried out to the girl.

The hapless Blossom-of-the-Broom had let herself fall on a stone, but hearing this, she rose quickly, and recognized at the window the pale features of Mademoiselle de Vaunoy.

"Have you seen Didier?" she asked.

"He is here," answered Alix, turning toward the bed

It happened that Didier's chamber was on the first floor, and that a full-grown vine spread out its vigorous branches, nailed to the wall, beneath the window of the room, so that it served as a natural ladder, with the help of which the sylph-like Marie ascended as lightly as a bird, and jumped through the window.

"Where is he? Where is he?" she exclaimed.

Alix showed her the bed.

The Blossom-of-the-Broom fell upon her knees beside bed, and passionately kissed the Captain's passive hand.

"How did I suffer!" she said, wiping a tear that did not have time to dry or shine in the middle of her smile. "I sang and screamed for so long hoping that he would hear me and recognize me. I trembled at the thought I might have arrived too late! Thank you, Mademoiselle Alix, thank you, my good demoiselle... He sleeps... He is unaware that his life is danger ...

"How do you know, this, Marie?" asked Alix, who thought of her father and was afraid.

"How I know it? But shouldn't I know everything that concerns him? Look at him! How handsome he is, Mademoiselle..."

The eyes of the two girls caressed the Captain's face at the same time.

"Yes," said Alix, sadly. "You are very fortunate, Marie. But is the danger that threatens him commonly known in the forest?"

"The danger comes from the forest, Mademoiselle. The Wolves went out tonight to kill my handsome Captain. Only God has allowed that they should not have not found his room yet, but it is necessary to awaken him quickly!"

"The Wolves!" Alix exclaimed in deadly terror. "Do they wish to murder him too?"

"No, not they, but only one villain, whose name I do not know, who came to the forest yesterday, and promised to leave the gates of the castle open so that the Wolves might enter and seize the treasure of the king and kill all the soldiers that were escorting it—including my Didier, who was to be murdered in his sleep. My father hates him, because he is a Frenchman, and although he said he would not strike him himself, he would not stand in the way of others doing so. I heard it yesterday, in our cabin, as I listened at my half-opened door when the name of my beloved caught my ear.

"Oh, Alix! I threw myself upon my knees before my father, and implored him to let me save my darling's life; but he refused, pushed me harshly from him, and locked me in my room. I wept bitterly for a long time, mademoiselle; oh, how bitterly! Then an idea rushed across my mind, and hope returned. See, Alix de Vaunoy, my hands still bleed, for I broke through the glass of my closed window, I tore down and burst through the wooden shutters, and came hither through the forest.

"The walls of the castle are lofty, mademoiselle; nevertheless, I recommended my soul to Heaven before I tried to scale them; happily, the Virgin of the Forest heard my prayers, I alighted unhurt within the walls, and here I find him, still unharmed, and you, Alix, watching, him like a guardian angel, next to his bed..."

She suddenly stopped. A cloud passed over her face.

"But why are you watching over him?" she asked Alix.

Marie's soul had just learned jealousy. But it was a fleeting look. Alix did not even need to answer her since, for the first time since she had entered the room, Marie looked away from Didier and saw the three corpses on the floor. She uttered a cry of horror.

Alix, however, had understood the look.

"Our Lady of the Forest has taken you under her special care, my child," she replied with dignity. "Two of those men who lie there were murderers, and came here to slay him. I knew them both. The third, whom I do not recognize, died in his defense—would he were still alive with his brave heart, for Didier is not yet out of danger. This strange sleep that nothing will disturb is most unaccountable, and I am aware that his enemies will go to any lengths to achieve his destruction."

The words were scarcely out of the mouth of the noble maid, than Marie, seizing the Captain's hand, shook it with all her force, exclaiming:

"Awake! We must go!... Ah! He does not respond!"

Alix de Vaunoy continued:

"I have read in some of those ridiculous romances my aunt takes so much delight in, that villains have been sufficiently vile to administer narcotics to their brave enemies that they might murder them in their sleep. What, if at supper—I was not there—they may have poured such poison in his wine? Lapierre would have done so, and gloried in the deed. It must be thus, or the noise of these demons rioting in the castle should have aroused him."

"Look, Alix, look! He is not moving!" Marie exclaimed leaning over the young man, shivering. "Ah! This sleep resembles death!"

"It may lead to it before long if we do not do our best to remove him. Give over weeping and calling, Marie, lest your cries bring the murdering villains to this room, and listen to what I am about to say..."

In the short time that had passed since Alix first entered the Captain's room, ten years' maturity of thought and self-possession had come over her; decision and energy sat hand-in-hand upon her lofty brow, and Marie, beheld the change with undisguised astonishment.

"Will you be strong?" asked Alix.

"I do not know... In the name of God, help me awaken him!"

"He will not awaken. You must help me to save him."

The Blossom-of-the-Broom submitted implicitly to the superior intelligence and determination of her self-denying friend.

Alix suffered cruelly, but had no time to rest. The sight of this child, whose joyful, unsuspecting love had killed her own hopes, only tortured her soul, without begetting hatred or envy. She was a noble girl, who deserved to have had a better father. She leaned over the Blossom-of-the-Broom and deposited a motherly kiss upon her cheek, still bejeweled with tears, and said:

"When you shall be married to him, Marie, be an affectionate, good wife, and give him back heart for heart... Yes, it is for the best... You will make him happy..."

"I do not understand," said Marie. "You were talking about saving him…"

"Yes, yes, you're right," said Alix, shaking herself out of her momentary reverie. "Let us only think of getting him away from this dreadful spot. Let's hurry and gather your strength, girl!"

Alix took Jude's dagger from the ground, passed it through the belt of her dress, as the fire of determination sparkled in her eyes. She gave Lapierre's dagger to her friend—who could not comprehend her actions—and said:

"You are a daughter of the forest, Marie. You know how to ride. You are in love, so you must be strong. We must be like men tonight, Marie. Do as you see me do; and if in bearing him hence, we should meet an assailant in the corridor, we must die to save him."

A heroic fire shone in Alix's eyes as she spoke thus. The Blossom-of-the-Broom stared at her for a moment and then bowed her head in silence.

"Are you afraid?" Mademoiselle de Vaunoy asked.

"No," answered Marie. "But I do believe that you love him, Alix."

Alix's enthusiasm dropped as if by magic.

"You believe that I love him?" she repeated in a muffled voice. "So you still wonder about it just as he may be dying You believe that I love him? But I know that he loves you, while I only dream of saving him, Listen to me, Mare: I have been very unhappy for a long time, but I would become even more so if I thought you were unworthy of him. Yes, I did love him," she added with sudden violence, "long before you, and maybe more than you.. But that no longer matters now."

"Oh, you are so wonderful," murmured the hapless Blossom-of-the-Broom, weeping.

Alix did not cry. She summoned to her lips one of those smiles filled with so much strength and suffering they they inspire fear and compassion in weaker hearts.

"Give me your hand, child," she said. "He is yours now. I no longer love him."

"But what about him?"

"He never truly loved me. See, I'll sacrifice one of my last, most cherished tokens of my love to you…"

Saying this, she put the copper medal she had taken from Lapierre the night he had tried to slay the young Captain in the streets of Rennes around Didier's neck. Marie did not have time to see the nature of that offering because Alix energetically continued:

"To work now, girl! Didier must not awaken inside my father's house."

Alix, with a degree of strength that was inconceivable after the attack of fever that had made such ravages on her form, lifted Didier's head from the pillow, and motioned to Marie to assist her by grabbing his feet. The Blossom-of-the-Broom obeyed meekly, like a child who obeys his master's orders without arguing. Together, the girls raised him in their arms; then, with a mighty effort, threw a blanket round his inanimate limbs, and bore him into the corridor, holding the four corners and carrying his unconscious body in it, as if it were a stretcher.

They sagged under the weight. Nevertheless, they crossed the long corridors of La Tremlays. The shouts and songs of the carousing Wolves resounded on every side, but, fortunately, having secured their booty, they took no heed of what was going on in other parts of the castle; and so the adventurous maidens bore the Captain without interruption down the stairs, and stopped to take breath in the courtyard.

The Blossom-of-the-Broom breathed heavily and trembled in every limb, whilst her companion—sustained by the heroic energy of her mind—was infinitely less fatigued. The forest girl looked at her with a mixture of admiration and fright.

Alix and Marie had known each other since childhood. They did not mind the difference in their respective social positions. There was a smidgen of deference in Marie's affection towards Alix, but it was mostly instinctive and had nothing to do with Mademoiselle de Vaunoy's fortune or rank.

As for Alix, she really loved Marie and as her soul was noble above all, the presence of a man coming between her and her less fortunate friend could not change her heart. Perhaps, if duty had not commanded it, she might have defended her claim to her happiness as it is the right of every woman to do, but her sacrifice had been made long ago, and she did not have to make the least effort to cherish her rival. And yet, she still loved Didier, with a deep and profound love, that would never die.

The Blossom-of-the-Broom, for her part, had never had any inkling about Didier's momentary liaison with Alix. If she had known about it, perhaps she might have rejected the marks of endearment from the rich heiress of La Tremlays, because Marie had the prickly pride of the student of nature, and her whole being was concentrated on the exclusive passion she felt for Didier. Yet, in the last few minutes, that veil had been torn away: she had discovered that Alix had been her rival, and Marie felt that Mademoiselle de Vaunoy was superior to most other women. Was she not right to fear her?

For a few minutes, the two young women remained immovable and mute, separated only by the body of the

Captain. Alix was thinking and looking round her to see whether any fresh means of escape were offered, while Marie looked sadly at the moon, the light of which illuminated the courtyard.

"What is this?" asked Mademoiselle de Vaunoy, pointing to a moving shadow against the far wall.

"It's a horse," answered Marie. "While I wandered through the courtyard, a servant of the Lord of La Tremlays, your father, came to tie him near the gate."

"Good! We will not need the key to the stables then! As for that of the gate, the Wolves have done us a favor—we won't need one. One last effort, girl!"

The horse was saddled and bridled, attached to one of the iron-rings in the stable wall. They lifted their heavy burden, bore him staggering to the animal, and at length succeeded in placing the Captain in a sitting posture on the horse's back. Marie mounted instantly upon the crupper, sustaining her lover in her arms.

"Go now!" said Alix. "You love him; you will be able to find a safe refuge for him."

The bridle was detached in a second from the ring. At this moment of their separation, the Blossom-of-the-Broom felt ashamed and regretful about her suspicions. She leaned over Mademoiselle de Vaunoy and kissed her on the forehead.

"You are good and generous, Mademoiselle," Marie murmured. "Thank you for both of us,"

The Wolves had indeed left the gate open. Alix struck the rump of the horse, which left immediately.

"May God watch over him!" she said.

The horse, led by the daring maid, passed through to the dark coverts of the wood.

Then, Alix sat down on the stone bench which is a required component of every Breton gate. Her goal had been achieved; her strength, born of her heroic will, suddenly dissipated as if by magic, and she became again what she had been only an hour before: a poor, broken girl, suffering from a fever and unable to move.

In the meantime, Master Alain, somewhat sobered up by the ghostly appearance of his master's daughter, had gone to report to Monsieur de Vaunoy the failure of their attempted attack against Didier.

The old steward had difficulties in locating his master. Hervé de Vaunoy, on hearing the first sounds of the Wolves' assault, had caused the horse which Alix had so fortunately discovered in the yard, to be caparisoned, and fastened to the wall, ready for any emergency that might arise; then, knowing the means he had taken to secure the King's troops in the barns, he had conducted the Wolves to the spot where the treasure had been deposited, intending immediately afterwards to mount and ride at once to Rennes.

His plan of action was no less simple than adroit: the death of Didier, he calculated, would undoubtedly be imputed to the Captain's undaunted courage in defending the gold entrusted to his care. The Wolves would be surely accused of the murder, and De Vaunoy's own riding in hot haste to Rennes would be ascribed to his wish to obtain reinforcements from the city. Everyone would feel sorry about this catastrophe that had snatched a young officer with so much promise in the prime of his life. Didier's well-known bravery would only add to the likely veracity of the tale that the Lord of La Tremlays planned to tell.

And his secret purpose would be better served by placing a couple of leagues' distance between himself and his new allies, the Wolves, whom he suspected planned to betray him.

After two hours of futile efforts trying to escape the surveillance of these dangerous allies, Hervé de Vaunoy finally managed to dodge them and rushed to the court-yard to find his horse.

There, in the shadows, he stumbled against old Alain who had been vainly seeking his master in every part of the castle.

At the first words that issued from old steward's lips, Hervé de Vaunoy felt as if a thunderbolt had fallen at his feet. The Captain lived, and everything had been for naught.

"What?" he exclaimed with a fearful oath. "You, despicable coward! I swear that Lapierre will…"

"He is dead," Alain sullenly interrupted.

"Dead—then the Captain must have awakened?"

"No, but his manservant, whom I could not remember yesterday, was none other than Jude Leker, the old Treml's squire!"

"Jude Leker!" Hervé gasped out, following the same line of reasoning as Lapierre earlier. "Then he knows he is Georges Treml, and that detested man still lives!"

"It was not my fault!" said Master Alain. "Jude Leker perished under our blows, but I remained alone in that room with that Didier, or Georges, who slept like a log…"

And? By God, will you tell me what happened next?"

"Well, as I was about to do the deed, I saw a person who…"

"By all the saints, who?" interrupted De Vaunoy, shaking the old man to the point of risking breaking his shoulder. "Who could have stopped you?"

"Mademoiselle Alix de Vaunoy, your daughter," answered the steward.

"My daughter?" Hervé stammered. "Alix?"

Then, suddenly straightening up, he exclaimed:

"You lie! You lie—or you're mistaken! My daughter is in her bed By all that's holy! Even if I have to kill him myself, I will not waste this opportunity that I bought at the risk of my very life!"

Hervé de Vaunoy violently discarded the old steward, who remained stuck to the wall of the courtyard, and rushed to Didier's room.

It was about five minutes after Alix and the Blossom-of-the-Broom had left. Mademoiselle de Vaunoy's candle was still burning on the night stand.

Hervé, whose normally cautious and prudent nature was now a thing of the past, stepped over the three corpses and rushed to the bed. It was empty.

"He's escaped!" he murmured in a strangled voice "And my daughter was here!"

He tore the sheets off the bed and trampled them in his delirious fury. Then, he dashed blindly towards the door.

But he did not pass the threshold. A pair of powerful arms blocked him and pushed him back inside with an irresistible force.

Hervé de Vaunoy raised his head and saw, standing before him, this strange character in a white wolf mask who had led the Wolves in the forest, and whose marvelous strength the unfortunate Jude had admired.

De Vaunoy tried to talk, but the White Wolf shut his mouth imperiously and walked slowly into the room.

"There is always blood everywhere you go, Monsieur de Vaunoy," he said in a low and threatening voice.

The White Wolf raised the lamp Alix had left, examined the faces of the three bodies attentively, and when he came to that of the gallant squire, he trembled slightly, the muscles of his face working convulsively beneath his mask, and he muttered between his teeth in a slow, melancholy voice:

"He had promised to defend his master… He was a true Breton! Alas! There is now no one but myself to cherish the remembrance of Treml living, or mourn him dead!"

"By God!" said De Vaunoy, who had succeeded in regaining his calm. "Tonight, I gave you five hundred thousand livres in beautiful crowns The least you could do is let me go about my own business… Let me out, friend!"

The White Wolf did not utter a single word in reply; his eyes glared like a tiger's for one moment through his mask, then turning to the door, he lifted up his hand; six or seven armed men burst into the room, raised Hervé de Vaunoy like a feather in their arms.

"To the Pit!" said the White Wolf.

Hervé de Vaunoy felt a large hand pressed against his mouth to prevent him from shouting.

Minutes later, he was lying on a stretcher being carried by four men, among whom he thought he recognized, despite their masks, two of his own servants, Yvon and Corentin. They carried him through the dark paths of the forest to the dreaded Wolf's Pit.

CHAPTER XXXII
The Chamber

It was with the greatest difficulty, that The Blossom-of-the-Broom maintained Didier's precarious balance in the saddle, as the horse walked slowly along the mossy glades of the forest, towards the charcoal-burner's hut.

Notwithstanding her ardent attachment to her gallant lover, and her determination to save him from the Wolves, or perish in the attempt, her strength was failing rapidly, and she had almost allowed the Captain to fall heavily to the ground, when the action of the narcotic administered to him began to gradually pass. The young man shivered slightly, and with the instinct of an accomplished horse man, strove to remain upright in his scat.

"My Didier!" Marie exclaimed joyously. "I saved you! Wake up!"

No wakening from deep sleep was ever attended with more delightfully romantic sensations than what waited on the youthful Captain in the forest of Rennes. The night was one of rare occurrence in Brittany, in the autumn of the year, for it was free from fog. The moon, hanging in the center of the azure sky, had doffed her usual shroud, and cast her silvery mantle over the whole. A light breeze breathed softly through the russet branches of the gnarled oaks, the tall tops of the elms swayed backwards and forwards, in the gentle wind.

As the young officer's sensibility returned, and he felt himself in that saddle which had become a second nature to him, he thought he was in a lovely dream, and kept his eyes close shut, lest their opening should mar the illusion of the scene.

As Marie whispered her fond congratulations in his ear, and the breeze played upon his fevered brow, the influence of the opium gave way more and more, until he raised his heavy eyelids, turned his face, and as he beheld the sweet, affectionate features of the girl, so close to his, that her golden tresses almost mingled with his own, and the sounds: "My Didier, you are safe," thrilled through his brain.

He shook himself, placed his hands upon his eyes, and marveled at the obstinate persistence of the dream.

Blossom-of-the-Broom drew his hands playfully away, and the illusion was dispelled; but still he was astonished at finding the maid mounted on horseback behind him in the forest, and though he endeavored to recall to his clouded memory the occurrences of the day, and an indistinct idea flitted across his mind, that his duty called him elsewhere, yet his situation, with Marie's slight arm round his waist, was too delicious not to be enjoyed, and he gave himself up to the delirium of the present, without thinking of the future or the past.

"So it is you?" he murmured, trying to sit up in the saddle bout of pure instinct. "You, here, with me on horseback, at this time…?"

The voice of the Captain expressed a stupefaction so profound that Marie could not repress a smile

"Yes, it is I," she said. "I will explain everything later… Do you feel any pain?"

She did not repeat the word "I saved you," that a first feeling of triumph had forced from her lips, because of that sense of tact that exquisite nature has given to girls of both the countryside and city. She had guessed what attraction danger and duty have for a soldier and that stopped her from revealing what had happened at the castle.

At intervals, Didier would address a few questions to her respecting their position, but The Blossom-of-the-Broom refused to satisfy his curiosity, until the woody arch became more dense above their heads.

Then, dropping lightly from the horse, she stood upon the sward, and gently compelled her lover to dismount.

The night air had done much to relieve his oppressed brain, but still the action of the opiate had not quite evaporated; his feet were numbed and useless, his legs refused to bear his weight, his head ached as if it would burst.

"I am confused," he said, trying to shake off the painful torpor in which he remained immersed in spite of himself. "This looks to me like an abduction, in which I do not play the role ordinarily reserved to an officer of His Majesty! Let's stop here, Marie. I need to get off… and I also need to rest…"

They had passed the last trees of the avenue and the dome of the forest was now above their heads.

Marie slipped from the rump of the horse and set foot on the grass.

"Wonderful!" Didier murmured. "Now it is you who is my squire! But what happened to my spirit and my strength! Help support me…"

He took a few steps and, staggering a few paces, fell at the foot of a chestnut tree, close to the narrow track, where he fell asleep immediately.

Marie drew the horse into the covert, gently placed his head on her knees, and remained motionless. He was safe; she was happy, and she watched him sleep peacefully with great delight.

Fifteen minutes passed; then she heard the measured tramp of men coming along the path. She held her breath, as she beheld four men bearing a litter on which a fifth, bound hand and foot, was stretched, directing their footsteps toward the Wolf's Pit. They passed in silence, but they were scarcely lost to view before she heard sounds of tumultuous rejoicing, mingled with songs, and the crackling of dry twigs breaking beneath the feet of many men, approaching from La Tremlays.

Frightened, Marie dragged Didier behind a shrub, then looked in stupefied amazement as the main body of the Wolves passed by, not in a manner somewhat similar to military discipline, as poor Jude had seen previous to the attack, but laughing, shouting, dancing, jumping, and carrying the pleasing burden of the five hundred thousand livres in little canvas bags, upon their backs.

The hardy sons of the forest had secured such a prize as never had fallen into their hands before, and having passed the night in drinking and revelry, they were celebrating their victory on their homeward route, with every demonstration of uncouth delight. The prize was great beyond all doubt, but the fact of its being taken from their mortal enemy, the Collector-general, rendered it doubly precious in their eyes.

We do not take it upon us to excuse the plunder of the guilty by our excellent friends, the Wolves. However, to those who would cast much opprobrium or blame at these poor peasants, we would ask a simple question: have you read the recent debates of the wine-growers' committees?[25] Have you also heard of the bold and

---

[25] The French Government intended to table a Law on 30 December 1840 that would have harmed the interests of the

strong daughters of Rebecca who do summary justice every night in Wales?[26] The Rebeccaites look a little like our Wolves, and our wine-growers would like to look a little like the Rebeccaites. In all these things, there are only differences in times, morality, and daring. Whenever the legal authorities oppress the weak, there will be a necessary, if not legitimate, reaction. This reaction may translate into mere gossip if the oppressed are journalists, Gascons or Members of Parliaments, but in violent reprisals if they are brave and too poor to wait half a century for the belated justice of the state.

In any case, right or wrong, the Wolves were drunk and very much pleased with themselves as much as if they had just done some kind of pious work; the money they had stolen felt even better in their pockets because it had been stolen from their sworn enemy, the tax collector, and we can affirm that no remorse disturbed their consciences.

Notwithstanding the darkness of the covert, the partial intoxication of the Wolves, joined to the necessity of no further secrecy, made them careless of what might be taking place in their immediate vicinity.

Marie trembled as she felt that an unexpected chance might lead to the discovery of the Captain's presence by his enemies, for from the smatterings of the conversation she had heard between Pelo Rouan and

---

French wine-growers and triggered numerous protests, including many violent ones.

[26] The Rebecca Riots took place between 1839 and 1843 in Wales. They were a series of protests undertaken by local farmers in response to unfair taxation. The rioters were often men dressed as women.

Yaumi in the hut, she thought the Wolves desired his death, but they passed by without incident.

Their rear was closed by the mysterious man in the white mask, the one called the White Wolf by the forest dwellers, who, far from appearing to partake in their joy, walked pensively along, in complete silence, with his eyes upon the ground, and his head bent down upon his breast.

When he passed by the Blossom-of-the-Broom, the girl shuddered and stretched her neck forward.

"Could it be him?" she murmured with emotion and fright.

The White Wolf eventually disappeared, like his "cubs," behind a bend in the road, and the Blossom breathed more freely. Everything soon returned to silence and, as always on a beautiful night, the mysterious and fleeting harmony of the woods descended from the tops of the tall trees.

It was only when a bitter breeze heralded daybreak that Didier conquered his lethargy. He felt crippled and frozen; his stiff limbs refused to move.

On awakening he was, just like before, astonished by her presence and asked question after question:

"You're with me," answered Mary. "Would you prefer to be somewhere else? Come with me... I have my own chamber in my father's cabin. You can find refuge there."

"But why not go back to the castle?" asked Didier. "There is a singular mystery about all this that I strive in vain to solve. My thoughts are confused... I vaguely remember that an irresistible sleep took hold of me yesterday when we were dining at Monsieur de Vaunoy's table... What is going on, Marie? I want to know!"

"You'll know everything soon, my handsome Captain," the Blossom-of-the-Broom said, smiling. "But your limbs are frozen... I do not like to see you shiver like this... It makes me cold to the bottom of my heart... Come with me. I'll lay you in my bed and watch over you!"

"Watch over me?" Didier repeated.

"As one watches at the bedside of those one loves," Marie added. "As a mother watches over her child. But come quickly!"

Didier was too cold and wearied to argue; his brain still throbbed, he had no mental will, and so consigning himself like an infant into Marie's hands, at her bidding he climbed with difficulty into the saddle, she bounded up behind him, and the good steed soon carried his double burden to the cross of our Lady of the Forest, where they dismounted, and turned their steps towards Pelo Rouan's cabin.

About a hundred paces from it, The Blossom dismounted.

"Stay here," she said in a low voice. "My father must not see you."

She walked slowly towards the cabin. The door was opened.

"Father?" said the Blossom-of-the-Broom putting her fair head within the open door.

No one answered.

"He is not back yet," she said with joy. "Praise God!"

She returned to the spot where she had left the Captain, and then, recommending the utmost caution, led him to the door.

"Hush!" murmured Marie. "Walk softly!"

The youthful couple moved as gently as if they feared to rouse the echoes of the forest with the slightest sound. They traversed the lower room, where the conversation had taken place earlier between the charcoal-burner and the devoted squire, upon tiptoe.

Marie's heart bounded lightsome and glad, as with a trembling hand she drew the inner bolts of her little chamber, and pushed Didier inside.

"Now," she said, closing the door, "we are safe, You're in my charge. My father never comes in here."

Alas! She had not noticed, as she passed through the outer room, that two fiery red eyes had followed their progress from behind a pile of straw that served as Pelo Rouan's bed.

No sooner were the lovers gone than a slight rustling was heard amongst the straw. The glaring eyes moved slowly upwards, and the sinewy, agile figure of Pelo Rouan issued from the straw.

"I thank Heaven for having conferred upon me the vision of a cat," he said with bitter emphasis. "I recognized that accursed Frenchman with my deluded child! By our Lady of the Forest, he shall die."

These dreadful words being uttered in a tone of profound tenderness and paternal love; however, proceeding to the mantelpiece, he took down an old musket from the wall, loaded it with the greatest accuracy, and looked well to every portion of the lock.

Having made these deadly preparations he opened the door of the cabin without making any noise, climbed, without the slightest effort up the straight slippery trunk of a lime-tree, that grew before the window of Marie's room, established himself amidst the branches so as to have a clear view into it, and waited for daylight with anxious heart.

Within an hour, the first faint streaks of grey became apparent in the east. Gradually, the dark veil was lifted from the face of the green earth; the joyous matins of the feathered songsters were heard throughout the woods.

Then The Blossom-of-the-Broom opened her windows and looked on the smiling scene.

Pelo Rouan's soul skipped a beat.

The girl kneeled down, and resting her clasped hands upon the sill, returned her fervent thanks to our Lady of the Forest, for the aid rendered to her in the hour of need, and then moved back to the bed on which Didier was lying still asleep, and whilst she sang a stanza of the *Lament*, prepared to offer him a cup of milk so soon as he awoke.

The chamber and its contents reflected the simplicity of the lovely forest maid; it was precisely of the same size as the somber room appropriated to the charcoal-burner's use, but the walls were coated with white plaster, and here and there were little bouquets of thyme and rue, held sovereign in those pastoral regions against attacks of fever, and every species of infectious ills. Immediately opposite to the window was a bedstead of black oak, resting upon the floor, and devoid of curtains, and above the head of it on a bracket were to be seen a small vase of holy water, a statuette of our Lady of the Forest, and a sprig of laurel blessed on Palm Sunday by the good Father at the parish church of Liffré.

The rest of the humble furniture consisted of one rush-bottomed chair, and a number of wicker baskets which the simple inmate dedicated to the uses for which band boxes are appropriated in female dormitories of the present day.

As Didier shook off the last remnants of the opiate and awoke to perfect consciousness, Marie approached the bed where he reposed, free from fear or shame, for her young heart was innocent of all guile; and she was pure as Eve when she first came on earth fresh from the hands of the Divine Creator.

Didier gratefully accepted the milk she offered to him, and having drank it, gazed on her with admiration and respect. The hearts of both at that moment were too full for their thoughts to find utterance through their lips.

But the sun, rising in unclouded majesty, cast its bright beams within the room, and Pelo Rouan quivered with rage, as he saw the manly outlines of the soldier's features traced in profile against the plastered wall. In an instant, the never-erring gun was raised to Pelo's shoulder, and his hand was on the trigger.

"This is lovely," murmured Marie.

Didier drew the maiden's head towards him, and imprinted an ardent kiss upon her brow.

The charcoal burner cocked the musket.

Suddenly, Marie's eye, as she looked upon the Captain, fell upon the copper medal that Alix had placed round his neck.

"What is this?" she asked.

Didier took the medal and his face expressed some surprise.

"What is it?" he answered slowly. "This is all I have in the way of titles and scrolls, Marie. I have always thought it was a token that a poor beggar—my mother—placed around my neck to encourage the charity of passers-by. But I don't understand, Marie... I thought I had lost it long ago. I looked for it in vain for a year! There is magic in what happened last night..."

Marie continued looking at the medal.

"It is strange," she said finally. "I have one just like it."

She quickly removed the cord that held the medal around Didier's neck and pulling at the same time her own from her breast, she went to the window to compare them.

Pelo Rouan had taken certain aim at the young man's breast, but had not dared fire, because his daughter's bosom had intervened between him and her supposed deceiver. Now, the moment was favorable for the infuriated forester's revenge. Again the gun was at his shoulder and his finger on the trigger.

Suddenly, a cry of joy from Marie resounded:

"They're the same! Totally identical!"

This momentarily caught the charcoal-burner's attention as he was about to fire.

He cast an involuntary glance towards her, and as he saw the two medals, a shout of ungovernable surprise burst from him, and the deadly musket dropping from his nerveless hands, fell harmlessly from branch to branch until it reached the ground.

Marie started at the sounds and was mute with fear as she perceived her father in the tree. Her first impulse was to turn and close the shutters, but Pelo Rouan made an imperative signal for her to be still and remain silent.

Meanwhile, Didier had closed his eyes and was lost in some daydream like any happy lover.

Pelo Rouan, swinging himself along the arms of the lime-tree next to the cabin, bounded on to the window-sill.

Marie had not dared make a move and the young Captain had not noticed anything.

Pelo dropped into the room, and catching up both the medals, devoured them with a lengthened, anxious gaze.

Then, the charcoal-burner suddenly pushed his daughter aside and advanced towards the bed.

"Do not kill him, father!" exclaimed Marie, weeping. "Please, do not kill him!"

Marie's plaintive cry roused Didier from his reverie, and he tried to sit upright, but Pelo's hand held him down upon the couch as a mother would a wayward child.

"Father! Father!" shouted Marie.

"Hush, girl!" said the charcoal-burner in a low voice.

Gradually as he scanned the soldier's features, a convulsive shudder shook his limbs; his bosom heaved; two round big tear-drops trickled down his blackened cheeks, and then he threw himself upon his knees, and affectionately kissed the Captain's hand.

"Why are you doing this, my good fellow?" asked Didier with still-increasing wonder.

"The voice too!" Pelo murmured to himself. "The voice too, with the features—and I did not recognize him!"

Didier thought that the charcoal-burner had gone mad; Marie thought she might be dreaming.

"Now I understand," Pelo continued, talking to himself. "I understand why that rascal Hervé de Vaunoy wished to kill him... And I, who did nothing to stop him... Who was it that saved him then?"

"I did, father," the Blossom-of-the-Broom faintly uttered.

"You, Marie, you, my own loved child!" Pelo exclaimed, pressing her shrinking form to his breast with

319

the proudest exultation. "Oh! Heaven, I thank you! You, my child, did what I should have rightly done! You loved him when I hated him! Your heart told you who he was when my eyes were blinded! You saved him when I would have killed him."

Then, turning to the astounded youth, he said:

"Oh, pardon, pardon, my good Lord Georges!"

"Georges?" the Captain stammered. "No, my friend, you must be mistaken..."

"Oh, no! No, I cannot be mistaken. It was I who tied this very medal around your neck, on that terrible night, twenty years ago, when Hervé de Vaunoy threw you into the lake, and would have drowned you. He's been after you for a long time, my boy! And I... Fool that I was to doubt your honor, when I saw you walking with Marie in the forest glades; as if a noble Treml would deceive a lowly maid! As if all that is noble and generous was not always reunited in the heart of a Treml!"

"But," tried to object Didier, who remained in-credulous, "in all that you have just said, I still see no proof."

"No proof? Are your eyes not those of old Nicolas Treml, a sainted old man whose soul is now in God's good graces. Your voice, your age, the medal, De Vaunoy's infernal hatred, he who stole your vast for-tune... Listen!" added the charcoal-burner, suddenly getting up, "you were about six years-old then, and God gave me a face that no one can forget after seeing it, even once..."

"But I do not recognize you," Didier interrupted.

Pelo darted from the chamber, rushed down the stairs, and the next moment, the noise of water dripping on the ground, was heard. A deathlike silence succeeded to the sound, and then a tall man, clad in a fantastic garment of white rabbit-skins, with a milk-white face and hair, and fiery eyes, plunged into the room, and with one bound reached the bed on which the young Treml still lay.

Again Didier regarded this strange creature with the most minute attention. He passed his hand across his eyes and forehead several times, as if recalling some long-buried thoughts.

The other man stood there, in front of him, motionless, looking visibly and violently anxious.

Then, as the flood of memory streamed back upon his mind, the Captain's eyes glistened, his features lighted up, and he suddenly exclaimed:

"Jean Blanc!"

"Yes! yes!" said the Albino, clapping his hands against one another with joy. "He remembers me! He remembers my name!!" he shouted, tears in his eyes. "My real name! Poor little boy! He remembers me!"

"Yes, yes, I do," said the Captain. "I remember you, and a thousand of other things, my friend, now crowd upon my mind. I was not mistaken yesterday when I thought I recognized the draperies of my room…"

"Because it was yours once, where you slept at La Tremlays. Heaven be praised for granting that the cold trunk of the noble tree should not lose its last green branch. May God and Our Lady be blessed for the joy that is now overflowing with my poor heart!"

There was a moment of silence. The Captain was lost in the memories of his infancy. The Blossom-of-the-Broom laughed and wept and thanked Our Lady of the Forest. Pelo Rouan, or Jean Blanc, leaning over his young lord's hand, savored the infinite joy that filled his soul.

After a few minutes, however, he straightened up. He frowned and all his features expressed a serious resolution.

"But now, that you are noble Georges Treml, your rank and heritage must be regained entire, and justice done upon that villain, Hervé de Vaunoy."

Jean Blanc did not need to provide long explanations to Didier, who already knew much of the story that he had heard from the mouth of the unfortunate Jude Leker, without ever suspecting that there could be the slightest relationship between him, a soldier of fortune, and Georges Treml, scion of a powerful family.

Circumstances, some say, make the man. This maxim is true, we think, and speaks well of the human condition. Who could deny that the son of a great house, stripped of his wealth by an infamous fraud, the natural protector of an entire suffering population, should not otherwise behave like a carefree soldier, having no other mission in life than to always fight well and occasionally to entertain himself. Now that Captain Didier had become Georges Treml, he felt a new sense of responsibility awakening in the heart; he understood what was required of him, because of his name and the memory of his ancestors. He had been brave; he now became strong.

"I will go to La Tremlays," he said. "And I will punish Monsieur de Vaunoy."

"I hope you do," Jean Blanc answered with a mysterious smile the significance of which Didier could not grasp. "Go to La Tremlays, Monsieur Georges, and wait for Monsieur de Vaunoy there."

Before parting with the White Wolf, the Captain shook his hand.

"The Treml must be indeed a noble race," he said. "And I'm proud to have a little of their blood in my veins. No base family can have servants like you, Jean Blanc, and I thank you."

"Jude did better than me," answered the Albino, modestly. "Jude Leker died for you, my boy. He would have wanted such a heroic death, because he loved you so very much."

"Poor Jude," murmured Didier "He was faithful and of pure heart."

"He was a Breton," interrupted Jean Blanc. "And, by the way, young Monsieur, it will be necessary for you to forget that you ever wore the uniform of the French King. The bones of your ancestor whiten here and they would rise against you if your sword remained loyal to that King in Paris."

The Captain did not answer. He buckled his belt, put on his hat, and prepared to leave.

On the threshold, he saw Marie who was leaning against the wall and had lost her happy smile.

A sad thought had occurred to her: what could the daughter of the charcoal-burner offer the heir of Treml?

Passing by, the young Captain pressed her to his heart.

"Jean, my friend," he said, smiling, "you would have been very wrong in killing me, because I who treated many noble ladies as mere fancy girls in the past, treated Marie as a noble lady. And if God grants me life, she will be treated like one by everyone else for the rest of her life."

Marie became joyful again. The Captain left. Pelo Rouan—with his whole heart in his eyes—had watched his new-found lord, until he disappeared beneath the trees. He then approached her daughter and kissed her on the forehead.

"My child," he said, "you are the image of your adored mother, and my only joy, comfort, and hope in this world. But let not the words the young lord said just now inspire you with hopes that must be disappointed. Mark me: the Treml must never marry anyone not of their noble rank. As long as I live, you can never become his wife."

The Blossom-of-the-Broom said nothing, but sighed and dropped her head upon her father's breast.

"Must I die then?" she murmured.

"God will make you forget him," said Pelo Rouan. "Besides our lives belong to Treml."

Pelo kissed her with a fond parent's love, re-blackened his face, resumed his charcoal-burner's dress, and left the cabin.

Marie dropped to her knees before the cross, prayed long and earnestly to Our Lady of the Forest, and then, completely worn out by mental excitement, and the extraordinary occurrences of the previous night, threw herself upon the bed and speedily forgot all her woes in sleep.

CHAPTER XXXIII
The Tribunal of the Wolves

Two hours after this extraordinary discovery, the great cavern at the Wolf's Pit presented a solemn and altogether unusual appearance.

The greatest order reigned throughout the cave, and the Wolves, masked and armed for immediate combat, stood, ranged in order around the council table of the elders, who were seated, four on each side of it, the head being occupied by the White Wolf himself, in a chair raised two steps above those of his lieutenants.

Profound silence prevailed, but at the end of a few minutes, the back ranks opened at a sign from the chief of the insurgents, and Hervé de Vaunoy, pale and trembling, with the expression of deadly fear upon his face, was half led, half carried, by two Wolves to the bottom of the table.

"Master," said one of the elders, addressing the White Wolf, "all has been done according to your wishes, and the assassin now stands before us for judgment. Is it your will that we should question him?"

"It is," issued from the lips of the White Wolf.

Père Toussaint then rose up and said:

"Hervé de Vaunoy, the deaths of twenty of our brethren have been caused by your deeds, their blood weighs heavily upon you, and you must die if you cannot prove your innocence."

"Was not our agreement fully carried out?" Hervé de Vaunoy answered. "You have the five hundred thousand livres I promised you. Why, therefore, is not your word properly respected?"

"Our word is worth nothing without the consent of the Master. We had not his permission on the occasion you refer to. You must adopt another line of defense if you would save your life. Yaumi, my boy, prepare the rope," added the old Wolf without any display of emotion.

The cold sweat stood on Hervé's brow as he made an ineffectual effort to mitigate the wrath of his judges.

"My good friends," he stammered, "some villains have belied me to you; take pity on me, I pray you. I swear that I have always had the kindliest feelings towards my poor vassals of the forest, and for the future I will be—"

"Shut up! You're lying!" said the White Wolf harshly, interrupting the trembling wretch.

"Yaumi, is the rope ready?" Père Toussaint said, calmly.

Yaumi replied in the affirmative, and the Lord of La Tremlays, turning slightly around, quivered from head to foot, with agony, as he beheld the fatal noose dangling from a beam in the background behind the ranks of the attentive Wolves. Then breaking out suddenly into a rage, he exclaimed:

"Scoundrels! By what right do you presume to judge me, a nobleman, and your liege lord? I swear by the Holy Mother that I will be avenged! Your stronghold shall be destroyed, and all of you smoked to death within it... But no, no, my kind, good friends... I do not know what I'm saying... Mercy, mercy, forgive me, my brain wanders—by Heaven! I swear I have never done you any harm... They lied to you... If only you could have watched me..."

"But we did," Père Toussaint said jeeringly. "We all know too well your kindness towards the poor folks of the forest."

"You are deceived," Hervé rejoined; "upon my word, as a nobleman, you are deceived. You have never known my real feelings towards you. Give me a few minutes' time that I may prove these facts... Ask Monsieur the Marquis de Nointel, ask my steward... my servants... Give me a reprieve, my friends, a small reprieve that I may prove the accuracy of my words."

"You wish us to question your servants?" Père Toussaint asked with a cold sneer.

"I do," Hervé replied, leaning on that frail reed, hoping to gain some precious time. "All, all of them will tell you of my tender solicitude for the stout sons of the forest, and the grace I have always implored for them from the Collector-general."

"So be it!" answered Père Toussaint. "We will not refuse you that act of justice."

Monsieur de Vaunoy started breathing more easily.

"Approach!" said Père Toussaint to two of the masked men who stood to the right and left of the Lord of La Tremlays.

The two Wolves obeyed and, taking off their masks, Hervé de Vaunoy was thunder-struck:

"Yvon!" he exclaimed. "And Corentin!"

"Well, now," continued Père Toussaint, "these two worthy fellows will tell us of your beneficence."

"Mercy!" said the nobleman, sinking to his knees.

The tribunal deliberated for a minute. The White Wolf took no part in the proceedings.

"Hervé de Vaunoy, the supreme council of the Wolves have judged that you should die by the rope, and you shall be hung—unless it shall be the will of our commander that you should live."

The White Wolf, who had remained mute during the preceding extraordinary scene, rose and said:

"Good. Yaumi, remain by this wretch, and let all the others retire."

This order was carried out as if by magic. The cavern was lit up, revealing huge underground tunnels and caves. The Wolves withdrew from various sides and soon their torches seemed to be no more than small specks of light, while they themselves, shrunk down by the perspective, and strangely lit in the middle of the darkness, took on the form of small human-shaped beings, like elves, or the strange demons that dance on the moors around a cross under the moonlight that the good people of Rennes have known since childhood under the nickname of *chats courtauds*.

The White Wolf then descended from his chair, and touching the kneeling Hervé with his foot, said:

"Get up!"

Hervé de Vaunoy got up.

"You are a dead man unless I interpose my authority between you and the rope."

"At what price shall I buy my life?" the nobleman eagerly inquired.

"Your life?" repeated the White Wolf with a strange expression on his face. "I shall not bargain with you for your life, for you are the murderer of my father and my wife."

"I?" De Vaunoy cried in the greatest astonishment. "But I don't know you!"

As the White Wolf' removed his mask, Hervé murmured in amazement:

"Jean Blanc!"

328

"Yes, murdering villain," the Albino shouted, "it is I, whom you deemed buried many years ago—I, whom you would have crushed as you would tread upon a worm. But the Almighty took me under his gracious care, and has protected me, if not for myself, but for the heir of Treml, the lost scion of that noble race of Christian knights."

"The son of Treml!" De Vaunoy exclaimed, affecting to be unaware of the existence of such a personage.

"Yes, he whom you have twice attempted to murder!"

Here, Hervé de Vaunoy thought that the Master of the Wolves was unaware of his third attempt.

"Yes, twice!" continued Jean Blanc. "And you knew not that his safety was your only shield! You knew not that had I been well assured that he was no more, nothing could have prevented your dying by my hand. How many times have I covered you with my musket in the forest, but forbore to kill you for the sake of that dear, lost boy…"

Hervé de Vaunoy shivered retrospectively at the thought.

"Many a time have you passed along the great tracks of the wood attended by your liveried assassins, and nothing was between you and certain death but the thought of young Lord Georges. Fifty times at least have I had my unerring musket at my shoulder: you were within a few paces of the muzzle, and yet a secret voice restrained me. Heaven be praised for granting me strength to resist that temptation, for now your testimony is necessary for the recovery of his title and his lands, and you must give it, Hervé de Vaunoy, if you wish to leave this cave alive."

"Do you know where he is?" Hervé de Vaunoy asked in a low tone.

"In his father's hall, in the house of his great ancestors, at the castle of La Tremlays."

"Ah..." said Hervé, pensive.

"Yes," continued the White Wolf, "but this time, you will not have an opportunity of getting rid of him. But now, to business. Do you wish to leave this cave alive?"

"At any time, and on any conditions you may name," replied Hervé who, for once, spoke the truth.

"Well, then, I will be frank with you: this once you shall go free. I do not say that, in the future I will spare your life again, for it is mine yet, to avenge my father's murder, and the death of my dear, outraged wife. No—Hervé de Vaunoy, you are mine. For certain reasons, I give you one chance of living, of fleeing my wrath; but to achieve this, here is what you must do..."

Then pointing to the table on which writing materials were placed, Jean Blanc said:

"Write—I, Hervé de Vaunoy, hereby declare that I recognize in the person of Monsieur Didier, a Captain in the service of Louis XV, King of France and Navarre, Georges, the grandson and legitimate heir of Nicolas Treml de La Tremlays, Lord of Boüexis-in-the-Forest, my late honored relative, in token of which I have here set my hand."

De Vaunoy wrote as Jean dictated, signed without the slightest hesitation, and then asked:

"Am I free to go now?"

"You are," Jean replied, after he had checked the document word by word and was satisfied no trickery lurked within it, "but again I bid you beware—come not

330

within my reach, for if you do, by our Lady of the Forest, one of us two shall die. Now, go!"

Hervé de Vaunoy did not linger. He walked randomly toward one of the points of light.

"Not that way !" said Jean Blanc. "Yaumi, bandage his eyes and take him outside. One last word Monsieur de Vaunoy. You will find at the castle the man whom you have here acknowledged to be the grandson of your benefactor, he whom you have so long deprived of his heritage. If you have one drop of the noble blood of Treml in you—which I much doubt—treat him as he should be treated, seek not to do him any harm, for there is a watch set upon every hair of his head."

Hervé de Vaunoy let Yaumi bandage his eyes, then he was taken up the slippery steps, took a breath of fresh air, and when the handkerchief was finally removed, he showed unbounded delight at his escape.

"You may well be rejoiced, villain," Yaumi muttered, "for where you have gone scot-free, many a more honest fellow would have left his bones. Well, it has worked twice for you, but if you are a wise man, you will beware of the third time."

"You are right, my friend," Hervé replied, for his insolence had returned to him with the knowledge of his safety, "but I will even do more than that, I will sell the domains of La Tremlays and Boüexis-in-the-Forest, and with the money they will fetch, I will buy property so far off that I may never again hear the accursed name of the Wolves! Farewell!"

And as he walked rapidly away, Yaumi said to himself:

"I regret that I did not allow the Wolves to hang him, when that villain fell for the first time into our hands. But the Master is more cunning than all of us. He must have a plan…"

The forest was traversed by the usurper on the wings of fear. He did not turn his head once round, and shuddered at every rustling in the bush, dreading to meet a hostile gun, but no danger beset the villain on his route.

When he finally arrived at the avenue of elms that bordered the approach to the castle, he removed his hat, wiped the sweat from his brow, and said:

"Holy Virgin! To have a rope round my neck twice in forty-eight hours is leading a rather rougher life than I like. I'll do as I said… With the price of the lands of La Tremlays and Boüexis-in-the-Forest. I shall always be a great lord, wherever I go… But who could have dreamed that that wretched idiot, Jean Blanc, was still alive? Ah, only let me once get him in my power, and we shall see whether he will ever cover me with his infernal gun again, in the woods or on the road!"

This pious determination being uttered, he walked slowly up the avenue, reflecting on what course he should pursue; a smile of satisfaction passed across his face.

"All is not bad, after all… I escaped miraculously from the clutches of the Wolves, and even if that declaration that I signed—which I can swear was extracted from me under threat of immediate death— may legitimize the heir of Treml—unless, of course, Monsieur Béchamel and the Parliament can find a way to delay his claims—which I rightly hope—still, that scribble is not enough to expropriate me. I still have that bill of sale from old Nicolas in good and due form. By the Holy Virgin! I have friends in Parliament, and exclusive possession of the Estate for twenty years is something that cannot easily be ignored or dismissed. Yes, I certainly would prefer it if that pesky Captain was dead and buried, but since he is alive and fate protects him, let him remain alive! I wash my hands of this, but I swear to never give him a sou of his inheritance!"

Monsieur de Vaunoy, while enjoying this interesting conversation with himself, arrived at the door of the castle. He went in.

After the departure of his prisoner, Jean Blanc remained for some moments buried in reflection, and then having reblackened his face, with the assistance of Yaumi—who had returned—he left the cavern, and proceeded to the hollow oak, carrying a pickaxe in his hand.

CHAPTER XXXIV
Jean Blanc

When Didier regained the castle, it presented the appearance of having been taken by assault, and the young officer could not repress his astonishment at what had taken place during the preceding night.

Jean Blanc and Marie had confined their narrative to what concerned himself alone, Jude's death, and his rescue by the two young women, and therefore he knew nothing of the attack by the Wolves, and the consequent loss of the five hundred thousand livres entrusted to his care.

The first person he met in the vestibule was the hapless Monsieur Béchamel, who appeared to have lost his rosy complexion. He was pale and his depressed countenance expressed only deep sorrow, It was he who told the Captain about the events of the previous night. He did it at length and in a very miserable voice.

"We were the victims of treason," he said, concluding his story. "The sergeants and the men from the constabulary were treacherously prevented from doing their job, and it's going to cost me five hundred thousand livres, Monsieur!"

"Yes, there was treason indeed," replied the Captain. "Do you have any suspicions? Do you know who the culprit may be?"

Monsieur Béchamel took a pinch from his tortoise shell snuffbox and looked at the Captain in an underhanded manner.

"Suspicions," he repeated. "Well, I might have some, yes, but what I do know is that I just lost five thousand livres; that is a cruel certainty, Monsieur. I would gladly give six months of my life to see you the owner in good standing of a vast estate."

"Why?" Didier asked, surprised.

"Because, as I said, I just lost five hundred thousand livres, and that, poor as you are, the Parliament can only hang you or decapitate you. I am saying this, Captain, with no intention to offend you and with all the consideration that is due to your title as officer of the King."

"You dare to accuse me of treason?" shouted Didier.

"Who else then?" answered Béchamel with melancholy. "Who better than I to do so? After all, I am the main victim here, and you do not hear me complain because it would take you such a long time on your salary to repay me my five hundred thousand livres."

Didier was in one of those moments where the heart is inaccessible to anger. His life had just undergone too serious of a crisis for him to vent his wrath on a man like Monsieur Béchamel. On the contrary, he felt some empathy towards him, because his grief was, after all, well motivated. His mind was still reeling from the revelations Jean Blanc had made to him. So, he spoke to the royal Intendant as he would have done with a reasonable person, and told him that his fortune would soon undergo a major improvement.

Béchamel shrugged.

"Some pitiful inheritance I could repossess, I suppose," he grumbled. "Two hundred écus of rent, at best. Still, if I can seize them, I will. But even if you were to repay me my five hundred thousand livres in full, you would still be in my debt, Monsieur!"

"Why?" asked Didier, who did not even try to understand what the other man was talking about.

"Because, since you ask, Monsieur," Béchamel replied, emboldened by the calm of his interlocutor, "last night, I was engaged to Mademoiselle Alix de Vaunoy…"

"And?"

"Well, this morning, I found her half-dressed in the room that you occupied, praying near the corpse of your squire. Do not ask for an explanation for this murder. This house is an abattoir, and I will not spend another night here, even if it would recover me my five hundred thousand livres. Alix was praying. Using the rights that I thought were mine, I asked her to go back to her room. She told me about you… I suppose she felt obliged to do so… in terms that did not allow me to doubt my misfortune."

"Poor Alix," muttered the Captain. "But do not infer anything that might impugn the honor of Mademoiselle de Vaunoy, Monsieur," he added with severity.

"I have enough certainties without needing to resort to suppositions," replied Béchamel. "Five hundred thousand livres, and my fiancée, for she told me that she would become a nun rather than marry me."

At these last words, uttered in a plaintive voice, the royal Intendant drew his watch from his gusset and rolled his eyes.

"Eleven o'clock," he whispered. "I'll bet that in the middle of all this fighting, no one will have taken care of lunch."

He hastily bowed to Didier and went to the kitchens.

Didier calmly reviewed his singular position, and perceived that Monsieur Béchamel would not be the only one to accuse him of treachery. Suspicions would naturally be attached to his sudden, singular, deep sleep, when he ought to have been on the alert with all the escort under his command. He reflected that the only way of freeing his honor from inculpation was to expose the villainy of Hervé de Vaunoy. But what about Alix? Alix who had saved his life! Alix who loved him and whom he had made so unhappy. Gratitude prevented him from making this disclosure, but his honor, dearer to him than life, had to be cleared. He impatiently waited for the return of Hervé de Vaunoy.

Distractedly, he took the way back to his chamber, the same he had occupied in his infancy, and, as he passed up the great flight of stairs that led from the courtyard to the mansion, the escutcheons over the entrance-door, and a hundred objects which on the day before he had not noticed, came back vividly to his recollection as old accustomed sights.

The door to the chamber was wide open, He went in.

On the bed in his own room, the body of the devoted Jude was reverently laid, the face still wearing its look of calm and noble intrepidity, and at the foot of the couch, Dame Goton was on her knees, reciting the verses of the *De profundis* for the repose of her old friend's soul.

Didier took off his hat and stepped forward. Hearing the sound of his spurs on the tiles. the housekeeper turned around. She had not met the captain before, and his sight caused him an emotion whose cause remained a mystery to her.

Didier stopped near the bed and stayed there for a long time while considering in silence the features of Jude, to whom death had not removed his expression of firmness and intrepid calm.

"Alas! Poor Jude!" the young man said when he had contemplated the body silently for a few moments. "God did not permit him to witness the consummation of his dearest hopes. He died before he saw the return of the grandson of his beloved master. He died, poor gallant Jude, one day too soon!"

Dame Goton Réhon ceased her mournful occupation, rose from her knees, turned towards the stranger, clasped her hands together, stared at him with the utmost eagerness, and, at length finding words, exclaimed in broken, anxious accents:

"Monsieur, Monsieur, my eyes are dim with age, and it is now twenty years since they beheld the darling Georges Treml, but, in mercy to a foolish old woman, tell me who you are?"

At that moment, the noise of the great gates rolling back heavily upon their hinges was heard, and the Captain, approaching the window, saw Hervé de Vaunoy entering the yard.

"Tell me—oh, tell me, who you are!" the house keeper repeated.

"So you, too, do remember Treml?" asked Didier.

"Oh, if I remember, Sweet Jesus!"

"Then follow me, dear lady," Didier replied, "and presently you shall hear the usurper of the domains of La Tremlays address me by my proper name and title."

The Captain, followed by the housekeeper as fast as her trembling limbs would allow, proceeded to the reception room, where he found his cousin Hervé de

Vaunoy, Mademoiselle Olive de Vaunoy, Monsieur Béchamel, and the King's officer from Rennes.

Without a moment's hesitation, the latter asked:

"Captain," he said, "yesterday evening, during dinner, you fell asleep. It is not natural. During your sleep, the Wolves looted the castle, I found myself locked in my room, with our men locked in the barn. What do you think of that?"

"I will answer you this evening," replied Didier, advancing towards Monsieur de Vaunoy.

The nobleman brought his sweetest smile.

"Holy Virgin, my young friend!" he exclaimed, opening his arms and meeting him halfway. "I have just learned things that fill me with joy. Brittany finds in you one of its oldest names, and I, the son of an excellent cousin. Let us embrace, my young relative. Monsieur Béchamel. Mademoiselle Olive, my dear sister, and all of you here present, I must now inform you that the real name of our dear Captain is Georges Treml…"

"…de La Tremlays, Lord of La Tremlays and Boüexis-in-the-Forest," added Didier.

Dame Goton who had arrived at the threshold had to lean against the wall, her legs being too weak to support her.

With tears streaming down her cheeks, she joyously exclaimed:

"I knew it, I knew it! My heart told me it was he! Oh! It is thus, I have often dreamed, that I saw him come back to the house of his great ancestors and reclaim his own—the sword by his side, the spurs upon his heels, bold, frank, and free, like a Breton of the true old blood!"

Mademoiselle Olive played with her fan, a game at which she excelled; the officer could not believe his ears; Monsieur Béchamel opened his round eyes;.

Damn! So he us no beggar after all, he thought.

"Such, indeed," Hervé de Vaunoy continued, not deigning to notice the housekeeper's interruption, "were the titles of your respected grandfather!"

"And such are mine!" Georges said firmly.

Well said! thought Dame Goton, who admired every word uttered by her young master.

De Vaunoy laid aside his fawning smile as he replied in the calmest manner,

"Monsieur and dear cousin, it appears to me that you have formed a rather false and highly exaggerated idea of your new position."

"Am I not the heir of my brave grandfather?"

"Undoubtedly, Monsieur; but—"

"But what?" Georges cried indignantly.

"But what indeed?" repeated Dame Goton under her breath.

Even the royal Intendant, now convinced of the validity of the Captain's claim, could not help but utter:

"But what?"

Hervé de Vaunoy smiled again.

"My young friend, I pray you; anger often prejudices a good cause, and never serves it. At my age, men do not make assertions lightly, and you may rely that the inheritance you will derive from Nicolas Treml—Heaven rest his soul—will not make you a very rich man."

Blood surged into the young man's face at this bold statement; but curbing his anger with the greatest effort, he advanced so close to Hervé de Vaunoy that no one could hear what he said, and whispered sternly:

340

"There is one being, villain, beneath your roof whom I esteem as much as I condemn you, whom I love as much as I detest you. Thank Heaven, Monsieur, that such a shield protects you from the fate you justly merit. I know you! I know how often you have tried to murder me; I bear upon me still the wound received from your paid assassins; I know that only last night…"

"Speak louder, cousin," Hervé interposed with in imitable effrontery. "Why should not this good company be partakers of our conversation?"

"Dastardly scoundrel! You are well aware that your daughter preserves you from my vengeance. She is as much of an angel as you are a demon! For her sake, I will be silent: but should you speak another word in op- position to my rightful claims, I may be tempted to scourge you from this house."

Hervé bowed with mock civility.

"My sister and you, Monsieur l'Intendant," he said, "please excuse the rusticity of my cousin's breeding in talking to me so long apart, but I cannot refrain from informing you—in order that you may appreciate it to its full extent—that his first act of generous parenthood has been to threaten to have me kicked out of my own house by the soldiers of His Majesty."

"Truthfully?" said Monsieur Béchamel, just to say something.

"How can that be?" added Mademoiselle Olive who pretended to understand what was going on.

"There is no link of generous parenthood between us, Monsieur," Georges answered, now exasperated to the highest pitch. "I am indeed threatening to have you kicked out, but not from *your* house, for this castle is mine!"

341

"You said it, my darling child!" Dame Goton exclaimed.

A sinister smile again crossed Hervé de Vaunoy's lips.

"So you believe, my young cousin, but you are, in fact, sorely mistaken. Let me absent myself one minute, the time necessary to go up to my office, and I will return to teach you many things that you ignore."

He bowed and left.

The Captain remained undecided, not knowing what to expect.

Monsieur Béchamel, the officer from Rennes and Mademoiselle Olive gathered to comment on this strange event that had just happened.

While everyone was so variously occupied, the blackened figure of Pelo Roan appeared on the threshold. He held under his arm a little iron chest, all rusted. Only Dame Goton noticed him, and she made a movement of surprise, but Pelo put a finger to his mouth ordering her to be quiet. He then glided noiselessly into the shadows cast by one of the large open folding doors.

Almost at the same moment, Monsieur de Vaunoy reappeared, followed by Master Alain the steward. He had in his hand a folded parchment.

"My young friend," he said with an air of insolent triumph, barely tempered by hypocritical smile, "I humbly beg you to excuse me if I made you wait..."

He took the parchment and read it. It was the deed of sale to Hervé of the lands of La Tremlays, Boüexis-in-the-Forest, and executed by Nicolas Treml de la Tremlays the night before he left for Paris.

Reading it, George became pale.

"it would seem," Monsieur Béchamel murmured, "that this document does not please this young man; but how on earth, then, shall I recover my five hundred thousand livres?"

"Hush!" Mademoiselle Olive intimated.

"Monsieur," said the Captain after a long silence, "there is here some kind of odious machination that I do not understand. How is it possible that you, a needy man, fed and clothed by my grandfather, could have amassed enough money to purchase these estates?"

"By economy and circumspection, my young friend," answered De Vaunoy mockingly. "With these virtues, a man may do much. But a truce to these questions. I hope you will never speak again of turning me from these walls; and I pray you, let there be peace between us."

"Never!" said Georges, pushing away De Vaunoy's extended hand. "For your daughter's sake, I can spare you and remain content that your infamy shall never see the light…"

"Monsieur my cousin," said De Vaunoy, straightening up. "My patience has its limits."

"Your infamy I said," repeated Georges. "But henceforth, there is war, eternal war, between us."

"Let there be war, then. Mademoiselle my sister, and you, Monsieur l'Intendant, you are witnesses that I pushed my moderation to its most extreme limits. So I believe it is my turn to be able to tell this Captain who has insulted me in front of all of you: Leave my house!"

"Oh, Blessed Virgin, he is going to expel my poor little Georges!" murmured Dame Goton.

The Captain recovered. He cast a glance of withering contempt upon the wily scoundrel, and strode towards the door.

Just as he reached it he found himself face to face with Pelo Rouan who took him by the hand and led him back to the center of the room

"Jean Blanc!" said the Captain, surprised.

"Jean Blanc!" muttered Hervé de Vaunoy to himself. "So he was Pelo Rouan all the time!"

He leaned over and said a few words in the ear of Alain who went out immediately.

"Why are you here?" he added out loud, addressing the charcoal-burner.

"I have come to render justice!" answered Jean Blanc in a deep voice."I have come to take from you those estates which you have possessed for twenty years by acts of the basest treachery and fraud."

Hervé de Vaunoy looked at the door. Master Alain had not yet returned.

"Hervé de Vaunoy," Jean Blanc continued, "you prevail yourself of a document signed by Nicolas Treml, our old lord, assigning the lands of La Tremlays and Boüexis-in-the-Forest to you for a certain consideration. But, as you well knew, you held them only in trust, for in this little chest, there is a another document signed by you…"

"What do you mean?" asked Hervé de Vaunoy, concerned.

Jean Blanc put the iron chest on the floor, kneeled next to it, and inserted his knife into the hinges. Rust had gnawed at the metal and the lid opened almost effortlessly. The box contained gold coins and a parchment that Hervé de Vaunoy must have recognized, because he rushed to grab it. Georges Treml pushed him away roughly away, and it was he who took the document from Jean Blanc's hands.

"I knew it!" he shouted after reading it. "I knew that there was some kind of fraud being perpetrated! Here is a statement signed by you to the effect that the estates could be repurchased from you by the direct and legitimate heir of Treml at the price of a hundred thousand livres tournois!"

"And here are the hundred thousand livres!" added Jean Blanc, striking the side of the chest.

Hervé de Vaunoy shuddered with rage in his heart and spittle on his lips were foaming.

The officer from Rennes, Mademoiselle Olive and Monsieur Béchamel were greatly astonished. The latter now conceived of a vague hope of recovering his five hundred thousand livres.

As for the old housekeeper, she marveled and promised in her heart a novena to Our Lady of the Forest.

At that moment, Master Alain reappeared on the threshold. He was followed by the servants of the castle, armed to the teeth, and the gendarmes of Rennes.

Hervé de Vaunoy's eyes shone brighter under his thick eyebrows.

"Secure all the exits!" he exclaimed. "Ten gold louis to the first to seize that rebellious, murdering robber!"

He pointed at Jean Blanc.

"This document is against me!" he continued, making an effort to contain his rage. "Although I am a ruined man, stripped of his estates, by Heaven and Hell, I will be fearfully revenged. Look well at this man, Monsieur the Marquis de Nointel! It was he who commanded the assailants who last night tore from you five hundred thousand livres, with the assistance of this traitorous Captain, who locked up the gallant officer and his men.

The gold in that coffer is the vile reward for his treachery and treason, and…"

"Oh, villain! Villain!" burst from the young man's lips.

Monsieur Béchamel was all ears, and the officer from Rennes was listening with interest.

"Can you deny, Georges Treml, that that audacious brigand who now stands beside you is the same person who directed the assault upon this house?

"If I had known this, I wouldn't have fired my musket at them!" grumbled Dame Goton, in her corner.

"And now, can you deny that the same murdering villain is rewarding you with this gold? The same villain whose very name consigns him to the gibbet and the rope! Soldiers! Seize the monster who for the last twenty years has rioted in the blood of so many of your gallant comrades! Seize on the leader of the insurgents—the notorious White Wolf himself."

"The White Wolf!" exclaimed at the same time Mademoiselle Olive, Monsieur Béchamel, the soldiers and the servants.

The latter prudently retired into the background, while the soldiers stepped forward to surround Jean Blanc.

"Arrest him!" shouted Monsieur Béchamel. "You detestable bandit! You will give me back my five hundred thousand livres!"

Mademoiselle Olive deemed it appropriate to faint at that stage.

Georges Treml drew his sword, determined to defend his faithful friend and Marie's father.

For an instant, a deathlike silence prevailed.

But Georges did not have to use his weapon. As the soldiers stepped forward, Jean Blanc, with one furious spring, leaped over the heads of his enemies to a window sill looking over the courtyard. The men were stupefied. The White Wolf stood up, turned around and, shaking his clenched fist, cried:

"Hervé de Vaunoy, you have lost! Even revenge shall be denied to you!"

"Fire! Fire upon that wretch!" Hervé shouted.

Snatching a musket from one of the soldiers, he leveled it at Jean Blanc's head.

But at the moment his finger was upon the trigger, Georges struck up the barrel with his sword, and the ball lodged harmlessly in the cornice of the room.

A laugh of derision and contempt burst from the charcoal-burner's breast.

"We shall meet again, one last time!" he said. "and then, all our accounts will be settled!"

He jumped down into the courtyard, and disappeared unhurt amidst a storm of bullets poured at random on him by the soldiers.

Epilog

The charges of treason and complicity with the Wolves in their attack on the castle brought by Hervé de Vaunoy against his cousin could not be supported for a moment.

Indeed, the scoundrel had calculated upon the chance of shooting Georges in the mêlée consequent on the discovery of Jean Blanc, and, his last hope having failed, he submitted to the loss of his title and estates with apparent resignation.

Monsieur Béchamel, Marquis de Nointel, was compelled to reimburse the King's Treasury for the loss of the five hundred thousand livres collected by him; an act of just retribution, in as much as the Collector-general had most undoubtedly robbed his Majesty of three times the amount during his fiscal government at Rennes.

Georges Treml, in becoming a Breton, did not cast off the feelings of respect and affection he had indulged for the French King, who had assisted him so materially on his uphill road in life. He did not offer the slightest opposition to the mandate of the Royal Courts at Paris, but stood between the good sons of the forest and the petty feudal tyrants who oppressed them, gaining back for the woodcutters, the shoemakers, and basket-workers, the prescriptive rights they had enjoyed from time out of mind, assisting them to pay the lawful taxes, and doing all the good a generous, noble heart could possibly suggest.

Within three years after the accession of the young soldier to his patrimony, not a Wolf was to be encountered in the forest of Rennes, but hundreds of artisans might be daily seen upon their knees before the cross of Our Lady of the Forest, returning their fervent thanks to Heaven for having given them back a worthy scion of the princely race of Treml.

Georges Treml de La Tremlays never forgot that, for the first twenty years of his life, he had merely been "Didier." In taking upon himself the duties and dignity of his new station, the young man did not assume the exclusive prejudices of his caste; a nobleman by birth, but for many years a soldier of fortune, whose sword had carved out his advancement, he determined to consult his domestic happiness alone in a choice of a partner for life and in his prosperity forgot not the humble Blossom-of-the-Broom.

An unexpected difficulty, however, a totally unforeseen obstacle, for a long time prevented the accomplishment of the dearest wishes of his heart: Jean Blanc had his own peculiar ideas of what was right, and persistently refused what he saw as a *mésalliance*.

And it was not some kind of game. No millionaire refusing to accept an indigent as son-in-law, no duke or a count declining an alliance with a poet, were more difficult to bend than the poor Albino, He, too, had his own rigid and inflexible ideas of honor, as strong as al the prejudices of the nobility of Brittany.

Didier ordered, cajoled and prayed in turn, and for a long time, all in vain. But one day, he had the good inspiration to swear on his faith as a gentleman and a Breton, that unless he wedded Marie, he would remain a bachelor for the remainder of his days, and Jean Blanc then gave way, under the conviction that it was imperatively necessary that the House of Treml should have heirs.

It was a day of unmitigated happiness when the lovely flower of the forest passed as a blushing bride across the threshold of the ancient castle of La Tremlays. She had no gaudy escutcheon to quarter with those of her noble husband, and add a new blazonry to the hundred shields suspended from the black oak walls, but amidst all the titled dames who smelled their painted bouquets in that vast mansion, none was comparable in beauty to the lowly Blossom-of-the-Broom. Rightly or wrongly, the Captain thought that counted for something.

Years rolled over the heads of the young couple unshaded by a summer's cloud. The line of Treml was in no danger of disappearing from the land for want of heirs, and as the lovely children of Georges and Marie roamed in the forest under the care and guidance of Dame Goton Réhon, they would occasionally meet Sister Alix of the great convent at Saint Aubin du Cormier, who would embrace them tenderly as tears ran down her cheeks. Sister Alix was beautiful, but her big blue eyes never smiled; the people of the forest interrupted their song as she passed by, as her pale forehead and her gloomy eyes breathed only sadness.

As for her father, Hervé de Vaunoy, his end was thus:

He had left La Tremlays to retire to Rennes. After a short while, he asked George for the permission to return for some effects he had left in his old office. Georges hastened to grant this request.

De Vaunoy came, escorted by a number of well-armed men. His office was the same room that had been old Nicolas Treml's own office, and it still contained that armoire from which the old Breton, before leaving

350

on his last trip, had drawn that hundred thousand livres so often mentioned in this story. That armoire still contained large sums left behind by Treml and De Vaunoy's own loot. That was the sizable fortunate that he had come to fetch.

He found no opposition from Georges, and resumed the road to Rennes that evening.

But his servants arrived at the town without him, and, frightened, told people that, at the edge of the forest, they had heard a musket shot and a bullet had passed over their heads and hit Hervé de Vaunoy in the chest. He had fallen off his horse and was dead before touching the mossy ground.

"We looked towards the place from where the shot was fired," explained the servants. "It was almost night. But through the darkening shadows, we saw a white figure jumping from branch to with superhuman agility until it was lost among the deep, dark foliage of the wood. So we ran away."

On the following morning, they found the corpse of Hervé de Vaunoy lying upon the sward, and close to it was the deadly musket that Jean Blanc had inherited from his father.